The Tailor's Daughter

LOIS BAER BARR

The Tailor's Daughter

A NOVEL

LOIS BAER BARR

Printed in the United States of America

Water's Edge Press LLC
Tucson, AZ
watersedgepress.com

ISBN: 978-1-952526-17-6
Library of Congress Control Number: 2023941069

Credits:
Cover and book design by Water's Edge Press.
Compostite photo frame image by Carollo Designs.
Cover images are property of the author.

A WATER'S EDGE PRESS FIRST EDITION

To the memory of my mother,

Ethel Cooper Baer (1924-2012)

Part One

Bialystok and Beyond

Prologue
The Bialystoker Apprentice

A bead of sweat dropped from Shlomo Toplansky's nose onto the black serge as he smoothed the fabric on the table. Pinning the onion skin pattern onto the wool, his young hands shook. Reb Dovid leaned over his shoulder so close that Shlomo smelled herring on the master's breath. When Reb Dovid went outdoors to have a smoke, Shlomo looked out at the spring day and began to hum an aria from *Pagliacci*. How can a man stay hunched over a machine? If only he could go back to the Nowy Teatr. If only Giovanna, the lovely soprano, would keep coaching him in opera and teaching him to read music, he'd sweep floors there forever. Although Giovianna had continued to give him lessons when she could, he hadn't worked at the opera since the Germans and the Russians had begun to wage war in their beautiful city. It was the year he'd turned sixteen. 1916.

That night Shlomo dreamed of himself in the heat of the spotlight singing "The Drinking Song" with Giovanna, but as sun lit the edges of the curtains, he awoke shivering. His baby brother Yitzhak, snoring sonorously, had wrapped himself like a blintz in the quilt. Shlomo threw clothes on over his woolen underwear and hummed the aria as Momma toasted yesterday's loaf of bread on the open fire. Heading out the door to the outhouse, Shlomo heard Poppa bang his newspaper, *The Daily Worker*, on the kitchen table and yell after him, "Vagabonds sing. You, you will be a tailor. Tailors always work."

Chapter 1
Crossing Over

The minute he stepped aboard the S.S. Victoria, Shlomo decided to become Sol. He carried the tailoring tools from his apprenticeship, a shirt collar, a parchment prayer scroll, sheet music from Giovanna, and a piece of paper with the address of his sweetheart Malke. His older brother Avrom had sent him money for a train to Hamburg and a spot in steerage. Avrom's money would prove the young tailor's solvency to immigration. Moreover, he had a letter from another Bialystoker offering him work in his tailor shop in the very city where Malke was working, Louisville, Kentucky.

Steerage was crowded, but Sol had expected that. He hadn't expected to run into Cousin Reuben from a shtetl near Bialystok. His farm boy cousin hugged him tightly. "Oy, you look so good. Such a fine suit."

"From my apprenticeship."

Reuben rubbed the lapel between his fingers. "Such fine fabric."

Sol explained, "Got it cheap. The fellow who ordered it skipped town before the Russian army put him in another kind of suit altogether." Sol hadn't seen Reuben in a few years and although they were only a couple of months apart in age, his cousin was now a head taller. If only he could make a suit for Reuben whose ragtag clothes were all right in the country but wouldn't make such an impression in America. Oh well, poor as he was, Reuben was a mensch. He introduced Sol to the others who quickly formed a minyan and commenced evening prayers. Sol chanted with them to be friendly. As more and more men joined in, he was the only one without a prayer shawl. The old melodies reassured him, the bowing and swaying helped him adapt to the movement of the ship. After prayers, the men showed him to an area of bunks where he could sleep among his own. The man who'd led the prayers said, "Stick close to us. We're your brothers, your shifbreeder. It's safer. There are some hooligans on this ship."

That night as Sol lay awake on the top bunk, the noise of snoring and grumbling stomachs made him miss Yitzhak. There was a stench that he attributed to himself as much as to anyone else. For a week he had traveled in a train with humans, animals, and bundles packed to the ceiling. No way to wash before you ate. Momma would have disapproved. How he missed the steamy baths he, Poppa, and his brothers took at the mikve every Friday before the Sabbath. Knowing he didn't have a chance of a real bath for the next two weeks, he worried about what animals might be living in the hinges and cracks of his bed or crawling on his skin. He tossed about on his bunk.

The man below gave a hoarse whisper, "Sha shtill! Quiet, a man must sleep."

Sol's thoughts turned to Momma's matzo ball soup and the arguments at the dinner table. Poppa liked to yell. No more fights with Poppa now. No more fights about music or Malke. The day he left, he went to see Malke's father, Calman, the Torah scribe, on the pretext of buying a prayer scroll for his new home, but in truth, Sol wanted to find out where in America Malke had gone. "A city in Kentoki," the scribe had informed him.

The day his sweetheart left, she promised she'd wait for him, but she was such a lively girl, such a beauty. Who knew? He remembered the first day he'd ever seen her, dancing in the street to celebrate her father's completion of a Torah scroll for a neighborhood shul. That night Poppa scowled. "They dance and feast tonight. But tomorrow it's back to black bread and onions." Poppa didn't know that Sol was going to look for Malke and marry her. What could Poppa do? Sol would be in America. Free.

The next day Sol stayed with the men of Reuben's minyan and chatted all day. He joined the prayers morning and evening. Too much praying. That night he felt restless in his bunk, so he got up to stretch his legs. He put his arms out to feel his way in the dark. Oy gevalt, he bumped his knee on something. He slowed his pace. The snores and moans reassured him. As he got to the side of steerage where the goyim bunked, Sol discerned a light and the smell of a kerosene lantern. A knot of men was shooting dice and one grunted, "Hey boy, watch out, you're stepping on our craps game." Sol wanted to try his luck, but a man as tall as Sol, even on his knees, grumbled, "Get out of here you dirty Yid."

Creeping along the wall, Sol smelled the tangy sausages of the Italianers. His fingers touched metal. A small ladder. He clambered to the top and wrestled with a heavy metal hatch until it opened a crack. Sol was slender enough to wriggle his way up out of steerage and onto on the second deck. The fresh sea air filled his lungs. He continued his foray and found a wide stairway that led to first-class. He ascended on tiptoes. Sounds of music and laughter led him to a nightclub. The aroma of cologne and rich tobacco wafted in the air. He peeked in to see a pale, heavyset man standing in the spotlight singing an aria Sol remembered from the Nowy Teatr. The tenor's voice was good, but he didn't hold the notes the way he should have. Sol put his hand on his abdomen and took a deep breath as Giovanna had taught him. As the song ended, Sol scurried away, hugging the walls of the ship to return to steerage.

The next night he waited until all his shifbreeder were asleep and ventured forth. Once again, he lingered by the door to the nightclub and looked into the room. Women in sparkling dresses with so much cleavage. Men in elegant tuxedos. Crystal chandeliers. Fine musicians. The same tenor performed, but tonight, he was sliding around the notes. He seemed out of breath. In his head, Sol corrected the errors, and before long, he was singing from his spot at the door. An officer walked up next to him and joined Sol in singing. The big man locked arms with him and they swayed to the music. As the tenor bowed to the applause, Sol and his new companion bowed to each other and laughed. Then, Sol could see the man's face change as though he were smelling something rotten. "Hey, what are you doing up here?" he asked. Sol's apology just made the man fiercer. He threatened to have Sol thrown off the ship if he didn't pay him hush money. When Sol said he didn't have any money, the man slammed him against the wall and ordered him to empty his pockets. Sol handed over his stash. Then, the officer dragged him back to steerage. He unbolted the door and shoved him down. "No more opera for you. Stay where you belong, boy!"

Shaken by that skirmish, Sol lay awake in the dark. The melodies of "La Traviata" alternated in his mind with worries about money for immigration. Why had he given his stash to that thief of an officer?

Next day, the sea was calm, so Sol shook off his jitters. He was joking with Cousin Reuben when his captor appeared and ordered Sol to collect his things. The goniff shoved Sol upstairs to the next deck. Sol Toplansky was sure he was finished. Was he going to be thrown overboard, locked up in chains? Like Daniel, would he be fed to the lions?

"What do you want from me? I told you I won't make no more trouble," Sol said.

"That lousy tenor met his maker during the night," the officer snorted. Sol looked bewildered.

"I told the music director you don't sing bad for a Yid. You owe me."

Next thing he knew, Sol was standing in the music director's office. The man motioned Sol to come closer. He ordered the petty officer to leave and looked over the terrified passenger from head to foot. The music director's scrutiny made Sol cringe when he realized the man was staring at the cracks in his boots. He felt the director could see the newspaper and cardboard he'd used to make his brother's boots fit.

"How old are you boy?"

Sol added a year to his age. "Twenty."

"What can you sing?"

He didn't tell the director that he only knew four arias and the rudiments of reading music. "Pagliacci," he said, thinking how Bialystokers had cheered for that clown's song.

Sol took a deep breath and thought of the sad face of the clown and began the famous aria. Hearing his voice resonate in the room, he sang lustily.

When he finished, the director said, "You'll do." He explained that Sol would perform after the magician. The director told Sol he could share tips with the accompanist, and he would get a small stipend at the journey's end. There would be no encores because the soprano would not tolerate waiting. In his free time, Sol was not to socialize with the patrons in first class although he could stretch his legs on the second-class deck. Meals would be taken in the crew's dining hall.

"You'll have the tenor's tux, but you'll need shoes. Those simply won't do," the director said, looking at Sol's boots with such disdain that he felt like a mangy dog. "I have an old pair of dress shoes that might fit you, but make sure you return them in good condition." The man got up and rummaged in a chest and handed Sol a pair of shiny black shoes.

Sol felt a rush of emotions. His shame turned to excitement at this opportunity. He was excited to be asked to sing, to be paid to sing, but he could hear his father's admonitions, and Momma wouldn't approve of his wearing a dead man's suit and a stranger's shoes.

The petty officer led Sol to a windowless room in second class. The cabin was not much bigger than the bed, and on that bed lay the Italianer's tuxedo. The officer informed him to show up promptly at 8 p.m. for his performance. That gave Sol all day to alter the suit. It was a big job, but manageable. There was no mirror, but finally the fit felt right.

Sol used his spare kerchief to add a pocket in the waist, the way Reb Dovid had shown him. The master had said, "You'll keep your money safe from Yankee goniffs." The old tailor scoffed at the idea that the streets of America were lined with gold. He told his apprentice that they were lined with pickpockets and murderers. "No place in the world is better than Bialystok," he'd said. As Sol recalled those admonitions he shook his head. His old taskmaster was turning a blind eye to the poverty and the violence around him.

In the afternoon, the pianist sent him some music but begged off rehearsing, saying he was too busy. Sol, not wanting to look foolish in his world debut, studied the melodies and did vocal exercises to warm up.

Sol stretched out for a little rest. My how his station had changed so quickly. Such luxury, a bed all his own. Maybe they would let Cousin Reuben move up and room with him? No, his cousin would never move away from the prayer group. Sol fluffed the pillow and got comfortable. A little snooze wouldn't hurt, but there was a chemical odor emanating from the closet. The closet turned out to be a tiny lavatory. Sol chuckled to think he wouldn't have to wait in a long line with his shifbreeders to relieve himself. To his delight, there was a basin, a faucet with running water, a bar of soap, a big white towel, and a drain in the floor. He scrubbed his body with great pleasure. Then he looked long and hard in the mirror. His hands shook as he held his long razor. Once he decided his beard and sideburns had to go, he worked slowly but skillfully. It wouldn't do to make his debut with cuts all over his face and neck. Cleaning up the red curls in the sink, he thought that now, no one would recognize him as the Jew from steerage, especially in the tuxedo.

Sol arrived early feeling pin pricks in his gut. Before they went on, Sol asked the accompanist to play some of the arias he'd learned in Bialystok, but the man feigned ignorance. Between the blinding spotlight and pianist's erratic tempo, the first number did not go well. The audience was restless and Sol knew he had to redeem himself. An elegant blonde in a gold sequined dress walked up to the stage. Sol took a step back. He had never seen such a short dress, or such deep cleavage. The woman put a stack of bills on the piano and smiled at the nervous tenor. Then she leaned toward the accompanist and said, "I know you play Italian opera. I've heard you. So, play."

Finally, the man agreed to play Verdi's "Di quella pira." Sol's vocal cords were relaxed, and his breathing was deep and steady as he fell into the role of the troubadour. He closed his eyes and became the troubadour ready to do battle to save his mother's life. He sensed the audience was convinced of his valor. While the last note still reverberated in the room, Sol saw the director standing in the wings next to the soprano motioning for Sol to get off stage. Sol took a hasty bow and exited.

The next day after breakfast, Sol sat in his cabin and sounded out songs from sheet music that the pianist had loaned him in exchange for a big cut of the tips. Afterwards, he strolled on the second-class deck.

He sneaked up to first-class to look at elegant things in the shop windows, but he dared not spend a cent because he needed money for a train to Louisville to find and marry his Malke, the dark-eyed daughter of the Torah scribe. Who knew, maybe someday he and Malke could have their own shop once they got settled in Louisville. Or could he support them with his singing? The audience had received him well. Could he concertize in America?

Two days later, Sol felt comfortable enough in his new station to think about maybe socializing after his performance. Sol had just heard that the soprano kept the music director busy in her boudoir after her performance. The coast would be clear, so he ventured back into first-class and discovered the casino. It was more elegant than the nightclub. Here he could double his money. After all, he'd won many a card game in Bialystok. Of course, back home, his brothers had always loaned him money and gotten a good return. Now he'd be playing with his own money. The risk terrified him, but the temptation was overwhelming.

Luckily, his boss was nowhere to be seen. There was a roulette wheel, games of dice, poker, and twenty-one.

"Signor Salomone," called out the tall blonde Italian lady who had rescued him from the piano player. She motioned for him to stand by her side at the card table. After a few hands he understood their game was like a five-card game he knew.

A German-speaking gentleman sporting a monocle and a finely tailored evening jacket sat next to Sol's fan, whom everyone called the Contessa. Last night the German had requested a Wagner aria that Sol didn't know. Now the man seemed agitated by Sol's presence. He murmured something to the player to his right, jumped up, and bowed to the Contessa, "I must beg your pardon. I am not in the habit of consorting with the help." He scowled at Sol and stomped out.

The blonde laughed and motioned for Sol to take the man's seat. She pushed half of her chips toward Sol. The gold from King Solomon's mines could not have thrilled Sol more. After winning a few hands, he felt like a king, indeed. When the dealer pushed a mound of chips toward him, the blonde whispered, "Bravo, Signor Salomone." Her perfume and the thrill of winning so engrossed Sol that he didn't see the musical director rush up to their table. He ordered Sol to step into the corridor.

"There has been a complaint," the director said. "You must not mix with the guests. I'll have to fire you if this happens again."

Chastened, Sol returned to his room and calmed his nerves by pacing the tiny space and doing breathing exercises. He wondered about the Contessa.

She could be thirty or forty, but she was so beautiful and generous. The next night as Sol made his entrance, his eyes searched the audience for her. She sat next to the snooty German fellow, drinking and laughing. When Sol took his place by the piano, the German made a disparaging remark and stormed out of the nightclub. The insult was obvious, but Sol decided to show everyone, especially the Contessa, what he was made of. It was his strongest performance yet. As the crowd stood to applaud, the soprano ran out to sing with him. His voice melded with hers in a glorious duet. The crowd loved their impromptu number, but Sol could see the scowl of the director as they took a bow.

Sol felt great satisfaction at his performances, but the days were lonely. He longed to try his luck at the games again but realized it was safer to stay in his cabin playing solitaire. Then one night the Contessa followed him out after his performance. She took his hand. Her gloves. Were they satin? Kid? He'd never felt such a smooth fabric. He looked into her eyes and saw laugh lines crinkle about them as she spoke to him in what little German she could manage. "Card game. My room. Tonight late. Wilkommen." The Italian lilt she gave to German was music to Sol's ears.

As Sol lay in his cabin, his better nature told him it was too dangerous to meet with her, but the cards and the Contessa's beautiful face kept flashing through his mind. She had been very insistent. Tempting as it was, he knew he should not consider her offer, so he closed his eyes and thought of his family in Bialystok. Momma, a devotee of Yiddish theater, would have loved hearing him sing. Better not to think of Poppa, but he did wish his father could see the meals he ate with the ship's staff. Of course, Momma would disapprove of his eating the meat. What delicacies, he wondered, would the Italian woman serve at her party? She was herself a tempting delicacy. Oy, better he shouldn't think of her.

As much as he tried to focus on his family, his Malke, their future, his mind kept returning to the card party. No doubt he could get to the woman's room without being seen, but was it worth risking his job? He owed the accompanist for more music, the petty officer wanted a finder's fee, and he'd had to pay for cleaning his shirt and collars. There was always the possibility of ending up back in steerage, which he'd discovered today now smelled worse than Bialystok's stockyards.

That morning he had visited his cousin. Reuben warned Sol that he had lice—it was rampant—and if Sol knew what was good for him, he should go back upstairs. "Of course, we miss you in the minyan. You made the prayers sound like we were in the Garden of Eden, but we have enough men."

When Sol gave Reuben some money, his cousin leaned over to hug him but pulled back with a laugh, "I wouldn't want you should get infested."

Instead Sol shook his cousin's hand. Reuben warned him, "You better get out of here and don't come back if you have a bundle of money. I don't trust some of these animals."

In bed that night, Sol thought about his performance and then about his morning visit to steerage. Thinking about the lice, he scratched his body and rolled over. He should get up and change out of his tux, but he was too tired. Before long he dozed off. A knock at the door woke him. He fumbled in the dark for his jacket. After another knock, he opened the door. At the door stood the countess, covered from head to foot in a hooded velvet cloak.

In her singsong attempt at German she said, "Come with me. We only have two more nights, and you, young man, should have some fun."

She took off the cloak to reveal a long black low-cut dress. She put the cloak on Sol. He grabbed the hem and ascended the stairs. Her perfume intoxicated him as they made their way to first class.

Musical laughter and chatter spilled into the hallway from her suite in the prow of the ship. What caught Sol's eye first was the panoramic view of the sea and the starry night, but he also spied a satin covered bed through the open door of her bedroom. The thought that he might be invited there stirred his desire.

Her friends greeted him with embraces. They'd tipped Sol generously when he sang Italian songs. They led him to a wide balcony where a table was set with champagne and foods Sol had never seen. One man showed him how to eat caviar. A liveried waiter poured him champagne. The guests toasted Verdi. They toasted Pagliacci. They toasted Enrico Caruso. They entreated Salomone to sing, so he did. He performed his four arias and some new art songs the pianist had sold him. Then they played cards and drank. Drank and played cards.

By morning, a soft gray light reflected off the ocean. It seemed to Sol as though a concert conductor had put his fingers to his lips wanting everyone to play pianissimo. Everything seemed still and full of possibility. Walking over to the railing, he felt the room spin. To regain his balance, Sol sat on a sofa next to his benefactress and kissed her hand.

"You are a most beautiful woman," he said. His voice was hoarse and his eyes could not avoid her cleavage.

She bent to whisper, "And you are a most enticing tenor, Salomone. Would you sing me just one more song? Perhaps a lullaby before we retire?"

Salomone stood to sing and toppled over.

"Accidente!" the Contessa laughed. "Salomone has drunk too much. He will not be much fun now. Giorgio, Tonio, help our friend to his room!"

The men held Sol up as they swayed their way down the hall. They were laughing and singing when Sol spied the music director leaving the soprano's room. Sol buried his face in Giorgio's chest to avoid being seen. Giorgio fiddled in Sol's pockets for his room key and helped him onto his bed.

A while later, everything was spinning again so Sol sat up, started to sing, and wondered where his friends had gone. Then he remembered seeing his boss and hoped he hadn't been seen. What a night! He had kissed the Contessa, hadn't he? He hadn't been unfaithful to Malke, had he?

There was loud banging on his door. Sol lurched to open it, expecting the Contessa. Instead, the director barged in, accompanied by the petty officer who wasted no time in pulling off the dead tenor's tuxedo jacket.

"You're not fit to wear those," the director said, pointing to the pants.

As groggy as he was, Sol understood, so he took off the pants but pulled his winnings out of the secret pocket before handing the trousers to the officer.

The director shook his fist at Sol. "You certainly won't be paid after this insubordination. I warned you about fraternizing with our guests."

After being escorted back to steerage, Sol spent the rest of the early morning nauseated from the stench and from too much wine. The hangover and his shame at being fired made him miserable, but he had to smile about the party. No one could take that memory from him. Exhausted, he curled up on top of his bundles and fell asleep.

Right after morning prayers, a bunch of thugs came over to ask Sol where he'd been all this time and how much money he had. Though terrified, Sol stared them down and didn't answer their questions. When one guy punched him in the gut, Sol hit him back.

"Ouch," the man said, laughing. "A fly could hit harder."

Another guy wrenched Sol's hands behind his back while a third searched his pockets. All they found was the red chip.

"Bigshot! Why are you waiting to cash this in?"

Sol didn't see the fist slam into his nose that sent him crashing to the floor. The men from the prayer group rushed over to beg the tough guys to leave Sol alone, but the thugs wanted blood and money, so they started kicking Sol. One man stomped on Sol's fingers.

"Oy, not my hands! I'll give you the money," Sol cried. He emptied his pocket of all the tips. The men grabbed the cash greedily, and one tossed him the red chip.

"Here singing boy, we wouldn't want to leave you strapped."

Another man kicked Sol in the ribs. When Cousin Reuben warned them he would call the authorities, the gang of men laughed and sauntered off. The fellows from the minyan helped Sol get up and cleaned the blood off his face and hands.

After evening prayers, Reuben and his friends took up a collection and gave Sol the money he'd need to show at Ellis Island. A few looked sheepish and asked him to pass their money back to them after he showed it to the officials. It was all they had.

In the morning they reached New York. Sol said warm goodbyes to his shifbreeders, but when Reuben hugged him tightly, he winced with pain and said, "Oy, cousin, if you wouldn't have helped me, God only knows what those ruffians would have done to me."

Sol rubbed the red chip between his thumb and fingers, a souvenir of his singing career and the elegant countess. A reminder of how quickly your luck can change.

Part Two

Louisville, Before the
Great Flood of the Ohio

Chapter 2
The Three Queens

Sol knew he was being scrutinized as he stood at the bottom of the cellar stairs before the heavy door. He had said the password, but still the door didn't open. He wiped his handkerchief across his forehead. Maybe he should just go back home, but he had that electric itch to gamble. He'd felt it all day stooped over the sewing machine in Maishe Yoffee's shop. Finally, the door opened. A ruddy-faced guy grabbed Sol by the collar and pulled him in. Sol could make out a ring of smoke over the heads of four men at a round green table. He stepped around boxes piled high by the doorway that he knew to be full of booze. Everyone knew Mendy Mendelson was making a fortune with bootlegged whiskey during Prohibition.

A baritone voice boomed, "Ain't you Shlomo Toplansky, the singing tailor?" Mendy himself waved a fat hand for Sol to approach.

"It's a pleasure, Mr. Mendelson. Here in America, everyone calls me Sol."

"And everyone calls me Mendy, but Solly, I gotta ask myself how such a young boy just off the boat can afford to ante up."

"Don't worry Mr. uh, Mendy. I came to play. I've got enough money."

"What's your idea of enough?"

Sol knew not to reveal what he had in his pockets or the stash he kept hidden in his waistband. He said firmly, "Enough."

Mendy flicked his cigar into an overflowing ashtray, shrugged his shoulders, and motioned for Sol to join his henchmen at the table.

"It's five-card draw," one of the men said as Sol sat down.

Sol nodded and took his cards from the dealer. Despite their rough appearance, Mendy's fellows were amiable players and reacted calmly when Sol won a couple of hands. Sol laughed at their coarse banter but paid close attention to the cards to get a feel for everyone's style of play. When Sol lost a hand, it didn't worry him too much because he was four bucks ahead.

"Can't win 'em all, can you?" said one of the players. That player didn't take risks, but the man next to him, a big guy named Ike, liked to bluff. The young fellow to Sol's right, kept getting miserable hands. Mendy reached behind his chair and pulled a bottle out of a box.

"Solly boy, how about a drink?"

"No thanks, Mendy." Sol had heard about the potent stuff that Mendy peddled, and he needed to keep his wits about him.

"Well, boychik, if you play with us, you should be sociable."

The others all had drinks in front of them. Sol couldn't refuse.

Mendy poured him a healthy glass of liquor and raised his own glass. "L'chaim."

Sol toasted back and took a swallow. It gave off a harsh heat. Mendy laughed at Sol's coughing fit and slapped him on the back. As they played, Mendy kept refilling Sol's glass until Sol put his hand over it.

"Okay, tailor boy, do you raise?"

Solomon Toplansky had a fine hand. He stared at his three queens and answered, "I raise."

As three players folded, Sol looked at Mendy Mendelson, and looked at the pot. He looked at his queens and his pair of kings. It seemed that the cards had come to life and wanted to tell him something. Then the Queen of Spades stared away in disgust, like his wife Malke would if she knew where he was. Oy vey, that spade, her scepter, looked sharp. Or was it a sword? Malke's tongue could be sharp as a sword. But he'd kept track of the cards and surely his three queens and a pair of kings would win. Was the king of diamonds winking?

"Boychik, are you dreaming? I see your raise and I call. What you got?" Mendy was in a hurry.

Sol put down his queens and kings with a flourish.

Mendy put down four jacks and said with a laugh, "I got the luck again tonight."

As the cards were being shuffled, Sol replayed the last hand in his mind. He hadn't lost track of the cards. Something seemed wrong. How did Mendy get that fourth jack? But he couldn't find his voice to protest, and he was feeling woozy. Mendy cut the cards. Sol could still see the fixed stare of the Queen of Spades. It stabbed Sol in his gut.

"Hey, tailor boy, are you in?"

Sol still had a fiver in his waistband. He had lost their savings, but if he left now, he'd still be able to make the rent. His heart pumped loudly in his ears. It was always hard to leave a card game, but he stood and said, "I don't have no more money, so I must beg your pardon."

Mendy wasn't buying it. "You ain't going nowhere, you shmendrick. Ike, check his pockets."

Ike was an ogre of a man. He grabbed Sol by the shirt collar and dragged him away from the chair. Sol's knees felt weak, so he didn't put up a fight. Mendy's henchman checked all his pockets and even under his shirt and pants.

"The guy ain't got a red cent."

"Bring him over here, Ike," Mendy ordered.

Mendy grabbed Sol by his belt, but just then Sol slumped over and said, "Mendy, I beg your pardon, I'm going to be sick."

"Well, get out of here, putz. This game is for the high rollers."

Sol was shoved out the cellar door of the tavern. His legs were lead going up the stairs. At the top he grabbed the railing and caught his breath. He wanted to get away before anyone decided to come after him, but he couldn't move. The little light over the doorway was circling his head and before he knew it, he was face down in the alley. He struggled to his knees and crawled over to a trash bin, got to his feet, pried off the lid, vomited, and passed out.

When he came to, Sol was too embarrassed to go home in his condition. He ducked into another alley and headed toward the Ohio River. Twenty bucks he'd lost. Malke would be furious but not as furious as he was with himself. His pace downhill picked up, and before he knew it, he was running. Not since the Old Country had he run like this.

Drenched in perspiration and reeking of bootlegged booze, he reached an old wooden dock. He climbed down the ladder to the little landing by the water and pulled off his shoes and socks and let his feet dangle in the river. Leaning down, he swished his handkerchief in the water, then dowsed his aching head. What had happened to his luck? Back in Bialystok he always won at cards. Even on the ship over, he'd won big pots. How would he tell Malke he'd lost so much money? Now they needed it for their new baby, their chubby, golden-haired Bess. And they were saving to bring Malke's mother Adel over. Oy vey, three women to feed and clothe. Three women in a two-room apartment, if he could keep the two rooms.

The current was swift. The water rushed away from him just like his luck. Maishe Yoffee, his boss, had promised him a raise, but even with a raise it would be tough. He thought of his friend Shimmie who had jumped off a bridge into the River Biala. The river had been so low that Shimmie had broken his neck. Here the Ohio River was deep. A horn interrupted his thoughts, and Sol looked at the lights of a barge reflecting off the dark surface of the water. He wiped his face again put his shoes and socks back on. Before long, he saw pink streaks upriver. Oy vey! Time to get home and sleep a little before Malke and baby Bess awakened.

Sol trudged back up Fourth Street. It was a muggy August morning. Approaching Jefferson, he saw Rabbi Zarchy heading to the shul, the strings of his prayer shawl flying from below his black jacket. Maybe Sol could change his luck by going to shul. Malke nagged him about going to synagogue. Once his mother-in-law arrived, there wouldn't be any two ways about it. They'd have to go with Mother Adel to the synagogue every Sabbath and every holiday.

"A good day," the rabbi said, greeting him in Yiddish as Sol caught up at the doorway to the shul.

"A gut yor," Sol said, wishing the rabbi a good year.

"So, to what do we owe this miracle, Shlomo?"

Sol grinned. "I know I don't come often."

"Often?" the rabbi laughed as Sol opened the door to the storefront where B'nai Jacob was now holding services. Zarchy put a prayer shawl on

Sol's shoulders and a yarmulke on his head and led him into the small chapel.

As the rabbi stepped in, the men at the front started chanting the prayers. Sol sang harmony, and the men sang louder. Soon they were all swaying, and Rabbi Zarchy called a descendent of the priests to come up to say the blessing before reading Torah. The rabbi quickly chanted the biblical passage, and a Levite was called. Then Zarchy nodded to Sol. He wasn't going to let this surprise addition to the minyan go unnoticed. The leader asked Sol his father's name and then chanted, "Shlomo ben Natan." Stumbling a bit on the opening, Sol managed to recite the blessing. As he scanned the open scroll, he thought about his father-in-law, Calman, the Torah scribe, his memory should be for a blessing. A saintlier man had never lived. Sol still had his prayer parchment, but they didn't have a place where they could nail up the mezuzah on their door. Sol touched the prayer shawl fringes to the place where the rabbi had his pointer on the Torah text. Then Zarchy shuffled Sol over to the other side of the pulpit as another man came to lift the Torah, dress it, and put it back in the ark.

When the service was over, the rabbi invited Sol into the kitchen for some coffee and a bialy. The coffee was strong, and the salty, chewy roll tasted like home, but Sol was worried about the time. "I have to get home, Rabbi. My Malke will think I've been murdered."

"Well, I'll walk with you and maybe you'll tell me what you were doing up so early," Rabbi Zarchy said, looking at Sol's disheveled clothes and bruised chin. "Or maybe you never went home?"

As they walked along Jefferson, Sol told Zarchy about the gambling and how he'd lost so much money. How he thought maybe there was something wrong with the whiskey.

Zarchy shook his head and stroked his dark beard. "The Talmud teaches 'Man has three friends on whose company he relies. First, wealth which goes with him only while good fortune lasts. Second, his relatives, who leave him buried in the earth. The third friend, his good deeds, go with him beyond the grave.'"

"But what should I do, rabbi? Do you think I've lost my good luck?"

Zarchy answered from Proverbs. "The lot is cast into the lap, but the decision is God's."

Sol frowned. Zarchy was harder to understand than their Rebbe in Bialystok.

"You're young and strong. Are you even twenty?" asked Zarchy.

"I'm twenty-two."

"You have a wife and a healthy baby. You make your own luck, Shlomo. And meanwhile, any time you need a good breakfast, come and pray with us. What a voice God gave you. The prayers never sounded so good."

"But Rabbi, what did it mean that I lost with the three queens and a pair of kings?"

"What do I know about cards? Maybe they cheated you. Maybe it was beshert. Maybe the three queens were a message for you, but you don't want to listen. Look, my young man, isn't your wife a queen?" The rabbi referred to Malke's name, which meant queen in Yiddish. Sol nodded.

"You mustn't neglect your profession. Did you know that God was the first tailor in the world? In Genesis: 3:17 it says, 'And the LORD Adonai made garments of skins for Adam and his wife and clothed them.'"

Sol felt a surge of pride.

"Well, be healthy, Shlomo, and don't be a stranger."

Trying to think what he would say to his bride, Sol paused in front of their tenement door. Again, with the jabs in his gut, he trudged upstairs. It was dark and silent, although there were slits of light below many of his neighbors' doors.

Bess stirred and whimpered as Sol entered their flat. He hurried to her crib, picked her up and took her into the hall. Holding the plump and fidgety bundle in his arms, he sang "Rozhinkes mit mandlen." The sweet melody of "Raisins and Almonds" relaxed her, and she molded her body to his. She squeezed his calloused fingers. Such a grip! She would have a violin. No, a piano. His little girl would shine on the piano. Bess began to wail. Such a voice. She could sing! Oh well, maybe she should decide for herself. It was America after all. She'd have whatever she wanted if he could just get the money to pay for it. He might have to give up music, but his daughter would not be denied.

Chapter 3
Fontaine Ferry Park

Bess pushed her five-year-old brother Calvin into the hallway. "Go wash your hands and face. Don't dillydally, or you'll make us late!" It was hot and itchy in her starched pinafore, but she was so eager to take the steamboat to Fontaine Ferry Park that she didn't mind her clothes. She could hear Momma in the apartment begging Bubby to go with them, but Bess's grandmother wouldn't budge. "Amusement parks. Bah!" Bubby had said. "That was where thieves made their living." Bess knew it was naughty, but she didn't mind if they left Bubby behind. Poppa in his linen suit stood quietly by the door. It was as if none of the commotion bothered him, Bess thought. Finally, Momma said it was time to go, and they hurried out.

There was a long line when the Toplanskys reached the Fourth Street dock. It would be her first ride on a riverboat. Momma held Bess's hand so tightly that her fingers hurt, and she tried to wriggle out of her mother's grip. At age six, she didn't need her mother treating her like a baby. As usual, Poppa had Calvin on his shoulders.

"Look at that, Poppa. Can we go to the top?" Calvin said, pointing to where the captain stood at the helm of the boat.

"If you behave, we'll go for a walk all around the boat."

"Calvin, get down and stand like a person," Momma said. "We're going aboard." She rifled through her purse. "Oy, I've lost the tickets! Where did I put the tickets?"

Sol put Calvin down and showed Momma the tickets. "Don't worry, Mollie. You gave me the tickets, remember? Calm down and enjoy yourself."

They filed onto the big boat and looked for seats in the shade. A tall young soldier Bess had seen in line moved over to share the only bench that was open. Poppa bowed to the young man and the soldier took off his cap and bowed in return. When the boat got underway, the captain steered out into the middle of the river. As soon as the boat got up some steam, there was a cool breeze and a calliope started to play. Bess pointed out a clock as big as a building on the far side of the river.

"That, kinder, is the Colgate Palmolive clock," Poppa explained. "The company what makes your toothpaste and soap. They brought that giant clock all the way from New Jersey."

"Such a country!" Momma said.

Sol asked Calvin if he wanted to go up to the captain's deck. Bess begged to go along, but Poppa asked her to stay behind to look after Momma.

"Sol, give an eye to the boy and don't let him run off."

Sol nodded and grabbed the boy's hand.

The soldier winked at Bess and offered her a piece of candy. Momma thanked him but said she didn't want her daughter to spoil her appetite. The soldier began telling Momma where he was from and lots of other stuff Bess couldn't hear. Why didn't Momma talk with her?

As the boat reached the park, the landing horn blew. Poppa and Calvin returned and took their seats. Momma and the soldier were still chatting. The young man was smoking a cigarette, and he offered Sol one. Sol thanked him but declined. The young man hurried off while Momma gathered their bundles. As they exited, Sol whispered, "What did that fellow want?"

"He misses his family," Momma answered.

The long wooden gangplank swayed in the water. Calvin jumped up and down on it.

"Calman, stop with the jumping!" Momma shouted. "You could fall in the river and drown."

Bess followed her family down the plank and pointed to an open spot halfway up the hill that led to the amusement park. They laid their blanket, one of many colored cloths covering the area, on a breezy spot. The barges' horns mixed with the laughter of picnickers, and the music floating down from the midway filled Bess with anticipation. Her first real concert. Poppa and Momma sometimes danced to concerts on the radio, but Bess had never seen musicians in person.

Momma proudly spread their supper out. Calvin skipped around with one knish in his mouth and one in his hand until Poppa pulled him down. Bess ate carefully so her new pinafore wouldn't get dirty. The food tasted so good outdoors, she thought. For dessert Momma had brought her favorite spice cookies with a big spot of grape jelly.

A lanky boy ran over and grabbed their picnic basket. Poppa caught the boy's foot and he fell. The boy scrambled to his feet and gave Poppa a red-faced grin.

"I didn't mean no harm. . . I's jist hungry," he said.

"Well, you should have asked for something," Momma said, admonishing the child.

Bess gave him her cookie, and Momma pulled out a knish from the basket. The boy stuffed them both into his mouth so quickly that Bess's eyes opened wide.

"Boy oh boy, they don't make nothin' that good at the orphanage!"

Sol reached into his pocket and gave the boy a nickel.

"Yippee! I'm gittin' me a ride on the Ferris wheel!"

Momma frowned and whispered something to Poppa, and he told her not to worry. They had plenty of money.

Bess wrinkled her nose at the dank odor that lingered after the boy left. It was a wonder that a boy from an orphanage was there at all, among all the picnickers. Orphanages kept children locked inside. They were dark and horrid. Weren't they? Her friend Millie had told her so.

"What's an arfinige?" Calvin asked.

"It's, God forbid," Momma said, "a home for children without parents."

Calvin looked puzzled, so Bess chimed in. "Orphans are kids who've lost their parents."

"And what's a Ferris wheel?"

Bess pointed at a big circle on the top of the hill, "See it? It looks like the paddle wheel on the boat." At age six, she'd only seen carnival rides in library books, but she liked pointing things out to her little brother.

"Can we go on the Ferris wheel?" Calvin asked.

"You're too young." Bess said.

"Momma?"

"No! Your sister is right. You are too little."

"And can we please go now, so we don't miss the music?" Bess urged them.

"We have time yet," Poppa said, "You're a worrier just like your mother. Let's have a little walk on the Midway."

But Momma insisted on the blessing after meals. Bess and Calvin fidgeted as Poppa and Momma chanted. Finally, they gathered their things and headed up the hill.

"I wanna go on the Ferris wheel!" Calvin insisted.

"I'm sure there will be something else you would like to do on the midway if we have time," Poppa said as they strolled past the rides. Huge roller coasters, the Loop-the-Loop, Dodge 'em Cars, and the Alpine Slide. Bess thought they looked scary.

As Bess asked again if it was time for the concert, Calvin darted off toward the Ferris wheel. When his family caught up, his mother grabbed him by the collar and scolded him.

"You must stay with us, Calman!"

Bess feared Calvin would ruin things the way he always did. Last Sunday he'd gotten so rambunctious while they were at Aunt Minnie and Uncle Sam's listening to Poppa sing on the radio, that he broke a china teapot which put Momma in a terrible mood and spoiled the gathering.

"Here we are children," Poppa said as they approached the carousel. "It's a beauty, ain't it?" Blue, silver, and gold horses with feathers and rhinestones bobbed up and down to a tune Poppa sang to Momma. *Oh, how we danced on the night we were wed.* Sometimes Poppa would dance with Momma and sometimes he would swoop Bess up into his arms and waltz her around the room. To Bess's delight they paused, and Poppa bought tickets. She chose a white bejeweled horse with a golden saddle. She loved rising and falling gently and waving to Momma and Poppa as they slowly spun around. Calvin, of course, wanted to stand on his horse, but Bess shook her head no and was happy to see he listened to her. As soon as the carousel slowed and the attendant helped them get off, Calvin begged to go again, but Momma and Poppa said no. One time was enough. He dragged his feet in the gravel all the way to the concert pavilion.

While the carousel was nice, Bess had waited all day for the concert. When they were finally seated, Poppa read them the program and told Bess and her brother what would happen. Sol pointed out all the different instruments as they warmed up to play. He promised that at intermission, he would take them up to meet his friend, the pianist. When the conductor came out and lifted his baton, Bess held her breath.

"The overture to *Marriage of Figaro*," Poppa whispered. Bess had never heard anything so beautiful in all her life. But it got better. There was a handsome tenor. Not as handsome as Poppa. The singer stood with a dark-haired lady in a long red dress with a red flower at her ear. Bess sat on the edge of her seat, her eyes glued to the performers.

Calvin fidgeted throughout all the numbers, until a singer dressed as a pirate came onto the stage followed by a group of men with swords and patches on their eyes. When the Pirate King jumped onto a treasure chest, Calvin hopped onto his seat. Bess pulled at her brother's legs hissing at him to sit down. Calvin whacked her on the head with his rolled-up program. Sol pulled him down and put him on his lap until the song was over.

At intermission people got up and wandered about. Poppa looked sternly at Calvin and warned him they would go home early if he could not behave. Calvin promised to be good.

"Hey," Momma said, "There are Fanny and Jake." She waved at her friends and said, "Hello!"

Momma kissed Fanny Broderson, and Fanny kissed the children.

"Oy Malke, look how pretty Bessele looks, pu, pu, pu!" Fanny said in Yiddish.

"Speak English, Fanny, and call me Mollie," Momma said.

"It's so warm. Let's get some lemonade," Jake said.

Sol nodded and loosened his collar. "A cold drink wouldn't hurt," he said.

As they wove their way through the crowd to the refreshment stand,

Momma linked arms with her friend, and Bess took Fanny's free hand.

Momma bragged. "What do you think of the children's sailor suits what my Sol just made? Calvin, show Aunt Fanny the sleeves."

But Calvin wasn't there. Bess looked all around to see where he had gone.

"Oy gevalt! Where is mein Calman!" Momma shouted. They pushed their way back to their seats, but the boy wasn't there. They couldn't see him anywhere in the pavilion.

"I bet he went to the Ferris wheel," Bess said.

"Yes," said her father. "Come on Jake, we'll go get him."

Bess asked, "Can I come?"

"No," Momma said. "You sit down on this bench and don't move. I don't want another child should get lost. Oy vey iz mir! What if he went down to the river?

"I'm sure he went to the Ferris wheel, Momma," Bess said. "If you let me go, I can help Poppa talk to the people in English."

"Yes," said Poppa, grabbing her wrist tightly. "Hurry, before he gets far."

It was getting dark and the lights of the rides and the aroma of spun sugar, popcorn and nuts, all things her momma would never let them have, were so enticing. Bess's eyes darted from the pastel-colored stuffed animals to the brightly lit ticket booths for the rides. How, she wondered, would her little brother pay for a ride? When they reached the Ferris wheel, Bess asked the ticket taker if she had seen a five-year-old boy with blond hair in a light-blue sailor suit. The woman said she hadn't.

Then Bess, Poppa, and Jake backtracked and watched the carousel as it circled, but no Calvin. Near the Loop-the-Loop there was a policeman. Jake rushed over to ask about Calvin, but Bess had to translate because the man couldn't understand Jake's English. The policeman said they should go to the lost and found at the entrance to the park, but the entrance was far away, and Bess was sure that Calvin would be at the Ferris wheel. So, they turned back. Poppa and Jake looked worried.

Bess knew Poppa must be thinking of the terrible things that had happened at fairs in the Old Country. There were accidents on the rides and even kidnappings. Things that Momma and Poppa had talked about when they thought she wasn't listening. Her memory of those awful things brought her back to Calvin. He was such a beautiful little boy. And so friendly. Too friendly.

When they got back to the Ferris wheel, Bess looked at all the little pods on the big wheel, but she only saw older children and adults. Then as the wheel lifted a new pod to the top, Bess saw a tiny boy in a sailor suit. She yelled to her father, "Isn't that Calvin up there sitting with a lady in a red hat?" Her brother was barely as tall as the safety bar.

"Calman," Poppa screamed.

Calvin waved at them, and when his pod returned to the top of the wheel, he took his hands off the bar, raised them, and yelled "hello." He looked so small that Bess forgot to be mad at him for a minute. She had to admire the little monkey, but then she worried he would stand on the seat like he had done at the concert. He was so high up. As she watched the wheel go around, she felt like the ground was moving.

"Poppa yelled, "They must stop that ride. He could slip under the bar."

They ran over to the man working the controls for the ride.

"Mein boy is too small. He could fall out," "Sol tried to explain.

"Til they go round twice more, I ain't stopping," the man said. "Why in heck you let such a small boy on the ride?" He barked in such a mean way that Bess stepped behind her father.

"Ignernt greenies!" the man exclaimed.

Bess puffed out her chest and shook a finger at the man. "Well, I'm going to get the police over there," she said. She turned and ran to the man in a blue uniform at the next ride.

"My baby brother is going to fall out of the Ferris wheel, and the man won't stop it."

The policeman followed Bess and ordered the operator to stop the ride immediately. The people got off pod by pod. Calvin's pod was at the top and it was swinging back and forth. Thank goodness, he was still sitting. You never knew with her brother. As he got closer to the ground, Calvin waved, grinning his monkey grin from ear to ear. Before the operator could release the safety bar, Calvin slipped under it and ran to Poppa excitedly.

"Boy oh boy, that was great! Can I go again, Poppa? Please!"

The woman in the red hat had now joined them.

"Thank you for taking care of my son," Poppa said.

The woman bent to Calvin and lightly pinched his cheek. "Oh! So, you aren't an orphan! I wondered about those nice clothes." She smiled at Poppa and said, "Well, you have him back safe and sound."

But Poppa wasn't as easy going. His face went red, and he smacked Calvin's bottom. "Ligoner. Liar."

"I'm not a liar," Calvin said. "I never said I was an arfin. I just said I lost my parents."

The woman in the red hat laughed, then waved her goodbye.

Bess did not laugh. "We're missing the music, and it's all your fault."

"Oy, Calman. You made your mother so worried," Poppa said. "No more Fontaine Ferry for you. We're going home."

When she realized that meant the outing was over, tears welled up in Bess's eyes as they marched back to find Momma and Fanny. She knew better than to ask her father to stay. Poppa rarely got angry, but when he did, you'd better watch out.

Momma saw them approaching and ran to her son. In a fierce hug, she spoke to him, "Oy, Calman, mein kint. My baby, you frightened me so."

Bess thought her momma ought to scold her little brother, but she just kept hugging him and saying his name over and over. When Jake told Fanny how Bess had gone for the police, Fanny praised her and gave her a chocolate covered cherry. Bess felt proud as she unwrapped the golden foil and popped the candy in her mouth. The chocolate was soft. She let it melt completely before she bit into the cherry. So sweet, but it didn't make up for missing the show. The noise of barkers, rides, bells, gongs, and throngs of people hurt her ears. Their night at Fontaine Ferry Park was ruined and it was all Calvin's fault.

Chapter 4
The Soldier

Mollie was relieved when Jake and Fanny insisted on driving them home from the park. The walk to the parking lot was tiresome. Both children were dragging their feet in the gravel.

"Sol, carry the boy," Mollie said. "I'm dying from the heat."

When they reached the lot, Jake pointed out his new car. Their shiny green roadster made Mollie a bit, as the Yankees would say, green with envy. Up front, Jake was pointing out the car's features to Sol, while in back, Fanny described their new place in Uptown. Mollie's head was spinning from the events of the evening, and she was getting one of her bad headaches, so she just nodded yes to everything. Fanny had a refrigerator, shiny white, an electric carpet sweeper, and a piano in the front room. Mollie wanted to feel happy for her dear friend, but this too she envied.

Gotsudanken, they got home quickly. Never was Mollie so relieved to see their blighted tenement. She couldn't wait to go to bed. She begged off Jake and Fanny's invitation to come over for dessert after they put the children to bed.

"Sol, you should go," she'd said to be polite, and, to her chagrin, he accepted. Hearing him singing softly as he carried Calvin up the stairs, she couldn't go back on her word. When they reached their flat on the third floor, Sol gave her a peck on the cheek and sprinted downstairs.

Mollie turned the lock to their two-room flat as quietly as she could. Her mother snored loudly in the rocking chair where she slept with her feet propped on a stool. The goose feather pillow and quilt from the Old Country softened Momma's makeshift bed. Mollie grabbed the children's toothbrushes, washrags, and towels from the cupboard by the sink.

"Bessele, go and help your brother wash up," she whispered as she looked for her headache powder. Bess hurried her brother out the door. Mollie poured herself a glass of water and downed the headache medicine in one gulp. She stepped out of the apartment to supervise, but her little Bess was managing. Thankfully, the hall was empty. No neighbors wanted to get into the washroom. The kinder had clean teeth and faces when they stepped out. Back in the apartment they put on their night clothes. Calvin marched straight to the bedroom without a peep. Mollie stayed in the main room where Bess slept on a little cot to listen to her prayers and kiss her goodnight.

She tiptoed into the bedroom and went over to the crib where Calvin was curled up in a knot. He'd outgrown the crib, but they had nowhere else for him to sleep. What a shame! Sol said he should sleep on a palette on the floor, but no matter how spotless she kept the place, there were vermin. She wouldn't have her baby boy sleeping on the floor. What a devil he was and what an angel he looked like when he was asleep.

She turned on a little lamp, opened a jar of cold cream, and wiped off her makeup. No doubt her Sol was playing cards with Jake and would lose track of time. She resented the cards, but now that Maishe's tailor shop was so busy, Sol never had time to sing. Playing cards was his only relaxation. Thanks God, Momma was asleep and didn't learn about what had happened at the park. Thanks God, Bessele had taken charge of little Calman and thanks God, Calman had let her. She hung her cotton dress up on a hook to air out, opened the window to the fire escape, pulled down the bedspread, and collapsed on the bed. A cool breeze was blowing, and the street noise had died down.

If only she could have gone to see Fanny and Jake's new apartment. If only they too could move. She tried to be happy their friends had been able to find a new and bigger place, but it wasn't easy. It seemed like they had moved to the other end of the earth. She missed them. Fanny and Jake didn't have any relations here, so the Toplanskys were their family. And without children, such a shame. A trial and a tribulation really, but that meant they had more money for nice things like a new car and an apartment away from this crowded, rat-infested neighborhood. Oh well, Sol and she were doing well enough working for Maishe Yoffee. Now that Momma was with them, Mollie could work full time and not just do alterations at home. Soon enough, they too would have the money to move, God willing.

Mollie thought she'd fall sleep as soon as her head hit the pillow, but the night's events had excited her. Even with the headache powder, her temples throbbed. She squeezed her eyes tight and heard the whistle of the freight train that passed through Louisville every night at ten. She didn't much like trains, with so many people all crowded together. But boats, they were worse. How she had let Sol convince her to step onto that riverboat she couldn't imagine. She hadn't been on a boat since the ship from the Old Country, The Rotterdam, and such a horrid journey that was. She'd been sick for the whole crossing. She wouldn't think about it. The train whistle blew one last time and the knot in her neck finally relaxed. She turned on her side, facing the breeze, and watched the curtain as it danced in and out.

She thought of the sweet fellow who had offered them his bench on the steamboat. He reminded her of the young soldier she met on the train on her trip to Holland. That awful, crowded train. Was it the cigarettes or his kind eyes that brought back the memory?

Only nineteen years old, Malke Kagan had been traveling alone from Poland to the Netherlands where she would board a ship in Rotterdam to sail to New York. Her brother Shmuel in America had sent money for the train and for passage on the ship, but she didn't have a travel visa for Germany. Her uncle had told her that when they came to check papers, she should go to the bathroom and hide, but what, she worried, would she do with her suitcase and bundles?

At the German border, a group of soldiers boarded the train, filling in all the empty seats. She could see that the soldier who stood next to her had no place to sit, so she moved her bundle and shyly offered him the seat next to her. He wasn't talkative, but he asked her where she was going and the words were similar to Yiddish. Later, he offered her half of his sandwich, but she declined, smiled, and turned her head to the window. As they got nearer to Berlin, the soldier said officials would soon check their papers. He took out his identity card and motioned for her to do the same. She shook her head no.

"No papers," she said, and he nodded and said, "Don't worry." As they pulled into the station, the soldier told her to put her head on his shoulder and pretend she was asleep. He put his arm around her. Mollie had never been so close to a man who wasn't a relative.

When the inspectors boarded the train, they demanded papers from everyone. "Ihre papiere, ihre papiere," they barked. Mollie trembled when the inspector stopped at her seat, but she kept her face against the soldier's woolen coat. To this day, she remembered his smell of wool and tobacco.

"Meine frau schläft," the soldier told the guard. Mollie understood that the soldier said his wife was sleeping. The guard stood nearby while he examined all the soldiers' documents. Satisfied, he eventually moved on to the next car.

As they pulled out of Berlin, the young man whispered, "You're safe."

Whether it was from fear or from the comfort she felt resting against the soldier's warm body, Mollie fell asleep and didn't wake until the young man nudged her. He told her they were close to the border and that he would be departing with his unit.

She sat straight in the seat and waited until the train chugged to a stop. Before he left, the soldier reached out for her hand.

"I wish you a safe journey," he said, squeezing her fingers lightly, smiling, his deep blue eyes sparkling.

Oh, Mollie, thought, on the brink of sleep, those eyes. She had never forgotten. That young man on the riverboat today had blue eyes, too, but he wasn't as tall as her soldier on the train, not as strong. And no woolen coat.

Mollie's every muscle begged for sleep, so finally she let her eyes close. Before long, she was dreaming of their sunny outing on the riverboat. But the sky grew dark, and bolts of lightning jolted her. She was rocking violently in a dark low-ceilinged room with people wrapped in blankets, retching in an enormous bucket, and rolling in filthy gray waves with suitcases banging and dead rats floating by and people yelling in so many languages. She tried to keep her head above the rising water, but she felt herself going under and began to scream.

Mollie woke to find Calvin in bed with her, his small arms clutching her neck. "Momma, momma, what's wrong?"

From the doorway came Sol's voice, "Calvin, haven't you made enough mischief for one night?"

"Momma had a bad dream again," Calvin said vaulting back into his crib.

"Malke, what's wrong?" Sol put his hand on her shoulder.

"I'm so thirsty. Could you bring me a glass of water and turn off the light so the baby can go back to sleep."

"I'm not a baby."

"Calman, gay shlafen," Sol said, commanding the boy to sleep.

As Mollie drank the water, Sol gently wiped her hot face and shoulders with a cool washrag.

"About the boat?" he whispered.

Mollie shook her head yes and finished the water.

"I'm here now," Sol said. "Everything will be all right."

Sol knew she had nightmares about the stormy crossing to America, but she had never told him about the soldier on the train. She had never told anyone. The young soldier belonged only to her.

"So, how is Jake and Fanny's new place?" Mollie whispered.

"It's nice and soon we will have a nice place too. I promise." He held Mollie close. She hoped her greenhorn tailor with the golden voice and hands could keep his promise.

Chapter 5
Uptown Yankees

"Here comes the streetcar, Momma!" Bess said jumping with excitement. Mollie bent to grab Bess's hand, but her daughter had hopped onto the trolley like a grasshopper.

"Bess, wait for Momma." Mollie examined a free seat to make sure it was clean. "Here, sit here."

"You look so pretty, Momma." Bess said as her mother checked her makeup in a golden compact. "Could I have some powder?" Mollie patted a bit on Bess's nose. "Oh, Momma, that smells so good. A shaynem dank," she said to thank her.

"Only English today, Bessele, "Mollie said and then laughed, realizing she'd used her daughter's Yiddish nickname.

It was worth the money to take the trolley. It was a hot afternoon, and they were running late. Her mother Adel had been so difficult about watching Calvin. "I raised six children with no help. I don't know why you need help with two," she'd said. She had a few choice things to say about the length of Mollie's dress and the matching white linen dresses her daughter and granddaughter wore. According to Adel, a color like navy or gray would not show the dirt.

"Momma, there's the Neighborhood House," Bess said.

"Oy, we almost missed it. Be careful," Mollie said as the girl jumped off.

"I have a surprise for you today, Momma."

"Well, be sure to keep your clothes clean. No playground for you."

As they climbed the steps of the Neighborhood House, Mollie's heart was racing. She was going to graduate from her English course and soon she would start citizenship class. Bess skipped down the hall and Mollie rushed to catch up. As Mollie checked her in at the children's section, she saw the new teacher, a pretty young woman, waving from the back of the room.

"Momma, that's the music teacher."

Mollie gave Bess a kiss, leaving a red Cupid's bow on the girl's cheek.

"Momma, don't forget I have a surprise."

"I won't," said Mollie using her kerchief to wipe the smudge off Bess's cheek. "Now be a good girl."

The classroom was crowded with all the women Mollie had studied with. Fanny Broderson had promised to save seats. Mollie spied her at the back of the room. Fanny stood and bent over to give Mollie a kiss.

"Malke, dos iz a shayn kleyd!" Fanny complimented the white dress trimmed in navy.

"Only English today, Fanny."

When their teacher Miss Beyer walked in, everyone rose. They recited the Pledge of Allegiance, and then Miss Beyer motioned for them to take their seats. She put on her reading glasses and opened a big envelope.

"I'm very proud of this group," Miss Beyer began. "Each one of you has worked hard to pass the English Level A test. I encourage you to enroll in Level B after Labor Day. In your Level B class, you'll study for the citizenship test. I know you all want to become citizens of the United States of America. Please come forward for your certificate when I call your name."

When it was finally Mollie's turn, she felt like a giant though she was only four foot ten.

After the ceremony, the women drank punch and stood shyly in little groups: Italians with Italians, Lebanese with Lebanese, and Poles with Poles. Mollie asked Fanny about Jake's promotion at the newspaper. Fanny leaned over to answer. People said they looked like Mutt and Jeff, but Mollie knew people teased them because they were pretty.

"You haven't been over to visit in ages," Fanny said. "You know how Bessie loves to sit with me when I play piano. I could teach her some songs."

Mollie wrinkled up her nose and tried to think of a kind way to tell her friend that she did not want her daughter learning the Second Avenue Yiddish songs Fanny loved. When they got a piano, Bess would learn classical music like her father.

"Oh, how sweet of you to offer. It's just we're so busy with the new orders. Maishe Yoffee wants him to be a partner, you know, but mine Sol wants us to have our own shop. Oh dear, I almost forgot. Bess said she had a surprise for me. I must go."

"May I go with you?"

"Of course, but let's hurry. I want to get home and show Sol mine certificate."

The two friends hurried down the shiny linoleum hallway. As they entered the playroom, Bess ran up and hugged them both. Mollie was horrified to see that one of her daughter's white knee socks was snagged. She was about to scold Bess for being so careless when the tall slender teacher walked up to introduce herself.

"Mrs. Toplansky, I'm Althea Rivers. Congratulations on passing your course."

"Thank you very much, Miss Rivers. This is mine friend Fanny Broderson."

"Pleased to meet you. Mrs. Toplansky, I wanted to talk to you about Bess."

Mollie winced. "Is there a problem?"

"On the contrary. Come, we've been working on a surprise for you."

Althea Rivers turned and led them to another room which had rows of music stands and a dilapidated upright piano.

Bess scrambled onto the bench and then onto a big book that enabled her to reach the keys. She splayed her fingers with a slight curve then looked at her teacher for her cue. Miss Rivers was such a graceful young woman.

"Ladies, Miss Bess will play 'Ode to Joy.'"

Mollie smiled with pride as Bess played the first notes. She recognized the tune and Fanny sang the words in Yiddish. "Alle Menschen seinen Breeder, (All men are brothers)." After the last note, Bess got up and curtsied. Fanny applauded with glee and Mollie wiped the tears from her eyes.

"What's wrong, Momma?"

"Nothing, mamesheine. You were wonderful."

"I noticed Bess picking out tunes on a toy piano, so I've been teaching her scales and some songs. She has a very good ear, and she holds her hands well. We've only been working on this piece a few weeks, so you can see she has talent. Bess should have piano lessons," Miss Rivers said. "She is at the perfect age to begin."

"Oh, thank you miss, Teacher, but we don't have piano for her to practice."

"She could practice at my studio, and she can use this piano when you come here."

"That would be an imposition."

"Not at all. Here's my card," the teacher said. "Let me know if you want to bring her for a free trial lesson, and we can work out something as far as payments. Bess tells me your husband made her dress and yours. I'm getting married soon, and I will need a trousseau. We could make a trade."

"I'll talk it over with her father. Thank you, thank you, Teacher," Mollie said nervously as they took their leave.

"If you can wait, mine Jake would give you a ride home," Fanny said.

"A shaynem dank, but it's out of your way, and Bessele loves the vagonetke."

"English, Mollie, speak English."

On the way home, Mollie thought about a piano. She and Sol had already discussed music lessons for Bess. A piano like Fanny and Jake's looked so elegant in their parlor. A piano was something Mollie wanted for her family, if only they had the room and the money. Well, if they had the money, they would have the room. Mollie shook her head sadly.

Bess interrupted Mollie's worries. "It's so hot. Could we stop for a root beer?"

Mollie looked in her coin purse and answered, "It would be nice to celebrate, but if we have a soda we'll have to walk home. All right?"

Bess agreed eagerly. They lingered over the tall chilly glasses and enjoyed the cool air blowing through the soda shop. And walking home wasn't so bad. The sun had begun to set and there was finally a nice breeze.

When they got home, the apartment was quiet. They tiptoed inside. It was only seven thirty, but Mollie's mother was fast asleep. As always, her Momma had her feet propped up on a stool, a goose feather pillow behind her back. Although it would still be light in the windows for quite a while, Bess would go right to bed. Mollie poured herself and Bess a cup of milk from the icebox. They stood together trying not to laugh at Momma Adel's gusty snores as they ate cream cheese and ryebread sandwiches with slices of cucumber. Bess got ready for bed without a word and pulled her folding cot from behind a cupboard. Her mother tucked her in and kissed her good night.

"Where's Poppa? Do you think he'll let me have piano lessons?"

"We'll see. You just say your prayers and sleep tight."

Mollie went into the bedroom upset that Sol wasn't home yet. She stood over Calman, her little boy, her beautiful, perfect, golden-haired angel of a boy, as he slept. They had named him in Hebrew for her father, may his memory be for a blessing, a more learned man had never lived, and in English, for their president, Calvin Coolidge. Poor thing, Calvin's ringlets were wet with perspiration. But worse, her baby boy was now five years old and could no longer stretch out to sleep in the crib. He was so active in his sleep, he banged about and got bruised, but now, he'd found his thumb and was perfectly calm. She took the thumb out of his mouth, so he wouldn't have crooked teeth. Bad enough he had a crooked thumb.

She removed her makeup in the fading daylight. As she rubbed glycerin and rose water into her hands, she thought about what the teacher had said, but how could they afford lessons when they were saving every penny to move out of their cold-water flat. When she left Europe, Mollie had thought she would soon have a house with a garden and indoor plumbing, fine carpets, mahogany furniture, and a piano. But where would they get all that on Sol's wages, and where would they put a piano?

Mollie paced in tiny circles wondering what was keeping her Sol. Then she sat on the edge of the bed. Despite angry thoughts, she stretched out on top of the covers and fell fast asleep until she heard the creak of their bedroom door and bolted upright.

"What, you're still awake?" Sol bent over Mollie and gave her a big hug and kiss.

"Sol, Sol, shah, shtill, you'll wake Calman. Why are you so late? I was so worried," she whispered.

Sol motioned for her to step out onto the fire escape. He helped her out, wiped his handkerchief on a stair for her to sit, and pulled a big roll of dollar bills out of his pocket.

"What, you have been gambling again? You promised you would only play penny pinochle with Sam and Jake."

"Well, I was feeling lucky tonight, and I was."

"Were you in that goniff Mendy's place?"

"Look, Malke, so much money. Fifty dollars!" Sol avoided the question.

"Tomorrow, you put that money in the bank. And I tell you this, if you touch it to play poker with those crooks again, I'll take Momma and the kids and walk out on you."

"Oh," Sol laughed, "and where would you go?"

"To Minnie and Sam." Although Sol's sister and brother-in-law had recently moved to Louisville, Mollie already thought of Minnie as a sister.

"My sister and Sam?" Sol was going to make a joke, but Mollie's eyes burned in fury, so he promised he wouldn't play high stakes poker again.

"Malke, my beauty, with this money what I won, tomorrow I'm going to show you something wonderful. I've found a new apartment uptown, and we could have our own tailor shop on the first floor. It's on East Broadway away from these filthy tenements."

Then he ran his warm hands on her shoulders. As he leaned in to kiss her neck, he whispered, "You always smell like roses."

She pushed him away. "You smell like smoke."

All night long Mollie tossed and turned. She wanted to move, but this was so sudden. Everything was so sudden. When she saw a faint light in the windows, she threw on her clothes, grabbed a towel, soap, and hurried out to the communal bathroom. She wanted to look her best when she inspected this new place what Sol had found. Back in the kitchen, she slipped a gingham smock over her dress. Calvin wandered out of the bedroom with sleepy eyes, but he had enough energy to slam the door and wake his sister and grandmother. "So much for a quiet morning to get ready," Mollie thought.

After breakfast the entire family took the trolley up Broadway. Most passengers had gotten off by the time they saw Brennard Flour Mills. "We're almost there," Sol said with a big grin. When they crossed Barrett Avenue, Sol pulled the cord to get off. As the family scrambled off at the corner, Sol exclaimed, "We're here. Look across the street, Mollie. That would be our tailor shop and our home." Then he turned her to look at the graceful white building behind them. "You see, the children would have a beautiful school. And look up the street at all the big houses with fine gardens. Someday, maybe, we too could have a house of our own."

They crossed the street. There was a barber shop on the corner. As Sol was about to knock on door at 1121, Momma Adel pointed to a stone church just one door away. She cursed and spat on the ground.

"Oh, Momma Adel," Sol said. "Not to worry. A church will bring business. And our new synagogue, when it's finished, will not be far, and up the block you could visit with the Cohens, and Mollie's friend Fanny lives up the hill too."

To Mollie he said, "Mrs. Zimmerman's grocery is just two blocks away, and the kosher butcher is close. This neighborhood will be good for business. Think how many people will walk by our shop."

A tall, pale man in a black suit and hat opened the front door to the shop.

"Mr. Schuster, please to meet mine wife and her mother and the children."

The man doffed his hat and said, "You know, Mr. Toplansky, I need an answer today. You take your time looking around, but come by my office and give me the deposit and a month's rent by five, or it will go to someone else. And you know the rent is due every first of the month. On the dot." Mr. Schuster shook Sol's hand, bowed to the women, and walked out.

The windows of the shop were covered in newspaper, but enough light filtered in to see the nice linoleum floor and ample workspace. Calvin charged up the stairs to a loft and grinned down at his family through the railing.

"Come down here this minute, you devil," Mollie ordered, "and don't ever put your head between the railings."

Calvin flew down the stairs crashing into his big sister. Bess shoved him.

"Children, behave," Sol said. "Let's go see our new home."

From the loft there was a door to another half a flight of stairs. The family waited in the dark landing as Sol opened the door to an apartment full of light. The kitchen and parlor had big windows. Sol rushed over and opened them.

"Look, Mollie. An icebox and a Coleman Cooker. Bess, you'll sleep in here and be nice and warm." Mollie frowned. She wanted her daughter should have a bedroom of her own.

In the big parlor, Sol said, "Here Calvin, we'll put for you a couch to sleep on. No more crib. You're a big boy now. Momma, now you would have some privacy." He pointed to an alcove at the far end of the room. "We'll put up a curtain and you could have Murphy bed what comes out of the wall. And here," he pointed triumphantly, "we would put radio."

"And someday, a piano for Bess," added Mollie.

"Yes, when we save enough, we'll buy piano."

"Now, the best!" Sol's eyes were beaming. He motioned them through the door next to the kitchen. A bathroom. Their very own bathroom with a bathtub.

"Now, you wouldn't have to wait for the neighbors."

Then Sol showed Mollie the little bedroom with a narrow window high up facing west. "Imagine how well you would sleep in here, Mollie. It's nice and dark. There's room to put a chifforobe for all the new clothes I'll make for you."

Mollie wondered how she'd like such a dark room. She thought she might miss stepping outside on the fire escape on hot nights, but the room had shiny wooden floors and fresh wallpaper with daisies and roses.

"So, nu," Sol asked his bride, "do you like it?"

Mollie smiled and nodded her head.

"Now, kinder, you would really like this." Sol led them out the back door and down a flight of stairs into a garden. There was an apple tree, a trellis full of vines with bunches of dark purple grapes, and a tool shed. A metal gate led to the alley.

"No more playing in the muddy courtyard. Now you have a yard."

"Doesn't it belong to all the tenants?" Mollie asked.

"Well, the man in there, a Mr. Vilcox, I believe," Sol pointed to a room behind the shop, "works all day, so he wouldn't be here when the children want to play."

"Who lives up there?" Bess pointed at an old lady looking out her window at them from the third floor.

"Her name is Mrs. Djedje, or something like that," Sol said, taking off his hat to the woman. "We'll make her acquaintance soon."

While Calvin stared at the apple tree, Bess looked at the big white wooden house next door.

"Who lives there, Poppa?" Bess asked. "It's such a big house. Do you think one family lives there?"

Before Sol could answer, Mollie admonished them. "You must never go out on Broadway. Too many trolley cars and automobiles. It's not safe. You'll always play back here," Mollie commanded.

Mollie thought with satisfaction how far the new home was from the tenements. And far from the taverns near the river. Here the distance might keep her husband home. Besides, with his own shop, Sol would be too busy to have time for gambling. She wondered what kind of people lived in the little row houses on the streets behind the alley. They looked so rundown, nothing like the lovely brick homes that lined East Broadway further up the hill. Mollie shrieked as her son was clambering up the apple tree. She grabbed his legs and yanked him back to the ground.

Just then a young girl appeared at the back gate.

"May I come in?" the girl said. The child wore a spotless white pinafore. Her light brown hair was held in two tight braids. She looked about the same age as Bess, but she was much taller.

Sol opened the rusty gate with a flourish. The girl's name was Naomi, and she was also six. Naomi told them she lived in the parsonage of Concordia Lutheran Church, and she was so happy to have a girl her age next door. She invited Bess to go to her house and play with her baby doll and meet her brothers and sisters.

"Thank you, Naomi," Mollie said. "Another time my Bess can come to play. But we have to go now. Sol, we'll be late to the owner's to pay."

The move went off like clockwork. Sol's brother-in-law Sam loaned them his car to move their valises, and Maishe Yoffee drove their furniture in his truck. Mollie and Sol said goodbye to Maishe Yoffee in the alley behind their new home on Broadway.

Sol hugged his former boss with tears in his eyes. "It isn't every day that a man helps you so much."

"Well, don't think I haven't had second thoughts. My best tailor and my finest seamstress are setting up shop as competition, but I guess you are far enough from my store. You are Uptown Yankees now." His kind eyes sparkled as he wished them good luck. "Here you should only have mazel and glick."

Chapter 6
A New Home

September 1928

And they did have luck and happiness. School began, but Bess and Calvin didn't go across the street to the fancy white school as Sol had promised. That was the Normal School where they trained teachers. The children went to a lovely school three blocks away. Mollie wished her kids could walk to school with their well-behaved next-door neighbors the Habermanns, but Naomi and her brothers and sisters attended the Lutheran School. So, Calvin walked with a whole passel of boys, and Bess walked with a girl named Nancy, who lived in one of the run-down row houses on the other side of the alley. A girl whose hands weren't always so clean.

Mollie didn't like that she could see that girl's house, and the rest of the rickety, wooden houses, from her kitchen window. She had heard that some of those houses held four, maybe even five families each. And their back yards were weed-ridden and muddy. Bess had come home from school one day and repeated a story Nancy had told her, how one of their neighbors had died in childbirth, and how the husband had been forced to put his new baby in an orphanage. Ach, Mollie couldn't think of a worse thing than having to give up a baby.

She didn't dwell long on that misfortune. Instead, she counted her blessings. And they were many now, thanks God. Sol was earning enough for them to have this clean place away from the old tenements downtown. And despite the poor neighborhood across the alley, here she could open windows on three sides and breathe sweet, fresh air.

That morning, Mollie had noticed with satisfaction that the grapes had turned deep purple. Soon they would make wine. And next harvest season, they would have vegetables, too, like in the Old Country. If her mother wasn't always breathing down her neck, the kitchen would be perfect. Mollie shooed Adel away from the stove. Would it hurt for Momma to let her enjoy her new kitchen and cook in peace? Momma grumbled, picked up her Yiddish Bible, and headed for her rocker. Mollie hummed a little tune as she stirred a big pot of freshly chopped vegetables.

It wasn't just the house she liked. Her Sol had chosen a good location for their tailor shop too. In no time, business was growing. He had a big sign painted for the front of the building that attracted new customers every day. Initially, she had objected to altering the owner of O'Rourke's Barber Shop's suit gratis. But it had been a good idea. Immediately, they started getting people O'Rourke had referred, and he kept her husband's business cards at his cash register. Although they were prospering, Mollie still had to stitch hems evenings after Bess and Calvin were settled in, but Sol promised her that he would hire a seamstress soon. Not only that, if things kept busy, he would hire someone to help her around the house. And, as they both agreed, they would get a piano for Bess.

Mollie liked the rhythm of their new life on Broadway. Saturdays, they walked over a mile to the new synagogue, and after their Sabbath meal, Sol's sister Minnie and her family would gather for tea and dessert in their nice sitting room. If Momma Adel was out visiting her friends, they'd turn on the little radio. Sometimes, Minnie asked Sol to sing something. If it was an aria, he sang alone, but the Yiddish songs everyone sang along.

The Toplanskys didn't socialize with their next-door neighbors, the Lutheran Pastor Habermann and his wife Clara. Mollie and Clara exchanged polite hellos. Much as she wanted to get to know the mother of such bright and well-behaved children, Mollie knew that Clara had even less free time than she did. Besides being the mother of six and having the duties of a minister's wife, her neighbor was a full-time nurse. Oy, imagine, cooking, cleaning, standing to greet parishioners and then running around a hospital. At least a seamstress could sit to work.

Mollie remembered the time Clara leaned over the fence and tried in

German to speak with her mother, who understood but never answered. Another day, Clara Habermann brought Momma bulbs to plant so that the Toplanskys would have tulips in the spring. Adel had yelled for Bess to come and explain what the wife of the "priest" was saying. Mollie wished her mother could finally feel at home and safe from their Christian neighbors. But Momma didn't trust the German speaking neighbors. Hadn't the Germans made their life miserable enough in Bialystok? Sometimes she called the pastor a Yankee goniff, a thief. Loud noises still made Momma think the Cossacks were attacking. Who knew, perhaps, she'd always fear the next pogrom.

Toward the end of September, just when Sol was finishing orders of clothes for the Jewish holidays, he told Mollie he needed to go visit his friend and former employer Maishe Yoffe. Even though it was a Thursday, his old poker night, Mollie trusted Sol was telling the truth. He'd been working so hard of late. However, when he got home after midnight, she assumed the worst.

"All you know what to do is throw out our money," Mollie yelled.

"But Malke, I lost bupkes, pennies."

Mollie shook her fists at him in fury.

Sol tried to take her hands, but she yanked them from his grip. Usually, they had their spats in whispers so as not to wake Bess on her cot in the kitchen, but tonight she exploded with insults. "Why must you play cards when we are just starting to make good money? You think you're a bigshot, but you're a waster. A no-goodnik."

Mollie wouldn't calm down, and Sol hated to make his pretty wife unhappy, so he went to the little strong box and unlocked it. He gave her the bank book and key and said, "Here, it's your money to control. From now on you are the banker."

Chapter 7
A Good New Year

It was decided that after the High Holidays Bess would begin weekly lessons with Althea Rivers (now Mrs. Althea Parmer) who had bartered a trousseau from them in exchange for lessons. She kept telling Mollie that Bess would make more progress if they had a piano, but they couldn't afford one yet. Sol's weakness for cards had put them behind again.

The fall had brought a good change in Momma Adel. She began to venture out, at first escorted by Bess, but later, she rode the trolley alone. Without knowing English, she could recognize the big B for Broadway and hopped onto the car nimbly for a woman her age.

One Sunday when Momma Adel was visiting friends and Calvin was with Aunt Minnie and Uncle Sam, Bess and her parents took a walk downtown to Chestnut Street and stopped as always to look in the window at Shackleton's Pianos. Through the window, Bess admired the baby grands.

Sol pressed Bess's shoulder as he said. "So sorry, but such a fancy piano is not yet for us."

"Where would we put such a big piano?" Mollie added.

On Monday they went back downtown after Poppa closed the shop. This time they ventured inside Shackelton's. Mollie admonished Calvin to behave like a decent person. A salesman approached them quickly, and when he learned the piano would be for Bess, he invited her to sit down at a lovely ebony upright and try it. Mollie and Sol beamed as Bess played a few new songs. Calvin and the salesman applauded.

"So, how much would such a piano cost?" Sol asked.

When the salesman told them the price, Mollie was dismayed. "Oy, Sol, it's so much money."

"Ah, but you could use our generous installment plan. You'd only have to put fifty dollars down to get immediate delivery."

Sol thanked the man and said they would think on it. As they walked home, Mollie whispered to Sol, "How are we going to get so much money?"

"You see how our account is growing. Have some faith in me for once."

But Mollie knew they owed the grocer lady money and electric would come due soon, so the purchase of a piano was postponed again.

The rhythm of daily life quickened with the coming of Rosh Hashanah and Yom Kippur. Momma Adel bustled around the house preparing for the Jewish New Year. Now that Momma got out more, she didn't criticize Mollie and the kids so much. Mollie was pleased to see her smile as she baked honey cakes and made little knots of dough encrusted with nuts that she kept in jars full of honey. They put the rugs outside and beat them. They turned the mattress in Mollie's bedroom. "Spotless," they said to one another as they finished by scrubbing the kitchen floor so clean that you could eat off it. All of this for the arrival of Sol's older brother Avrom, who now was called Abe, and his family.

The brothers had been hired this year to chant the High Holiday services. Mollie hoped it would turn into a real job for Sol because she knew he missed singing. Moreover, it would mean extra income and a modicum of prestige. But there was competition. Not that the fellow could sing like her Sol.

Brother Abe lived in Indianapolis, and he would bring his wife Hettie and their two children, Pinkie and Sarah, in his big new Studebaker. Mollie wrote her sister-in-law Hettie to say that she and Abe would have their bed. After all, they were used to the best, but Hettie wrote back and refused. Hettie insisted that she and Abe would stay in a hotel, and only the children would stay in the apartment. In the letter, Hettie said she and Abe would have a second honeymoon. Mollie knew that the honeymoon would be not having to worry about little Pinkie. He was five like Calvin but such a handful. Sweet, but Pinkie was so slow-witted and a devil sometimes. Lucky thing, Sarah, who was a bit older than Bess, was a smart cookie.

It was a warm October afternoon when Sol's brother and his family arrived at 1121 East Broadway to drop off the kids. Before the valises were even unpacked, Calvin started begging Uncle Abe to take him for a ride in his new car. Cousin Pinkie always imitated Calvin, so Adel pulled her grandson aside and admonished him to behave like a mensch.

Rosh Hashanah morning Sol and Abe left early to don their white prayer robes and to warm up their voices. Mollie didn't need warming up. The kitchen was sweltering, and she was dashing about getting the kids ready.

"Oy gevalt," Mollie yelled as she slipped and fell. By her hand was a green marble. Last night the kids had been playing the new game Abe and Hettie brought them, Chinese Checkers. When Pinkie lost, he threw the board up in the air and the marbles spun all over the living room and even into the kitchen. Mollie bit her tongue but thought it was her luck to find the last one.

The women and children left the house at ten. Calvin and Pinkie skipped and ran all over the sidewalk. Mollie trusted Bess and Sarah to make the boys stop at the corners. She was starting to sweat in her linen suit and wondered how Hettie could stand to wear her fox stole. Oh well, it felt so good to walk arm and arm with her sister-in-law, and she knew they would have time to have a nice long schmooze since services would last all day. Adel brought up the rear complaining in Yiddish about her bunions.

The children scampered up the stairs to the women's section of synagogue. Fanny Broderson had saved seats in the front so Mollie and Hettie could see their husbands lead the chanting. Mollie was so proud of Sol and was sure he would make a good impression. As the men, wrapped in their prayer shawls, were immersed in supplications to God, the women upstairs kept up a steady buzz of gossip. Fanny, Hettie, and Mollie admired one another's holiday clothes. Fanny asked about Bess's music lessons and Mollie reported she was doing well. Fanny invited Bess to come play on their piano, but Mollie whispered to Fanny that, God willing, soon they would have a piano of their own. Hettie bragged how smart her Sarah was, how well she read and wrote. She didn't say much about little Pinkie except how good natured he was. Adel told the women to be quiet and pray. "The cantors' wives should set an example," she said as she showed Mollie the place in the prayerbook.

Before the noon break, the temperature upstairs got so hot, Mollie felt woozy. She went downstairs to the lady's room. Her face was crimson in the mirror. She moistened her hanky and slipped into a stall to loosen her corset. From inside she heard one woman tell another how good the cantors sounded. Mollie was rebuttoning her dress to go out and chat when the other woman said that any tenor would sound good with such a baritone.

"If you ask me," the woman said, "my nephew Mordechai sings as well as that tenor. What's more, my nephew comes daily to the men's morning prayers. Why should they give the job to that tailor when he isn't even a regular at the minyan?"

Mollie waited in the stall until the women left. When she leaned into the mirror to reapply powder, her face was on fire. What else did those women know of her Sol? What were other people saying? Another woman walked in and wished Mollie a good sweet, blessed year. Mollie smiled and wished her the same, but inside she felt sick.

At noon, Mollie and Hettie left shul to make sure everything would be ready for the holiday dinner. They found the children playing tag with other kids on the front walk and sent them back in to stay with their Bubby. Strolling home, Hettie praised Sol's singing. Mollie smiled and tried to forget the awful woman in the bathroom.

"Your Sol is such a hard worker. Soon you'll have a house."

"Well, business is good..." Mollie said. She wondered whether a tailor could ever make enough money to have a big house like her sister-in-law's in Indianapolis.

"My Abe says you have to be a fool in these times not to make money. His customers say he should put money in the stock market, but instead Abe's going to open a bakery next to the restaurant. That's the good thing about a restaurant, he says. 'People always gotta eat.' And, lucky for you, they can't go around naked, right?" Hettie laughed.

Eight days later came Yom Kippur. They rushed to eat the chicken in the pot and get to synagogue before sunset. The whole congregation stood in silence as the brothers harmonized to the ancient prayer asking God to annul all vows that would be made in the coming year. Then as they stood and pounded their chests in a communal confession of sins, Mollie felt faint and had to sit down. Her mother frowned at her and prodded her to stand but she could not.

"I need air, Momma. I feel so dizzy." So, the children walked their mother home. She served them some milk. They were too young to fast. And even though she would be fasting for twenty-seven hours, the milk didn't look the least bit tempting. Mollie fell asleep as her head hit the pillow.

The next day Mollie woke up refreshed and ready to fix a bite for the children and set the table for breaking the fast. The adults wouldn't eat until well after dark.

Lucky Hettie. She had a cleaning lady and didn't have to lift a finger. And yet that morning Mollie felt so bad for her sister-in-law. Hettie never did well at the prayers that listed your sins. Who knew why, but Mollie suspected that Hettie blamed God that Pinkie was so slow. Or maybe she blamed herself. Poor Hettie had to be so patient with Pinkie's childishness, and that burden would never change.

All morning the women stood in the hot synagogue pounding their chests and listing their sins. At midday there was a break to go home and rest. Adel didn't go home. Instead she said she would catch a catnap in her seat.

Mollie returned with Hettie for Yizkor services. The prayers for the dead always left Mollie feeling so sad. It was painful to remember her dear father. She left immediately after the memorial service even though she didn't like to miss the blowing of the ram's horn that ended Yom Kippur. That part of the service, truth be told, was the best. If the shofar blower was good, those blasts were so long and so loud you could feel them in your gut.

As she walked home up Broadway, Mollie could see the moon rising, and it was dark enough that cars had their headlights on. It still surprised her to see automobiles near shul. Growing up in Bialystok, the Jewish neighborhood was quiet as a graveyard on Yom Kippur, or as Poppa, may his memory be for a blessing, used to say, "So quiet, you could hear the rabbi's beard grow." Here even some Jews drove on Yom Kippur.

When everyone else returned from services to break the fast, Mollie sighed that the peace and quiet had been so brief. She smacked Calvin's hand as he reached for a bialy and said, "First you must pray. Go, take Cousin Pinkie to wash his hands."

They gathered in the kitchen to light and bless the braided blue and white Havdalah candle that signified that they had transitioned from the Holy Day to the new day. The chopped herring, egg salad, and sweet noodle pudding disappeared. After breaking the fast, everyone gathered in the back yard to watch Sol and Abe begin building the sukkah, the little hut where they would take their meals during the week-long Feast of Tabernacles. At ten, Mollie and Hettie announced that it was time for the children to go to bed.

Sol asked Mollie if she'd mind if he accompanied Abe and Hettie to the hotel. His brother wanted to talk to Sol about something. Instead of working on the sukkah, they would build it in the morning. It had been such a long day, and Mollie would have liked to just close the bedroom door with her husband and rest. Why didn't Sol tell Abe that whatever it was, it could wait until morning. But off the men went with Hettie, leaving Mollie to get the children calmed down and into bed.

Finally, after the young ones were asleep and Sarah and Bess had quieted their giggles and whispers, Mollie collapsed onto her bed. Around midnight she heard a truck rumble down the street. Sol should have been back long ago. She put on her robe and tiptoed through the kitchen. Sarah and Bess slept in an embrace. What angels when they weren't in cahoots. Bess with her straight golden-brown hair and Sarah with her dark curls. Mollie went out to the back landing and sat down to wait for her husband.

Such a starry night. The High Holiday services had gone well. Ach, she was so proud. Sol's sweet tenor voice melding with his brother's resounding baritone. People had made such nice comments. Well, most of them. Fanny said she was sure that they wouldn't hire that skinny nebesh Mordechai with the screechy voice. Her girlfriend was sure the board would hire Sol as the cantor, so Mollie could look forward to putting more money away.

When she heard a church bell toll one, Mollie started to worry. What if Sol and Abe had gone gambling? But Sol had promised never to play poker with the men at the tavern, and anyway Abe was not a gambler. He had a good head on his shoulders. He wouldn't let his younger brother waste his money. But maybe Abe had gone back to the hotel, and Sol had gone to play by himself. Just a week ago there had been a shooting at Mendy's Tavern. What if Sol was hurt? God forbid--or dead? How he could make her insides churn with worry.

Tiptoeing up the back stairs, Sol smiled widely at Mollie. He bent to kiss her, but she pulled away and shook a finger at him.

"You, how could you? You make me worry so much. Where were you all night? You played poker. You lost the high holiday money."

"Oy, Mollie! Why do you worry so much? I didn't play poker. Abe and I took Hettie to the hotel, but we weren't sleepy, so we went and visited by Sam and Minnie. We had some schnapps, and then we took a long walk down by the river."

"You ate trayf! You went to that oyster place on the dock."

"No, we didn't have oysters, but we sat by the river and talked like we used to in the Old Country. It was so warm, we thought about swimming."

"In that dirty river what could give you a disease?"

"We didn't swim, but I told him how the store is going, and he approves of all what we've done. He says his restaurant is booming. People are spending money. They want new cars, new clothes. He thinks we'll be a big success. He's even thinking of opening another restaurant. We were in such a fine mood."

"You went to play poker," Molly interjected.

"No, I promised, remember? You hold the purse strings, right? We walked all the way down to the water tower, and Abe said he wanted to give me his money from the shul."

"The money that the synagogue paid him this year?"

"Yes, Mollie, yes! Abe says I need life insurance, but these twenty dollars we'll use for down payment on the piano. Oh, and I forgot to tell you. Sam heard that the rabbi and the board are in favor of hiring me. Now are you satisfied?"

The next day as Mollie washed the breakfast dishes, she watched the activity in their garden below. Abe and Sol finished the frame for the Sukkah. The children tired of gathering leaves and pine boughs for the roof and began to run and yell like wild animals. Soon they tumbled in laughter on the ground. Even though it had been a lot of work to take care of everyone for ten days, Mollie would be sorry to see Abe's family go home. She often felt alone and in need of company, and it was so wonderful to see the cousins play together.

After supper, the families wished one another a good year and said their goodbyes. Pinkie and Sarah would sleep in the hotel with their parents that night so they could get an early start in the morning. Abe promised they would come back soon to hear Bess play piano. Hettie was sure her niece would have her own piano by the next High Holidays.

After supper, it was so peaceful. They listened to the classical music hour on the radio as Bess and Calvin played their beautiful new game of checkers with marbles. Such fine wood and shaped like a Jewish star. As she rested her feet and leaned on Sol, Mollie thanked God her kids were so bright and healthy.

That night, Mollie had indigestion again, and she was calculating in her mind all the things they would need soon. Impossible. They couldn't afford a new piano now. Then she tried to remember the last time she had had her monthly bleeding. Not so long ago, she hoped. Oy gevalt, could she be pregnant again? Sol would love to have another baby, and she would too, but oh, the work. And the money. She looked at Sol sleeping peacefully. Such a good year they had had. If only God would grant them strength and prosperity in the year to come.

Chapter 8
Be Happy, It's Purim!

FEBRUARY 1929

Fanny sat in the window seat watching for Bess and Calvin. Spring had come early to Louisville, perfect for their visit. Such a show the trees made. Dogwood, magnolia, azaleas, redbuds. The hyacinths in blues and purples with their heady perfumes. Her garden was like paradise. All it needed was children to run around in it.

Sol and Mollie's kids would spend a few days with her and Jake. Mollie needed bedrest. Doctor Rubel's orders. Oy, she hoped Mollie could keep the baby. But oh, how she herself wanted a baby. Spring meant a daily parade of baby buggies up and down the street. Each chubby pink face begging to be picked up and held.

What was taking her Bessele and Calman so long? Fanny had planned to celebrate a perfect Purim with the children. Each and every year at Purim, Jake and Fanny watched other people's children dress up for carnivals and parades in synagogue. And each and every year, she would think, "Next year. Next year I'll have a baby to bring to shul." But that hadn't happened. So, Fanny always pretended to be happy.

It was a commandment to be joyous at Purim. After all, it was a celebration of the Jews' narrow escape from annihilation. The King of Persia's minister, an evil man named Haman, plotted to kill all the Jews. It was the only Jewish holiday when Jews were supposed drink to the point that they could no longer distinguish Haman's name. Jake always complied, though Fanny was sure he was also sad.

Fanny jumped up when she saw Calvin and Bess running up the street ahead of their bubby. She ran outside to help the old lady up the steps.

"Good morning," Fanny said, bending down with open arms to receive her visitors.

"A gut yor," Adel said, wishing Fanny a good year and nodding her hello.

Fanny covered Bess and Calvin with kisses. "Oy, children, such a good time we're going to have. Go inside and leave your bundles in the hall. Wash your hands and go in the dining room and see what we're going to do today." She turned to Adel and invited her in, but the old lady said she had to get back to her daughter.

"Is Mollie better?" Fanny asked with her hands on her face.

"Not to worry. It will be as God decrees," Adel said and spat three times.

Fanny told her to wait a minute. She ran inside and grabbed a basket that was filled with dried fruit and Purim pastries shaped like triangles. Fanny returned to find that Adel was already advancing down the street.

"Wait," Fanny called after her. "I wanted to give you this for the family." She handed her the basket and wished her a happy holiday. The old lady thanked her, then kept trudging down the street.

Back inside Fanny sat with the children at the table. "We are going to have such a Purim. Are your hands clean?" Fanny could see that Calvin and Bess were eager to try the pastries she had stayed up all night to bake. "Would you like a glass of milk and a hamantaschen pastry?" As the children dangled their legs and sipped the milk, Fanny put a triangle filled with poppy seeds and another filled with prunes on their plates. "Do you know why we make these with three corners?"

"Yes," Bess answered proudly. "They are like the hat that the bad man Haman wore."

"These hats are good," Calvin said with a mouth full of pastry.

Fanny told them what she had planned for the day. First, they would put some coins in the charity box. Then they would fill the baskets and deliver them to friends. After lunch, they would make their Purim costumes.

"I want to be Queen Esther," Bess cried.

"Of course, you do. I have such pretty things for you to wear. And Calman, you must be King Ahasuerus."

"Okay, but do I get to have a sword?"

"Uncle Jake made you a scepter. It's like a sword, but you must you promise to be very careful."

"Now Bessie, you put nuts and dried fruit in these bags. Calman you put the bags and an orange in each basket." As Calvin went around the table filling the baskets with the goodies, he stopped by Bess's station to steal a nut or a raisin. After a while he started sneaking the pastries. Bess grabbed him, he shoved her, a basket fell on the floor, and all the goodies spilled out. Both children froze.

"Don't worry, that we'll keep for us," Fanny said. "Calman, why don't you go in the backyard and scare the rabbits away from my flowers." On his way out, the boy slammed the door, and Bess apologized to Fanny with a chagrined look.

"Oy, such a devil your brother is."

Bess had to agree.

After lunch, the children helped Fanny deliver the Purim baskets around the neighborhood. Bess and Calvin were so sweet and friendly to everyone. When people asked about Mollie, Fanny just said her friend was busy helping Sol get the spring clothes finished. Better no one should know their troubles. Although what could you do? Mollie was beginning to show.

"Happy holiday!" the children yelled as they skipped from place to place. Such energy, they had. Fanny felt like skipping with them.

The rest of the day was also a joy. After lunch Fanny and the children prepared their costumes. It was easy. For Calvin she had painted a cardboard crown with gold paint. Bess would wear Fanny's long silk scarves over her holiday dress. Fanny opened a box of her costume jewelry for Bess to select something. A rhinestone necklace caught the girl's eye.

"Oh, Aunt Fanny, this is so pretty."

Fanny put the necklace on her head and said, "An elegant Queen Esther." She motioned for Bess to stand on the dressing table stool so she could see the effect.

When Jake got home from work at the newspaper, he took Calvin to the basement to finish the scepter. Thanks God, they were busy for an hour and

Fanny and Bess could put out dinner in peace.

The children were very hungry and quiet at dinner. Then Fanny washed the dishes as Jake sat with Calvin on his lap. What a father he would make, Fanny thought as he quizzed them on the story of Purim.

"So, how did a Jewish woman become a queen of Persia?"

Bess piped up, "Queen Esther won the beauty contest to become the new queen. Her brother Mordechai told her not to say she was Jewish. And a bad man told the king to kill all the Jews."

"Who was the king's evil minister?" asked Jake. When Bess answered "Haman," Calvin started to bang the table with his new scepter.

"Easy, Calman." Jake laughed as he grabbed the toy. "It's okay to make noise, but you promised me, no funny business with the scepter. Better you should use these to drown out Haman's name tomorrow." He handed the children brightly colored metal rattles. Calvin immediately started turning the rachet until Fanny said, "Calman, please to save the rattles for synagogue."

The next day Jake walked the children to school on the way downtown to work and Fanny got busy at home. First, she cleaned the kitchen. Then she made the kids' beds. She picked up Bessie's pillow to fluff it, held it to her nose, and breathed in the little girl's sweet smell. How nice for Bess and Calvin she thought, to sleep in a bedroom in real beds. Oy, if only Sol and Mollie could move closer and have a nicer place. Maybe soon, she thought. Then she went back to the kitchen to prepare their lunch.

It was decided the children would not go back to school after lunch so they could have baths and get ready for services in synagogue.

"I can take a bath by myself," Calvin protested as Fanny tried to scrub his back.

"Okay, but keep talking, so I would know you didn't drown." In the bedroom, Fanny combed Bess's hair to get out the snarls.

"You're so gentle, Aunt Fanny. Momma just pulls the tangles out."

Fanny smiled and said, "You are going to be the prettiest Queen Esther in shul."

After dinner they took Jake's car to hear the reading of the Book of Esther.

The shul was only a couple of blocks away, but Calvin had begged to go in the car. The front hall was full of parents applauding their costumed children marching about. Soon Rabbi Zarchy clapped his hands and announced the reading of the Book of Esther would commence.

"Do we have to go upstairs?" Bess asked Fanny.

"No, sweetheart, you and Calvin go with Uncle Jake and enjoy yourselves."

Bess twirled to make her silk scarves flare out and took Jake's hand. Calvin had already gone into the main sanctuary to see what the other boys were doing.

Fanny looked down from the balcony as the rabbi chanted the story. Each time Haman's name was said, the children jumped up and twirled their rattles. The men stomped their feet. Fanny didn't know so much Hebrew, but she got the gist. Yet another woeful Jewish tragedy, but such a satisfying ending. Haman would hang, and Queen Esther's brother Mordechai would become the king's new minister. The reading got more and more boisterous. Afterwards, the men let the boys run about. All the little Queen Esthers ran upstairs to be with their mothers who shook their heads and said, "Every year, it gets like this."

Fanny and Bess laughed when Jake put Calvin on his shoulders. But, oh my goodness! "No! Not the scepter! Not the rabbi!" Fanny yelled down, "Jake, the boy! Give a look."

Luckily, Jake realized Calvin was about to crown Zarchy on the head.

"Time to go home," Fanny said to Bess, and then she motioned for Jake to leave.

The next day the children stayed home with Fanny. Calvin played in the yard and Bess sat at the piano with Fanny and they played from her sheet music of Second Avenue Yiddish songs and Broadway hits. Fanny showed Bess how to play "Chopsticks." So fast, she learned it. Then for the "The Flea Waltz," Bess played the chords and Fanny the easy tune. Mollie wouldn't like this stuff, but the little girl always practiced so long and hard. Why couldn't she have some fun? As Fanny made lunch, Bess picked out "Bye Bye Blackbird" by ear.

"Oh, so good you play, Bessie," Fanny exclaimed from the kitchen.

On Thursday afternoon, Bess had her music lesson. They took the trolley to Mrs. Parmer's studio. Fanny and Calvin had ice cream sodas at the Oak Leaf Coffee Shop while Bess was with her pretty teacher. Mrs. Parmer wasn't so happy when they went in to fetch the girl.

"Bess says you have a piano, but did she practice at all?" the teacher asked.

Fanny replied, "Oh yes, Mrs. Parmer. She has played the piano every day." She didn't want her Bess to be in trouble. When they got home, she'd make sure she practiced good.

"Oh, well," Mrs. Parmer said, "I'm sure she's upset about her mother. Please give these to Mrs. T." She handed Fanny a bouquet of tiny roses and violets.

On the trolley, Bess fretted about her awful lesson and whispered to Aunt Fanny, "Please, don't tell Momma I was bad." Fanny promised she wouldn't breathe a word. "And, is Momma okay? I miss her so much."

"Yeah," Calvin echoed Bess but louder. "I miss Momma!"

Fanny was so embarrassed and worried the children might cry. "She's fine. Please don't worry." She patted Bess's head and gave them both a lemon drop. Calvin cuddled close to Fanny and said, "Thanks, Momma. I mean Aunt Fanny."

That night in bed she told Jake how Calvin had called her Momma. He laughed and then he got serious. "If only." Fanny got weepy and said she didn't know how she would be able to take the children back. It seemed they just hadn't had enough time together.

"Do you think it would be terrible, if I kept them home from school tomorrow?"

Jake frowned but then he knew how sensitive Fanny was and how much she loved the Toplansky kids. "Well, I guess it wouldn't hurt."

In the morning Fanny took them to the park. She sighed to see that their outfits were looking shabby. Mollie always took such pride in how they dressed. Fanny guessed that with all that was going on, Sol and Mollie didn't have time to make new clothes for them. "The shoemaker's children go barefoot," Fanny said to herself in Yiddish, and then she got a wonderful idea.

After lunch they went downtown to Kauffman-Strauss Department

Store. Calvin loved riding the elevator and seeing all the floors go by. When they got to the fifth floor, of course, he wanted to get back on and ride down, but Bess tugged him off.

"Behave, Calvin. Don't you want to see the pretty clothes," Bess said looking at all the colorful spring outfits.

The saleslady complimented Bess and Calvin's good manners. Fanny was so proud and happy. For Bess, she bought a blue dress trimmed with white satin ribbon and a matching ribboned hat.

"Oh, Tante Fanny, the hat is beautiful, and this is my first store-bought dress! Thank you so much." Bess hugged Fanny who gave her a big kiss on the forehead and said "Trog es gezunter hait. Wear it in good health."

For Calvin she got a tweed jacket and was looking at matching short pants when the saleslady brought a pair of knickers in his size and said, "The young boys are starting to wear these now."

"Big boy pants!" Calvin exclaimed.

They fit, so Fanny bought them. Fanny saw Bess admiring a tweed cap for her brother.

"Yes, why not? We'll take the cap also," Fanny told the saleslady.

That night at supper, Fanny was tired but happy. When they finished eating, Calvin and Bess played a noisy game of Crazy Eights on the floor. Jake sidled up to Fanny as she washed the dishes and whispered, "I bet you'll be happy to have some peace and quiet."

Fanny shook her head no and tried to hold back tears. "Oy, Jake, this is so wonderful. We had such a day shopping, and the kinder were so well behaved."

"Children, show Uncle Jake your new clothes."

"I have knickers," shouted Calvin who threw the deck of cards in the air and ran out of the kitchen to find his new pants.

"Hey, come back here. If you have big boy pants, then you'll have to behave like big boy," Jake shouted as he motioned for him to come back and clean up the mess.

"Sorry, Uncle Jake," Calvin said as he picked up the cards.

"Maybe better you and Uncle Jake should go and work on something in the workshop," Fanny suggested.

"Swell," the boy answered and ran to the basement.

"Bessele, you could practice your lessons, no?"

"Oh, yes," the girl answered and went to the parlor. Fanny thought to herself how well the children behaved. No need to hit them, like their bubby did.

After the kids were in bed, Jake called Sol to see how Mollie was doing. Fanny was upset to hear that her friend was in the hospital. Her first thought was what if Mollie died. Her mind raced. Would she and Jake take care of the children forever? Then she felt guilty. "Jake, you must go to the morning minyan before work and make a prayer for Mollie."

Jake shook his head, "No, Fanny, I wouldn't want to say Mollie's name out loud." But Fanny insisted he should go and say the prayer to himself.

In bed that night Jake said. "I know this has been wonderful for you, Fanny, but ..."

"I know, Jake, I know. They're not ours."

"Well, you are a good friend, and you know you're always my best girl." Jake pulled on her waist, "Come here, my beauty."

"Not now, the children will hear," Fanny whispered.

"So, we'll be quiet," Jake said, wrapping his strong arms around her and kissing her on the neck and shoulders.

Jake fell sound asleep after they made love, but Fanny was fretting. She wasn't a good friend. She resented Mollie. How, she wondered, could it be that God gave everyone children but her. Even if Sol and Mollie lost this baby, they still had the most lovable children in the world. It made her heartsick to think that the children would have to go home, but she knew they would.

Chapter 9
Motherhood

In her bed in the maternity ward, Mollie stared at the ceiling. The other mothers were nursing their babies. Visiting hours were over, so the proud fathers and Sol had gone home. Sol was as sad as she was. Sadder. He, not Mollie, had cried when the doctors said what they already suspected: Mollie had lost the baby. She had bled so much that she was sure she too would die. But Dr. Rubel reassured her, "You are fine, Mollie. You will get back your strength, and you can have more children,"

Did she want more children? God should give her the strength to get up out of bed and take care of the two she had. Mollie pulled the covers over her head and curled up in a ball. Her insides hurt, and she just wanted to sleep. She wanted to go home and get into her own bed and be left alone. After the babies were taken back to the nursery, one of the nurses came to see if Mollie needed something for pain. She did. The pills wouldn't take away her worries, but at least she would sleep.

The next morning Mollie went home. Momma Adel made special teas and beef barley soup for Mollie to regain her strength. Mollie wasn't hungry, just tired. Sol had put a red velvet box of chocolates by her bed. He tucked her in and closed the door.

"If she doesn't eat, she won't get strong," Adel grumbled loudly so Mollie could hear. Then she heard Sol talking calmly and sweetly to her mother.

Mollie had been asleep for only an hour when Sol poked his head in the bedroom and announced, "The children will be home soon. Would you like to change into a nice dress?" Mollie shook her head no and turned away from him. Sol sat on the bed and whispered, "You're going to be fine, Mollie." She didn't answer. Sol sang softly in Yiddish, "If I were to lose you, I couldn't live anymore." Mollie got up and Sol helped her change into a house dress. He led her to the parlor and eased her into a chair, pulled up the ottoman for her feet, and wrapped her in a blanket. Then he got her a cup of tea.

Mollie stared into space. Next thing she knew there was a racket on the steps and Momma was yelling, "Sha! Shtil, kinder. Your mother is resting."

Bess burst into the parlor and ran to kiss her mother. Mollie tried not to cry as Calvin ran in and wrapped his arms around her.

"Careful with your mother, children," Fanny warned as she closed the door. "How are you feeling, Mollie?"

Mollie shrugged and said, "I've felt better." In a flat voice she asked if the children had behaved themselves.

"They were wonderful!" Fanny answered.

"Momma, Mrs. P sent these flowers for you!" Bess put the bouquet in her mother's lap and then took off her coat and twirled around. "Look at the new dress that Aunt Fanny bought me. And look, the hat matches."

"I got new pants, big boy pants. And look at my new hat!"

Mollie's eyes grew big. She was stunned and didn't know what to say. Then she exploded. "Who asked you to do that? We dress our own children. We're not paupers."

"I just thought..."

"You thought? You didn't think. These clothes must go back to the store. Children take them off and put on your own clothes."

Calvin stamped his foot,. "I'm keeping the pants."

Bess started to cry, "But Momma."

"You see? Now they don't obey me. You've spoiled them. You always spoil them with candy and foolishness. They're not your children."

"I know, I know, but sometimes they need a treat."

"So, you take my children for a few days, and you think you know how to raise them? Maybe it's best you don't have your own. Maybe God did right."

Fanny stumbled backwards like a balloon that had just been pricked. When she could breathe, she cried, "You ungrateful person. How can you say such a thing? Malke Toplansky, as God is my witness, I never want to see you again." Fanny ran out the door.

Calvin and Bess were bawling. Momma Adel grabbed them and told them to stop. Then she hobbled over to Mollie and helped her get up.

Mollie went back to her room, closed the door, got into bed, and cried.

Chapter 10

The Golden Dream

Business was steady and the stipend from the synagogue for chanting prayers helped a little, but still Sol never managed to save enough to make a down payment on a piano. Customers were slow to pay, so he was keeping his suppliers at bay. Their bills they could put off, but the rent was another story. Their landlord Mr. Schuster appeared at their door every first of the month, and he always let Sol know that there were plenty of people wanting to rent such a choice location. Bess's lessons at Mrs. Parmer's new school were costly, and without a piano for her to practice on daily, it almost seemed like lessons were a waste of good money. At least Mollie had finally stopped nagging Sol about getting a piano. His wife knew where every penny went.

Just that morning Sol had awakened from a wonderful dream. A card game. He had won a pot of golden coins to a blaring trumpet salute and a fat man accompanied the trumpets on a golden piano. At the end, the piano man turned and smiled at him with a mouth full of golden teeth. It was Mendy Mendelson! Odd, since Sol hadn't gone back to Mendy's in ages. Well, not since he'd won that big pot and moved to Broadway. In fact, he'd only played pinochle at his brother-in-law's place or at Jake Broderson's, now that Fanny and Mollie, thanks God, had kissed and made up. The dream was a reminder that he had been itching for a high-stakes game. The gangster's appearance was probably due to something he'd heard about Mendy opening a fancy schmancy new spot on Market Street. It would be so good to get out of the apartment. Out of the store. Many days, it felt like the walls were closing in on him.

Mid-morning Sol took the kids rowing on the river, and despite the calm waters and warm sun, it wasn't so enjoyable. Bess was bored, and Calvin was so fidgety that Sol brought the boat in earlier than he had wanted. That afternoon he caught up with things in the shop, and at dinner, he was itching to go to Mendy's new tavern. So, he told Mollie that he had to help Maishe Yoffee fix some new equipment.

"You?" Mollie arched one eyebrow. "You are going to help fix a machine?"

"Well, Maishe asked me, so I have to go, don't I?"

Mollie said yes, but her eyebrows knit an ugly knot that made Sol hurry out the door.

The night air was cool, and for the first time in weeks, Sol felt like his old self as he walked down Market Street. He had heard that you just walked right in the front door and went to the backroom. Mendy had bought a restaurant that went bankrupt. Now it had a neon sign announcing its new life, "Mendy's New Tavern." Sol made his way through the crowd to the back where he knocked at the door. Evidently, not everything had changed because it was Ike who opened up, grabbed Sol's arm, and pulled him in.

"Well, Solly, we ain't had the pleasure of your company in ages! To what do we owe this honor?" Ike said. Then to the gamblers at the tables, "Look fellas, the cantor of the synagogue has come to play with us schlubs."

Sol greeted them with a grin although he worried that word about this could get back to Rabbi Zarchy.

Mendy said, "Pull up a chair and sit down. We're just getting started. Ike, you know, and I think you know Jackie and Max."

The men nodded to him.

"How do you like the new place?" Mendy said.

Sol looked around. There was a big, shaded lamp over the felt-covered game table. No more liquor crates around the room. In the corner by the window were some potted plants, and from the corner of his eye he saw a little piano. "It's nice," he answered.

"Hmph. Nice. It's more than nice."

The backroom of the new tavern wasn't a palace. Sol struggled for words and tried, "Mazel tov. It looks very profitable."

That amused Mendy, who slapped him on the shoulder. "How's the tailoring business now that you're an Uptown Yankee from the Highlands?" Mendy asked.

"Not bad."

"You on top of Phoenix Hill? In one of them big houses?" Ike asked.

"Not exactly."

"Then you're at the bottom," Jackie interjected.

When the laughter died down, Mendy asked, "Are we going to kibbutz or play cards?"

He handed Sol the deck. "Tailor boy, let's see how well you cut."

Money and conversation flowed back and forth for an hour or so. Sol lost track of time, but he didn't lose focus on the cards, and he didn't accept when Mendy offered him a drink. His luck had been good, and he now had a couple extra bucks in his pocket.

Ike dealt and Sol picked up a king, a jack, a ten, and a seven. The first go around, Sol discarded his seven and picked up a five. Everyone stayed in. Mendy puffed away at his cigar and Ike had his tell of humming. He hummed when he was bluffing. Max was picking up too many cards, so he must have bupkes. The fourth go round Sol's heart pounded as he picked up a queen. The pot had grown. Finally, Jackie called the game. Sol had a huge smile on his face when he showed his straight.

Sweeping the cash towards him, Sol said, "Gentlemen, it was great playing with you again, but I got to get home to the family." He knew there would be objections, but he couldn't risk his winnings.

"Not so fast, tailor boy. You know you gotta give us a chance to win some of that back," Mendy said, hulking like a giant at Sol's back.

"But tomorrow's a workday," Sol sputtered and tried to stand.

"No buts about it. Sit your backside down in the chair and put your hands on the table. We're all among friends, you know." Mendy sat back down and smiled broadly, his golden tooth gleaming.

Trapped, Sol sat down. Mendy pulled out another deck of cards. He handed Sol the deck to examine. Sol won another hand with a pair of aces. Mendy stubbed out his cigar and growled at Sol.

"Look tailor boy, you got thirty-five bucks of our money there. How about we make a deal?" Sol sat there and listened. When Mendy offered a deal, you better listen.

"You need any muscle at your shop? Got any clients who ain't paying that maybe need persuading? With all that moolah, you could hire Ike. Ike, show Sollie what we do to people who don't pay."

Ike took out a gleaming knife and stabbed it into the table inches from Sol's hand.

Sol had the sinking feeling that if he didn't lose some of the money, he might lose some blood. And he wasn't hiring Ike to cut off the fingers of customers who didn't pay. His business would be ruined if people suspected he was in with Mendy and his mob.

"Look," Sol said, his mind racing to come up with a safer idea. "How's about I make you a nice three-piece suit, and I'd throw in an extra pair of pants for free. A nice heavy wool tweed. Good for the winter."

Mendy appeared to be thinking it over. "Yeah," he said, "I'll come in for a suit, but I want to pay you for it fair and square. Because I'm a businessman like you." Mendy laughed and lit another stogie. "Listen, I got another idea," Mendy said, jerking his head and toward the corner of the room with the potted flowers. "You see that pretty little piano?"

Sol followed Mendy's gaze and stared at the piano. He nodded.

"Go ahead," Mendy said, "take a look."

Sol walked over to examine the piano. It was a blonde spinet. Pretty and small enough for their parlor.

"So, Solly, what would you offer me for this beauty?"

"Mendy, I could pay you the thirty-five bucks."

"What? That piano what my dear departed mother played in Odessa? I couldn't part with that beauty for such a measly sum. Sit down and try it."

Sol sat at the piano and lifted the fallboard. The piano was dusty, so he wiped the keys with his handkerchief and played scales all the way up and down. It needed a little tuning, but the tone was bright, and the action was perfect. Mollie might like the golden flowers painted on the fallboard and the legs. Bess would love it. It was fancier than the black piano they had looked at every week at Shackleton's, the one they hoped to afford one day. Sol wondered where Mendy had gotten such a fancy piano. Maybe better not to think of that.

"I can't give it to you for less than fifty bucks," Mendy insisted.

Sol sensed that Mendy just wanted to push him around. He wanted Sol to know that no one came into his house and walked out on top. "How about half price on the suit?"

"Enough. No more dickering. Let's say you give me twenty-five bucks for a down payment and delivery on Monday. Free delivery. But you pay me fifty cents every week for a year. You ain't gonna get a deal like that any place else."

Sol calculated a year of payments, and while it was more than they could afford to pay at the time, he realized it was a very good price for a piano. Not only that, he had no other choice, not if he wanted to make it home without being followed by Mendy's thugs. Maybe it was meant to be. Maybe this was exactly what his dream had meant.

"All right Mendy." Sol shook Mendy's hand.

Mendy took out a sheet of paper and wrote a bill of sale, and Sol signed his agreement to make fifty-two payments. Sol counted out twenty-five bucks, keeping ten to take home to Mollie.

Sol said his goodbyes to Mendy and his boys and vowed to himself never to come back. Outside, a nice breeze had picked up. Sol walked briskly toward Broadway thinking of how he would frame this news to Mollie. Bess, on the other hand, would be thrilled with her little spinet with golden flowers. The clock at City Hall said ten o'clock. He'd better hurry.

Chapter 11
The Gilded Piano

OCTOBER 22-29, 1929

At breakfast the next morning, Sol announced to the family that Bess would have a piano.

Mollie gave her husband a quizzical look, but Bess interrupted it with her excited response.

"When, Poppa, when? Did you buy the black upright from Shackleton's?"

"No, not that one," Sol said. "A prettier one. A blonde spinet with golden flowers."

Adel grumbled under her breath.

"Oh, it's a beauty, Mollie, and it will fit better in our front room than the upright."

Mollie's eyes shot daggers, but then she shrugged her shoulders, shook her head, and turned away.

"The piano is being delivered on Monday, October 28," Sol said.

Waiting for the delivery from Mendy's boys wasn't the only thing making Sol anxious. All that week he had been reading about runs on banks. Mollie was tense, and Adel muttered a litany of calamitous predictions. Only Bess was hopping about the place happily. When delivery day came, Bess begged her parents to let her stay home from school to be there when the piano arrived. Sol relented. Calvin tried the same ploy, but Mollie said he was going and there was no two ways about it. The scowl on Adel's face let Sol know she disapproved of letting a child miss school.

All morning Bess clambered up and down the stairs to the tailor shop to announce that the piano still hadn't arrived.

"Patience, Bess," Sol said. "You could help here, to take your mind off," he suggested. But after she botched a button, she was sent back to the apartment.

At noon Calvin came home for lunch and announced there was a truck in the alley. He headed out the door to see everything firsthand, but Mollie grabbed him and scolded, "You stay out of the way. You could get hurt. You too, Bess."

Sol watched as Ike and two giants he didn't recognize maneuvered the piano out of the truck. They maneuvered it expertly into the parlor. Then one man carried the bench up as though it were a box of feathers. When he untied the rope on the bench, Calvin opened the lid and shouted, "Would ya look at those women!" He grabbed an armful of sheet music, and the lid slammed down with a bang.

"Feh!" Mollie exclaimed yanking him away. The sheet music scattered on the floor revealing vaudeville dancers dressed only in feathers and beads. Ike gathered the pages up and tucked them into his jacket saying, "I don't think this was part of the deal."

After the men left, Sol showed off the piano's features to his wife and daughter. Bess was speechless as she ran her fingers over the golden flowers. Calvin banged on the keys with abandon. Momma yelled, "Get away teivel. Your hands are dirty."

Sol added, "Never bang on a piano. If you want to play it, you must have lessons like your sister."

That evening, Minnie, Sam, and their kids, Joe and Dotty, came over after dinner to see the new wonder. Mollie proudly showed them how it fit so nicely in the room. Mother Adel grumbled that furniture had been moved right in front of her alcove so she would, no doubt, bump herself at night.

Mollie said, "Oh, Momma, you know you love music too."

Uncle Sam wanted Bess to play them something.

"Sit down everyone, please," said Sol.

Mollie, Aunt Minnie, and Dotty sat on the sofa by the window. Sol told Adel to take the seat of honor, the big armchair. He and Sam brought in kitchen chairs. Calvin and Joe sat on Mollie's new floral rug.

Her back straight as a board, Bess played a minuet and a march.

"Play something your Poppa can sing," said Aunt Minnie.

Sol joined Bess and asked her what she would like to play. She pulled out a sheet of music and whispered to him that she wanted to play the very first song she had played for Momma.

Sol announced, "Bess will play 'Alle menschen zaynen brider' to the tune of Beethoven's 'Ode to Joy.' You should all sing with us."

All men are brothers,

Yellow, brown, black, white

Nations, races and the climates

nothing but a made-up tale.

Minnie, Dotty, and Bess had sweet soprano voices that blended with Sol's. Mollie and Sam sang along zestfully but off key. The little boys crooned in made up Yiddish thinking they were the monkey's eyebrows. Adel tapped time with her foot as the two families sang and danced. They celebrated as the world outside their apartment on East Broadway was in a downward spiral.

On Tuesday, October 29, the stock market crashed. In the days that followed, banks failed, businessmen jumped out of windows, bread lines formed, and desperate men and women hopped onto cross-country trains in search of jobs.

Chapter 12
The Golden Garden

In the eleven months since Bess's piano arrived, Poppa hadn't missed a payment. They'd had to pinch their pennies, but now the piano was almost theirs. Bess had fallen in love with the gilded piano the moment she set eyes on it, but she didn't realize she would now have to practice two hours every day but the Sabbath. Momma and Poppa's rules. How she resented them on days she could hear Calvin and his friends playing down in their garden. And yet, once her fingers began climbing up and down the scales, she often forgot everyone and everything around her.

All summer long Calvin had played outside, while Bess had been expected to help Momma with chores and still practice piano. But most afternoons she had had time to go into the backyard and skip rope or play jacks with Naomi. Kids from the crowded rowhouses on the other side of the alley came to play. Girls like Nancy Dillard brought their tattered dollies, and from next door Johnny Habermann and other boys flocked there to play marbles, stick ball, or tag with Calvin. Now that it was fall, Bess would have no time for fun. After practicing, she had schoolwork and chores. It was unfair. Calvin went out to play after dinner, while Bess had to help Momma.

Worse than that, her beloved Mrs. Parmer was becoming a strict taskmaster. It seemed that no matter how hard Bess worked at the scales, she didn't do them fast enough or her hand position wasn't quite right.

"You aren't spending enough time on the exercises," her teacher said.

How did Mrs. P know that? Bess did do the dratted scales, but they were so tedious. It was much more fun to play pieces she liked. When her parents weren't around, Bess played the popular tunes Aunt Fanny loved and her mother disdained. Anything was better than music theory workbooks. She hated having to memorize the different keys and what sharps and flats they required. Sharps and flats were annoying.

"Sharps are like cherries on a sundae. They brighten things up," Mrs. P said. Why did her teacher have to bring up cherries. Before they got the piano, her mother had always taken her across the street from Mrs. P to the drugstore to have a chocolate phosphate with whipped cream and a bright red cherry on top. Now, there was little money for anything but her lessons, certainly not fountain treats. They didn't even have the money to take the trolley to her teacher's studio at Fourth and Oak.

"Bess," Mrs. Parmer said, sounding frustrated. "You didn't complete the questions about F major and minor in your notebook. I have a boy a year younger than you who can play the scale for any key I ask without a minute's hesitation."

When Bess's eyes got teary, Mrs. P put her hand on Bess's arm and said, "I know this is harder than you thought, but I don't want you to waste your talent." Mrs. P showed Bess a clipping of a girl wearing a ribboned medallion around her neck.

"You may not believe it, my dear, but you can play rings around other children your age. In a year or so, if you work hard, you could compete at statewide contests."

Bess nodded, even though she just wanted to go home after her lesson with Mrs. P and play in the yard with Naomi and Nancy or go over to her Cousin Dotty's and cut out paper dolls.

"I promise I will practice more this week," Bess said, knowing her promise was as weak as her voice.

"And finish the theory exercises."

"Yes ma'am."

The walk home with Momma was quiet, and Bess was glad her mother didn't press her by asking her if there was something wrong. It seemed her mother had things on her mind as well. Inside, Mollie hung her scarf on the peg by the door and shooed Bess into action.

"I've got things to do in the shop, while Poppa is making deliveries. You get busy practicing and please to bring up the clean sheets when you're finished."

Bess felt miserable. With her mother downstairs and Bubby out visiting a friend, she could grumble out loud. "It's not fair. It just not fair." Her voice echoed off the walls. She smashed her fists on the keys and slammed the fallboard shut. Remembering Momma downstairs, she wished she hadn't made so much noise and hoped the sound hadn't carried to the shop.

She went to the kitchen and looked out at the garden. The shadows were long, but it was still sunny in the yard. There were still a few golden delicious apples in the top of the tree that Calvin had missed. She could see Calvin shooting marbles with his buddies by the shed. Then she saw Naomi and Nancy come into the yard and begin chalking up the sidewalk for hopscotch. She had done none of her duties as she tiptoed across the kitchen floor and out the back door, and she didn't care.

Bess was on ninesies hopping toward "home" and beating Naomi and Nancy, when she heard a boy named Ricky yell at her brother, "Gimme back that marble, you dirty kike."

Before Bess could react, she heard Naomi telling the boy to take it back. "You can't talk to Calvin like that."

"What's it to you? I thought you was a kraut."

Naomi ran over to Ricky and said, "You better apologize, or else."

"Or else what?" the boy said as he took a step backward toward the alley.

"Bess, grab him. Nancy, hold the gate," Naomi ordered. Nancy ran to the gate and Bess grabbed Ricky by the shirttail. As the boy turned and shoved Bess away, Naomi punched him in the nose. Blood spurted from his face, and everyone stood stock still. Then the boy slugged Naomi in the belly and ran out the gate.

Safe in the alley he yelled, "I'm gonna come back and whup all you kikes."

"You can't play here anymore," Calvin yelled.

"Who's gonna stop me?"

"Our cousins are ten times bigger'n you," Calvin called as the boy disappeared.

"Oh, Naomi, look at you," Bess said. "You have blood on your clothes."

"Y'all was great, Naomi, but I hope that Ricky don't take this out on me an' my brothers. I better git home," said Nancy, who then hurried out.

Naomi looked at her hand and saw that a bruise was forming. "I'm in big trouble. My father and mother don't approve of fighting."

Bess nodded. Momma and Poppa would be mad as well. "Come on upstairs, Naomi, and we'll clean you up. Then we can figure out what you can tell them."

"Why Bess, you know I can't tell my parents anything but the truth."

Bess winced. She knew how strict Pastor Habermann was with Naomi. And yet they loved her. It would be all right, Bess thought. Naomi was standing up for us. That had to matter more than punching a bully.

That night at dinner Bess and Calvin were quiet. Bess had made Calvin swear he wouldn't tell their parents what had happened. She didn't want them to know she'd been down in the yard when she was supposed to be practicing, and she didn't want her friend to get in trouble. And yet, it hurt that a boy who always played in their yard would call them such an ugly name.

When everyone went to sleep, Bess lay awake in her daybed. If only she had been the one to hit the boy. Then Naomi wouldn't be in trouble, but if she had hurt her hand, Momma would hit her harder than Naomi had hit the boy. Pastor Habermann wasn't the only one with a temper. And Bess was certain Momma would forbid her from playing outside in their yard for a very long time. Tomorrow, Bess thought with resolve, she'd practice extra hard.

Chapter 13
War Stories

Adel wanted to finish darning while there was still light in the kitchen window. She went at the socks as if they were Cossacks, jabbing them as swiftly as her swollen fingers allowed. When she finished, she made sturdy knots in the heels, knots that her daughter's family would walk on in the damp Louisville winter. Then she cut the thread with her two remaining teeth. She pressed out the socks with her hands, placed them in the basket, and looked out the window.

Why, she wondered, hadn't her granddaughter returned from the upstairs neighbor's apartment? That Miss Dodge, always offering her Bess cookies that could be made with anything, lard or suet. Not Kosher, for sure. And why did Bess call that woman Grandma?

Adel put her sewing basket on the pine shelf and opened the blinds, shivering as the wind whistled through the warped window frame. Pulling her shawl higher up around her neck, she stepped over to the stove to stir the soup her daughter had left simmering. Oy vey, the barley was sticking. It would burn. When the long wooden spoon hit the soup bone, she thought of Basia, of blessed memory. How her sister liked to suck the marrow. Adel considered taking out the bone and enjoying the delicacy, but better she should save it for Sol. Her son-in-law needed his strength.

A clattering in the stairwell announced her granddaughter's arrival. The door creaked open and slammed shut. The old woman went over to Bess and pulled a rag from her apron pocket, spat on it, and wiped a smudge off of the girl's winter chapped cheeks.

"Bessele," she asked in Yiddish, "Zug mir, did you eat the landlady's cookies?"

"Neyn, Bubby," Bess said. Adel watched as her granddaughter brazenly wiped cookie crumbs off her sweater. The girl stuck out her chin and challenged her grandmother. "Di Bubby Dodge told me Civil War stories. How come you never tell me stories, Bubby?"

"Stories! Who has time for stories? The things I saw, better you should never know. Better you should study or help your tate-mame downstairs in the shop." Adel picked up the poker to stoke the coals in the iron stove.

Bess flinched although her grandmother had never hit her.

After Bubby Adel put the poker back into the stand, Bess smiled and said in her Louisville-inflected Yiddish, "Grandma Dodge tells me stories about beautiful ladies in long wide skirts and handsome men with silver swords and chestnut horses. Her family had a farm. A horse farm. And they drank sweet minty drinks on. . . um . . . di groise veranda." Her granddaughter made a sweeping gesture with her right hand. Adel squinted at Bess, turned to pick up her Bible commentaries, and moved to the window to read.

Bess continued, "And Grandma Dodge showed me pictures of when she was a girl with her hair in curls down to her shoulders." Bess made curling gestures around her straight sandy colored hair that Malke had bobbed the night before. She walked over to her bubby, "And she tells me all about the Civil War."

Adel sat down in her rocking chair and pulled her woolen cap down on her shorn head. She coughed to clear her throat. "I don't know from stories, but I know from war. Sit down. Zet zikh avek."

Bess sat down at the little table and propped her elbows on the oilcloth. Then she rested her head on her fists as her grandmother got up from the chair by the window, put her book next to the sewing basket on the little pine shelf, and slowly sat down at the table.

"Nu, where to begin? Shall I tell you how the soldiers burnt our field and our old mare caught fire and ran down the street? For two days the family hid in the root cellar. We heard the soldiers' boots stomping overhead and pots and dishes falling. Cupboard doors slamming. For two days we stayed there in the dark eating raw beets and potatoes and fighting off the rats with our shoes. With our shoes. When it got quiet, my little sister Basia, for whom you were named, ole ha-sholem, ran to the outhouse. She didn't come back. My brother Jacob found her clothes in the woods. Covered in blood."

The old woman began to wheeze. "You want I should tell you more?"

Bess sat silently in the darkened room, her legs dangling from the chair. Through the stove's Isinglass window, bright red sparks and flames glowed. Adel closed her eyes and saw the burning horse running through town.

"Oh, Bubby," Bess said, her eyes glazed with fear.

"So, my story isn't as nice as the neighbor lady's?" Adel sat down in her rocker, picked up her Yiddish Bible Stories, and began to read them to herself.

Chapter 14
Help Wanted

1933

Readying the shop for the day's business, Sol raised the blinds and saw a Negro in a well-cut striped suit standing at the door. The man tipped his hat and smiled. Sol unlocked the door and let him in.

"Jackson Clay's the name, and sewing is my game."

Sol extended his hand to the man and said, "Solomon Toplansky, pleased to meet you."

"Well, well, well. A handshake from a white man. As I live and breathe. But I reckon the answer is still no."

"I don't know the question."

"As y'all can see by my suit, I am a master tailor. Come from a long line of tailors. So, I wonder if you be needing any help?"

Sol motioned the man to come closer and examined the underside of his lapels.

"Yes, good cut and fine stitching, Mr. Clay."

"Jackson, if you please."

"Jackson, I don't have enough business to keep me and mine wife busy at the moment."

"Yeah, that's what they say everywhere I go."

"Well, maybe in the spring when Derby Day is closer. People always have money to go to the races."

"Now, ain't that the truth," Jackson said with a laugh. "Well, sir, if you need any help at all, basting, deliveries, sweeping the store, give me a call. Y'all can reach me here." He handed Sol a card with the address and telephone number of The Paddock Saloon.

"A tailor and a bar keeper?"

"Oh, that is my cousin's place. He watches out for me."

Jackson Clay tipped his hat and left. Sol noted the zigzag stripes on the back of his suit. That was a new one! He put the man's business card in the drawer where he kept his tools.

Not a half an hour later, another Negro walked in. This was a tall muscular man in a tan uniform that fit well but looked frayed at the cuffs.

"Mr. Toplansky, I'm Mr. Brennard's chauffeur."

"Would this be the Mr. Brennard of the flour mills across the street?"

"Yes, sir. Mr. Brennard would like to see you."

"Well, he can just come right in."

"Oh, no, sir. He's busy now. He would like you to come by his office to talk to you about some tailoring work."

"Yes, I'll just check my book," Sol said as he opened his daybook and saw blank pages. "That would be fine. What time?"

"Four o'clock. You give the receptionist this card, and she'll let you see him."

At lunch Sol told the family what a strange morning he'd had. Two Negroes had come in. One asking for work and another offering work.

"What kind of work would a shvartzer offer?" his mother-in-law asked.

"He didn't exactly say. I'm supposed to go to his boss's office this afternoon. To Mr. Brennard."

"The owner of Brennard Mills?" Mollie asked.

"Yes, the very same man."

"Oy, Sol, he must want a nice spring suit. Maybe two."

"I don't know, but a man who is too busy to come in and get measured, must be a very wealthy man."

"Or very lazy," muttered Adel.

"Sol, you must take your sample fabrics," Mollie paused. "Oh dear, your samples are moth eaten. And we don't have a new book of men's suits either. You should go right after lunch and get new ones. Calvin, put that cutlet back until you finish what's on your plate."

After lunch, Sol went to the fabric store. They agreed to loan him samples, but he would have to return them if he didn't need material. The fashion book he had to buy.

At 3:45 Sol showed up at the office of Brennard Mills with his measuring tape, fabric samples, and a book of men's suits.

"I have an appointment with Mr. Brennard," Sol told the receptionist. She looked like Sol was delivering a package of dead fish when he handed her the card. She showed Sol where to wait and wait he did. Three men went through to the door marked. J.J. Brennard. One looked familiar. The president of the bank on the next block. Sol had never met him, but the man had stepped in once when he was speaking to the loan officer. "Hmm," he thought, "even the bank comes to him."

An hour later, a lady in a well-cut wool suit came out and led him to Mr. Brennard's office. Sol took a deep breath as he crossed the soft carpet. Mr. Brennard stood and extended his hand across a mahogany desk as shiny as a mirror.

"Always nice to meet a neighbor. Sorry for the wait. Have a seat."

"Not to worry, Mr. Brennard. It will be my honor to make a suit for you."

"For me?" Brennard looked surprised. "Mr. Toplansky, I need uniforms for my staff: the butler, the chauffeur, and the valet. What am I saying? That son of a gun left me high and dry."

"Well, just in case, I can show you some beautiful fabric and the latest in men's suits."

"I'm not one to follow fashion," Brennard said with a chuckle. "But these pants are feeling a bit snug, I can tell y'all that." The man motioned Sol to come over to him as he stood.

Brennard towered over Sol and pointed to his waist. A fine leather belt was holding up the man's pants because his buttons were not buttoned.

"Sir, if you could undo this, I could see if there is what to let out."

Brennard not only unbuttoned the pants. He took them off, handed them to Sol, and walked into another room and closed the door. As Sol examined the seams, he heard a toilet flush. The man had his own private bathroom in his office!

Brennard came out and lit himself a cigar that smelled like nothing Sol had ever smelled before.

"You do have room in a side seam to let out the waist, but I would rather do it in my shop so I can press them."

"Just do it here, Toplansky."

"But I don't have my scissors."

"Here, use this." Brennard handed him a small red knife with many tools.

As Sol snipped away the stitches, rather clumsy ones at that, Brennard took a call and began giving orders. Sol couldn't wait to tell Mollie about this big man standing in his office smoking a fancy cigar and talking on the phone in his gatkes.

When Sol finished, Brennard took the pants and put them on. "Good job, man. At last, I can breathe."

"I could let out your jacket and vest if you come by the shop."

"Fine idea. I'll have James drop them off." Then Brennard buzzed his secretary who appeared instantly. "Miss Lee, please show the gentleman out."

"Thank you for coming by Mr. Toplansky. If you do a good job on the uniforms, I'll tell my friends and neighbors. Oh, I almost forgot this." Brennard handed him a long white envelope.

Sol hoped it was a deposit.

"My wife put in samples of the fabric she'd like. Her card is in there, so you can set up an appointment to go by the house and measure everyone. I like a man who's prompt, and I like keeping business in the neighborhood, if y'all know what I mean."

Sol nodded and took his leave. That night Mollie was disappointed to learn that Brennard only wanted uniforms and that his chauffeur would be dropping off his boss's jacket to be let out.

Momma Adel said, "See, I told you the man is lazy."

Lazy or not, Mr. Brennard was true to his word and told friends about Sol. Unlike Brennard, they came into Toplansky's Tailor Shop for suits and dresses. In March, Mendy Mendelson, who'd been a steady customer the last few years, ordered a linen suit for the Kentucky Derby. Soon Sol and Mollie couldn't work fast enough. She was getting more irritable by the day. And one evening when the kids were being particularly rowdy, she burned her hands taking a pot of stew off the stove. They weren't serious burns, but she wouldn't be able to sew for a few days.

That night in bed, Sol remembered Jackson Clay. He promised Mollie he'd go and talk to him. She reminded him that she also could use a hand in their home.

"The lady who works for Mrs. Habermann has a daughter who's looking for work."

Sol agreed that she needed a hand with housework and cooking, but first, they needed help in the shop. He didn't tell Mollie that he'd noticed a slight tremor in his hands. Why worry her about nothing.

The next morning, Sol strolled down West Market Street to The Paddock Saloon. As Sol stepped in, the floor felt spongy, and his eyes had to adjust to the dark and smoke. It was easy to pick out Jackson Clay at the crowded counter. He was the only one not leaning over a drink. Jackson sat ramrod straight eating boiled eggs and sipping beer. Jackson saw Sol in the mirror and whispered something to the man next to him who staggered off the stool to an empty table. Then Jackson stood to greet Sol.

"Good to see y'all, Mr. Toplansky. How about a beer?"

"No thank you. I don't drink in the morning."

Jackson introduced Sol to his cousin Leroy and asked him to pour Mr. T a cup of coffee.

The coffee was lukewarm and thicker than molasses.

"Leroy, make the man a fresh cup of coffee."

"Oh, that wouldn't be necessary," Sol said as he placed his steady hand over the one that was a bit shaky. He thought maybe coffee was making him tremble.

Jackson grinned, wiped egg crumbs from his face, and said, "I hear tell y'all been mighty busy."

"How did you know that?"

"I have my ways."

"Well, we do need help. I might even get a truck. But if I hire you, you must promise me you'll never touch liquor when you're working."

Jackson pushed the beer away, "Y'all won't be sorry, Mr. T. I promise I won't never touch a drop on workdays. If I'm lyin', I'm dyin.'"

And in all the time Jackson worked for the Toplanskys, he never showed up with alcohol on his breath although of a Monday morning, Jackson was often sullen.

Sol and Jackson worked together well, and it was a great relief to have help in the store. Mollie let Sol know how disappointed she was not to have help in their home, but they just didn't have the extra money. She'd have to wait until just before Passover of the following year to hire a young girl named Annabelle Rowan to clean and help out in the kitchen.

Chapter 15
Bad Hair

SPRING, 1934

Annabelle's mama, Ida Rowan, had worked for Pastor Habermann's family since she could remember. Now there was a job at their next-door neighbors. Annabelle was of two minds about leaving Jackson School. On the one hand, she was the star pupil of her seventh-grade class, winner of every spelling bee of all the Negro schools since first grade, but on the other, her family needed help. Ever since Pappy had died, things had been tough. Her older brother wasn't much help, Lord knows. He couldn't keep a job because he always thought he knew best, and bosses didn't like that.

The first day at the Toplansky's, Annabelle's head was buzzing. There were so many rules in the kitchen and such specific ways of cleaning. She wanted to do a good job 'cause that's just how she did things. But right off the bat she made the old grandmother spitting mad. Washing up from breakfast, Annabelle had used a red dish towel to dry the butter knife. The old lady grabbed the knife and the dish towel and yelled for the boy. He ran out into the yard and buried the knife! Annabelle watched out the kitchen window in horror as he dug a little hole.

The sister—the old lady called her Bessie Lee—said, "Hey, it's not hard. We follow the rules of Kosher. We separate milk and meat because of laws in the Bible."

Annabelle nodded and said, "Like the Good Book says, you shouldn't cook the calf in its mother's milk."

"Yes! So, just remember the blood and think of the red towels. Always use the red towels for meat dishes and the blue for dairy." Then the girl gathered her books and left for school with her brother. Annabelle was sad and jealous, but mainly she was scared to be alone with the old lady, whose eyes never left her.

When the grandmother showed Annabelle how to do the washing, she couldn't understand what the old lady said. But Annabelle sure enough wouldn't wash the red dish towels with the blue ones. Lordy, the boy would have to bury them too. After scrubbing linen and hanging it up to dry, Annabelle was getting hungry. She and her Momma hadn't eaten breakfast so as to get to work early.

At noon Missus Toplansky came upstairs to prepare lunch. From the shiny white breadbox, she pulled out a big dark loaf and began to slice it. The kids burst into the kitchen and dumped their schoolbooks on the daybed in the corner. Before the boy could get near the table, the grandmother growled at him. He and Bessie Lee went to wash their hands. As the family took their seats, Annabelle noticed there was an empty chair.

Missus Toplansky said, "Please, to sit down, Hennybelle." Annabelle couldn't believe she was supposed to eat with the white folk. Missus Toplansky said, "We only have one table, so please to join us." Stupefied, Annabelle sat down. Hungry as she was, Annabelle barely ate a bite.

There was a lot to report to Mama as they walked home in the heat of the afternoon. Her mother laughed about the boy burying a knife in the yard. "It ain't funny, Mama. That old lady follows me like a hawk. And I'm afraid of making another mistake 'cause I can't understand them so well. Sometimes I can't understand them at all."

"They's talking in Jewish," her mother explained.

"Do you think they'll actually pay me?"

"Oh yes, of course they will. Mrs. Habermann says they are fine God-fearing people. So don't you worry. You'll get three dollars a week, and fifty cents you can save."

Annabelle was relieved. She had plans for that money. If she worked for Jews, her brother Willie had said, she'd never make any money. He told her Jews were Christ killers. He swore they drank the blood of Christian babies at their services. It was bad enough her mother was working for the Lutherans, he had said, but Jews, they was bad news. Annabelle asked him how come he knew so much since he'd never in his whole life kept a job more than a month with anybody: Jews, Catholics, Presbyterians, or Baptists, like they was.

Her brother had her worried, but pretty soon Annabelle got used to the family and their ways. Well, the grandmother still gave her the heebie jeebies. One day Annabelle went into the old lady's alcove to clean and saw her without her bonnet. The woman had no hair. Had she shaved it? Did she have lice? Just thinking about it had Annabelle feeling itchy all day.

Bessie Lee was a good egg though. Annabelle liked to hear her play piano, especially when Mr. T sang along. The blond-haired boy Calvin was not a bad kid, even though he hurt her feelings the first day. He'd pointed at Annabelle and said, "Gee, you look like the Tar Baby in that straw hat." That wasn't funny, but Annabelle was too upset to say anything. Sometimes Calvin was sweet, like his father. He picked daisies from the garden and left them for Annabelle. One day he brought her a golden delicious apple right from the tree, spit on it, polished it on his shirt and gave it to her.

Annabelle said, "Well, ain't you an angel!"

Mrs. T said, "Oh yes, mine Calman is just that, an angel. Wash the apple, Hennybelle."

Bessie Lee laughed and said, "The perfect name for you. Angel."

And even though it was sure enough hard work, Annabelle got used to the routine after just a few weeks. Each day had its special chores. Mondays she cleaned the shop before it opened. Polishing the wood up in the loft, she thought of the choir in their church. Sometimes Mr. T sang while he worked, and the sound echoed on the wooden walls. Thursdays were her favorite day. She dusted everything. When she dusted Bessie's shelf, she sometimes read a few pages of the girl's library books. She liked the sound of the ivory piano keys as she cleaned them. She polished the big brass candlesticks and the silver spice box that the family would use on the Sabbath table. Best of all, on Thursdays the old lady did marketing which gave Annabelle time alone.

The old lady's return would be announced by the squawking of a big old hen down in the yard. Then Annabelle would run down and take the basket of vegetables to wash and pare for the chicken soup. As she worked at the sink,

Annabelle couldn't help watching the old lady down below making short order of that unlucky chicken. She admired how fast the woman slit the bird's throat and then patiently flicked off every feather. Then the grandmother would come upstairs, hack up the hen, soak it in saltwater, and put it in the ice box. Annabelle wasn't partial to washing the old lady's bloody apron.

The house smelled great on Fridays. Sometimes the old lady made noodles and hung up them on a string to dry. Others she made fluffy balls of dough that floated on top of chicken soup. The hen's fat she fried up with onions. Annabelle loved eating rye bread with that golden fat and onions.

One Thursday as Annabelle cleaned Bessie Lee's hairbrush, she thought how pretty and straight the girl's honey-colored hair was. But just the day before Bessie Lee had come home from school crying that the kids had made fun of her hair. That morning Annabelle had helped the girl braid her hair and tie it with beautiful ribbons. Then at school, they had called her "Topsky" 'cause her braids made her look like Topsy on the cover of *Uncle Tom's Cabin*. Bessie Lee had let Annabelle borrow her copy. It was a good story. She wondered why Bessie Lee was offended to be compared to such a spunky character. Well, she supposed no one would want to be called a slave girl. Bessie Lee had torn out her braids and thrown the ribbons on the ground. Annabelle picked them up and handed them back.

Bessie Lee sobbed, "You keep them. I won't ever wear them again."

For her part, Annabelle hated her own hair. How she suffered when she tried to comb it. And it looked so nappy. At home she couldn't see herself, but at work, she could. She loathed seeing herself in the little bathroom mirror. How fine she would look with honey-colored straight hair like Bessie's. Well, if she changed the color, Mama, a deaconess at the church, would beat the living daylights out of her. Her mother thought "Thou shalt not change the way God made you!" was the Eleventh Commandment. She scoffed at parishioners who lightened their skin or hair. But Mama never said nothing about straightening your hair. Her friend Flossie had done it, and her hair looked great. Flossie wrote up the recipe, and Annabelle had saved enough money to buy the ingredients. She had a plan. Next Thursday while the grandmother was out shopping, she would have time to straighten her hair. It would be shiny, sleek, and straight like her friend's.

When the big day arrived, Annabelle had everything she needed in her apron pockets to make her hair straight and beautiful. She arrived at the work early so she could get lots of chores done before the old lady left the house. When she got there everyone was running around so busy, they barely said hello. They was making such a fuss about the kitchen. Bessie Lee and Angel brought boxes of dishes and pans from the basement. Adel and Mollie were scrubbing the icebox, the stove, the cabinets and counters with boiling hot water and smelly soap. Then they spread oil cloth on the kitchen counter and lined the cabinets with newspaper. Calvin took the breadbox down to the basement. Before the kids left for school, Bessie Lee told Annabelle they were getting ready for Passover. They wouldn't be eating any bread for eight days. Finally, Mrs. T went downstairs to the shop. Annabelle knew that as soon as the old lady left for the market, she'd have to work fast and keep her eye on the clock.

At last, the old lady gathered up her baskets. Today, she had extra ones. As soon as Annabelle saw her at the bottom of the back stairs, she went to the bathroom and read the recipe once more. She had even brought her momma's measuring spoons because this recipe had lard: boiled eggs, lard, red devil lye. A special shampoo to take it all out. She carefully added the six tablespoons of lye and four tablespoons of water to the mashed eggs and lard and rubbed the mixture all over her head. She tied an old rag loosely on her head and went to the living room to roll up the parlor rug and wash the floor like they had told her. Her scalp stung and the smell was awful! It was a good thing all the windows were open.

While she was moving the rug and chairs back into place, she heard the old lady coming up the back stairs. She heard the clucking of the bird and watched in fear as the woman went into the bathroom. Annabelle was confused. What was the old woman doing in the bathroom? She would never kill the hen there. And according to the clock in the parlor, it was time to wash off the relaxer. No way she could do it in the kitchen. No way she'd get lard in that sink. Besides, the old lady could come out any minute. She tiptoed up to the bathroom door and heard water running in the tub. Was the hen getting a bath? Annabelle went back to the parlor and finished dusting. Her scalp was burning. She couldn't wait for the old lady to get out of there.

Finally, the grandmother went downstairs. The hen squawked as if she knew her end was near. When Annabelle opened the bathroom door, she was horrified to see two big fish swimming in the bathtub. Now she'd have to wash out the relaxer in the tiny sink and fast. Her head was on fire. Her throat and eyes burned too. She shampooed out the mixture as quickly as she could and scrubbed the stinking mess out of the sink. This better be worth it.

She combed her hair with her big steel comb admiring what she saw in the mirror. Smooth wavy hair. My, my, didn't she look fine? Back at home she would cut her bangs and trim her hair to shoulder length. She knew her mama would be angry, but she was thirteen years old and a working girl. Mama would just have to accept that. Flossie's directions said not to pull your hair tightly, so she best not braid it.

Soon the family assembled for lunch. First, the grandmother came up from the yard with her bloody apron. Annabelle took it to soak in cold water with bleach. While Missus pulled lunch from the icebox, the children came banging into the house out of breath from running home. Finally, Mr. T came up from the shop. After the old lady washed her hands at the kitchen sink and said a prayer, they all sat down.

"Annabelle, what's that funny smell?" Calvin asked as he turned to pass her the tuna salad.

"Where are your braids?" Bessie Lee asked.

Annabelle's hand went up to adjust her hat and a little clump of hair came out in her hand. She jumped up from the table and ran into the bathroom. She took off her hat and more hair broke off. She touched her head on top and more hair fell. What if she lost all her hair? Her mother would say God was punishing her. Annabelle didn't want anyone to see her, but she couldn't go home. She'd lose her pay. She might never come back if she left now. If she lost her job, her mother would whup her for sure.

She felt tears welling up in her eyes, but she wiped her face with her apron and said to herself, "Annabelle Rowan, you best just act like nothin' happened." She put the hat on, and more hair fell out. Now she was worried about shedding all over the house. She had no choice. She ripped off her hat so hard that the brim tore. Then she combed and pulled at her burning scalp until hair stopped falling out and she was left looking like a raggedy headed boy with a bald patch by her ear. She sat on the toilet feeling miserable. There was a soft knock on the door.

Bessie Lee asked, "Are you okay? Can I come in?"

Annabelle opened the door a crack. The girl stepped in and closed the door behind her.

"What happened to your hair?" Bessie Lee asked.

"I just wanted straight hair, but I look awful. And I done ruined my hat." Annabelle shoved her hat into the waste bin and slammed down the lid.

Bessie Lee stood there for a spell. Then she said, "It's not so bad. You just need to trim it all the same length. Momma keeps hair scissors in this drawer. Let me help you."

Bessie Lee evened the hairline in the back and put the scissors on the sink for Annabelle. Annabelle had taught the girl never to hand anything sharp directly to anyone. With a glum look, Annabelle cut off the rest of her bangs in front. She shrugged at her reflection and said, "I look dreadful."

The girl said, "Oh no you don't. The short hair makes your eyes look big and pretty."

"You lyin,' but thanks for saying so."

"Well, you better get back to the table before Calvin eats the food off your plate. The tuna is almost gone."

Everyone was silent when Annabelle sat down at the table. Then the old lady said something in Jewish, and Mr. and Mrs. T answered her at the same time. Next to Annabelle, Calvin was stifling a laugh. Every dish on the table was empty, but on Annabelle's plate was tuna fish and a canned pear with lettuce and sour cream. She ate quickly with her head down choking back the tears.

When she got up to clear the table, the old lady yanked her by the hand. "Kum da!" she ordered.

"Oh Lordy," thought Annabelle, "I'm in for a whupping now." The grandma sometimes gave Calvin punches that left welts on his pale skin.

The old lady led her to the parlor and drew aside the curtain to the alcove where she slept. Annabelle remembered the day she'd seen the old lady's shaven head. Was the woman going to get a razor and shave Annabelle's head? Hit her with her walking stick? The grandmother reached up to a hook on the wall, took down a blue muslin bonnet, and handed it to Annabelle.

She didn't like the look of the cap, but the old lady motioned for her to put it on. Annabelle had heard them say "thank you" enough to know how to say it in Jewish.

"A shame an' dank," she mumbled.

The woman shook her head and cocked it to one side. She tied the bonnet for Annabelle. Then she stood back, put her hands on her hips, showed her two remaining teeth in a smile, and said, "You velcome!"

Chapter 16
The Evil Eye

1934

The last day of Passover was a special day, so Bess and Calvin were home from school. Her brother was in the back yard playing with Cousin Joe. It was a sunny day, perfect for being outdoors, but Bess had so much homework. Her belly was hurting and she thought it must be all the matzoh she'd eaten. Thank goodness, no more matzoh after today.

Everything felt tight. The waistband of her skirt, her shirt. Everything put her on edge—Calvin shouting with their cousin in the yard, Annabelle humming at the sink as she scoured the pans, Bubby snoring in her rocking chair, but most of all, her stupid math problems. Her head ached as she fidgeted at the table, reading her workbook exercises. This stupid boy Bob has a coin collection with nickels and pennies and there are three times as many pennies as nickels. His collection has a face value of $41.60. Boy, he was rich. And how is she supposed to know how many nickels and pennies he has? Doesn't he have any quarters or dimes? Bess tried different amounts, but nothing added up, so she slammed the book on the floor. The noise woke Bubby. who shuffled over to the kitchen table.

"Bessele, what's wrong? The homework? Oy! Tell me the problem so I can help you."

"You? How could you possibly help me? You can't even speak English!" Bess yelled at her grandmother.

Bubby Adel raised her finger to scold her. "It is forbidden to talk to your elders this way." But before her grandmother finished, Bess had kicked her workbook under her daybed and was heading out the door. Bess had no idea where she was going, but she thought she would explode if she sat in the kitchen one minute more. She ran down the back stairs, past the boys, out through the back yard, and into the alley. As she slammed the rusty gate, she heard Calvin yell, "Hey, Sis, where are you going?" She just kept going, crying as she ran.

When she reached the top of Phoenix Hill, she wiped her eyes. At the front gate of Cave Hill Cemetery, she thought of going in but didn't want to be there alone. So she walked to Bardstown Road, and before she knew it she was in front of her favorite haunt, the branch library. At the desk was Miss Steele, the nosy librarian, who said hello to Bess and asked why she wasn't in school.

"A holiday," Bess said. Miss Steele nodded and went back to stamping due dates on a lady's books.

Bess went to the children's section and sat down. She wasn't quite as mad at the world. Maybe a book would take her mind off everything, but nothing in the children's section interested her. If she went to the adult section, she knew Miss Steele would rush over. So, Bess went into the stacks where they kept bound copies of her favorite magazines. Sometimes she looked at the pictures in *American Girl* or *Collier's*. Although she loved the covers of *McCall's* and *Vogue*, the impossibly slender women with impossibly long necks made Bess even more self-conscious about her own body. Short and plump. She slid the copy of *Vogue* back into the rack.

When she was sure the librarian could no longer see her, Bess pulled a bound volume of *The Saturday Evening Post* off the shelf and sat on the floor. Paging through the issue, she found a story that she had read before by a man called Fitzgerald. She had liked it so much that she found one of his novels, but Miss Steele wouldn't let her check it out. It was so frustrating to be treated like a child.

The story was about a girl named Bernice. Bess remembered now that Bernice felt out of place, too. The story started at a country club dance. Bernice's cousin Marjorie, much prettier than Bernice, danced with all the boys. But Bernice wasn't comfortable around boys. Bess knew just how Bernice felt. Out of pity, Marjorie convinced her friend Warren to dance with her awkward cousin. Warren thought it might be a lark, but he quickly got tired of the quiet girl, so, he decided to try out his new line on her. "You've got an awfully kissable mouth," he told Bernice, lying through his teeth.

Bess remembered how mean Warren was, but also, she wondered how it would feel to be kissed by a boy. She closed her eyes and thought of the time Cousin Joe had kissed her, but just then a terrible pain struck her belly, and her panties felt wet. Alarmed, she looked about to see if she were still alone. Then she slid her hand under her skirt. When she brought her hand out, it was bloody. Oh God, she was bleeding. What was wrong with her? She thought she must be very sick. Maybe God had cursed her for being wicked to Bubby. Bess heard Miss Steele's steps as they clicked nearer on the tile floor and didn't know what to do.

"We're closing soon," Miss Steele said, "so if you want to check something out, you'd best do it quickly." Bess stood up with the bound volume in front of her.

"Oh, dear girl, you're dripping on the floor," Miss Steele said.

"I don't know what's wrong with me," she said in a shaky voice.

"Come with me." Miss Steele led Bess to the part of the library for "Staff Only." In the bathroom, Miss Steele's voice became kinder.

"Don't worry," she said. "You're not sick. It's all normal. When you get home, tell your mother, and she will explain it. You're fine." Then she told Bess to wash up and that she'd bring something she could put in her underpants.

As Bess stood there scrubbing the stain, she felt more blood dripping down her legs, and she doubted Miss Steele. This was a curse, and she was going to bleed to death.

Miss Steele knocked on the door and entered. Bess put the skirt in front of her and the librarian handed her a white oblong package and two safety pins.

"Inside there is a Kotex pad. It has cotton inside. Pin it to your panties and get home quickly. Your mother will explain everything. I'll wait outside for you."

Bess pinned the oblong pad to her damp underwear and put her skirt on.

Not knowing what to say to Miss Steele, she left with her head down. She dared not walk too fast What if the pad leaked. It rubbed between her legs with every step, and the cramps were starting up again. When she got home, darned if Annabelle wasn't still messing about in the kitchen. Annabelle rushed up to her with a worried look.

"Where y'all been?"

Bess didn't answer. She decided she would lock herself in the bathroom.

Annabelle said, "Your grandmother is taking a nap, so best be quiet."

A nap? That was a bad sign.

Once inside the bathroom she inspected the damage. The pad was bloody. She grabbed some newspaper from the box by the toilet and wiped herself. More blood. There was a soft knock at the door.

Annabelle said softly, "Bessie Lee? Are y'all okay?"

"Leave me alone!" Bess snarled.

"You sure you don't need help?" Annabelle insisted.

Thinking maybe she could use some help, Bess whimpered, "All right, come in."

As soon as Annabelle stepped in, Bess told her to guard the door.

"What's wrong?" Annabelle handed her a hankie to wipe her eyes. When Bess kept on crying Annabelle said, "Y'all just having a bad day. Nothing is worth crying over."

"I'm dying."

"What?"

Bess showed Annabelle the bloody pad.

"Oh that? It's 'cause you are a woman now. I know it's sure enough scary the first time, but you'll get used to it. Your momma keeps rags in this bag that you can pin to your panties."

"But it hurts so bad."

"Yeah, them cramps hurt like the devil sometimes, but that's just part of the curse. My mama said it's all because Eve ate the apple."

Bess looked at Annabelle and smiled. For the first time that day, she felt like the world had stopped spinning out of control. "I was so awful to Bubby."

"Yes, that's true, but womenfolk get crabby when they bleedin'. Sometimes I want to break things, but you just got to put up with it. It won't last but four or five days."

"Four or five days!"

"Listen, Bessie Lee. You gonna be all right. I gotta get home soon. Should I go and get your momma?"

"Yes. Thank you, Annabelle."

When her mother came in, she asked, "What's wrong?"

"I'm sick, Momma. I'm bleeding."

Momma hugged her and said, "Nu, Bessele. It's something all women do. Now you too."

"But I'm only twelve."

Momma gave her a sympathetic look. "You'll be thirteen in July. This just means you're growing up."

"Momma, are you sure I don't need to see Dr. Rubel?"

"No, you will be fine, mamale. Today you will use my special panties, and tomorrow I'll buy you your own. In the panties you will pin rags that are nice and soft."

"I have terrible cramps."

"I'll tell your bubby to fix you a cup of tea for that."

When Bess ventured out of the bathroom, Bubby was pouring hot water into a cup. Bess knew she should apologize for yelling such terrible things at her, so she walked over to the stove. Bubby turned, slapped Bess on the cheek, and said, "Kenahora!"

Bess's face stung and her head buzzed with hateful thoughts like hitting her grandmother back. She turned and ran into her parents' bedroom, slammed the door, and pushed the chair under the doorknob so no one was getting in.

Her grandmother rapped on the door with her cane. "Bessele, effen di tier! Open up this minute."

Bess ignored her and flopped onto Momma and Poppa's bed where she rolled into a ball.

Before long, Momma was back upstairs, "Bessele, Bessele, open up, mamale."

Bess got up and opened the door a crack to let Momma in. Pointing to the red mark on her cheek, she asked, "Why did Bubby hit me?"

"Oy, Bessele, she wasn't angry with you. It's what they do in the Old Country to keep the Evil Eye away when you bleed for the first time. So you should be safe. Your bubby didn't mean to hurt you. She hit me when I became a woman. Poor little girl, it's been a bad day."

"Oh, Momma, I said hateful things to Bubby, and I was so mad and ashamed, I wanted to go far away where I'd never see her again."

"So, where did you go?"

"I ended up at the library."

"Did you start bleeding there?"

Bess nodded.

Momma put her arm around her and said, "Then you come home, and your grandmother hits you. Oh, mamale. I hope this should be the worst that would happen in your long life. Tomorrow will be a better day."

"Well, it couldn't be worse," said Bess. "Do you believe in the Evil Eye?"

"Maybe yes. Maybe no. You know I kept a red thread on the crib for you and Calvin. It couldn't hurt to chase the Evil Eye away."

"Do I have to go to school tomorrow?" Bess feared getting blood all over the place.

"And why not?" Momma said. "My first time, I was sent to school, and somehow I made it through that day."

After she'd finished the tea and rested a bit, Bess remembered her unfinished math assignment with a shudder and went to retrieve the dratted workbook. Tucked inside the page she was working on was a sheet of paper with Calvin's messy cyphers and all the answers. Impossible, she thought, her brother's math skills were worse than hers. But not Bubby's! Her grandmother could figure rows and rows of numbers in her head. He must have translated, and Bubby had figured out every single problem.

Chapter 17
The Prize

"Momma, why are you still in bed?" Bess said. "There's so much to do to get ready for the contest."

"I have to rest a little to recover from the tumult of Passover," Momma said. "I wouldn't be able to go to your piano contest tomorrow. Your father will take you to Frankfort."

"But you promised. Why can't you come? What's wrong?"

"Nothing is wrong. I just need to rest. Why are you home from school so late?"

Annabelle came into the room and tugged at Bess's elbow. "Your momma needs to sleep, child. I'm just gonna fix her bed a little, so, you go and set the table. I made y'all brisket and roasted potatoes and peas."

Usually, Bess laughed when Annabelle called her child because she was all of a year older, but today it was irritating.

At dinner Momma was sullen. Bess wondered whether her mother was pregnant again. That would explain why she needed bed rest. Bess was so upset she couldn't taste her food. Should she skip the contest? But she'd worked so hard to make it into the semi-finals. She and her school nemesis Mary D were representing Louisville. Everyone at the table ate silently, including Calvin, until Bess said, "Poppa, we have to be up early tomorrow to get the first the train to Frankfort."

"Yes, we'll get up early, Bessele, but I'll drive us in my truck. Your bubby is coming too."

"The truck?" Bess could not hide her disappointment. The plan had been to meet Mrs. Parmer and her husband on the train. Now Bess would be showing up at the concert in an old, dented delivery truck with her grandmother who had no teeth, well only two, and two niceties in English which were "ten kew" for thank you and "plitcha mitcha" when she met someone new.

"It ain't fair. Bess gets to go to Frankfort, and I gotta go to school," Calvin grumbled, but no one paid attention.

After dinner, Bess put her sheet music into her satchel and polished her good shoes. She sat at the piano and practiced the trills in the Lecuona piece. She had fallen in love with "Malagueña" the first time Mrs. Parmer played it for her, but Mary D had said it was too new. In her opinion, the judges preferred classical composers. "You know," Mary D said, "I did come in second last year at twelve years of age." How could Bess forget?

Annabelle had pressed Bess's new green taffeta dress and left it hanging on a hook in the bathroom. Now that she was bulging in different places, Bess thought she looked awful in most of her clothes, but the new dress fit like a dream. Momma and Poppa had outdone themselves.

That night Bess didn't sleep well. Momma moaned through the night, and at dawn, Poppa came into the kitchen to fill the hot water bottle. He tiptoed but still it woke Bess. Then, at 6:30 a.m. Poppa woke her from a nightmare. She was playing the piano in a fit of anger, banging it with her fists, but no sound came out.

After breakfast, Bess spied her brother getting into the back of the truck, and she told Poppa. Calvin came back to their apartment shaking his head. "Pop caught me, so I guess I can't go and cheer for you." Bess felt guilty for tattling and relieved Calvin didn't realize it. She gave a hug to her loyal fan and then got into the truck with Poppa and Bubby.

As they crossed the railroad tracks, Poppa pointed out a group of men with packs on their backs waiting to hop a train. "A shame a man should live like that."

Bess replied that Mrs. Dodge thought men who really wanted work could find it.

Poppa said that although things were better, there still were too many people unemployed. "Think how long it took our friend Jake to find that job in California."

Further into the country, there were mansions atop the hills. "Give a look at that palace," her grandmother said, pointing to a white colonial home. "Yankee gonevim!" Bubby Adel called Americans "Yankee thieves." Even though she didn't read the workers' newspaper like Poppa, she was disgusted by lavish displays of wealth.

The hills were blooming with dogwoods, redbud trees, and azaleas, and everyone's mood changed. Poppa started humming a song. Bess had never seen Bubby so excited. Her grandmother pointed out birds and taught Bess their names in Yiddish. She showed Bess trees that she remembered from her childhood. Bubby could be so irritating, but it was nice to see her enjoy the scenery.

"Such a beautiful green grass!" Bubby exclaimed.

Poppa said, "We are lucky Kentucky is not like Kansas and Oklahoma what have nothing but dry land and dust blowing in the wind."

Bubby ignored Poppa and called out to the horses. "Such a horse for a Czarina. My sister Basia, of blessed memory, for whom you are named, loved horses. We rode bareback on our horse as fast as it would go, and we'd fall off and laugh and laugh."

Bess asked, "Didn't you get hurt?"

"Oh, no," Bubby answered, "We rolled on the tall grass and got back on."

"That's a good lesson, Bessele," Poppa said. "If you fall off the horse, you get back on."

"You think I'm going to make mistakes today, don't you Poppa."

"No, of course not, but sometimes you get so angry when you do."

Poppa's words changed her mood. Dark thoughts buzzed about in her head. Suddenly, she felt under immense pressure to win. And she was embarrassed to be going to Frankfort with her grandmother in tow. Bubby didn't look like the other family members who would be at the contest. Although Momma and Poppa spoke English with an accent, they were always nattily dressed. Bubby just kept mending her old clothes that reeked of mothballs.

They'd been driving for two hours when Bess spied the new State Capitol

Dome! Bess had studied it in school, but it was even more beautiful than the pictures. Before long Bess realized that Poppa had passed the capitol four times. They were lost.

The contest was being held at an old plantation on Limestone Hill Road. She would be disqualified if she was late. Eventually, Bess spotted a sign for the contest. They turned and found Limestone Hill. As they pulled into a long tree-lined lane, Bess felt like they had driven into a movie. "Yankee gonevim." Bubby shook her head.

"There aren't any Yankees in this place," Bess said. She could imagine ladies in long dresses in horse-drawn buggies riding down this lane, dashing men riding thoroughbreds, and colts darting around in the immense pastures. As they grew closer to the mansion with graceful white columns and a wide porch, the colorful outfits of the contestants and their families reminded her of stories Mrs. Dodge had told her about sipping minty cold drinks on the veranda of her family's plantation. How would she get her bubby up all those steps to the porch without drawing attention? Maybe Poppa would take Bubby to park the car, and she could go up alone. But he had other ideas.

"I'll drop you and Bubby off here, so she won't have to walk too far," Poppa said.

"Oy vey iz mir. Everything hurts me," Bubby said as they slowly made their way up the stairs. Bess was sure every eye in the place was on them.

Mary D ran over just as Bess found a rocking chair in a far corner of the porch for Bubby.

"Hey, Topsky, your father made you a new dress! The bias cut covers your bulges." Mary D patted her on the stomach. Bess stepped back and wanted to turn and walk away, but as always, her nemesis just kept talking.

"I saw y'all pulling up in your poppa's truck. You could have come with us. We have plenty of room in my daddy's car. Where's your momma?"

"She isn't feeling well."

"That's too bad. Who's this?"

"Bubby, this is my friend from school." Bess introduced her grandmother.

Bubby nodded gravely at Mary D, and Bess was relieved she hadn't smiled. "Plitcha mitcha," Bubby said.

"It's a pleasure," Mary D said with suppressed laughter in her voice.

"Come on over. I want to introduce you to my momma." Mary D dragged Bess over to a tall well-dressed woman.

"Momma, this is Bess Toplansky, the girl from my school."

"Well, hello, Bess. Mary Dianne has told me all about y'all." The woman extended a gloved hand to shake Bess's. "It's a wonder y'all can play an octave with those tiny hands. But Mary D says you are a fine musician, almost as good as she is. Mary D tells me it's your first time at the contest. Hope you don't get the jitters. Best of luck to you."

Bess felt confused. Mary D's mother had smiled and greeted her warmly but still she had hurt her feelings. And didn't she know it was bad luck to wish a performer good luck? Mrs. Parmer had told her in her last lesson that you never said good luck before a performance. She looked around the porch hoping to find her teacher, but all Bess saw was a sea of musicians and their parents.

"Come, let's get some lemonade for your granny," Mary D said. As they stood in line for refreshments everyone said hello to Mary D. This was her third time at the competition. One woman bent Mary D's ear and invited her family to come visit their horse farm in Lexington. Bess felt invisible.

The woman motioned another friend to come over. "Amy Lou, meet the girl who's taking first this year!"

When Mary D smiled and thanked her modestly, the friend said, "It's your first time in the senior group and this year is your year."

A gong sounded, and a gentleman took a megaphone and instructed the contestants to assemble in the grand ballroom. Bess followed the crowd into an entryway with a sparkly crystal chandelier like in the movie theaters, and Mary D stayed close by her side.

In the big salon, the master of ceremonies thanked the Breckinridge family for allowing the Piano and Violin Teachers of Kentucky to use their lovely home. He explained the course of events and where the junior and senior musicians would compete. He said the pianists would play in the ballroom and the violinists in the dining room.

Thank goodness, she thought. It wouldn't be hard to get lost in this place.

At 11:30 the contestants would reconvene in the ballroom and the finalists would be announced. Lunch would be served on the veranda for those who had reservations, and the others were welcome to take advantage of the lovely grounds to have their picnics.

Mary D whispered, "I don't recommend the luncheon here. We're having lunch at a club with old friends. I would have invited y'all, but they don't allow Jews."

Bess didn't hear any other announcements after that.

Total chaos ensued as the musicians filed out to find where they would be playing. Bess shook off Mary D by ducking into a powder room. She sat at the long mirror pounding her fists in anger and telling herself not to cry.

"Hey, what's wrong?" Mrs. Parmer was behind her.

"Mrs. P, thank goodness you're here," Bess exclaimed jumping up from the stool.

"Hey, don't you just look perfect," said Althea Parmer taking Bess's hand and giving her a twirl. "Such beautiful fabric, and that green sets off your honey-colored hair. Your parents are the best."

"Momma couldn't come."

"So your father said."

"The doctor says she needs bed rest. I think she's um, pregnant again," Bess said blushing.

"Oh, well, Bess, sometimes bedrest is important. But your father and grandmother and John and I are all here to root for you."

Her teacher could make her feel like everything was going to be as easy as pie.

"So, Miss Bess, it's your first contest, and you should savor every moment. Don't pay attention to anyone else. People may say and do things to rile you, but you need to focus on your music and enjoy playing." Then Mrs. Parmer gave her a hug and reassured her that everything was going to be fine,

Bess walked into the grand ballroom with her head held high. Mary D motioned for her to take a seat she'd saved, but instead Bess took a seat at the end of the row. She sat quietly and enjoyed the other pianists.

Bess was the last to perform. As she adjusted the piano bench, she thought about what Mrs. P had advised. She didn't *play* the "Soldier's March" by Schumann. She *was* the "Soldier's March." The audience applauded loudly, and when Bess bowed, she saw her teacher and Mr. Parmer nodding their heads vigorously. Then the emcee instructed the performers to wait in the entranceway. Bess joined the musicians in the hallway nervously awaiting the decision of the judges. She hoped she would be chosen for the finals after lunch.

Bess saw Mary D talking to a tall blond violinist in a well-cut gray suit. He looked very dashing. Although Bess was envious, she was relieved that she didn't have to listen to that chattering magpie. She went out onto the veranda and waited until the musicians were called back for the big announcement.

First, she heard names of pianists from Lexington, Paris, and Richmond. Then Mary Dianne Porter. Well, Mary D had played well. When her own name was called, Bess felt joy and relief.

Mary D ran over to Bess. "I knew we'd both make the finals! I'm so excited I don't know how I'll eat any lunch. Don't you wish your mother were here?"

Mrs. Parmer congratulated her student and Mary D. Then she asked whether Bess and her family would sit with them at the luncheon. Bess thanked them but declined. She was glad to see Poppa and Bubby winding through the crowd toward her.

"So, our little girl made it to the final round!" Poppa said. "We're so proud of you."

Bubby spit three times to ward off evil spirits and patted Bess on the head. "Goot girl," she said.

"Nu," her father said, "let's have our picnic. I found a nice spot."

Thank goodness a few other families had brought baskets of food. Not all the contestants' families were going to the luncheon or to fancy clubs in shiny cars.

They spread their quilt in a shady spot under a big oak. The smell of freshly cut grass filled the air. Bubby breathed deeply, picked a little bunch of clover and said, "This is how it smelled in the Old Country."

"But Bubby, you always say your village was muddy and smelled of horse manure."

"Bessele, you have to know which way to point your nose."

As they were unwrapping the brisket sandwiches, Poppa saw a boy sitting alone not too far away. It was the tall blond Mary D had been talking to.

"Bess, go and invite that boy to join us. No one should eat alone."

Bess felt shy, so Poppa yelled over, "Please to come and sit with us and have what to eat."

The boy bowed to the family and thanked them. "I am Walter Schreiber," he said shaking Poppa's hand.

Poppa introduced the family and offered Walter a sandwich. Bess didn't know a boy could eat so delicately and slowly. She noticed that his jacket had been let out and not so expertly. His shoes were well polished, but the soles were thin. Bess translated for Bubby that the boy was living in Paducah and that he was German. Bubby muttered insults about the Germans. If Walter understood, he didn't let on. He complimented the food and especially the spice cookies.

"In Berlin we would have a cheese plate or a nice coffee with cream after lunch."

"Oh, we don't eat milk and meat together," Bess said.

"I too am Jewish." (Walter pronounced it "Chewish.") "However, we don't bother with the dietary laws." Bess didn't translate that for Bubby.

When Bess stood to clear up their picnic, Walter stood and helped Poppa stand. He offered his hand to help Bubby, but she shooed him off, got on her knees, and stood slowly.

Poppa reminded Bess that they needed to leave immediately after the contest to get home before sundown for the Sabbath. Then he and Bubby wished Bess and Walter good performances, and Bubby spit and said, "Ptu, ptu, ptu."

Walter said,"Toi, toi, toi is what we say in German. It is to ward off the Devil."

Bess laughed to think that such a mature boy would say the same thing as Bubby. As they ambled back to the contest, she asked to see his violin. It was the most beautiful one she had ever seen.

"It is Italian, and my sister has one that is almost identical. She is my twin and . . ." Walter went silent and looked away. Bess wanted to know more but there was an announcement that the contest would resume in ten minutes.

"Oh dear, we didn't warm up, and I'm feeling so jittery," Bess said.

"My mother was a concert pianist, and she used to warm up like this before a performance," said Walter as he closed his eyes and rubbed his palms slowly up and down. "Do it until you feel a tingle. Stop. Then rub vigorously until they feel hot. Don't think of anything but the feeling in your hands. Block out the audience and just feel your hands." The two stood together in the shade and rubbed their hands. Bess did it and was amazed how the motion calmed her jitters.

As they stood in front of doorway to the mansion, Walter asked her about her teacher's husband. Bess told him that Mr. Parmer was a violinist and directed a small orchestra that performed around Louisville and taught at the university. Walter said there was no one to give him lessons in Paducah. Perhaps he should come to Louisville for some lessons. Bess felt a funny flip flop in her chest. Mary D's shrill voice broke the spell. "Wait for me, Topsky!" Bess turned and saw her get out of their shiny black car.

Walter bowed and said, "Toi, toi, toi. And Bess, you must promise me to warm up your hands as I showed you." He walked inside as Bess waited for her dratted schoolmate.

"I see you met that German boy," said Mary D, out of breath from running up the stairs.

"He had lunch with us," Bess said proudly.

"Well, I could barely understand a word he said."

"He speaks better English than a lot of us."

"Oh, you're just used to funny accents. Anyway, there's something peculiar about him. He seems kind of prissy."

"Well, I bet he will play the pants off everyone here. And if you are going to say mean things, please, don't sit next to me."

Bess hurried into the ballroom and sat in between the boy from Lexington and the girl from Richmond.

The violinists played first. Thank goodness there was no screeching or flubs. Bess hated when musicians made mistakes. Walter played the

"Capriccio" movement from Stravinsky's violin concerto. Bess had never heard it before, but it made her feel like dancing. The rich sound, the tricky chords, and the tempo were executed perfectly. The audience applauded but not as generously as they should have. Was Mary D right? Maybe in this venue classical composers were better. Walter smiled at Bess as he sat down.

There was a short break before the piano finals, and Mary D made sure to grab the seat next to Bess. The girl chattered on about the violinists and finished saying, "Your foreign friend played well." Bess couldn't believe she'd said such a thing. She turned her head away to ignore the running commentary. Finally, she turned to Mary D and said, "Shush!"

Bess tried to do the warmup Walter had recommended, but she felt black thoughts buzzing in her head. She barely heard the other pianists perform. But there was no way to block out Mary D who played the Mozart sonata perfectly. The audience loved her. She smiled triumphantly at Bess as she sat down and whispered, "Good luck, Topsky."

When the judges called her name, Bess jumped up. Her fists were clenched. She marched onto the stage and sat at the piano. Fury had erased all memory of her piece. The head judge said, "Miss Toplansky, we are waiting."

The only thing Bess remembered was that Mrs. Parmer had told her over and over to start "Malagueña" very softly. Out of nowhere the first chord came and not as soft as it should have been. The crowd gasped. Then as the music worked its way quickly from pianissimo to fortissimo, her hands took over. She had never played the somber lower chords with such force. The shimmering trills in the high keys floated off her fingers. The battle between the bass clef and the treble not only expressed her anger but also the sweetness of the music. When she finished, there was complete silence. She stood and bowed as the audience began to applaud politely, and then Walter and Mr. Parmer stood and yelled, "Brava."

All the players filed into the hall while the judges deliberated. For the first time in her life, Mary D was quiet. Then they were called back to the room and onto the stage. Walter won the violin competition. That was no surprise. Before she knew it, she heard her name. "Miss Bess Toplansky, of Louisville, second place."

Bess stepped forward, and one of the judges hung a red ribbon around her neck and congratulated her. The crowd clapped warmly, and Bess smiled as she curtsied to them. She could see her Bubby and Poppa standing at the back applauding and waving.

Then they called out, "Miss Mary Dianne Porter, of Louisville, first place." There was thunderous applause and Mary D bowed her head as the judge put the blue ribbon on her. A young girl and boy brought bouquets of red roses for Walter and Mary D. As they lined up on the stage for pictures, Mary D made sure to stand next to Bess. Flashbulbs popped and Mary D resumed her chattering. Bess didn't feel angry anymore, just proud of how she had played and happy that her Poppa was the first to greet her as she stepped into the lobby.

"Oh my, Bessele, you were outstanding. Please to collect Bubby on the veranda while I bring the truck around front." Mr. and Mrs. Parmer handed Bess a basket of daisies. "I'm sure the judges had a tough decision," Mr. P said. Mrs. P nodded her head and added, "You played perfectly. The most dramatic interpretation I've heard."

Walter walked up smiling broadly. "You were so wonderful. I've never heard a violinist as good as you," Bess said. Walter laughed and bowed deeply. He extended his hand to congratulate her and said, "Lecuona himself could not play his showy piece better. Now you must learn to play Gershwin and Stravinsky. Forget the classical composers."

Bess wished he had hugged her, but he said something she would savor for a long time: "You, Miss Bess Toplansky of Louisville, were robbed."

Not knowing what to say, she stammered her thanks and added, "I need to find my grandmother." As she turned to go, Walter said, "Wait, here's my card. You must write to me."

Before she could get outside to the porch, Mary D's mother walked up to congratulate her. "What an adorable girl you are. Who knew someone so little could make so much noise?" Reeking of whiskey, she laughed loudly at her own joke. Bess noticed she tottered a bit. Mary D took her mother's arm to steady her. A look of embarrassment on her rival's face quickly became a smile as Mary D said her goodbyes to Bess.

Bess found Bubby dozing in the same rocker she'd first led her to. She had a chain of clover on her lap. Bess touched her grandmother's hand. "Bubby, it's time to go."

"Bessele, you played so well. A leben af dein kopf." She kissed Bess's head and handed her the clover chain. Bess curtsied and put it on. "A sheynem dank, Bubby." Bubby rarely praised anyone, so Bess savored her congratulations. And then of course, Bubby spat to ward off evil spirits.

All the way home, Bubby watched the course of the sun. Bess stared at her father's shaky hands on the wheel. Was that why he didn't play cards anymore? She wanted to ask whether he had gone to the doctor, but she knew how touchy he was about the subject.

When they pulled into their back alley, there was a bit of gasoline and a bit of sunlight left. Bess helped Bubby out of the truck and then took off running up the back stairs to find Momma.

Her mother was sitting at the Sabbath table and Annabelle was pulling stuffed veal breast out of the oven. It smelled delicious.

"Well, would you look at that ribbon. I knew y'all was gonna win!" Annabelle declared.

Calvin ran into the kitchen, spied her ribbon, and began to hoot, "You won! You won!"

"I won second place. Momma, how do you feel? You look so much better," Bess said.

"I feel a little better, but I am so happy you won."

"Mary D got first," Bess answered with a twinge of regret in her voice.

"Well, I am sure you played beautifully," Momma said kissing her on the forehead.

"It was wonderful. I've never felt so free with my playing. Mr. and Mrs. Parmer were pleased."

"That's good."

"Walter said I was robbed."

"Who is Walter?"

"He's a wonderful violist. Better than Jascha Heifetz, and he thought the judges were wrong"

"Well, you must not say that to anyone else," Momma said. "You must be gracious. Next year, you will play even better, and you will win first place. And then you must also be gracious."

As Bess stood with Momma and Bubby to light the Sabbath candles, she felt calm and happy to be at home. No one talked much at dinner but Calvin, who had them laughing at shenanigans his buddies had been involved with at school. Bess was sure he had also been part of the mischief.

That night when Bess kissed her mother goodnight, Momma asked her about the boy named Walter.

"Oh, Momma, he's so handsome and has such good manners, and he's from Berlin."

"So you met a Yekke."

Bess looked at her quizzically, so Momma explained, "A German boy and from Berlin. Soon your family from Bialystok won't be good enough."

"No, Momma, I am really proud of you all." Then Bess whispered, "Are you going to lose another baby, Momma?"

Her mother shrugged and said, "Better we should talk about good things. Like how you won this beautiful red ribbon which we will hang in the store for all our customers to see."

Chapter 18
Pen Pals

MAY TO AUGUST, 1936

A year's worth of letters from Walter Schreiber lay in a shoe box under Bess's bed. When no one was in the kitchen, she read and reread them. His first letters had been long and full of stories about Berlin and London, where his family had lived when he was a boy. He and his twin sister had studied and played violin together so long that they had a trick of stopping in the middle of a performance and switching violins.

His father was a chemical engineer, although the only work he had found in the United States was as a traveling salesman. Walter's father sounded like a tyrant. His mother was a beautiful and talented pianist who had played solos with orchestras from Copenhagen to Madrid. When his sister got tuberculosis, his mother took a position as the accompanist of the Berlin Opera, but in 1933, she was fired along with all the other Jewish musicians she knew.

When Walter was thirteen, they lived in an apartment in the middle of the city next to a park with a zoo and formal gardens. He described standing with neighbors on the rooftop of their building watching the Nazis burn books. The Schreibers decided that the family had to leave Germany. Walter and his father would go first. His mother would stay in Berlin with his sister because she couldn't get into the United States until her tuberculosis was cured. The family would be reunited, they hoped, in New York, where both his parents would have the best chance of finding work.

Bess loved Walter's sardonic words, and she could see the elegant places that he described.

*So, Bess, you see, nothing panned out for my father in New York,
but an acquaintance wrote to him from the bustling metropolis,
Paducah, Kentucky, to say that a position at a chemical firm had
opened. Father and I arrived to discover that the friend had left for
a better job, and here we were in this one-horse river town knowing
not a soul. Because we are from Germany, the members of Temple
Israel welcomed us. They consider themselves German aristocrats
since their families came here to peddle clothes a hundred years
ago, but they are not. At first, they invited us to all their parties,
but Father found excuses. And we never went to their quaint little
temple. Well, we never went to services in Berlin, except to show
the world we were Jewish at Yom Kippur, so why go now?*

In another letter he mentioned a Jewish girl who took violin lessons from
him. Bess was glad Walter only wrote about her twice. Occasionally, he sent
Bess poems or songs he liked. Mainly, he wrote about pieces he was studying
and compositions he had written. He wanted Bess to hear his collection of
Duke Ellington and Benny Goodman recordings. And he gave Bess advice
about everything.

*Little Bess, I sometimes think of you stretching so far to reach the
pedals. I was thinking you could put extenders on your shoes, so I
asked my father to fiddle around with that idea in his spare time.*

Bess had liked Walter's letter up to that point. The idea of foot extenders
angered her. Some of the girls at junior high called her Little Bess to distinguish
her from a tall girl also named Bess. She really regretted telling Walter about
that nickname. Poppa had always told her boys liked shorter girls. But so far,
no boys other than Walter had ever paid attention to her.

Bess wrote Walter that in the fall, she would enter Atherton High School
for Girls. Her life would be consumed by homework, orchestra rehearsals,
piano practice, and doing the bills for Poppa. She could imagine Walter
dozing off reading this, so she told him about the crazy slang expressions
that peppered her brother Calvin's speech and all his misadventures. She told
him how Annabelle had given her brother his nickname Angel and that all

his friends called him that now. Calvin ran around with their older cousin's crowd and that worried Bess. Somehow, he always had money to burn.

What she didn't write was how worried she was about Poppa. His eyes got so tired he didn't read his newspapers, and sometimes his hands were shaky. She did say that she kept the ledger and balanced the books at the end of the month. It was the bane of her existence. In his next letter, Walter suggested how she could improve her bookkeeping. His intentions were good, but Walter could be overbearing.

One afternoon in May after going to the movies with Cousin Dotty, the two girls sat in the backyard, ate cookies, and looked at her cousin's movie magazines. They debated about which star kissed better. When Dotty did a pantomime with her back to Bess of a man caressing her, Bess almost fell off the bench laughing. She couldn't resist telling Dotty about Walter's letters and the photos he had sent of himself in Berlin with his family. She ran upstairs and brought down a bundle of letters and put them on the picnic table. She handed her cousin a photo of Walter and his family.

"Wow, look at his father!" Dotty thought he was more elegant than William Powell from *The Thin Man*. "But isn't Walter a little young for you?"

"That photo was taken five years ago, Dotty. Anyhoo, look at his mother's dress. Did you ever see anyone more elegant? She is so lovely."

"Personally, I like the dresses your mom and dad make. Is that his sister? She's pretty."

"It's his twin sister Charlotte. She plays the violin too."

"Too bad Paducah is so far away," Dotty said.

"Walter is going to come take a lesson with Mr. Parmer, and Mrs. Parmer wants us to play a duet."

"Can I meet him when he comes? Pretty please?"

"Hey, what are you two up to?" called Naomi Habermann, who had let herself into the back yard. Dotty and Bess were so busy gabbing about the photos that they hadn't heard the creaky gate.

"Golly, look at all those letters," Naomi said.

"She's writing to a German boy in Paducah. Can you believe it?"

"The fellow you met in Frankfort at the contest last year?"

"Yes," Bess answered. She passed the plate of cookies to her neighbor, embarrassed that there were only two left. She never could resist spice cookies with jam.

Naomi looked at the pictures wistfully. "My father has been to Berlin, but now with all the ugly things that are going on, he won't go back. Does Walter talk about the Nazis?"

"A little. His parents decided to come to America after they watched them burning books in a public square in Berlin."

"Oh, the Nazis don't just burn books in Berlin," Naomi said. "They burn them all over Germany. It's terrible there. Father says Hitler is dangerous."

Naomi picked up a cookie and took a bite. "Bess, do you think I could write to Walter? I really need to practice my German."

"Well, he's so busy giving music lessons. I don't know whether he'll have time to answer." Bess couldn't say no to her neighbor, but she didn't want to share the closest thing to a boyfriend she'd ever had. "And besides, you are pen pals with people all over the world already," Bess said trying to dissuade Naomi.

"Yes, but my last pen pal from Germany stopped writing."

Bess shrugged her shoulders and passed an envelope with Walter's address so Naomi could copy it.

Dotty wanted to be his pen pal too, but Bess was sure her cousin would forget to write the first letter. Naomi wouldn't.

"Thanks, Bess," Naomi said. "You're a real pal. At Lutheran School, they won't let us sing or do anything in German anymore. I could use the practice before we go to Atherton High. I've heard the German teacher is impossible to please."

After the girls left, Bess felt foolish for giving out Walter's address. Then as the school year ended, Bess learned that Naomi was writing to Walter every day, and he answered promptly. Horsefeathers! There was no way to stop her friend once she got going. In mid-July Naomi was going to Bible Camp for a month. Maybe the budding friendship with Walter would wither.

Soon after Naomi's departure, Walter's letters stopped. Bess tried to think if she'd said something insulting, but she couldn't remember anything bad.

She kept writing. Toward the end of July, the postman brought back several letters marked "Undeliverable at this address." Now, she was worried. Naomi hadn't mentioned anything about Walter in her postcards from camp, so she would have to wait for her neighbor's return to see if she knew anything.

Finally in August, Naomi and her siblings returned from camp. She was so tan and slender. "You look like Esther Williams," Bess said.

"Hey, you have a great tan too. Especially for someone who says she didn't do anything but practice piano," Naomi said with a laugh.

"Well, I helped my grandmother with the gardening."

"Listen, did you hear anything from Walter?"

"Nothing for a while."

"Me neither."

"I'm worried. Why isn't he writing?"

"I don't know. Before I left for camp, he asked for my father's help in getting his mother and sister out of Germany. Dad wrote his last remaining contact in Berlin, but so far there's been no answer. Things are terrible there."

Bess asked her neighbor what she thought of the Olympics in Berlin. Naomi said she didn't think the Americans should go, and Bess said her father agreed. Poppa especially didn't think Jewish athletes should go, but Bess wanted them to go and win gold medals.

The next morning Naomi rushed over to Bess's with a letter from Walter. Bess was picking tomatoes from Bubby's truck garden.

"This letter came the day I left for camp, and Mother just gave it to me."

Bess and Naomi sat at the picnic table. As Naomi pulled out the letter, colorful stamps fell out. She picked them up and put them back into the manila envelope. Her translation from German to English flowed easily as she read.

July 3, 1936

Dear friend Naomi,

*I hope this letter finds you well and reaches you before you go
north to your camp in Wisconsin with your brothers and sisters.*

Please thank your father for his concerned inquiries on my family's behalf. You may tell him now he need not bother any more.

Please, tell Bess I apologize for not writing. She must keep up her practice because though she may be small in stature, she has the soul of a giant when she plays. I regret she and I never played Beethoven's "Spring Sonata" together.

I wish you both much success in your new school and in your lives.

The canceled stamps inside the envelope are for you, Naomi. I know you, like me, are an avid collector. The sheets of Beethoven stamps are for Little Bess. Tell her to guard them in a safe place, dark and dry, because they are extremely valuable. Ask her to make my apologies to the Parmers, for I shall not be coming to Louisville to take a lesson. Nor shall I ever play the violin again.

And to you my dear new friend Naomi, I wish you much success in life and bid you farewell because I shall never write or speak in German again.

Sincere regards to you both,
Walter

Bess held back tears. "What is wrong with Walter?" she said finally. "I think something bad must have happened to his mother or his sister. Or maybe it's his father."

"Walter sounds so grim, doesn't he?" Naomi said.

Bess nodded. "I'm scared. He doesn't sound like himself," she said.

"He was so eager for my father to help him get his mother and sister out. Sounds like he's lost hope."

"Oh, Naomi. What if something happened to his sister Charlotte. What if her tuberculosis got worse?"

Naomi shook her head. "Let's not think the worst. My father promised he would write one more time to his friend in Germany."

"Well, we have to do something. Does your father know anyone in

Paducah."

"I don't think Walter is there anymore." Naomi pointed to smeared ink on the big envelope. "This says Cincinnati, Ohio, I believe." She handed the envelope to Bess who studied the postmark and agreed.

"Let's go and ask your dad to contact the pastors in Cincinnati and Berlin."

"Not now. He's writing his sermon. We can't bother him."

Naomi put her hand on Bess's hand and said, "I have, um, something I need to tell you. Walter sent this for you before I left." Naomi reached into her pocket and brought out a small photo. "He must have put this in my letter by mistake."

Bess stared at it. Walter's blond hair spilled across his forehead. His eyes looked so serious. He was in the same wool jacket he had worn in Frankfort. On the back, it said, *Paducah, Kentucky, 20/6/36, For Little Bess who plays like a giant. Walter*

"Why didn't you give this to me before?" Bess asked crossly.

"I'm sorry. I guess I was so busy packing for camp, I forgot." Naomi said meekly.

"You forgot? How could you?" Bess picked up the photo and the sheets of stamps, ran up the stairs, and slammed the door shut.

Annabelle looked up from the sink. "What in tarnation is eatin' you?"

Bess ran into the bathroom and sat on the commode holding the manila envelope. Her head swirled with black thoughts. Walter was in big trouble. His family was in danger and Naomi was a selfish, thoughtless, shameless excuse for a friend.

There was a knock on the door. Naomi whispered, "Bess, I'm so sorry. Please come out."

Bess's eyes were full of tears when she opened the door, "You are a terrible person, Naomi Habermann! I am never going to speak to you again."

"Please, Bess can we go back outside and talk?"

Bess was going to say no, but she saw the way Annabelle, her grandmother, and Calvin were staring at the two of them. She pushed Naomi aside, flung open the kitchen door and ran down the stairs. She ran up the brick alley with

Naomi right beside her. She was quickly out of breath and felt like her sides would split. Near the top of the slope, Bess stumbled, and Naomi caught her. Bess pushed her away.

"Come on, Bess. You know you can't outrun me. Let's go to my house where we can talk in private."

Bess shrugged and followed. She stood in the doorway to her friend's bedroom, still resistant, her arms akimbo, but Naomi grabbed her hand and tugged her onto the bed. Bess got up and sat down on the floor.

"I'm really, awfully sorry, Bess. I meant to give you the picture before I left for camp, but I forgot."

"How could you forget? I mean you, of all people. That's like stealing."

Naomi got down onto the floor close to Bess. "Well, there was another reason. I mean, you know how my sister Ruth can be. She grabbed the photo and commented, 'Look who finally has a boyfriend.' I grabbed it back so she couldn't see Walter's inscription to you. Then I locked it in my diary for safe keeping. That's how it ended up with me at camp. I carved a little frame for it, so my bunkmates couldn't see the back, and I put it in the window by my bed. Everyone thought I had a boyfriend. It felt swell even though it was a lie." Naomi paused and added in a whisper, "You are right, Bess. I did steal it."

Bess stared at Naomi in amazement. Naomi was tall and slender, not pudgy like Bess. She had wavy brown hair, unlike Bess's dishwater blonde, poker straight, useless hair. Bess had always thought all the boys who came to their house from Lutheran School wanted to be Naomi's boyfriend. But that was not the case. For Naomi to lie about something, she must really have felt bad about herself.

"I mean it, Bess. I feel terrible. It was a big mistake. We have to make up, and we have to figure out how to help Walter. Please, forgive me." They sat quietly for a while. Then Naomi gently put her arm around her neighbor and asked, "Do you forgive me?"

Bess hugged Naomi back and said, "Yes. I get angry fast, but I get over things just as quickly."

"That was some inscription. I think he's sweet on you," Naomi said softly. "Could I see it one more time?"

Bess pulled out Walter's picture. She stared into his eyes for answers. If only she could talk to him. But where was he? She read what he'd written on the back again. Her family was proud of her playing, but they never said she played like a giant. A giant!

"Oh, Naomi, he has to be okay. He just has to be."

Part Three

The Great Flood

Chapter 19
Down by the Riverside

PADUCAH, KENTUCKY, JANUARY 19-24, 1937

Torrential rain, like Walter had never seen, began falling early in January. The landlady at their boarding house said not to worry, she'd seen many a flood, though never in the winter. Despite her assurances, the water had risen precipitously in the last two weeks. Now it was snowing and sleeting. The only good thing was that school had been called off, and he was grateful to not have to go to Paducah's pathetic excuse for a high school. From the windowsill of their parlor, Walter watched the muddy water of the Ohio rush down Sixth Street. Ice lined the rooftops and covered the debris from toppled houses. A dead mule and an uprooted tree floated by.

Like the tree, Walter felt rootless and alone. Father was on the road again. He'd lost track of time. Dreary days and nights blended, so he hadn't realized at first that the electricity had been cut off. He grabbed his coat and lay down on the couch. As always, events of the recent past preoccupied him.

Hard to believe that just a few months ago, Walter and his father had left Paducah for Cincinnati with such high hopes. Father had finally gotten a job as a chemist, and Walter could attend a good high school and study with a renowned violinist. Cincinnati had a symphony and an opera. The whole family could live there.

Everything fell apart after they received a package from Germany: Charlotte's violin. Inside was a letter from Mother with the news that his twin sister Charlotte had died. Moreover, his mother wrote that she wouldn't be joining them in America.

His father spiraled into despair and rage and most of his fury was aimed at Walter. Then Father's work at the laboratory became so erratic that they dismissed him. After that, they'd had no choice but to return to this dreary backwater town, where Father went back on the road selling chemicals.

Yesterday or the day before, the water had started coming into the first floor. The landlady had banged on his door yelling, "Come on boy, the Red Cross is evacuating us. Grab your valuables and get a move on."

What valuables? He had his violin and Charlotte's, but what good were they now. Walter decided to lock his door. He had no food. No water. Soon he descended into a blackness unlike any he had ever felt even in Cincinnati. It took all the energy he could muster to resist the urge to throw the violins into the icy water and jump into the current after them.

By late afternoon the water was rising faster than before. As the sky darkened, Walter stared out the parlor window until all he could see was a lantern in the attic of the house across the street. He heard the steady paddling of rescue boats. Weak from hunger and cold, he dropped onto the sofa and fell asleep.

He dreamt he was in Berlin with Charlotte and Mother. Crystal chandeliers lit a pathway through a theater with red carpets, red satin walls, and tall gilded mirrors that reflected the light. Onstage Charlotte stood playing Beethoven's "Moonlight Sonata," luminous in a silvery white dress. Her eyes shone and she swayed as her hand deftly moved the bow. Mother in a long black velvet dress sat serenely at the piano and motioned to her precious boy to join them. "Walter, don't give up. Walter darling, you must play."

Sirens woke Walter. He untangled himself from the blankets and walked to the window. The early morning sun peeked through clouds for the first time in weeks. The sweetness of his dream vanished with the realization that the carpet was wet. Water had begun to seep into the room. If it got worse and if the violins got wet, they would be ruined.

Walter's first thought was that his father would be furious. Perhaps he should take the violins up to the attic where the landlady let them store their things. But after walking up the stairs, he couldn't budge the swollen door. He felt dizzy and weak from hunger. The door to their rooms creaked as he went back in. He put both violin cases on the top shelf of a bookcase that separated the living room from the bedroom.

The blast of a boat's horn summoned him to the window.

"By order of the police," came a voice through a bullhorn, "everyone in this neighborhood must evacuate." Walter peered down and saw a tugboat approaching. He looked at the violins on the high shelf and, on impulse, grabbed his sister's antique Guarneri. He opened the window and yelled.

"Help!" At first his voice croaked from disuse, so he tried again, "Help! Please, help!" But the boatman kept going. Though the boat was full of people, no one had looked up. Not one single person had heard his cry for help.

His desire to be rescued surprised him, but not the rebuff. Life seemed like an endless series of rejections. He lay back down on the couch. He was thinking how he could save his sister's violin, when he heard noise coming from the street. He got up to look out the window and saw a rowboat a block away. This time he would not be missed. He took off his woolen scarf and waved it out the window. As the rowboat approached, he saw it was a family of Negroes. He called for help and waved the red scarf furiously, until the man who was rowing waved back.

"Y'all need a ride?" he yelled.

"Yes. Yes, please," Walter answered.

The man steered toward the boarding house and tied the boat to the fire escape. By then Walter had started climbing down.

"Y'all got a fiddle in that case? Toss it here, boy. You gonna need two hands to get on board nice and steady," commanded a gray-haired lady.

Walter passed Charlotte's violin to the old woman and then climbed into the boat as gently as possible.

The man rowing the boat introduced himself. "I'm Saul Robertson. This here's my family. My wife, Mary, my daughter, Nellie, and my wife's momma. Everybody calls her Miss Verna."

"I'm Walter Schreiber. Thank you for taking me. You don't have much room here."

"Y'all think Noah worried about room on the Ark?" Miss Verna said.

"We goin' to the Grace Church, Walter, if y'all wanna come with us," said Mr. Robertson.

Walter said yes. He knew exactly where they meant. It was a stone church on a hill where he played a concert with an organist shortly after they had come to Paducah.

The boat made slow progress through the water, and the rocking made Walter drowsy. When he tried to focus, everything seemed too sharp in contrast: the sunlight off the water, the dark faces of the family.

"You shiverin' child," said the old woman with the violin in her lap. "Mary, put my quilt around the boy." When Walter was wrapped in the quilt, the old woman rubbed Walter's icy hands.

"You have calluses on your fingertips."

"I used to play the violin," Walter said softly.

The grandmother told Walter that her granddaughter Nellie played banjo as well as the fiddle. Walter nodded but asked no questions.

A motorboat glided by leaving a wake that felt like it would capsize the boat. Walter wasn't a good swimmer. That was yet another thing that had disappointed Father.

"Whoa, what's the hurry?" Mr. Robertson said with a laugh as he steadied the boat.

Walter wondered how the man could find anything funny about their situation, but he admired Mr. Robertson's composure.

A few blocks from the church, Mr. Robertson spotted a woman trapped on her roof. As they got closer, he called out to ask if she wanted help. She hollered down that she wouldn't leave without her cat.

"I don't rightly know whether they'll take a cat at the shelter, but we sure enough don't mind sharing our boat with one of God's creatures."

Nellie—she looked to Walter to be about thirteen—shimmied up a drainpipe to get the woman's cat. Her limbs were long and nimble. She handed the cat to her mother and climbed back up to help the woman get down to the boat. The woman lost her balance getting into the boat, fell, and almost tipped the little rowboat over. Walter felt the boat rocking as if it were in slow motion. Once the woman found her seat and the boat settled, they were on their way, the cat trying furiously to escape his owner's hold on him.

Soon they saw the church steeple, and the old lady praised Jesus. Mr.

Robertson helped everyone out of the boat and tied it up behind a hedge of bushes well above the flood line. The ragtag group trudged up the hill. When they got to the church, a volunteer met them at the door. Walter and the lady with the cat were sent to the community hall, and the Negro family was sent off to another building. Everything happened so fast that Walter didn't even have time to thank his rescuers.

The church was full of refugees, people like him who had stayed too long.

The woman led him to a cot. "You're lucky," she said. "There are only a few left." At the end of the cot was a blanket, and Walter realized he was still covered in the quilt the Robertsons had given him.

As a woman was explaining where the washroom was, Nellie ran up with Walter's scarf. "Y'all gonna need this."

"Y'all can't be in here," the woman said, chiding Nellie who rushed off before Walter could thank her and give her the quilt.

"Some of them jist don't know their place," the woman said. Then smiling at Walter she said, "Before you settle in, we need to register you." She led Walter to a table where another volunteer kept a list of the refugees.

Since Walter was only seventeen, she asked where his parents were, and he said he wasn't sure. He had had a phone call from his father three days ago from Clarksville, Tennessee, and he had expected him back any day.

"Well, we post these lists at City Hall and the *Paducah Sun* publishes them, so your father will find you."

"If he's alive," mumbled Walter.

"I'm sure he's fine," she said cheerily, "but y'all don't look so good. Lie down and rest. A nurse will check you over presently."

Walter felt woozy and collapsed onto the cot. When his head cleared, he used the blanket to cover Charlotte's violin. Then he fell asleep wrapped in Miss Verna's quilt. It was a fretful, dreamless sleep, and every time he awakened, he wondered where he was. Finally, he fell into a deep slumber.

It was dark when he woke to hovering voices. The church hall was lit by candles and kerosene lamps, which gave the scene a ghostly presence.

"The boy has a fever, and he looks malnourished," said the nurse to the volunteer as she pushed up his coat sleeve to take his pulse. When she saw the scars on Walter's wrists, she said, "We need to keep a close watch on this one."

For three days Walter drank the juices and ate the sandwiches and cookies that were brought to him. He got an enormous inoculation against typhoid that left a welt on his arm. The nurses jotted down everything he ate. When he was able to get up, a male volunteer took him to the bathroom. It was lit by candles and there were buckets of flood water to throw down the toilets. There was boiled water in big containers for washing.

After four days, Walter felt strong enough to explore a bit. He grabbed Charlotte's violin and wandered into the main sanctuary where he'd given that concert almost two years ago. Fifteen and full of ambition. Walter scoffed to think of how sure of himself he had been. The sun sent rays of color through stained glass windows depicting the life of Jesus. Walter rubbed his hands on the elaborately carved lectern that stood before the altar. He remembered the lovely sound of the organ, but he couldn't remember what he had played. As Walter walked up to the organ, he started humming the "Pachelbel Canon." Yes, that and Bach concertos. The acoustics had been excellent, and when they finished playing, the audience rose and applauded furiously until he and the organist played an encore.

Afterwards, Father had laughed at the ovation and said, "After all, what do those peasants know?"

But at least he didn't criticize Walter. It was the first time in a long time Father had been satisfied.

Walter sat in the front pew, his unkempt hair lit by the sun filtering through the blues and reds of the windows. He thought of the awful time he and his father had spent in Cincinnati, especially the day they received the package with Charlotte's violin. Inside was a long letter in his mother's hand recounting how Charlotte had died of tuberculosis. His father had crumpled the letter and tucked it into his pocket. When Walter asked to see it, Father tossed it into the fireplace.

After that, his father became sullen and more demanding. No matter how many times Walter asked why Mother wasn't joining them, Father refused to answer. Finally, he yelled, "Walter, stop whining and act like a man for once. Your mother is not coming and that is that."

While Walter no longer wanted to study at the Cincinnati Conservatory, his father kept pressuring him to prepare for the audition. Walter went through the motions. On the day of his audition, he didn't play well. So, he was not surprised to receive a letter stating that he had been rejected.

"You are a useless failure and your lessons are a waste of money," his father had said.

For once, Walter agreed with him. After that he began to contemplate how he could extricate himself from his impossible life. He would not create a spectacle by jumping off a roof. He didn't have a gun, nor did he want to leave a bloody mess behind. He knew you could take pills but didn't know what pills they were.

One evening when Father had to stay at work late, Walter found the solution in the medicine cabinet. His father's straight razor. Without hesitation, he filled a bathtub, removed his clothes, folded them neatly, submerged himself in the water, and cut his wrists.

When he woke the next day in the hospital with his wrists bound in bandages, Walter realized he had failed yet again.

Walter jumped when he felt a hand on his shoulder. It was the volunteer who had signed him into the shelter. "You're looking a lot better," she said. "Sorry to say this, but we don't allow people in here. The pastor is strict about that. I'm glad you're feeling good enough to go traipsing about, but lunch is soon."

Although her cheery voice irritated him, Walter answered politely, "Would it be all right if I stroll around a bit more. My legs are so stiff."

"I don't reckon it would harm anyone."

Walter wanted to find the Robertsons. He had to at least thank them for their kindness. He looked in other rooms in the church but didn't find any other flood victims, so he went around to the back of the church. He saw a Negro child going into a wooden tool shed and slamming the door tight. Walter knocked and was told to come in. A dozen or more people were crowded inside. Two infants were sleeping in a wheelbarrow, and Walter saw Mr. Robertson sitting on a step ladder. His mother-in-law was sleeping on wooden palette next to him.

Walter approached quietly and asked, "How are you?"

"We fixin' to leave as soon as we can," Mr. Robertson said. "We goin' to find somewhere with proper facilities. It just ain't healthy like this."

Walter asked if the family was all right.

"Nobody is sick, but I suspect we will be if we stay."

Walter wanted to know if they had been inoculated against typhus. The man said they had been, but they weren't allowed to go into the church to relieve themselves. He said they had had to dig a ditch in the frozen ground to answer the call of nature.

"This is terrible," Walter said. "But is it safe to leave now? Is the water still rising?"

"You bet it is. I helped sandbag this church. And look how they thank us. Oh well, we're all alive. Praise the Lord."

Walter was about to ask about the rest of the family when Mary and Nellie walked in carrying buckets of water.

"Here, Daddy. Now we can wash up."

"We have a visitor," her father said.

"Well, I won't disturb you," Walter said, "I just wanted to thank you for saving me."

"That sure was a time on that boat. The water liked to take us under," Mr. Robertson said.

Mrs. Robertson asked, "How you feeling, Walter? Y'all look so much better."

"Yes, I am better, and I don't know if I would be alive if you hadn't rescued me."

"Since you're feeling better, maybe you could play us something on that fiddle of yours," Saul Robertson said. "My women have lovely voices, and my daughter plays the fiddle too."

"Oh, I don't know. I haven't played in a while," Walter said.

The grandmother opened her eyes and egged him on. "I bet y'all still play just fine."

"I've given up the violin, and anyway, it's not mine."

"Well, if you change your mind," Miss Verna said, "you know where to find us."

Walter went back to the church social hall and sat down to lunch with the volunteer and the other displaced white people. There were kerosene heaters everywhere and light came in from the tall windows. It made him angry that it was so much warmer in the main building and that the Negroes were not allowed to use the toilets. After lunch, he was tired, so he stretched out on his cot. He lay there thinking of his dream of Charlotte playing the violin in her flouncy white dress. For some reason Nellie reminded him of his sister. Well, Nellie must be about the age his sister had been when he left Germany. The most vivid thing about the dream was his mother's invitation to play the violin. "You must live, Walter," she had said.

Walter knew what he had to do. He took his sister's violin back to the tool shed and found the Robertsons packing up their things.

"Here, I want Nellie to have this fiddle," Walter said taking the bow and violin out of the case.

"Oh no, son, we couldn't take it. It's too fine."

"It doesn't matter. I don't have use for it anymore, and I want her to have it," Walter said dramatically. He held out the beautifully carved instrument. Even though Nellie kept her hands behind her back, Walter could see in her eyes she was eager to hold the violin.

The man laughed a deep baritone laugh. "People would think we done stole this. But why don't y'all play us something?"

"As I said, I don't play anymore, but would your daughter play for me?"

Nellie held out her hands eagerly. Walter asked her whether he should tune it, but she shook her head no and sat down. To Walter's amazement, she hummed middle C and then A and plucked the middle string. Like his sister, Nellie had perfect pitch. Walter watched her work slowly, cradling the violin on her lap. Her long fingers turned the peg to tune the A string. Then the chords: A and G, G and D and so on. Charlotte's beautiful instrument was badly out of tune.

Finally, satisfied she had tuned it well, Nellie played a spiritual Walter had never heard. The mother and father clapped softly, and the grandmother harmonized with a smooth contralto voice. "Wade in the water, children," she sang as other families nearby joined in. "God's gonna trouble the water," they sang over and over.

Walter admired how sweetly Nellie played the melody, and he felt a knot in his chest begin to loosen.

"That was good and very appropriate for our situation," said Walter.

"Oh, you don't know the half of it," Nellie said. "That song was sung in the fields and by our folks who ran away. Now we're running from misery again."

"We sang, now you play," said the grandmother, who looked sharply at Walter. There was something commanding in her voice, but Walter still couldn't bring himself to play.

"No, but I'll come back later and bring you some sandwiches. Nellie, will you take care of the violin 'til I return?"

Nellie nodded.

Walter hurried away, wiping tears from his cheeks. He went to his cot and got the grandmother's quilt. Then he went to the makeshift reception desk and said, "I need more sandwiches, please."

The woman looked pleased that he was hungry again. She went to the pantry and found a few cheese sandwiches and a box of crackers.

"Where y'all from?"

"Berlin."

She looked quizzical and then said, "Oh, y'all mean jist north of Lexington? I have kin there."

"Exactly," Walter answered and chuckled to himself. It was good to feel superior again.

He took the quilt and the food back to the shed behind the church. He thanked Miss Verna for the use of her beautiful quilt and gave the food to Mrs. Robertson. She opened the crackers and passed them around to everyone in the shed. Then she cut the sandwiches in quarters and passed them out. Walter smiled as Mrs. Robertson stopped Nellie from eating hers.

"Don't forget the blessing, child!"

Nellie asked Walter why he wasn't eating, so he took the piece of sandwich she offered him and nibbled at it. Nellie took a tiny bite of her square. The way she dabbed her lips with a handkerchief reminded him of Charlotte and how she loved the tea sandwiches at a café near their home in Berlin. He knelt on the cement floor and listened as the little children listed the foods they missed, like eggs and bacon and animal crackers. If only he could provide a tastier spread.

Walter asked Nellie to play another spiritual, so she played "Swing Low, Sweet Chariot." That one he knew. He hummed softly as she played, and the Robertson's sang along. When it was over Miss Verna patted Walter's knee and said, "Now, I know y'all wanna play for us, so what's stopping you?"

Nellie handed Walter the lovely, amber-colored violin. Walter took it and leaned his chin on its surface. It was still warm from Nellie's face. He remembered how he and Charlotte sometimes traded violins. He closed his eyes to gather his composure, then he thought of a jazz recording he'd heard by Sam Morgan, "Down by the Riverside." Walter chose a slow tempo like the one that Nellie had used for the hymn. After the opening bars, the family began to sing along, picked up the pace, and Walter followed their lead.

I'm gonna lay down my heavy load.

Down by the riverside, down by the riverside, down by the riverside.

When the Robertsons stood up and started clapping, he stood up also. Walter swayed to the music and played verse after verse. When they finished, someone asked him to play "Amazing Grace," but Walter didn't know it. He handed the violin back to Nellie and listened intently as she played. Harmonies, instrumentation, and improvisations of that haunting melody filled his head. It made Walter want to weep out of gratitude, so he turned away and wiped his face with his sleeves.

When the song was over, Walter hesitated to ask Mr. Robertson something. He didn't want to impose. But he needed to ask. "Mr. Robertson, sir, when you leave here, I'd like to go with you."

The grandmother raised her eyebrows. "You sure you want to cast your lot with us?"

Mr. Robertson said, "I suspect we'll be wandering quite a while."

Walter stammered, "Oh, sir, I don't want to be an extra burden, I just want to get out of this place. And now that I'm back on my feet, I could maybe help some. I'm stronger than I look."

"Why naturally, son. I give y'all my word. We won't go anywhere without you."

Walter thanked him and got up the courage to request one more thing. "I know the currents are dangerous, but when we leave, could we first row back to where you rescued me so I can get my violin?"

Chapter 20
Search and Rescue

"Siz a plagen, a curse!" Bubby said at breakfast, and Calvin agreed. This rain was bugging him, and the snow was useless. With all the flooding you couldn't have a decent snowball fight. Missing school for so long was great, but he needed action. He needed to get out.

It was cold and dark inside even though they had the monkey heaters, lanterns, and those big smelly candles from Pastor. So far, the flood had only come up Broadway to about a block away from them. Poppa said that the hill that began by them and led up to the Highlands might save them.

The next morning, Momma announced they were going next door to get typhoid shots. Shots? Calvin hated them, but he knew there was no fighting with Momma. He stood shivering from the cold with Momma, Bubby, and Bess in a long line on the sidewalk in front of Concordia Lutheran Church.

"If Poppa ain't getting' a shot, I ain't getting a shot," Calvin muttered.

"Poppa can't get a shot," Bess whispered in his ear. All the while they waited, Calvin jumped around and complained. Every time he tried to escape, Bess pulled him back in line.

"You're fourteen years old. Stop acting like you're a baby," she said. When they finally got into the social hall for their turn, Calvin looked at the giant needle like it was a snake about to strike. It took both Momma and Bess to hold him while the Red Cross nurse administered the dose.

Calvin's arm ached as he helped Bubby walk back home. He had a choice: see to Bubby or work in the church soup kitchen with Momma and Bess.

Poppa opened the shop door and said, "Now, was that so bad?"

"No, Poppa," Calvin said grudgingly. "Poppa, you need me to deliver anything?"

"No, thank you, son." Poppa sat down and lit up a smoke, his hands shaking like anything. "Help your Bubby upstairs and make sure the monkey heaters have oil."

Bubby pushed Calvin away. "I'm fine, go and help the Christians."

Calvin started toward the church but turned back. He was more interested in the rescue boats lining up at the edge of the floodwater just beyond the barber shop. He pulled his muffler up over his face, so Poppa wouldn't see him sneak past.

At the corner of Barret and Broadway was a makeshift dock for deliveries and rescue. A big knot of men stood in front of OK Storage. Calvin spotted two coppers sitting in their car. Calvin knew the one leaning out the window giving orders. He had ducked away from that officer more than once. The man's partner was talking on a new-fangled radio. Calvin approached the car and when the officer got off the thing, Calvin asked what it was.

"This, son, is our new system to talk to headquarters and get orders."

Calvin's attention turned to a small Coast Guard motorboat slowly approaching the dock. Nearby were canoes, a big rowboat, rafts made of planks and whiskey barrels, and a boat, maybe ten feet long carved out of mahogany. Calvin skirted around the crowd to admire the mahogany boat, its oars ready in the oarlocks, as if waiting for a boy to put them into motion. Calvin was running his hand over the smooth wood when Mr. O'Rourke, the owner of the barbershop next door, noticed him.

"Hey, my boy, how's your old man doing? He feelin' any better?"

"About the same, thanks."

Mr. O'Rourke smiled. "Well, let me know if he needs anything. What're you up to anyway, young fella."

"I just came to see if you all needed any help here."

One man guffawed and said, "Well, if we need midgets on our rowing team, we'll let you know."

"No joke," Calvin said doggedly. "I'm an expert rower."

"Well, we're fine for now, but if you're so eager, you could help with the loading and unloading," the barber said.

So, Calvin helped women and children get out of the boats. They were a sorry lot, bundled in as much as they could wear, carrying whatever food or possessions they could manage. Some had their pets. One old lady had a bird cage covered in a blanket and her parrot squawked like the devil. Calvin carried boxes of emergency provisions from trucks that kept rumbling down from Phoenix Hill and loaded them on the boats.

It had started to drizzle again, and the rain froze on everything it touched, but Calvin didn't mind. His face was numb, and his hands were cold despite his woolen gloves. This was better than being couped up in the soup kitchen at the Lutheran Church. He needed action, and he liked joining in the banter of the men.

Finally, the rain stopped, and it warmed up a bit. Some of the men went to get lunch so there were only three men left at the makeshift dock when a Red Cross truck delivered boxes of medical supplies for Louisville City Hospital.

A red-faced man at the oars of a big rowboat called Calvin over. "Well, boyyo, we could use someone to sit in the prow to keep things steady."

The other man at the oars asked, "You sure you can swim?"

"I'm a terrific swimmer," Calvin said. It was a lie. He could barely tread water.

"Well, get in then, and sit down and stay down and be sure you follow orders."

"Aye, aye, captain." Calvin smiled and clambered into the boat.

"It's no joke, son. The water is running swift down by the hospital."

Calvin didn't know the two men who were rowing, but he'd seen them around the neighborhood. Maybe they worked at Brennard Mills across the street. One had his hat down low on his forehead. His name was Charlie and the other was a red-faced giant. At first the two men had trouble rowing together, so the boat rocked a lot. That was great! Even better, when they were under the train bridge, Charlie put his oar up, tapped the overpass, and grinned. Calvin was fascinated to see street after street covered in water shimmering with iridescent oil. Abandoned cars were submerged and furniture and junk floated by. People stood on rooftops and waved at them.

When they got to Louisville City Hospital, Calvin helped unload. Afterwards he figured they would head back to the barbershop, but the coppers at the hospital dock had gotten a call on their new-fangled car radios for a pickup of medicine for someone stranded at the Brown Hotel. But first, they had to go to the man's apartment on Oak Street and get his stuff.

A rescue mission sounded swell, but it was getting late, and Calvin's parents would be wondering where he was. He'd be in big trouble if he didn't turn up soon, but he didn't want the men to think he was just a punk. What's more, the adventure of being on a boat going downtown to the Brown Hotel was so tempting that he never considered asking them to take him home first.

The rising moon shimmered like a big white balloon on the purple-gray water. When they reached Fourth and Oak, Calvin recognized the sign for the soda fountain where he and Momma used to wait for Bess while she had piano lessons. His stomach growled at the memory of the ice cream sodas. He hadn't eaten lunch. The men pulled up to an apartment building down the street from the Parmer's music school. The first floor of the building was submerged. The men debated how to get into the building and up to the third floor. They decided Calvin should shimmy up the fire escape ladder and try the window on the second-floor landing and go find apartment 302. They hoisted Calvin onto the ladder, and he got up to the second floor in seconds. The window wouldn't open, so he climbed up to the third floor and banged on a window. He explained to the bewildered man who opened it that he needed to pick up something from number 302. The man let him in and led him by flashlight down the dark hall to his neighbor.

"How do, Jenny. Seems you've got a kid willing to take Don his things." The woman invited Calvin into her apartment with a huge smile of relief.

"Wait right here, honey." The place smelled like lady's perfume. There were three women in the living room sitting around a card table where they had been playing cards by candlelight.

"Y'all don't know how important this is," the woman said as she handed Calvin a small suitcase. "My husband has asthma and needs his nebulizer to breathe. It's made of glass so mind how you carry it. Well, it will be safe tucked inside his clean clothes. Poor guy hasn't changed in days. They've been broadcasting from the hotel nonstop. Y'all just ask for Don in the WHAS newsroom. It's on the fifth floor. Can you remember that, honey?"

Calvin shook his head yes.

"Thank you so much."

When Calvin smiled, the woman patted his wavy blond hair. "Y'all look just like an angel," she said.

"People call me Angel," Calvin replied, and the women at the card table laughed.

"Well, Angel, I want y'all to get yourself a little something." She reached into the dish of coins on the table and gave him a quarter. "Be sure to tell my husband that I'm fine here with my mother and sisters. And tell him, well..." The woman sounded like she was going to cry. "Tell him just to stay put where it's dry and warm and let Foster and Pete go out looking for stories."

Calvin had a little leather pouch under his shirt where he kept important things, and he tucked the coin into it before heading into the hallway to return to the boat.

The man who had let Calvin in led him back to his apartment and out the window.

"You be careful, kiddo."

It grew darker as they rowed north on Fourth Street. The going was slower since the current was against them. There were candles and lanterns in top floor windows of most places, and as they passed other boats, they always waved their flashlights. At a certain point Charlie asked Calvin to switch places with him and take over his oars. Calvin was glad to because it was getting colder by the minute. Rowing would warm him up.

As they passed the public library, Charlie pointed his flashlight at the statue of Abraham Lincoln. "Look boy, Honest Abe's walkin' on water." Lincoln's face looked grim. Soon they pulled up alongside the Brown Hotel where the doorman and bellboys were at the second-floor mezzanine windows to watch for boats and help people get inside. Charlie handed Calvin a flashlight and the suitcase.

"Boy, you deliver this. We'll tie up and just step in and get warm. But you best be back down here in ten minutes so's we can take you home. Don't lose that flashlight and don't dilly dally. Y'all hear?"

Calvin said he wouldn't. He climbed into the big hotel. He had never been inside the Brown. It looked mighty fancy with all the men in their fine suits sitting at tables lit by lanterns. Big gold mirrors magnified the glow of crystal chandeliers lit by candles. Gripping the suitcase, Calvin asked a gentleman who was sitting on a red velvet couch smoking a cigar how to get upstairs.

Calvin shone the flashlight up the dark stairwell and counted the floors as he climbed the three flights.

In the fifth-floor hallway, there were a couple of tables with kerosene lanterns, so it was easy to find the makeshift headquarters of the news station. Calvin poked his head into the open door and saw the newsmen around a table. A woman put her finger over her lip and came out into the hall.

"This suitcase has Don's medicine," Calvin said.

"He's upstairs taking a rest, young man," the woman said. "Could you run it up to room 809?"

By the time Calvin got to the eighth floor, he was out of breath. But not like the newsman in 809. He was wheezing something awful. Don took the suitcase from Calvin, opened it, and pulled his contraption out of its box. He put in medicine with a dropper, squeezed a rubber ball and sucked slowly on a big mouthpiece.

As soon he was breathing better, he said, "You are a lifesaver, kid." Then he handed him a dime. Calvin backed up to refuse it, but the man put it into Calvin's pocket. Don put the nebulizer to his mouth and inhaled a second dose.

"Much obliged, son," Don said.

Calvin placed the dime in his pouch and left the newsman. On his way to the stairwell, he passed an open door. Inside a smoke-filled room were four men playing cards. He stood in the doorway mesmerized by the sight of a game lit by kerosene lamps and the sound of coins jingling. Boy oh boy. Poppa would love this.

One guy noticed Calvin and yelled, "Hey, kid, how did y'all get here? You a fish?"

Another fellow laughed and said, "Maybe he's a card shark. Wanna play a hand of poker?"

"No thanks," Calvin said. "Maybe another time. I'd sure like to, but I gotta get back to work at the rescue boat."

"Oh, a rescue worker," the man winked. "They're recruiting 'em young."

"You want a sandwich for the road?"

Calvin was hungry, but he thought he should get a move on, so he thanked the men and headed down the stairs.

Back on the main floor, he nodded to the doorman, then looked out the big window he'd climbed in earlier but saw no boat.

"They left, kid," the doorman said. "Had an emergency."

Calvin's shoulders dropped in a sigh.

"Don't you worry though. They said they'll be back soon, and you should just stay put."

Calvin zigzagged his way through the guests on the mezzanine and found himself a comfortable chair. Pretty swanky, he thought. It would be nifty if his friends were with him. Then he thought of Momma and how she'd be worried, and he couldn't sit still. His stomach growled, and he remembered that tray of sandwiches upstairs and the invitation to play cards. He went over to the doorman and told him he'd left something upstairs.

"I won't be gone long," he said. "Tell the guys to wait for me."

The doorman nodded.

Calvin retraced his steps to the eighth-floor room where the men were playing cards.

"Hey, kid, you're back. Come on in and have some refreshment."

"Hello again. Seems like I've got a break." Calvin looked hungrily at the sandwiches.

"Go ahead, take what you want," said a redhead with a friendly smile.

There was ham and Swiss on rye and bologna on white. Calvin hoped the bologna wasn't pork. It sure tasted good.

"I think we might have a bottle of root beer. Or there might be milk in there," said the red head.

There was one bottle of root beer and half a dozen bottles of Falls City

Beer in a bucket of melted ice. The root beer was still cool. Calvin used the church key to pop off the top. He hadn't tasted anything so sweet in a long time.

One of the men motioned to him to sit down on the bed so they could get back to their game. Calvin had made fast work of the sandwich and took another, then he sat behind a man in rolled up shirt sleeves with his tie loosened. Unlike the others, this man didn't join the friendly banter. He was so focused on his cards, he barely took notice of Calvin. They were playing five card stud, a game Poppa had taught him. Calvin noticed that the quiet man liked to bluff, and he had taken a couple pots with lousy cards. Calvin sipped the root beer and studied how each of the players was acting. He noticed that the chubby man across from him got intense when he had good cards and he let the ash on his cigarette grow until it flopped onto this belly. Don't lay that card, Calvin thought, scrutinizing the quiet man's every move. And as if the man read his mind, he dropped an eight instead.

The woman from the newsroom walked in and announced, "Pete's bushed, so Mike needs to take over."

"Well, shoot, Peggy," one of the players said. "Pete can't play cards, so who's going to sit in for Mike? You?"

The woman shook her head. "Me in this den of iniquity? Did it ever occur to you to open a window and get some fresh air? Come on Mike, shake a leg."

"I'm coming," Mike said with a laugh. "Just let me collect my winnings."

The quiet man groused. "Dammit, you just grabbed the biggest pot."

"Cool down, I'm sure we can find a fourth," said the redhead.

"I can play," Calvin said, bouncing off the bed.

The redhead squinted and then looked at the grouchy guy who shrugged his shoulders. The heavy-set man said, "Well, then. Let's see what you know. It's a nickel to ante up. I'll loan you the nickel if you need it."

"Nope, I've got thirty-five cents."

"Hey, you are loaded, but you know, kid, you should never tell what's in your pocket."

Calvin sat down as Mike said his goodbyes.

"Are you all news reporters?" Calvin asked.

"No, Mike's the only newsman. We're just lucky travelers stranded in your fair city," said the red-haired guy. "I'm Nelson, by the way."

"My name is Calvin," he said putting his dime on the table and pocketing a nickel.

Then the other man said his name was Harry and the quiet man with rolled up shirtsleeves just said, "Let's get this show on the road."

Nelson handed the pack to the grouch to shuffle who handed it to Calvin to cut.

"Aces are high, and twos are wild," Nelson called as he dealt.

It was keen to play cards again. Hmm. Not a bad hand. A ten, a jack, two and two eights.

"Hey, kid," asked Nelson, "what happened to your thumb?"

Calvin was touchy about his crooked thumb. He shrugged and answered, "My thumb's been this way since I was born."

"Hey, shut up and play," said the guy with rolled-up sleeves.

"Come on, Carson, this is a friendly game," Harry said.

Calvin thought maybe Carson was bluffing again.

Harry won the first hand. Calvin should have known his cards were good. He'd burned a hole in his vest. The second hand, Calvin won fifty cents with an inside straight. Nelson, the friendly guy who had offered Calvin the sandwiches, won the third. The fourth hand, Calvin had three aces and was pretty sure the grouch, the guy whose playing he'd observed from the bed, was bluffing. As the pot got bigger and bigger, Nelson got out and then Harry stubbed out his cigarette and said, "I fold."

Now it was just Calvin and Carson.

"I'll raise you." Carson gave Calvin a look that said he meant business. The other guys watched in silence.

Calvin said, "I'll see your nickel and raise you a dime."

Carson looked at him intensely. "Okay, kid. I call. Let's see what you got."

Carson put two jacks on the table. Calvin smiled from ear-to-ear as he lay down his aces and pulled in the pot. The other two men got up from the table and grabbed some beers. Carson sat there, his face flushed.

"This was swell," Calvin said rising from his seat, "but I gotta get my boat ride home."

"Not so fast, boy. You don't leave a card game like that." Carson jumped up and grabbed Calvin's collar.

"Hey, Carson, it's a game. Sit down and let the kid go."

Calvin felt relieved and hurried out of the room, his pocket jangling with change. The stairwell was just by the room, but as soon as the door closed, he realized he had left the flashlight. He thought he should go back, but he was afraid that Carson fellow would make him stay and play another hand, so he groped his way down in the dark. He sure didn't want to meet up with that bum again.

Calvin kept one hand on his pocket and the other on the wall. He was seeing stars in the darkness, when there was a flash of light and heavy footfalls from above. He picked up the pace figuring he was about down to the fifth floor. The footsteps got closer, and bright lights shone on his face.

"Hey bigshot, you forgot something, didn't you?" It was Carson carrying two flashlights. He was waving a big one in front of him as though it were a billy club.

"That's real kind of you mister," Calvin said.

The man aimed both lights in Calvin's face and growled. "You don't just up and leave a poker game like that." Carson grabbed Calvin and pinned him against the wall, but Calvin ducked out of his grasp.

"Oh, yes sir, I mean no sir, I won't. Thanks." Calvin grabbed his flashlight out of Carson's hand and busted through the door of the fifth floor. He sped down the hall toward the newsroom with the man right behind him. The newsmen looked up when they got to the open door. One man stepped out and said in a low tone, "What's the rush? Can we help you?"

"Oh we're fine," Calvin said relieved to see Carson turn tail and head back to the stairs. The newsman motioned Calvin into the makeshift station. The big clock on the table read nine p.m. Horsefeathers! His family was sure to be frantic. Don, who now wore a freshly starched shirt and was breathing normally, waved at Calvin. He motioned him to sit down by him as he answered the phone and pulled a ribbon of words out of a machine. Mike, the fella from the poker game, was announcing the news at the big microphone.

"Hey, it's my friendly delivery boy," Don said as he finished writing a note and handed it to Mike. "You want to listen for a while?"

Mike reported five drownings—two boats that had collided and capsized. Then Don handed him an announcement. "The family of Calvin Toplansky is urgently seeking any information about the whereabouts of their son. He is fourteen years old, blond with brown eyes."

"Hey, that's me," Calvin shouted.

Mike laughed and announced, "Well, that is WHAS efficiency for you. We have Calvin right here. If the Toplansky family is listening, or if you know the Toplanskys, tell them their son is safe and dry on the fifth floor of the Brown Hotel in the WHAS newsroom."

Within the hour, Pastor Habermann showed up to fetch Calvin and take him home. Mr. O'Rourke, the barber, waited for them in a rowboat outside. Although Pastor and the barber rowed smoothly up Broadway, Calvin was worried they might hit something in the dark and capsize, like the unlucky devils, they'd reported about in the newsroom. He wished he hadn't lied about knowing how to swim. The water, he knew, was very deep in some spots and the current was swift. One of the drownings had been a boy his age. Calvin sat quietly. A light snow was falling and Calvin trembled from cold and fatigue. When he saw the towers of Brennard Flour Mills, he was relieved.

The barber tied up the rowboat just a ways from his shop.

"Hurry up, Calvin," Pastor Habermann urged as they got out of the boat. "Your mother and father are worried about you."

Poppa opened the shop door. He hugged Calvin tightly. "Calman! Thanks God you are home. You worried your momma sick." Poppa shuffled slowly up the stairs. Pastor shined his flashlight, and Calvin trudged up impatient to tell his story and worried about his punishment.

Momma shrieked with joy. "Oy vey, Calman, how you worried us. Danken Got, you are back. Are you all right?"

Bess hugged him and then remembered how upset she was. "What in the devil made you run off like that."

Momma shooed Bess away and hugged her boy again, "Are you cold?"

"Momma," he said wrapping his arms around her, "I'm fine.

"Oy vey, your clothes are all wet. You'll get sick. Bessie, boil some water so Calvin would take a hot bath."

"No Momma, dry clothes are all I need."

Bubby sat at the kitchen table wrapped in her quilt. She scowled.

Poppa asked, "Have you eaten anything?"

"Yes, at the hotel."

"You ate trayf?" Momma asked.

"Just a soft drink and cold sandwiches."

Pastor Habermann asked if they needed anything else.

"No, Pastor, now that our Calman is back, we are fine. We cannot thank you enough for all what you did."

"Well, all you need to do is call. We've got plenty more batteries for that if you need them," the pastor said pointing to the Farm Radio he'd loaned them. Then he doffed his hat and went back down the shop stairs.

Calvin was glad to see their neighbor go. Pastor was so stern, and Calvin wanted to tell the family his story about the hospital and the fancy lobby of the Brown and what the WHAS reporters looked like. Of course, he would skip the poker game and the man who tried to beat him up with a flashlight. That he would tell his buddies. Calvin enjoyed being the hero and not the punk who whined about getting a typhoid shot.

When everyone finally went to bed, and when he thought Bubby was asleep in her alcove at the other end of the parlor, Calvin tiptoed into the kitchen. He wanted to give Bess some of his poker money, but she was fast asleep, so he headed back to his bed in the parlor. Groping in the dark for the couch, he felt footsteps. Bubby Adel grabbed him and shook his shoulders.

"A shonde un a carpe. A disgrace! How dare you disobey your tatemame."

"Anshuldik, I'm sorry." He tried to answer her in Yiddish, but all he could think to say was, "I'm sorry, Bubby. I didn't mean to make everybody worry."

Thankfully, his grandmother did not hit him but retreated to her Murphy bed at the other end of the room. From the couch, Calvin could hear Bubby muttering angrily, then he heard her familiar prayers, then her familiar snoring. His arms were sore from rowing, especially the arm that got the shot. He tossed about remembering the people he'd met and what he'd seen that day. He had rowed all around Louisville on a boat. He'd helped Don. Saved his life maybe. And won at poker. The world outside his home seemed bigger and more exciting than any pot of coins.

Chapter 21
The Field Glasses

"Bess, take this pot of your pea soup up to Miss Dodge, please," Momma said.

Bubby called after as Bess headed out the door. "Bessele, don't forget, she should pour it into her own shissel, do you hear?"

How many times had Bess heard that? "Don't let her put her ladle in our shissel. Don't forget our shissel." Bess chuckled to think how her Bubby had always mistrusted Grandma Dodge.

Bess knocked on her neighbor's door. She felt guilty about not taking the time to have a proper visit with Grandma Dodge in weeks. What with all the work from the flood and Annabelle still missing, Bess had only been able to run up and drop off batteries or food. She knocked again. It was sad how her neighbor had declined so much since she retired from the department store just a year or so ago. Bess was about to rap again when she heard a rustle and the familiar creek of the floorboards. Miss Dodge didn't have carpets anymore, so Bess sometimes heard the old woman shuffling about during the night.

Miss Dodge opened the door a crack.

"It's just me, Granny!" Bess said.

Miss Dodge squinted because the hall was dark, but when she realized who it was, she opened it wide.

"Why it is you Miss Bess! We haven't sat down for a chat in a coon's age."

Bess followed her old friend inside. "How are y'all doing Granny Dodge?"

"Oh, I spect I'm doin' well enough. Y'all must be too busy with this dratted flood to come and see your Granny."

"Yes ma'am. Things have been busy, but I have missed our visits. Here's some split pea soup I made myself."

"Why Bessie, you know I am partial to pea soup, and I reckon maybe I have a ham bone in the ice box just to spice it up a bit."

"Oh, that will be nice," Bess said, thinking it sounded revolting. "Oh, and we need that pot back now to make our supper."

"Well, I'll just take it to the kitchen and put it in another pot if you'll light a lantern for me. Fiddlesticks, I can't find the light anywhere."

Bess saw a flashlight and turned it on. She hovered over her friend as she went to the kitchen.

"Now, I'll be fine. Y'all go in the living room and sit down so we can have a proper visit."

Bess sat on the couch she'd always admired. The magenta brocade was faded and the seams looked about to split. Bess wondered why Miss Dodge didn't turn on the lights since the electricity had gone back on a couple of days ago, but she bit her tongue realizing what the answer might be.

"Miss Dodge, do you need any help?" Bess could hear pots clattering.

"Oh no, I'm just making us some tea. But if you would be so kind as to light a lamp? We don't need to sit in the dark, do we?"

By the dim light from the kerosene lamp, Bess could see how bare it looked. The oak chest of drawers and the gilt mirror were gone. The curio cabinet, which used to be full of treasures, now only held a few chipped cups. Miss Dodge used to let her take out the porcelain figurines and play with them. She had always praised Bess for being such a careful child. Seated on the soft flowered carpet, Bess would play with the graceful horses—dappled, ginger, bay, and black. Shepherds with flutes, sheep, shepherdesses with staffs and garlands of daisies. But best of all, the ladies in hoop-skirted gowns and dashing gentlemen in gray uniforms. It dawned on her that these were the only toys she'd had as a little girl. Bess would waltz the porcelain figurines about, reenacting the balls that Grandma Dodge remembered from her youth.

Those ballrooms, Grandma Dodge had reminisced, glowed with the light of a thousand candles. Miss Dodge would fan herself with a big lace fan when she told the stories about how her father had taught her to dance the Spanish

Waltz. She had been heartbroken when he went away to war.

Miss Dodge walked back in and said, "Oh, you miss my old knickknacks. I just got tired of dusting them," she said and sighed. "Now let's have our tea."

Miss Dodge placed the tray on the coffee table. "Oh, dear I have forgotten the sugar."

Bess walked over to the window. She picked up the field glasses that Granny's father had used as a confederate officer. From up here you could see all the way to Gray Street and beyond. The brown water of the Ohio River that had covered so much of Louisville was finally receding. And yet, the little shacks and shotgun houses across the alley were still surrounded by pools of water. Bess thought how lucky they were that the flood waters had never reached Poppa's shop.

"Here's the sugar. Now, you just sit right down and tell me what you've been doing at school. Is it your schoolwork keeping you from playing the piano?"

"No ma'am. Atherton is still closed, and I'm not sure when it will reopen," Bess answered as she sat down. She wondered whether Miss Dodge realized there hadn't been any school for a month or that Atherton was a shelter for Negroes. She decided not to broach that topic. Miss Dodge's view on Negroes made Bess uncomfortable.

"You used to come here almost every day after school, and you were so partial to my butter cookies."

Bess remember how Bubby worried the cookies might have had lard. "Oh, did you use butter?"

"But of course. Butter is for cookies, and lard makes the flakiest pie crusts. Wouldn't you just give your eye teeth for a cookie now?"

"Oh gosh, yes. But what I really loved were your stories about Bardstown, especially the one about the secret passageway."

"Heavens to Betsy, I haven't thought about that one in a while."

"I'd love to hear it again," Bess said.

"Well, Miss Bess, let me see if my memory serves me right." Grandma Dodge paused. "I guess this is one thing a girl never gets over. When my father went off to war, he promised he would write us every day and visit whenever he could. At first, Mama and I got letters regularly filled with stories about our men's victories over the Yankees. Daddy would send us pressed bachelor's buttons and wild roses from the fields where they encamped. He composed verses about his brave compatriots whose sabres would be raised no more. But then the letters became less frequent, and after the Battle of Perryville, they came no more." Miss Dodge stopped and closed her eyes.

Bess had studied Perryville in school, so she knew it had been a terrible defeat for the Confederacy. She didn't know what to say, so she said nothing.

"We never stopped writing to Papa and praying for him to come home safely. One night I dreamed that he had come to kiss me on the forehead while I was asleep, and when I awoke there was a blood red rose on my pillow. It gives me goose flesh to think about it, even now after all these years."

"Is that the rose you pressed in your Bible?" Bess remembered Bubby scolding her for holding the neighbor's Christian Bible, when Bess tried to tell her the story.

"Yes, Miss Bess, it is. Well, I dreamt several nights that I felt my father's kiss on my forehead, and I always awoke to find a rose in the morning. One night, I vowed that I wouldn't close my eyes even to blink, and sure enough I heard footsteps in the darkness, and I felt the brush of my father's beard on my face. As I cried, 'Daddy,' a shadowy figure slipped out of the room and down the stairs. I followed him in the darkness into the library where he disappeared completely. The next morning, I asked my mother about it, and she just shrugged her shoulders and said, 'Y'all must have been havin' a beautiful dream.' But in the kitchen, I heard the cooks talk about preparing food for Massah and his men who were hiding out in the passageway. That afternoon Yankee soldiers near broke down our doors, demanding entry. They tramped through the house pushing over cabinets and throwing books out of the bookcases, but they didn't find any hidden soldiers. The Union men stole everything from our garden. They slaughtered our chickens. They took all our beautiful horses. But the worst thing was that after that day, I never saw my father again."

"Didn't you ask your mother whether your father had really been there?"

"Of course, y'all know I did, but my mama could be so mule-headed.

Then, just before she died, I musta been sixteen, she told me about my father's secret visits and the hidden passageway behind the fireplace. That, she said, led to where my daddy's men had stayed, waiting to escape to safety in Tennessee. After a lot of searching, I found a brass pull in the floor of the fireplace. I gave it a tug, and a section of the wall opened to a stairway. Cobwebs hung everywhere, but I just had to explore that dark tunnel. It went down quite deep and at certain parts water had seeped in, so the stairs had almost rotted away. I kept brushing off little critters crawling on me, and at one point, I fell through a step and twisted an ankle. Somehow, I managed to extricate myself and kept going until the tunnel ended at a big door. I worked hard to move the big iron bolt and push the heavy door open. I groped in a dark room stumbling about until I found a door to the outside.

Light poured in. I saw the little pasture that led to the woods where our soldiers must have escaped. Right by our house were some tree stumps. I figured the Yanks had chopped down the trees that had hidden the entry for firewood. I could imagine those blue coats camping there, feasting on our chickens, not even knowing that my daddy and his men were a few feet away.

I propped open the door with a big rock and explored the secret room. It was bigger than I realized. There were remnants of hay where horses and soldiers had bedded together, bits of used candles, old gourds, and shards of broken pottery. There was a button on the floor from a Confederate uniform. I wondered whether it might be my father's and whether there might be something of his in that room. I so longed to find a keepsake of him. And after much searching, in an alcove, I found my father's diary and his field glasses, which I have treasured all my life."

At this point in the story, Miss Dodge got weepy, like she always did. She used to get up and look out the back window with the field glasses, but today she just sat there.

"Do you still have the diary?"

"I beg your pardon?"

"Your father's diary. What happened to it?"

Miss Dodge paused for a moment and shook her head solemnly, "Now didn't I tell you about how the Yanks came back and burned our barn? Well, my window was open, and the curtains caught fire and so many of my pretty things went up in smoke."

Bess hadn't heard that version before. "Did the whole house burn down?"

"Oh my, no. My mammy rescued me and Mother. Then, Mammy, bless her soul, and the groom and stableboy put the fire out."

As Bess remembered the story about the Yankee raid, there were no men left on the plantation and the women had fended for themselves. And how had the Bible survived but not the diary? As well as losing her hearing and eyesight, poor Miss Dodge was getting forgetful. Then Bess recollected something Annabelle had once said about not knowing any Dodges in Bardstown. Annabelle often visited Bardstown because she had lots of family still living there.

Miss Dodge stared at the window. "I reckon we're lucky nobody had to rescue us from the rooftop. And to think that the water stopped just two doors down Broadway. Your momma told me your presser's house just toppled over. So many folks lost everything."

Bess fidgeted in her chair and started to get up.

"Now Miss Bess, how about I fix us some more tea," Miss Dodge said.

But the light was fading in the window, and Bess needed to get back downstairs, so she made her apologies. "I'd love to stay longer, but I have to set the table and get supper going."

"Now don't forget your pot. And I can't let you go home empty handed," her neighbor said as she got up and went to the window. "I want you to have these field glasses that my daddy used at the Battle of Antietam."

Bess picked up the pot and smiled but stepped back. "Oh, I couldn't take a family heirloom."

Miss Dodge put the binoculars around Bess's neck. "They only collect dust, and I can't see much through them anymore. Truth is my sight is about gone."

"Thank you. That's so kind."

"Oh no, it's your family that has been generous to me. Especially your mother. She is uncommonly generous. Still, I don't know how she can let that colored man sit down at her table."

"Well, Jackson helps Poppa," Bess answered briskly. "I don't know what we'd do if he hadn't come back to work."

"Honey, I hope I can repay your family soon. Your President Roosevelt says that better times are coming, but I think he's leading us to rack and ruin. Oh well, I reckon my good times are all behind me. Now go on, take those, and give your family my kindest regards."

Bess hugged her neighbor. Grandma Dodge was skin and bones. Walking down the stairs, Bess felt unsettled. Miss Dodge had never said such mean things before. It was sad to see her neighbor in a bad way, but she truly hated her remarks about Jackson and about the president. In her house, FDR was like Abraham Lincoln, no, he was like Moses.

When Bess walked into their apartment with the field glasses around her neck, Momma arched one eyebrow into a question.

"What are you wearing around your neck?"

Bess stepped closer, took the binoculars off and held them up. "Field glasses. Miss Dodge gave them to me."

"Oh no, you mustn't keep such an expensive gift."

"But Momma, Miss Dodge only wanted to thank us for all we've done," she said.

"Well, that wouldn't be necessary. Take them back upstairs right this minute."

"I think she would be hurt if we didn't keep them. Anyway, she says they were her father's, from the Civil War."

Her mother grabbed the field glasses and took them over to the window. She pointed to a small mark on the bridge that said, Nippon. "Give a look, Bessele! They were made in Japan!"

Bess's throat felt tight. But what about the secret passageway? And the diary? The faded rose? Annabelle's comment haunted her. Maybe there was no Dodge Plantation in Bardstown ever.

"If you ask me," Momma said, "your Grandma Dodge bought these at a five and dime."

Chapter 22
Mrs. Parmer's Dress

Bess sucked in her stomach and pulled gently at the side zipper of Mrs. Parmer's dress. Oh gosh, it closed! She stepped carefully onto the toilet seat to get a better view of herself in the little mirror over the sink. The golden orange silk set off her honey brown eyes and hair. She took a deep breath and put her palm on her waist. What do you know? With all the extra chores and meager rations, she had lost weight. On Mrs. P the dress fell mid-calf, but on Bess it was a full-length gown. She held a hand mirror and turned to see the beadwork in the back when the bathroom door flew open. The jolt nearly knocked her off the toilet.

"Oy, Bess, sorry," Momma said. Then she took a good look at Bess and shook her finger.

"What are you doing in Mrs. Parmer's gown?" her mother cried. "Your poppa and I worked like dogs on that dress. I nearly lost my eyesight on the beading."

"Mrs. P loaned it to me," Bess replied, raising her chin with pride.

"What do you mean loaned? Get down. Who stands on a toilet?"

Bess was too excited about her reflection in the mirror to step down.

"Oh, momma," Bess said, "moving her hands over the beaded sleeves. It's just thrilling. I've been invited to play a recital next Sunday at a very elegant club."

"Nu, what kind of a club?"

"The Pendennis Club."

"That club what don't allow Jews? There you will never play."

"But Momma."

"Sha! I forbid it," Momma said pulling Bess down. "You won't play anywhere you can't walk in the front door. Now, take that dress off before you pop the seams. Your father worked so long on that dress to pay Mrs. Parmer for your lessons. The pattern he made himself from a picture in the newspaper of that Duchess of Vindsor, Vallie Shimshon. The silk alone cost a fortune."

"But Momma, Mrs. P arranged the recital for me, and it pays twenty dollars.

Momma's eyebrows shot up. She hesitated, but she shook her head no. Knowing she could never change her mother's mind, Bess nodded and began to undo her dress. Momma shooed Bess's hands away from the dress and struggled to lower the zipper. When it finally slid down, she said, "You can't breathe in this dress. How would you sit to play piano?"

With the gown across her arms, Momma said, "This dress you must return as soon as you can. Why would you want to wear a dress to look like that terrible divorced woman, that Vallie Shimshon? Instead of standing on toilets admiring yourself, you should go and help your father with the bills. Or help Bubby in the kitchen. Here, put it away carefully."

Bess felt like Cinderella. She had so many duties now. Because of the flood, they hadn't seen Annabelle in weeks. Momma wasn't feeling well in the mornings, so Bess had become laundress, cook, and her brother's watchdog.

No siree! She would not take the dress back. Mrs. P intended for her to wear it, and she would wear it. She was playing the recital. If she played, they could pay Mr. Schuster the back rent. So that was that. She held the gown to her face and breathed in the scent of lavender sachet, put the dress in its box, and slid it under her daybed in the kitchen. Somehow, she would get out of the house on Sunday afternoon and get to the Pendennis Club.

The next day, Bess turned her attention to breakfast and the day's soup. There was hardly any food on hand. Peeling the last potatoes in the bin, Bess knew that after lunch, she would have to walk in the freezing cold to Zimmerman's Grocery. The coldest thing would be the look on Mrs. Zimmerman's face when Bess signed the book to buy on credit. And she had to buy enough to feed the five of them and their presser Jackson Clay.

Jackson had been sleeping on a palette in Poppa's shop because his house had toppled over and floated away. Until they finished the wooden pontoon bridge that linked his part of town with Broadway, he'd stayed in a terrible shelter. With Jackson back, Poppa's mood improved because there was actual work going on in the shop even if it was just Jackson working on uniforms for the band at the Negro high school.

That night Bess couldn't fall asleep. Her mother and father were squabbling in the bedroom. Her mother was worried because Poppa refused to see Dr. Rubel about the tremors in his hands. Her father changed the subject to the alterations of uniforms for Ft. Knox that had just arrived. The bushelling, he called it. "No," she heard her mother say, "the bushelling won't be enough." They owed the rent, the doctor, the pharmacy, the coal bill, Mrs. Zimmerman, the fabric store, the electricity, the telephone. Bess knew that they were behind on the rent, but she hadn't realized how deeply in debt they were. Would they lose the shop, the apartment, and everything they owned?

Before dawn, Bess woke up drenched in sweat and freezing cold. She'd dreamed the landlord Mr. Schuster had posted an enormous red eviction notice that covered the shopfront door. Neighbors and friends stood on the sidewalk and stared as their clothes and furniture floated down Broadway in muddy water. Bess pulled the feather quilt up over her ears and replayed Poppa and Momma's argument.

Knowing how much money her family needed, Bess was even more determined to find a way to get to the Pendennis Club. If she said she was visiting Cousin Dotty, her Aunt Minnie would tell her mother that she hadn't seen her. It wasn't fair. Calvin came and went as he pleased, and since his rescue mission with the rowboats, he was a neighborhood hero. But Momma watched Bess like a hawk. She fell back asleep until Momma was in the kitchen lighting the oven for breakfast.

"Bessele, could you go and start the furnace? It's such a blessing, now that we have heat again," Momma said.

As a child she'd been terrified of the cellar. Bess hated starting the furnace, but Poppa's hand shook too much to light it, and she needed to stay on Momma's good side. She threw on her coat and boots and ran down to the cellar. It felt like she had spent most of the flood in this basement. Calvin and Cousin Joe had sandbagged outside around the cellar windows, while Bess and Dotty kept the basement floor mopped dry. They sandbagged the furnace to keep it and the coal bin as dry as possible. Two days ago the city inspector had checked the basement and declared the furnace functional, so they were able to use it again.

How wonderful it had been to feel the warm air taking the chill out of their bones. For weeks they'd tried to keep warm with monkey heaters, layers of clothes, hot water bottles in their beds, all the extra blankets piled high. Whenever they complained, Bubby told them how it was every winter in her village. Nothing was more bitter than the sharp wind that blew through their house, but this, she said, had been worse. Bess agreed this was the coldest winter she could remember.

Bess cleaned out the ashes and scooped coal into the opening. The coal pile was dwindling too, just like their pantry, just like the bolts of cloth and spools of thread in the tailor shop. Unlike shop supplies and groceries, coal couldn't be bought on credit. After she threw the coal into the belly of the furnace, she lit the pilot light.

It was an anxious week. Knowing she was going to deceive her family, it was hard to act normal. Whenever Bess found a little time to practice, that helped steady her.

On Wednesday afternoon, Annabelle came back lugging two bags of groceries. Momma shrieked with joy and hugged the girl, saying over and over "You are all right. You are all right." Bubby Adel pulled out a handkerchief and sobbed.

Bess said, "What a relief. Where were you? How is your mother?"

"We all fine, but hold on, Bessie Lee," Annabelle said as she put the bags on the counter and caught her breath. "Let's put this stuff away."

"Give a look at this!" Momma said as Annabelle unpacked cans of tuna and green beans, bags of coffee, cornmeal, and flour. There was even butter and a little bottle of cream.

"Here, Bessie Lee," Annabelle said, grinning as she placed a big can of beets on the table, "I know how you like your beet soup."

"My gosh, Annabelle, how did you come by all this food?" Bess asked.

"Best not ask. My brother brings us lots of stuff. And we don't ask where he gets all of it. Lordy, Lordy, I shudder to think of it."

Bess knew that many stores had been looted, but she certainly wouldn't turn up her nose at this windfall.

"I coulda brung y'all more but you don't eat most of what Will gets us."

Momma wiped a tear from her eye and said, "Oy, Hennybelle, we were so worried about you."

"Well, we sure enough had some bad times. We stayed with the white folks at a church, but we didn't feel welcome there, to say the least. Then Will got himself a boat. Lord knows where that came from. He rowed us to our auntie's house up on a hill, where we was dry and warm the whole time. Our whole family, cousins and dogs and cats, were all packed into Auntie's two room house, just like Noah's Ark."

With Annabelle's return to the Toplansky's, Bess was relieved of her extra work, which allowed her more time to practice the pieces for the program. She still hadn't perfected her escape plan.

Sabbath it was cloudy and cold, but it didn't rain. As they walked to synagogue, heading south away from the river, the air smelled cleaner. Not the nasty mix of gasoline and dead fish that still hung over their neighborhood to the north. Momma and Bess trudged slowly with Bubby. Calvin and Poppa had left earlier because Poppa had to chant the opening prayers.

When they arrived, they made their way up to the women's section. Bess, preoccupied with her upcoming recital, mouthed the familiar prayers, but her mind was elsewhere. She needed to get away to practice piano, but Momma, who was a stickler for two hours of daily practice, never allowed her to practice piano on the Sabbath. Hearing Poppa's sweet voice, Bess relaxed a bit and got an idea. As Bubby always said, "A wise Jew figures things out."

After shul, they went home and had some rye bread and a salami that a do-gooder from shul had brought them. Momma had tried to refuse the charity, but the woman said that since the food had been sent all the way from a kosher butcher in Cincinnati, it was a sin and a disgrace not to take them.

And anyway, didn't the Toplanskys always provide food for poor itinerant rabbinical students? And didn't they have the colored presser staying with them? Momma shrugged her shoulders and took the salami and the bread just to shut the busybody up. She knew that everyone in the shul would hear that she'd taken charity.

After lunch, everyone planned to take a nap, but Bess said she was going to visit Naomi. Instead of going into the parsonage, she went over to the church. Entering by the back door, she tiptoed down the basement stairs to the Sunday School. It smelled musty, but it was dry. Since it was a bit higher up the hill than their building and the parsonage, the church had not taken water in the basement. Bess went to the farthest end of a long passageway to the social hall where she knew she could play the upright piano, and not one soul would hear her. She got her first piece the way she wanted it, but in the opening of the "Moonlight Sonata," Bess sensed footsteps behind her. She turned around with a start. It was Pastor Habermann in work gloves, overalls, boots, and a scowl.

"Does your mother know you're practicing on the Sabbath?"

Bess closed the piano fallboard and swung her legs around on the stool. She had no idea what to say, so she asked where Naomi was.

Pastor Habermann said she was up at their high school fixing meals for the shelter. "If you are going to work on the Sabbath, you might want to join Naomi at Atherton High and lend a hand. They are still caring for close to a thousand people who've lost their homes."

Bess asked him whether he'd gotten any word as to Walter Schreiber's whereabouts, but the pastor shook his head no. Then he told her that Paducah and Cincinatti had also flooded. Bess knew that already. The worse thing was not even knowing where on earth her friend was or if he was even alive. Knowing she had to put that out of her mind for the present, she asked if he knew when Atherton would open again. With a shrug he said he thought it would be as soon as the Red Cross could find shelter for the Negroes staying there. So no school for a while.

Pastor Habermann's news gave Bess an idea. She left the church through the front door, mulling over the details. Bess unlocked the shop door and closed it quietly. She needed privacy to call her girlfriend Phyllis from the shop telephone, which beside the church's, was the only telephone on their block. Since the first day at Atherton, Phyllis Leibmann and Bess had been fast friends. Phyllis lived in a spacious house in the Highlands, which had escaped the flood entirely. Bess and Phyllis were among a handful of Jews at Atherton High School for Girls. It was great to hear her friend's voice on the other end of the line. Phyllis promised to do anything Bess needed her to do. That resolved, Bess ran upstairs to help put supper on the table.

After supper, her aunt and uncle and cousins Dotty and Joe would resume their Saturday night gatherings for the first time since the flood. Now that some of the downtown roads were passable, they had driven. As always, Aunt Minnie wanted to hear "Malagueña," which Bess planned to play for the recital, but then Dotty requested show tunes. It felt so good to return to their normal routine that the family lingered in the parlor until midnight. After everyone left, Bess hurried to bed. The kitchen was always extra warm after the Sabbath since they kept the oven on day and night to avoid the sin of turning anything on. Bess slept well.

On Sunday morning, Bess did her usual chores. While state law prohibited business on the Lord's Day, it was an ordinary workday for them. Poppa adjusted the blinds so no one would see him and Momma stitching away at the soldiers' uniforms. The sun poured in through the cracks in the blinds.

Bess was delighted to see the sun. A sunny, sunny Sunday! Bess took the damp linen outside to dry. Thanks to a huge plank of plywood Jackson had placed in their backyard, Bess managed to walk around without sinking into the swampy ground. Meanwhile, Momma promised to make beets and cabbage for dinner from the provisions Annabelle had brought them. Of course, Bess wouldn't be home for dinner if all went well.

Momma had given Bess permission to visit her friend Phyllis and eat with her family. Bess was relieved. Usually Momma didn't let her eat there because she thought the Leibmanns were careless about how they kept kosher. But the sunny day had improved her mother's disposition. Momma told her to go and enjoy the time with her friend. She gave Bess a little linen handkerchief she'd embroidered with fleurs-de-lis to give to Mrs. Leibmann. Momma hated for Bess to go anywhere empty handed, and there was nothing else in the house to send.

"Enjoy yourself," she said as she kissed her daughter's forehead. Momma looked at her satchel and said, "Are you going to study? You deserve a rest, mamale, you've been such a help."

"Thanks, Momma, but Phyllie is going to help me with math."

Bess had already placed her music and the silk dress in her school satchel, and now she walked up Barret Avenue to Morton Street confident no one was wise to her scheme. Bess had called Mrs. P to tell her that the driver from the Pendennis Club should pick her up at the Leibmann's. Bess saw Phyllis watching for her from the big bay window in their front parlor. She walked in, hugged her friend, and whispered, "Is the coast clear?"

"Everything is copacetic," Phyllis said. "Moms and Pops have a shindig at the club."

They hurried to Phyllis's bedroom giggling all the way. Bess changed into the silk gown. Looking at herself in the full-length mirror, she twirled to see the chiffon swirl around her.

Phyllis squealed with delight as she pinned a cream-colored satin flower behind Bess's ear. Then she dabbed some lipstick on Bess's lips and stood back to admire the effect.

"Tell me how you got this job again?"

"Well, the Parmers get calls all the time to recommend performers. This time it turns out the Pendennis was looking for someone to play a classical piano recital."

"And who better?" Phyllis said.

As they waited in the parlor for the driver, Phyllis kept telling Bess how perfect she looked. Bess knew she looked fine, but she still felt strange. The dress was big in the shoulders and tight across the bust. She could pop a seam during one of the reaches to high or low octaves. Phyllie told her not to worry because she looked as skinny as a bean pole. Bess flushed with pride.

"Hey," Phyllis said, "maybe I should go with you to turn the pages."

Bess rolled her eyes, and they both fell into a fit of laughter. Phyllis didn't know a musical score from a baseball score.

"Yes, I know, I'm a butter fingers. I'd probably skip a dozen pages, and your big debut would end in a flash." Phyllis asked her if she wanted a snack.

"No thanks, I couldn't eat a thing."

Just then a big black car pulled up the driveway and a handsome black man in a gray uniform came up to ring the doorbell. Bess kissed Phyllis cautiously so as not to smudge her lipstick.

"I can't wait to hear all about it. You'll be swell," Phyllis shouted from the doorway.

Introducing himself as Luther, the driver apologized to Bess for being a few minutes late and helped her inside. In this snazzy car, Bess felt like the Hollywood stars she'd seen in Movietone newsreels. Maybe someday she would be driven up to Carnegie Hall in a big black Oldsmobile with leather seats like this. But Luther halted her reveries by pointing out the boarded-up houses and stores. He told her downtown was still a mess, but he would get her to her concert right on time because he knew which streets were dry.

"We had quite a time at the Pendennis Club. You know the police set up headquarters with us. The club was the highest point in all downtown Louisville, like an island in a sea of muddy water." Luther told her he'd driven the police chief. His stories made the trip through the eerily quiet downtown go by quickly.

"Well, Miss Bess, here we are," Luther said as he parked in the portico of a palatial building. He accompanied her to the door. Bess thanked him for driving her.

Luther answered, "Now I have to go pick up a member, but I'll be back for you after your concert, after y'all eat your supper. Break a leg."

That was Mrs. P's expression. Bess took a deep breath and peered into the club. Suddenly she wondered if she was ready for her debut after all.

Chapter 23
The Recital

The butler welcomed Bess. Her face flushed from the warmth as she walked in. Ablaze with light everywhere, the place stunned her. The black and white marble floor glistened like a giant checkerboard. Everything shone. Brass fittings, glass prisms, crystal chandeliers. As the butler led her to the women's sitting room, she saw gentlemen in tuxedoes heading up the widest, most graceful stairway she'd ever seen. In the sitting room, the butler led her to a leather chair next to a fireplace with a marble mantle.

The butler pushed up an ottoman so her feet wouldn't dangle. Bess asked him who would raise the piano bench for her, and the butler answered that he wasn't sure they'd ever raised it.

"I don't reckon anyone so tiny has ever played here," he said. "I'm sure we can find you a cushion."

"No, a cushion will slide." Bess said.

"Well Miss, I know just what to use," he said, and he went to retrieve the telephone book from the alcove.

"Thank you, that will be perfect." Bess reached out to take it, but the butler promised he would see to it that it was on the bench for her performance. He asked if she needed anything else and left.

The longer she sat there, the warmer she got. Her palms began to sweat, and she worried she'd perspire right through the linen dress shields she'd worn to protect Mrs. P's beautiful dress. Oh, if she ruined it, she'd be mortified. She'd forgotten to ask the butler about the page turner that had been arranged.

If Phyllis were there, she at least could have taken Bess's mind off her worries. After what seemed like ages, a grim-faced woman in a black velvet gown walked in and introduced herself. She pulled off a long white glove and shook Bess's hand.

"I am Miss Pendleton. I'm to turn your pages for you, my dear."

"It's nice to meet you," Bess said. She smiled then pulled her clammy hand down to her side and pressed it onto the fabric of her dress.

Bess handed the woman her music and began to explain the order of the program, but the woman motioned Bess to follow her upstairs to the ballroom. Ascending the marble staircase, Bess felt even warmer. The woman led her into a ballroom so fancy that it looked like it should be at the White House. Crystal chandeliers and candles at every table made the soft yellow walls glow in sharp contrast to the men in black tuxedoes. Laughter and the clink of plates being removed from tables filled the air.

At the microphone stood a portly figure. He bowed to Bess and smiled. As he raised a big glass of amber colored liquid, the crowd got quieter. "Gentlemen, as we celebrate our opportunity to rebuild a greater Louisville after the flood, we also celebrate a young talent who graces our fair city. Please welcome the winner of last year's Kentucky State Music Competition for piano, Miss Bess Toplansky."

The man bowed at Bess and stepped forward to shake her hand. "How's your daddy doin'?" Bess was too nervous to try to figure out how the man knew Poppa.

Flashbulbs popped as she began to play, something she hadn't expected. Why would someone be taking photographs? Oh dear, she'd lost her place and skipped a measure. Another distraction came from the hum of the men who had resumed their after-dinner conversations. There was polite applause when she finished the Mozart piece. As she stood and bowed, the photographer aimed the camera at her. What if they put her picture in the paper? As Miss Pendleton arranged the music for the "Moonlight Sonata" on the piano, Bess told herself that her parents wouldn't find out anything. They only read the Yiddish press.

The Schumann March went well now that her fingers had become accustomed to the velvety smooth action of the Steinway. It was tuned to perfection. Next was "Malagueña," which she was tired of, and yet the gentlemen appreciated it. With the opening chords of a Bach prelude, Bess fell into a reverie sensing herself and the gentlemen settling into the music. The clatter of coffee cups and silverware had ceased. The place was silent when she finished, and then there was loud applause. As she stood this time to bow, Bess knew they might want her to play an encore. Mrs. P had suggested "The Hungarian Rhapsody," as it never failed to impress. Sure enough, the master of ceremonies called out, "Encore," and the club members followed his lead.

Bess started the piece with an imposing lift of her hands and attacked. Toward the end of the rhapsody, as her left hand reached the lowest keys and her right hand raced up the higher octaves she leaned into the keyboard and played with an abandon and delight she hadn't felt in so long. When she finished, she raised her head up and her hands went up into a high arch and fell dramatically on her lap. The men cheered as she stood to take a bow.

The master of ceremonies came up to thank her and to walk her off the stage. He accompanied her downstairs and back to the sitting room.

The butler was waiting and greeted them. "Good evenin' Mistah Brennard," and he turned to Bess and said, "Y'all sure played nice."

"Yes, she was a hit. We'll be asking you back here, for sure. Now, y'all tell your momma and daddy hello for me, you hear?" He handed Bess an envelope and asked the butler to accompany her to supper.

"Yes, suh, Mistah Brennard."

Suddenly Bess realized that the master of ceremonies was none other than Mr. John J. Brennard of Brennard Mills just down the street from them. A few days ago she had delivered a bill to his office. She was about to say something when Brennard bowed and left the room.

Bess followed the butler through the hallway and down to the main floor. At the far end of the lobby, he opened a door to a narrow passageway that led into the kitchen. A tall woman in a white bonnet and apron led her between the ovens and grills to a butcher block table set for one. Bess put the envelope into her coat pocket before hanging it on the chair.

"Good evenin', Miss," the woman said. "Sit down. Y'all must be hungry."

The kitchen was buzzing with women washing and drying dishes and polishing silver. Bess smiled and squeaked out a weak thank you. She sat down dazed and disappointed. Bess hadn't known what to expect, but she certainly never imagined eating her supper alone in the kitchen. The woman brought her a big glass of water. "Y'all must be parched. We all stood by the dumbwaiter and heard you play. You make a mighty sound for someone so young."

"Why, thank you. That's so kind."

"Your dinner won't be but a minute, so just you relax."

Bess sat and examined the enormous kitchen. It had a smoky sweet smell like the smell at the Habermanns on Sundays. As she waited, she thought it was such a coincidence that the man whose flour mill was two blocks from their store was a bigshot at this club. Then she got irritated thinking how many times she had delivered delinquent bills to his receptionist and how unfriendly she was.

"Hope y'all like this," the cook said as she placed a plate in front of Bess. There were green beans, yams, and a big round reddish pink slice of something in the middle. It looked like raw meat. Bess realized with a sick drop in her empty stomach, it was ham, garnished with a yellow ring of pineapple and a red cherry. For goodness' sake! It was one thing to go behind momma's back and play here, but this she could not do. Bess jumped down from the high table and grabbed her coat and satchel from the other chair.

"I apologize," she said to the cook, "but I'm not feeling well. I should just be getting home. Thank you for your kindness."

 "But Luther ain't back to fetch you. Y'all supposed to wait here. How about some coffee or some tea? A bite of toast? Or maybe some consommé with sherry would settle your stomach."

Bess shook her head. "No, thank you. How do I get out of here? Please."

The woman shook her head and led her through the stoves and cabinets to a door.

As Bess scurried out, the woman yelled after her, "Now y'all be careful. That alley is still wet and slippery."

Bess pulled the silk dress up to her knees and hurried down the brick alley. Before long she was out on Third Street. Everything looked so different in the dark, and she couldn't remember Luther's winding route down drier streets. Her mother would expect her home from the Leibmann's soon. Anger boiled inside her as she ran down the street. Her mother had been right. She never should have set foot in that place. That Mr. Brennard in his fancy tuxedo that he probably hadn't paid for and that snobby lady in her long black dress and gloves. The nerve of them to shuffle her back to the kitchen and then to serve her ham. She was out of breath when she turned down Guthrie. Now even the sidewalks were wet. Fear replaced her anger. Downtown was quiet as could be. So many of the stores were still boarded up. You could hear the gush of water in the sewers. Before she knew it, water was up to her ankles, so she had to slow down as she made her way home. She hoped she was heading home.

Chapter 24
Borscht

Bess heard a church clock strike eight times. St. Paul Church. She must be going in the right direction. Then the rumbling of a truck splashing its way down the street sent her into the entryway of a store to avoid getting drenched. She resumed her walk but sensed a car was following her. What if the car splashed her or she slipped? Her mother would kill her if the dress got ruined.

The car pulled slowly alongside her. She looked straight ahead and quickened her pace. Her heart was pounding. The car pulled a few yards ahead of her. The driver rolled down his window and yelled, "Hey, Miss Bess, it's me, Luther. I been lookin' for you. Why didn't y'all wait for me?" Luther parked, got out, and opened the door for her.

Bess smiled with relief as he helped her into the car.

"Now what's the big hurry?" Luther asked, but Bess was too upset to talk. She just shook her head and sat there blinking to keep back the tears.

"I hear tell y'all played some mighty beautiful music."

Bess couldn't answer.

"Now, why y'all so quiet? What's wrong, Miss Bess."

Bess took a big breath and tried to answer. "I just. . . I never. . . never should have played there."

"Well, I know they pay a pretty penny."

"Oh, they paid me, but then they shooed me off to the kitchen to eat all by myself."

"Well, I'm sure that kitchen wasn't empty, lest you mind eatin' with Negro folks."

"Oh, no!" Bess said. "You're right I wasn't alone, and the cook was very kind." She surely didn't want to hurt Luther's feelings. "It's just that they fed me ham and I'm. . . We're Jewish."

"Well, what do you know! I bet you the first Jewish gal to play a recital at the Pendennis Club," Luther said with a chuckle. Then he saw in the rearview mirror that Bess wasn't laughing along. "But I can see why you'd be angry. Lord, don't I know it..."

Bess realized that Luther was driving her back to the Leibmann's, so she interrupted him, "Please, sir, I don't live on Morton where you picked me up. We live on East Broadway and Barrett. At 1121. You picked me up at my girlfriend's house."

Luther headed to Baxter Avenue so he could come down Broadway and let Bess off in front of her house. He slowed down to look for the numbers as he got to the Lutheran Church.

Bess said, "This is it, but could you take me to the alley?"

"Whoa, this gal walked in the front door of the Pendennis, and now she's sneaking down alleys?" Luther laughed again. He stopped in the alley and let her out. Bess shook his hand and thanked him.

"Everything's gonna be fine, girl. You just stop frettin," Luther said as he doffed his cap and got back into the car.

Bess listened to the rumble of the Oldsmobile on the bricks and tried to think what she would say to her parents. It was way past their dinnertime, and she imagined they'd all be in the parlor listening to the radio. As she stood in the alley for a moment to catch her breath, she heard rats banging about in the garbage cans. She shuddered and darted so fast across Jackson's plywood plank that she almost tripped. She steadied herself. Falling and ripping the gown would be the perfect end of this disastrous evening.

At the door, Bess removed her wet shoes, then turned the knob. The apartment reeked of cabbage, and it was strangely quiet and dark. Where was everyone? There was a light under the door of her parents' bedroom, so she knocked.

"Kum," her father said. He was lying on the bed reading the workers' newspaper, *Der Forverts*.

"Bessele! Thanks God you are back! Your momma called everywhere, and no one knew where you were. Mrs. Leibmann said she hadn't seen you."

"Oh, Poppa, I feel terrible. I lied to Momma. But where is everyone?"

"Everyone is out driving around with Uncle Sam looking for you."

Bess felt so ashamed that the whole family would know what she had done.

"So, where were you, Mamele, to worry us all so?"

"Oh Poppa, Momma forbid me to go, but I went anyway, to play a recital at the Pendennis Club."

"At that fancy club you played?" her father asked. He folded the *Forverts* and put it on the nightstand. "I want you should tell me everything."

Bess felt better seeing that Poppa wasn't angry, but she didn't know where to begin.

"Nu, what did you play?"

Bess told him everything: the kindly chauffeur, the marble floors that looked like a checkerboard, Mr. Brennard, the photographers, the dreamy Steinway grand, and her program.

"Nu, did they like it?"

"Yes, they stood and applauded, and I played the "Hungarian Rhapsody" as an encore. It went perfectly, Poppa. But after the recital they shuffled me off to eat alone in the kitchen and gave me a plate of ham. I was so furious, I left. Then I got lost coming home trying to find the dry streets. Momma was right. I never should have played there. I am sorry I lied. Anshuldik mir."

"Come here and don't cry." her Poppa caressed her and stroked her hair. "What a beautiful flower in your hair. You are my beautiful Bessele, and I don't want you should ever be unhappy."

Bess wiped her eyes and pulled the envelope out of her coat pocket, took out the twenty-dollar bill, and handed it to Poppa.

"God in heaven! So much money! This you must keep for yourself, Bess. Save it for your studies."

"No, Poppa, I did it for us. This will pay the rent and the coal bill."

"Don't worry about the bills. Let me handle that," her father said, putting the bill back in her pocket.

"But Poppa, you can't work as much now, and Momma's getting sick. . ."

"My hands are not so bad. I just need to rest sometimes. And what makes you think your mother is sick?" Poppa grabbed Bess's hands with a firm grasp.

"I hear her throwing up in the bathroom every morning."

Pulling on Bess's hands, Poppa sat up in bed. "I have some good news to tell you. Your mother is doing fine, and this baby she's going to keep. I'm sure." He gripped her hands tightly and said, "You are icy cold. You should heat up that delicious beet and cabbage soup your momma made for us. Or is a girl who plays "The Hungarian Rhapsody" on a Steinway grand piano at a fancy club too good to eat borscht?"

"Poppa, will you sit with me?"

"Maybe in a few minutes."

Sol lay back down, and Bess tiptoed out of the room. She went into the bathroom and undressed. Thankfully, her teacher's dress looked fine. She took the flower out of her hair and put on her long underwear and a robe. She washed and dried her face and hands. Then she put the dress into its box and took it down to the store so it wouldn't reek of beet and cabbage soup.

When she got back upstairs, Poppa was stirring the pot on the stove.

"Sit down, Bessele," he said as he poured a steaming bowl of soup.

Bess ate the borscht with a roll and butter.

"Nu, how is the borscht?"

"It's so good. I am soooo hungry."

Bess told Poppa about Mr. Brennard sending his regards. "Maybe he thinks the twenty dollars will pay his overdue bill, but I'm going over there tomorrow with another one."

"Oh, Bessele, not to worry. It's just for some alterations, and he has sent a lot of work our way."

Then she told Poppa how nice the cook had been and how Luther, the driver, had opened doors and treated her kindly.

"Many people will open doors for you, Bessele, and they will treat you special. I promise you," Poppa said.

Part Four

After the Flood

Chapter 25

Mr. Brennard's Suit

END OF AUGUST 1937

Sitting on a barstool at his cousin Elroy's Paddock Tavern, Jackson Clay sipped sweet tea. He'd promised himself never to touch liquor again the day he was spared from the flood. Truth be told, he liked sitting at the bar and gabbing more than the taste of liquor, and since his cousin's place opened early, he could get his breakfast. Most of the morning regulars stared down into their first drink of the day and would stumble out of the bar sometime in the afternoon. Before the flood, he was sometimes among them. But today, an important day, it felt good to be at his best.

The owner of the Brennard Mills was coming to the tailor shop to have a suit made, and Mr. Toplansky wanted Jackson to take the measurements. Besides that, it was possible, if Mr. T's hands didn't get better, that he, Jackson Henry Clay, would be trusted to make the suit. He wiped the crumbs of boiled egg off his lips, finished off his iced tea, and left a nickel on the counter. As he walked out, Jackson pulled his straw hat low on his face to shade his eyes. It was going to be a scorcher and a long walk.

Boy oh boy, seemed like he'd just left work, he thought as he approached the tailor shop. What a night he'd had, working on the Shawnee Park Boy's Band uniforms. He still had the keys to the place from when he'd stayed there back in the winter during the flood. Jackson tried to give the keys back, but Mr. T wanted him to keep them. It was quiet in the shop and quiet upstairs, so Jackson took the band uniforms from the pressing area and examined them. Mighty nice if he did say so himself.

He'd always had his side jobs that he worked on at home on his mother's sewing machine, but her machine was lost in the flood. Besides Mr. T's Singer was so much faster, and Jackson hoped to make a tidy sum with this order. Maybe someday he'd have money for his own shop in the West End.

He turned on the fan and ran a rag over the big cutting table and the windowsills and took out the pattern books. He opened the drawers and got out Mr. T's notebook and the pencils. He rooted around in the drawer for the tape measure and saw Mr. T's lucky red chip. It was sad Mr. T couldn't hold the cards anymore 'cause that man did love a good card game.

He hoped Mr. T would be in shape to greet his customer because Mr. Brennard might let a Negro take his measurements, but he wouldn't never buy a suit made by one. In fact, Jackson was surprised the man did business with a Jew. Mr. Brennard had been ordering uniforms for his household help from Mr. T for years, but until now had never ordered something for himself.

Jackson could tell by the slow steps on the stairs that Mrs. T was coming down.

"Morning, Mrs. T. How you doing today?"

"Not bad. Thank you, Jackson."

Jackson thought she looked terrible. She had dark circles under her eyes. She was still carrying the baby high, but she looked thin every place but her belly.

"Will Mr. T be down soon? Mr. Brennard's appointment is at nine."

"He's right behind me."

Jackson pulled down the bushel basket of clothes left for alterations. Last thing she needed was to be lifting heavy things. He put a pair of pants on Mrs. T's sewing table and helped her into her chair. It was obvious she was uncomfortable, and that made him fidgety. He paced bit and thought maybe he'd press the garments she had finished last night but thought better of it. Best not get the shop heated up before Mr. Brennard came.

"Should I go and help Mr. T?"

Mrs. T shook her head no and pointed at the stairs. Sure enough, Mr T was making his way down.

"Good morning, Jackson." Mr. T shuffled over to the window and adjusted the blinds. "It's a sunny day today. A good luck day, don't you think?"

Mrs. T muttered under her breath as she opened a seam and Mr. T hummed a song.

At 9:30 the bell on the door rang.

"Good morning, Mr. Brennard," Sol Toplansky said. He extended his hand to his customer.

Mr. Brennard shook his hand and said, "Good morning, Sol. Good morning, Mrs. Toplansky. You are still the prettiest seamstress this side of the Mississippi."

Mrs. T usually smiled when customers flirted, but today she just nodded, pursed her lips around the straight pins and kept working.

"With that baby on the way, y'all must be looking to move up to the Highlands."

Mrs. Toplansky pulled the pins out of her mouth and answered, "Oh, we're fine right here. Bess is close to her school, and we have good neighbors."

"Well," Mr. Brennard said, "I wouldn't be partial to living next to the German Church, but it's a free country."

"So, we need to measure you for the suit," Sol said, taking Mr. Brennard's hat and helping him off with his jacket.

"Jackson would assist me to take your measurements. I'm teaching him a little bit about the trade."

Jackson saw the look of surprise on Brennard's face but knew to ignore it. "Mornin' Mistah Brennard," he said. He was tall enough to look Brennard in the eye, but he didn't.

"Mornin', boy," Brennard answered.

Brennard stood stiffly as Jackson laid the yellow tape along his arm. Mr. T stood by and watched every measurement and reached out to move the tape measure when it wasn't just right. He double checked the notebook as Jackson jotted down the numbers. Normally Mr. T trusted him, but Jackson knew this was a show for Mr. Brennard's sake.

Satisfied that the measurements were exactly right, Sol took a few steps back and nodded. "So," he said to his customer, "the first fitting would be right after Labor Day. Then I wouldn't have your suit ready for the final fitting until after our holy days." Sol looked at a calendar and gave Brennard a date in early October.

"That's just fine. We're not going to Washington, D.C. until October 20. We're going to the White House to tell FDR we need to ensure the Ohio River never floods our fair city again. Your president is busy building dams and giving handouts to workers, but he needs to protect the people who put America to work."

He's your president too, Jackson thought.

"Yes, Mr. Brennard, the flood was terrible, but I still see people in bread lines," Sol said.

Yes, sir, Jackson thought, tell the man.

"Well, I don't want to say what I think of those free loaders in front of your wife."

Mrs. T rushed to say, "So, Mr. Brennan, the suit would be ready in plenty of time for your trip. Would your wife maybe need a suit? Or an evening gown? Tell her I do the best beadwork."

That Mrs. T wasn't one to let an opportunity slip away, Jackson thought stifling a chuckle.

"Well, she goes to a French tailor in Cincinnati, but I thought I'd give our local talent a try."

Jackson noticed the man's chest puff out in satisfaction. Mr. T just smiled. Jackson wasn't the only one swallowing a pride sandwich.

"Speaking of local talent, Toplansky, how's your daughter Bess? She sure did herself proud at the club. She can come back and play for us any time."

"Thanks, Mr. Brennard, but our holidays are soon, so, she has to stay up on her schoolwork. She doesn't want to get behind right at the beginning of the year."

"Now, how much do I owe you?"

As a rule, Mr. T told regular clients they could pay later, but Mrs. T smiled her first smile of the day and said, "Half now and half when it's finished." She knew how much her husband had paid for the material. Jackson had never touched finer fabric.

"I'm still not sure about a wool suit for the fall," Brennard said. "It's always so hot in Louisville and I can't imagine October in that cesspool Washington."

"You wouldn't be hot in a merino wool suit, Mr. Brennard, believe me. Did you ever see a sheep sweat? You would wear this suit for a long time and in good health."

Brennard laughed and handed Sol $25.00.

"Thank you," Mr. T said.

"My pleasure, Sol. Good morning to you all. Mrs. Toplansky," Brennard said, doffing his hat to her as he left.

Mrs. T smiled until the door closed. That woman could cut with her words, but she knew how to manage people, better than the boss most times.

Jackson looked through the slats in the blinds, "Would you all believe the man came from down the street in his limousine?"

"Well," Sol said, "maybe he came from home, or maybe he's going to a business meeting downtown."

"I don't know, but if he doesn't do some walking soon, he's gonna need a new belt."

Mr. and Mrs. T laughed. Mr. T sat down at his table and said, "I'll draw and cut the pattern this afternoon after the sun goes down a little bit."

That afternoon Jackson made deliveries and got back to find Mr. T sleeping at the cutting table. The pattern was only half drawn on the tagboard paper.

"Mr. T, you all right?" Jackson said a few minutes later, to be sure Sol really was just sleeping.

"Oh, I'm just a little tired. My eyes get blurry sometimes, and I have to rest them. You know I want to be sure to draw this right."

"Do you want me to finish the pattern? I can stay late and cut it. I'll close the blinds so no one sees me."

Mr. T looked sheepish. "No, Jackson. I wouldn't mind your help, but I don't know how I can pay you extra for the tailoring work."

"Look a here, Mr. T. I'm not short of money. I've got these band uniforms and then it will be the fall racing season and I'm never short of business and seeing as you let me use your machines. And how many meals have I eaten with you folks?"

"For meals you would always be welcome, Jackson. But you go home now. I might get in trouble with your union."

Jackson laughed at the idea of a Negro in a union. Not in Louisville, anyway.

The next morning, the pattern was still not finished, so Jackson repeated his offer. This time Sol didn't hesitate. "If you could stay after we close, we can draw it together and then you'll cut the Italian wool."

Jackson nodded. It was an honor, this trust. As they worked, Jackson asked Mr. T why he put the darts where he did. Mr. T said it would hide Brennard's paunch.

"Reckon I don't have fat cat clients like you. I mainly make the suits too big for the kids so they can grow into them."

At dinnertime, Jackson declined Mr. T's invitation to join the family, and he kept on working. At seven he went upstairs and told Mrs. T that he'd cut the material if Mr. T wanted to take a look.

"No," she said. "Sol's resting now. Would you like something cold to drink?

"No, thank you, ma'am. I've got a taste for catfish and cornbread."

At the mention of catfish, Mrs. T grimaced and Jackson laughed, "I suspicion y'all wouldn't eat nothing at the Paddock.

"It's just that we have rules against eating the fish what swim in the bottom of the river."

"I understand, Mrs. T. To each his own. I mean we all have our own ways and that's just fine. Well goodnight," Jackson said. He paused for a moment on the back stairs to listen to Bess finish a piece he'd never heard her play before. Sounded like a show tune. That gal could tease the keys.

The streets were beginning to cool down, and he was hungry. He headed down to the Paddock for some dinner and conversation. In the evening most of the drunks had wandered out, and the working folks arrived after a long day, thirsty and itching to talk. Cousin Leroy had hired a bartender, so sometimes he chewed the fat with Jackson for a spell.

"Hey, Leroy, how's business today?"

"Not bad. How about you?"

"Well, I'm thinking I'm gonna be making a rich man's suit."

"Now who might that fat cat be?"

"That's something I ought not be tellin'."

Jackson wanted to brag a bit, but the man who sat down next to him looked familiar. In fact his uniform came from Sol's Tailor Shop. No doubt about it. He remembered thinking that suit was for one mighty big man when he'd pressed it.

"You looking at my threads?"

"Just admiring the fit. Do you wear that chauffeur's uniform everywhere?" Jackson smirked.

"None of your business, but I'm still on duty. Waitin' for my boss down at the Pendennis."

Jackson didn't know what to say.

"I know who you is, and I know you got your own tailorin' business on the side," the driver said, "and I suspect you gonna be makin' Mr. Brennard his new suit. He told me he was worried about Toplansky. Said his hands was shaking like anything this morning."

"Well, I'm not. And Mr. T's hands may shake, but he's still the best tailor I know."

"That may be true, but my boss thinks the wife is gonna do the work."

"Mr. T and only Mr. T does the men's tailoring in that shop."

"Well, all I know is Mr. Brennard said we was gonna drive up to Cincinnati if the suit ain't right. What I don't git is how you stomach workin' for them Jews."

Jackson looked at the man. He was light-skinned and strong. Maybe he was Mr. Brennard's bodyguard as well as his driver. And the way the man squinted at him, Jackson really didn't want to get on his bad side, so he thought twice before he continued the conversation.

"I don't know whether you a God fearin' man."

"I am."

"And I don't know whether you all read the Good Book."

The chauffeur didn't avert his gaze, but he didn't answer, so Jackson kept going.

"Well, you know how Moses was taken out of the river by Pharoah's daughter? I feel like Mr. Toplansky and his family took me up out of the flood and saved me. When I had nowhere else to go, they gave me a place to live, and they fed me when they didn't have much to eat themselves. So, I know they God fearing people."

The man was quiet. His stare made Jackson squirm until finally the chauffeur chuckled and said, "Tell you what, I'm not drinking no more right now, but next time I come in here you can buy me a top-shelf whiskey."

"Leroy, next time this gentleman comes in, you pour him a glass of Four Roses on me."

The chauffeur shook Jackson's hand. Told him his name was James.

"Well, James, how's about some sweet tea for both of us?"

Chapter 26
The Substitution

This is my exchange, this is my atonement, this is my substitute, this rooster will go to its death and I will go to a long life of peace.

—Prayer for *Kapores* ritual to be done before
Yom Kippur, the Atonement Day

Tuesday, September 14, the eve of the Day of Atonement

Bess awoke to the slamming of doors and her grandmother's cane banging on the kitchen floor.

"What's going on, Bubby?"

"Your mother's going to the hospital."

"But the baby's not due for a month."

"What does God know from due dates?"

"I want to go."

"No, you must stay home with Calman and do the Yom Kippur sacrifice for me."

Bubby pulled a handkerchief out of her bosom and untied the knot. She showed Bess a roll of quarters and told her to go buy a hen and a rooster at the Haymarket and take them to the shochet to be butchered. The ritual slaughterer would know a needy family to give them to. Then they should go to school.

"You know where I keep my basket," Bubby Adel said. "And here is the prayer. Calman must hold the rooster over his head, and you must hold the hen. Don't forget, three times you must wave the chicken over your head while you say the prayer."

"But Bubby, you know I don't believe in such superstition. Killing chickens so humans can live? And last year I got scratched. . ."

"Scratched? You got scratched! The kapores is important. You want your mother should lose the baby? Or the baby should be born, God forbid, deformed? You want your father should die from his sickness? For me, I don't care, I wish the Almighty would take me already, so you wouldn't have another mouth to feed, but as long as I am alive, I will take care of my family. You will do this Bess. And don't buy no black chickens. They should be pure white. Go now before they run out of the perfect ones."

Her bubby slammed the quarters on the kitchen table, tied a bonnet over her wig, grabbed her cane, and walked out. Bess went to the window. She could see her mother and father getting into a cab parked in the alley. She heard her grandmother clattering as quickly as her old bones would allow her down the back stairs.

Back in her daybed Bess pulled the covers over her and tried to go back to sleep. For once it was cool in the kitchen and now, it was so quiet. But peace did not last long, for a few minutes later, Calvin nudged her shoulder.

"Sis, where's my breakfast?" Calvin asked.

"Fix yourself some toast and then we gotta get going."

Calvin spied the roll of quarters on the table. "Hey, who left us this fortune? I can double this before you can whistle 'Dixie.'"

"Leave it alone. It's Bubby's money for the kapores. We have to go to the Haymarket to buy a rooster and a hen and say the Yom Kippur prayers. Bubby can't do it 'cause they're taking Momma to the hospital. The baby's coming early. So get a move on. If we don't hurry, we won't get to school before the bell." Bess realized that if she was going to honor her grandmother's wishes, she would have to move this very minute.

"This ain't breakfast," Calvin said as he stuffed a kaiser roll into his mouth.

"I'll buy you doughnuts if you go with me. I dread this business of holding the live chickens and I need you." Bess shook her head. "At least she doesn't expect us to kill them. Now go get dressed."

In the bathroom Bess saw spots of blood on the floor. This had happened once before, the last time Momma lost her baby. Bess wiped up the blood and rinsed out the rag. Maybe it would almost be better if they lost this one too. How would they take care of another child when Poppa was so sick? And her foolish bubby, spending so much money for a stupid superstition. As Bess washed her hands, she was ashamed of thinking such bad thoughts about the baby. Instead, she should be worried that her mother might die. If Momma died and Poppa couldn't work…, what would they do? She had never forgotten that poor man whose wife had died in childbirth. He'd had to put his baby in an orphanage. Bess shuddered and decided she'd better carry out Bubby's wishes. What if the stupid ritual worked?

"Come on, Sis. Shake a leg."

Bess and Calvin left lickety split. As they walked down Broadway to Brook Street, Calvin bragged that he could parlay $5.25 into a fortune. Bess tried to divert his attention by telling him how their grandmother used to kill the chickens herself.

"You were a baby. You probably don't remember when Bubby would swirl the bird over her head and say the prayer and then she'd snap its neck off with her bare hands. What a racket those chickens put up. They must have known the end was near. Then Bubby took the dead birds to the rabbi to make sure they were ritually perfect before taking them to a family that couldn't afford a holiday meal."

"Yeah, I remember that. Look, Sis. You see the kids down that alley? They're pitching pennies, and if you just give me a penny, I can win us some breakfast money. It's on the way to the market anyway."

They grew closer to a knot of kids about Calvin's age and an older boy standing at the edge of the alley, maybe fifteen like Bess or older, certainly taller. Bess didn't like the looks of the group, but they waved to Calvin. It was clear they knew him.

"You know the ropes, Angel, you gotta touch the wall and the winner is the one closest." Bess laughed to think that Annabelle's nickname for him had caught on, but she wasn't happy that he wanted to pitch pennies.

On the first toss, Calvin's penny landed on top of another player's coin pretty close to the wall, but the last player put his coin within millimeters of the wall. So he asked for another penny from Bess.

She shook her head. "No, we have to get going."

"Just give me the penny, Sis." Calvin sounded angry.

Bess gave in and handed her brother a penny. On the next toss, Calvin's coin took a bad bounce on a raised brick and didn't even hit the wall.

"So, who's your girlfriend?" the tallest boy asked Calvin.

"This is my big sister, and I better not see a one of you bothering her."

The tall boy shrugged, and one of the younger boys giggled. The game continued, and Calvin won a few pennies and lost a few. Bess felt sorry for the younger kids who kept losing money. Especially a boy her brother knew, a kid named Billy. She didn't think she'd ever seen a scrawnier kid. So rag tag and dirty, she wondered how her brother even knew him.

"Okay, Sis, I can feel my luck coming. Give me another penny."

"I don't have any more pennies, just the money from Bubby."

Calvin whispered, "Well, fork it over. I need a quarter, and then I'll leave, word of honor."

Bess figured the fastest way to get out of there was to let her brother play and win. "Okay, but just this one time and that is it."

Calvin winked at her and told the players, "Okay, men, I'm going to up the ante. Who's got the guts to pitch a quarter?"

Only a few kids had quarters, but they were willing to take Calvin's dare. Bess was amazed. So much money. She had to wonder how much time Calvin actually spent in school.

He pitched his quarter, and it rolled a bit and landed right smack on the wall. The four other boys came close, but Calvin was clearly the winner. Billy looked desperate when he saw Calvin take his quarter off the ground and pocket it. Calvin announced he had to get his breakfast and go to the market.

"Hey, not so fast," Billy said. "Ain't we gonna do tips."

"Not today, I owe you one and you know I'm good for it."

At the end of the alley was the Haymarket Bakery. "Hey, Sis, I'm treating for the doughnuts," said Calvin, now all smiles.

As they pulled doughnuts out of a greasy brown bag, Calvin said, "Let's skip school and go see how Momma is doing. We'll just tell Bubby we did the kapores."

Bess didn't like the idea, but she did really want to see her mother. The blood in the bathroom had scared her.

"If you want to buy the kapores we can go to the market after the hospital. And," he smiled, "I made enough money to take the trolley."

On the trolley, Bess didn't talk at all. Calvin finally said, "Look, Sis, we'll be there an' back in a jiffy. Don't worry."

"I don't care about Bubby's kapores but poor Momma and Poppa. This has been a terrible year." What Bess was also thinking about was that she was only fifteen and Calvin was fourteen. Would she have to take care of the family? Could she?"

"Hey, Sis, get up. Next stop is Jewish."

The dark brick hospital building was a familiar sight. Bess and Calvin ran up the front steps. The lady at the reception desk was attending to a big family, so she didn't see the two of them slip into the stairwell. They knew their way to the women's section. The first person they saw was their grandmother napping in a chair in the hallway. They peered into Momma's room and tiptoed in. Poppa seemed to be asleep, but he sat up and put his fingers on his lips and motioned for the children to go back into the hallway. Bess couldn't stop staring at their Momma who had a rubber tube in her arm and fluid in a glass bottle hanging above her head. Bess didn't want to leave, but Poppa gave her a gentle nudge into the hall.

"Come away from the door. Your momma needs her rest."

"She looks so white," Calvin said.

"How's she doing, Poppa?" Bess said. "Tell me the truth."

"Dr. Rubel says she has a good chance, but they want her to stay here, in bed, until she has the baby." Sol nodded and breathed out a big sigh. "Anyway, what are you doing here? I thought you were going marketing for the chickens."

"Yup, we did it," Calvin said before Bess could think of what to say.

"Look, you kids shouldn't be here," Poppa said. "And aren't you supposed to be in school?"

"But we were so worried about Momma, we had to see her."

"Well, you won't help her making noise out here, so go on home and help Annabelle get everything ready for your dinner tonight before the fast."

Bess saw Calvin grimace and knew how he hated the meal before the big fast. But he didn't talk back to Poppa. The two kids were quiet as they walked out of the hospital. They didn't like the way their mother looked.

"Good thing Bubby was napping. I'd hate to lie to her," Bess said knowing that most of the time Bubby guessed the truth anyway.

Bess knew Calvin resented how often their grandmother disciplined him. She was the only one who didn't think Calvin was an angel. Bess told Calvin what Bubby had said about wanting to die and Calvin said, "Well, life might be a heck of a lot easier without her." Bess felt the same way, but she felt terrible thinking it.

"We should go to school."

"Nah, it's late. Let's get a snack. Anyways, you don't want to mess up your perfect record by being tardy, do you?"

Bess shrugged. She had never skipped school. It felt strange, but when Calvin was pitching coins, she hadn't worried about Momma. A few blocks from Jewish Hospital they found a little diner. Calvin ordered a bologna sandwich and Bess ordered a cup of coffee. She wasn't going to chide her brother for ordering non-kosher meat, but she did tell him he shouldn't gamble.

"Do you want to end up owing everyone money like Poppa?" She'd overheard enough angry talk between her parents late at night to understand the effect of Poppa's urge to gamble.

"Hey, I won, didn't I? And Poppa, he's the best poker player around."

"Hmm. Maybe, but did you see the kid who lost his quarter? He probably won't eat today. That's because of you."

"Billy shoulda never bet. He's not a pro. I'm a sure thing with pitching pennies."

"Yes, but Calvin you could have lost our money."

"Nope, it's more skill than luck."

"Listen, Calvin, our family has always worked."

"But Poppa can't work no more, and Jackson keeps talking about setting up his own shop or going up North. If he leaves, what'll we do?"

"Yes, but some way or another we'll work and tonight we'll have a meal without your gambling money. Annabelle is making your favorite, chicken croquettes."

"Yeah, but there won't be much. And how are we supposed to fast tomorrow on two measly croquettes." Calvin gobbled the last of his sandwich.

"But the point is, we'll eat."

"I might just have me another sandwich," said Calvin.

Bess didn't hear him. "Momma sure looks bad. I hope she isn't going to lose another..." She stopped abruptly.

"Sis, you think I don't know Momma lost those babies?"

"Who told you?"

"Cousin Joe. And know what? I think we should go buy some white chickens just in case. Maybe Momma could use some help from the Man upstairs."

Bess smiled. "You might be right. Then we better get to the market fast because the slaughterer closes early before holidays."

"Good thing we'll have money left over after we buy the darned poultry."

"I think we should give that to charity too."

"I'll put a dime in the pushkie, but the rest is ours. I won it fair and square, and charity begins at home, right, Sis?"

Bess shook her head. Her brother seemed to be on top of the world, while most days she felt confused and worried.

The Haymarket was quiet when they got there. Some of the trucks were taking up their awnings and others were pulling away. They went to the stall where their bubby always did business and asked for a white cock and a white hen.

"Well, y'all kids came kinda late to be getting that today. I only got a couple of spotted roosters left."

Bess felt stricken. Surely this was a sign that she was being punished for giving in to Calvin instead of doing as Bubby wanted.

"You know, a couple of your people bought other poultry for their holiday. I do have a pair of white ducks, if you gotta have white, but they'll cost you."

"Mister," Calvin said. "You all got something cheap like quails or pigeons?"

"Take the ducks or leave them. I'm closing for the day."

"Calvin, we have to buy something. The shochet closes pretty soon." Bess addressed the vendor. "We'll take the ducks."

Calvin grudgingly handed the money over to the man.

"All right," Bess said. "Now we've got to hurry."

"I know a shortcut," Calvin yelled as he sprinted down the alley with the ducks honking madly in the basket.

"Hey, wait, Calvin, we need to do the prayer first."

Calvin looked at Bess as though she were crazy. "Whoa, Sis, how are we going to get home and do the prayer and get to the slaughterer in time? I say we do it right here."

Calvin put down the basket. He untied the lid and one of the ducks flew out and scampered away. He shoved the other duck back into the basket and told Bess to keep a lid on it. He ran down the alley and caught the duck.

"Phew that was close," he said, wrestling to keep the agitated duck in his grasp. "So, what's the prayer anyway?"

Bess reached into her pocket and pulled out the little card in Hebrew her grandmother had given her. She didn't read Hebrew as well as Calvin, who'd had a bar mitzvah, so she handed him the prayer and told him to hold the male duck while she held the female.

"How do we know which is which?" The ducks were squawking and wriggling.

Calvin held one up over his head and said, "Well, this one is bigger, so it must be the male. Okay, let's get this over with." He held the duck over his head and made three circles and read the prayer. "This is my atonement, this is my substitute, this rooster will go to its death and I will live a long life of peace." Calvin put his bird back in the basket and handed the smaller one to Bess. She held its neck with both hands. The bird struggled as she circled it over her head. Calvin said the prayer for her and then they put it back into

Bubby's market basket and tied the lid tightly.

When they got to the butcher shop, they saw the handwritten sign. "Closed until 7 a.m. Thursday."

Bess sighed with exasperation. "I knew this would happen," she said.

"Come on, we'll go around the back," Calvin said.

They knocked at the slaughterer's door and waited and waited. Finally an old lady shook her finger sternly at them through the window. When they didn't budge, she opened the door a crack and yelled, "Farmacht."

"Now, what do we do?" Bess said.

Calvin shook his head, then lifted his head and smiled. "I know," he said. "How about we let them go loose at Cave Hill Cemetery."

"But they're supposed to go to charity. That old lady is Bubby's friend. She'll tell Bubby she saw us for sure."

"I guess our goose, or our ducks, are cooked," Calvin laughed.

"Calvin it's not funny. We lied to Bubby and now the ducks haven't been killed by a kosher butcher and we're not even giving them to someone needy."

"Well, I guess I know someone needy all right. Follow me Sis."

Calvin took off like a shot. Even lugging the ducks, he set a fast pace. It seemed like he knew every alley in their neighborhood.

Bess was out of breath as they approached Baxter and Broadway. They stopped at a rundown house by the alley that ran behind their apartment.

"It's around the back. Look, Sis, let me do the talking.""

Calvin knocked at the door of a basement apartment. A haggard woman opened the door and a kid in a droopy gray diaper ran out the door. The woman yelled, "You get back in here or I'll tan your hide."

"What do y'all want?" she said as she yanked the toddler hard and motioned them both to come inside.

"Uh, ma'am, we're friends of Billy's."

"He's not here. He's at school. Y'all must be one of his durn gambling buddies, I reckon."

"Oh, no ma'am," Calvin said with his butter wouldn't melt in your mouth smile, "We are classmates, and I, we, just came from the church. From St. Paul's to be exact. The priest told us to give you these ducks."

Calvin opened the basket, and the ducks squawked and flew about. The toddler ran after the bigger one and the bird arched its neck and bit the kid on his hand. The kid let out a scream, and then a baby started crying.

"Now look what you all done. What am I supposed to do with these animals?"

"Eat them. Do you want me to kill 'em for you?"

"Nah, my oldest son will be home soon enough, and he'll do it."

"Do you have something my brother can put them in?" Bess asked. "We have to take this basket back home."

The women pulled a box full of rags out from under a bed and emptied it onto the table. Calvin placed the unhappy ducks into the box and then the woman put the lid down and placed a skillet on top.

"Well, I reckon the kids will be right happy of a good meal. Y'all didn't steal them ducks I hope."

"No ma'am, we bought. . . I mean the priest gave them to us. Anyways, you better make sure they have some air to breathe."

As they walked down the alley, they saw Billy traipsing home. The boy was even dirtier than he'd been that morning.

"Hey Billy," Calvin said.

"Hey Angel. If you're lookin' to pitch pennies, I ain't playing. My mother is gonna tan my hide for losing money this morning. I was supposed to go buy milk."

Calvin dropped his chin. "Yeah, well. Actually, we left a pair of ducks for your family to have for dinner."

"What do you mean?" Billy squinted at Calvin.

"A duck. Didn't you ever eat a duck?"

Billy grinned and said, "A course. We eat duck durn near every day and on Sundays we have steaks."

"Look, here's the quarter you lost this morning. Guess y'all should stay away from them games, Billy. You don't have the toss."

Billy hit Calvin on the back. "You sure can be a pal sometimes."

Bess was beaming as they walked down the alley toward home.

"You were terrific! Did you see the smile on Billy's face?"

"Yes. I'm glad we did it. Anyways, we still have $1.75 left."

"Well, you better put that in the pushkie tonight before we light the candles."

"All of it?"

"All of it."

When they got back, Annabelle was setting the table.

"I left y'all's croquettes in the iron skillet. You can just heat them a little bit." She took off her apron and left.

Bess reminded Calvin to put his winnings in the charity box. "Oh well," he said with a big grin, "There's more moolah where that came from."

Bubby arrived around three o'clock and said that Momma was doing well enough. She said a little prayer and put a coin in the charity box. Bess worried about Bubby's look of surprise at the added weight in the tin box. As they washed their hands in the special bowl before lighting the candles, Bubby Adel looked quizzically at her granddaughter's arms. "No chicken scratches this year?"

"No, Bubby," she said with an uneasy feeling in her gut.

"When will Popppa get home?"

"He is staying at the hospital. Your mother needs him," Bubby said.

They ate in silence, blessed, and lit the candles.

The meal before the Day of Atonement, even when her cousins from Indianapolis came, was never Bess's favorite. They ate early and quickly. Then they were supposed to fast for over twenty-four hours, until you could see a star in the sky. And Bubby wouldn't let them leave a light on anywhere but in the bathroom. Usually, the whole family ran out after dinner in a sweat to get to synagogue and hear Poppa chant "Kol Nidre." At least tonight they didn't have to hurry. They wouldn't be going to shul. After Bess and Calvin finished the dishes what would they do? You couldn't play piano, you couldn't listen to the radio, you couldn't read a schoolbook, you couldn't even tear toilet paper.

At nine o'clock, Bess lay on her bed and watched the candles flicker out. Nothing felt right. It was so quiet without Momma and Poppa in their bedroom chatting or arguing. She wouldn't mind talking with Calvin, but he must be asleep. He had the conscience of an angel. She smiled at the name again. Well, he wasn't a bad egg. Calvin had looked at her once during dinner and almost broke out laughing. She had done a terrible job of looking after her brother, but it had been such an adventure. She dreaded going with Bubby and Calvin to synagogue in the morning. It would be a whole day of standing and confessing and striking her chest with her fist. How on earth could she have wished Momma wouldn't have the baby or that Bubby were dead. Bess had a lot to atone for this Yom Kippur.

Chapter 27
Breaking the Fast

WEDNESDAY EVENING, SEPTEMBER 15, 1937

"Bessie, I made your favorite, whitefish salad," Aunt Minnie said, spreading some fish on a bialy and passing it to her niece. "You haven't eaten a thing. Take some noodle kugel."

Normally Aunt Minnie's table would be crowded for breaking the fast, but Poppa and Bubby were at the hospital taking care of Momma. So, it was just Bess, Calvin, Aunt Minnie, Uncle Sam, and Cousins Joe and Dotty around the dining room table. After having firsts and seconds of everything, Calvin and Joe wiped their faces and stood to excuse themselves.

"Great meal! Thanks, Aunt Minnie," Calvin said, then kissed his aunt on the cheek. "Don't walk home in the dark by yourself, Sis. I'll be back in a bit," he said as he and Joe headed to the door. No doubt, they were going to meet up with their friends.

"Not so fast," Uncle Sam said. "I could use some help putting up the sukkah."

"Pop," Joe said. "Why bother putting it up again? You know the landlord won't let you put it on the fire escape."

"Maybe, but Sol and Mollie won't have a sukkah this year, so we have to make a place for the family to eat for the week of the festival."

Minnie and Sam lived in an apartment over their pawnshop. It was spacious, but unlike Sol and Mollie, they didn't have a backyard, just an inner courtyard where laundry dripped on crisscrossing lines from floor to floor.

Joe and Calvin shrugged and climbed out the window to the fire escape to join Uncle Sam. Inside the women put on aprons, bright gingham ones sewn for them by Mollie, and started cleaning up. Dot would wash and Bess would dry. They told Aunt Minnie to go sit and rest, but she insisted on clearing.

"You look so worried, Bessele," Aunt Minnie said as she covered up the leftover fish salad and put it in the icebox.

"I am just thinking about Momma."

"Your mother is a strong and healthy woman, and she will get through this."

"But she looked so bad and…"

"I was there today, and she looked better, I promise you."

Bess wished she had gone to see Momma instead of spending the entire day in synagogue with Bubby. Somehow having lied to Bubby made Bess think she had to make up for it by staying with her and chanting the prayers. Not just that, but she was truly sorry for having had such ugly thoughts of not being able to afford a baby. How selfish could she be?

"Bess, what is up with you? You are never so quiet," Aunt Minnie asked.

"Yeah, cat got your tongue?" Dotty wanted to know. "It's something else, isn't it Bess?"

Sometimes Dotty didn't get Bess's feelings at all, but this time she read her like a book. "Do you promise you won't tell Momma and Poppa?"

"Spill the beans, Bess," Dot said. "Mum's the word."

Bess looked at the kitchen window. Uncle Sam or Joe could come in at any time, and Calvin would kill her if she confessed.

"Let's go into the parlor," said Aunt Minnie. "We can finish the dishes later."

Aunt Minnie took Bess's hand and led her to the parlor.

"I feel bad that I lied to Bubby," Bess said and proceeded to tell Aunt Minnie and Dotty every detail about the kapores. Aunt Minnie shook her head about Calvin pitching coins in the alley, but she approved of them giving the ducks to Billy's mother. Dotty wanted to know more about Billy's family.

"Their place smelled so dank. I'm sure it flooded in January. And I've never seen such scrawny babies."

"Well, don't feel so bad. You did the mitzvah of giving to the needy, and anyway I can't believe your grandmother still does the sacrifice. It's another superstition from the Old Country," Aunt Minnie said decisively.

"And no need to worry your grandmother," Dotty said. "What she doesn't know won't hurt her. Right, kiddo?"

"That Calvin takes the cake," Aunt Minnie said with a chuckle.

As if on cue, Calvin burst into the parlor. "Hey, come out and look at our work!"

Grateful for the diversion, Bess followed him out to the fire escape. Calvin and Joe were beaming with pride, but the sukkah looked sad. It was just a little cubicle made of an old army surplus tarpaulin, nothing at all to compare to the lovely booth they had every year in their back yard. Bess tried to find something to compliment. Telling them the pine branches smelled good was all she could manage.

Later, as she and Calvin walked home from downtown through the dark streets, Bess tried to keep her mind off Momma. She asked Calvin whether he thought Bubby would be able to climb through the window to get to the sukkah.

"Oh, she'll get out there," he said.

"Well, I think we'll have to help her. It won't be right if she can't be with us." Bess sighed and slowed her steps. She stopped at the corner and looked up at the stars. "Everything just seems wrong now. We've always had a wooden sukkah in our back yard, big enough for lots of guests. It's my favorite holiday, and it won't be the same with Momma in the hospital."

As they made their way down the alley, they could hear hammering. They arrived at the back gate to find Jackson and Pastor Habermann putting up their family's sukkah.

"Hey, Rev. Hey, Jackson," Calvin yelled out. "Good work!"

"Get over here, Calvin, and help us," the pastor ordered.

Bess pitched in too by cutting boughs for the roof and bringing up the decorations from the basement, and soon the festival booth was complete. As they admired their work, Bess said her family would be so honored if the Habermanns would eat in the sukkah with them for the Feast of Tabernacles. No sooner had she extended the invitation than Bess felt she had spoken in haste. What if Momma had to stay in the hospital? How could they celebrate the holiday? But she couldn't take the invitation back.

"The honor would be ours," Pastor Habermann said solemnly.

"And you have to come too, Jackson," Calvin said.

"Oh, I reckon I have eaten my share of meals in this little shack, and you gonna have a mighty big crowd to feed with all the Habermanns."

The sukkah really was pretty. Bess wished Momma and Poppa could see it. At least one thing in their lives was normal.

That night Bess was awakened by the telephone. She ran down to the store and answered. It was Poppa.

"We have a baby girl."

"Is Momma okay?"

"Danken Gott, your mother is fine, and your new sister is a beauty with dark eyes and hair just like your momma. Her name will be Toviah."

Chapter 28

The Festival of Booths

It was hotter than blazes in the Atherton High School for Girls auditorium as Bess slumped at the piano. She had flunked an algebra quiz and wasn't looking forward to rehearsing for *The Mikado*. She was fed up with the piano and wished she could be doing anything else. Be anywhere else. She had so much schoolwork and now there was a baby to take care of. Momma hadn't regained her energy, and Bubby Adel spent most of the time dozing in her rocking chair. The new baby was the least of their worries.

Poppa's ailment now had a name. Parkinson's Disease, and they were told it would only get worse, not better. If it weren't for Jackson, none of the tailoring work would be done.

To make matters worse, the rent was late again. So, as soon as Mr. Brennard paid for his suit, Bess would run the money over to Mr. Schuster. Last week when he stopped by for payment, Bess had asked for an extension. His look had been as black as his hat and coat. The man must have ice water in his veins to wear that outfit in this heat.

"A penny for your thoughts," her friend Phyllis said, plopping down next to Bess on the piano bench, nearly bumping her off.

"They're not worth a penny," Bess said, forcing a laugh.

"When can I come see the baby?"

"Do you want to come eat in our Sukkah?"

"Sure. Well, maybe. When does Sukkoth start?"

"It's next week. If you come Wednesday, we'll have potato latkes and homemade applesauce." Bess knew she had to bribe her friend. Phyllis hated picnics, but she loved potato latkes.

"Look, I'd better skedaddle. I've got a tennis lesson. I'll let you know tomorrow."

After Phyllis left, Bess started warm-up scales, but her fingers wouldn't cooperate.

"Sounds like you could use some help here, Topsky," said Mary D, who had a way of sneaking up on you.

Bess slammed the fallboard down and jumped up, "Where did you come from? And why are you still calling me that childish name?"

"Don't be a sorehead, I was just joking."

"Why can't you call me Bess like everyone else?"

"Oh, don't be so fussy. I just came by to help you out."

"I don't need your help. Have you forgotten I was the winner of last year's state contest?"

"Well, they couldn't very well give me first prize every year, now, could they?"

"If you're so good, why did Mrs. Satterwhite choose me to accompany *The Mikado*?"

"I'm sure I don't have the slightest idea, but my mother says Satterwhite feels sorry for you."

"Feels sorry for me? Why?"

"She feels sorry for your people."

"My people. Do you mean my family? Because they don't live in a big house on a hill and parade around in a shiny limousine? Or do you mean Jews? Do you mean the Jews in Germany?"

"Look, Topsky. Sorry, I mean Bess, I just wanted to help. I wasn't trying to hurt your feelings."

Bess opened her eyes wide. She had never heard Mary D apologize to anyone.

Just then, Mrs. Satterwhite, who was directing the musical, hurried onto the stage, her arms full of scripts. "Places, please!" she said, barely looking at any of the girls. "Here, Mary D, hand out the music, and we'll practice 'My Object All Sublime.' Yesterday you sang this so slowly it sounded like a funeral dirge. Bess, set the pace and don't follow them. Play it as though you were playing for King George."

Bess had to smile at the idea of the king in Atherton's auditorium. As her classmates stepped to their spots, Mrs. Satterwhite set a brisk tempo and Bess began to enjoy the lilting music and the funny lyrics.

Walking out of rehearsal she sang, "My object all sublime/ I shall achieve in time/ to make the punishment fit the crime/the punishment fit the crime." Bess wanted to catch up with Naomi who was at her social service meeting. Thank goodness she spied her friend in the hallway. They hadn't walked home together for a week or so. Bess needed to talk.

"Hello, Bess. You look happier than I've seen you in ages."

"Well, rehearsal went great and would you believe Mary D actually called me by my real name."

"No fooling? What a snob."

"Isn't that just the truth. And she said that Mrs. Satterwhite chose me to accompany the operetta because she pitied me and my 'people.'"

"Well, I never. I hope you gave her a piece of your mind. But enough about Mary D. I have something important to tell you. I got a letter from Walter this morning. Has he written to you?"

"Yes," Bess said. "It's so exciting. He's coming to Louisville to take lessons from Mr. Parmer. The Parmer's offered to let him stay with them. Sounds like he's doing better."

Just before the Jewish New Year, Walter had written to say that his sister had died of TB in Berlin the year before. Bess had stayed for the memorial service at the end of Atonement Day to pray for Charlotte even though Bubby warned her she shouldn't. It would tempt the evil eye for a young girl to go to a service for the dead.

"Yes," Naomi said, "And it will be wonderful to finally meet him."

As the girls rounded the corner onto Broadway, Bess saw the dark shape of her landlord at the shop door.

"Naomi, I have to go," Bess said, and she shot off running.

When she reached the shop door, the landlord was pushing the doorbell repeatedly.

"Hello, Mr. Schuster. It's nice to see you again. Is there something I can help you with? My mother is just home from the hospital, so she may be in bed and not able to answer the door." Bess hoped to inspire some compassion for her family.

"I need to talk to your father."

Bess led him around to the back, perspiring as they walked up the stairs. She paused at the kitchen door.

"If it's about the rent, I can bring it in just a few days as soon as Poppa gets paid for an important job. It's almost finished."

Mr. Schuster didn't answer her. Bess opened the door, and the landlord barged into the kitchen. Momma was in Bubby's chair rocking the baby. She greeted Mr. Schuster and invited him to sit down, but he remained standing, stiff as a statue. Toby started to cry, and Momma told Bess to get Poppa.

Poppa shuffled into the kitchen and greeted the landlord. "A good year, Mr. Schuster. How nice to see you."

"Gut yor," Schuster said, clearing his throat. "Mr. Toplansky, I am here with bad news."

"I'll have the whole payment, this month and last, in just a few days. You know we always pay."

"Yes, I know, but I have someone who wants your shop space as well as the apartment, and they are willing to pay a big increase, so you see, I have no choice in the matter. You must vacate by the end of October."

"But we've been good tenants, taken such good care of this place. Nine years we've lived here. Now? With the baby? Surely, we could make some arrangement. I can take on more clients, wealthier clients."

"It isn't possible. I'm sorry," Schuster said.

His tone was so final that Bess heard a soft cry escape from her mother's throat.

"Now, if it'll make it easier, you don't have to pay any more rent. I'll keep your deposit, and we'll call it even." With that, the landlord let himself out.

That night Bess listened to her parents talking in bed about how they would get by. Poppa kept saying maybe he would get better, and Momma kept saying he would get worse.

"What are we going to do?" Momma asked. "We can't count on Jackson forever."

"Yes, but you can do alterations."

"There's not enough money in alterations, Sol."

"If we sell the machines, it could tide us over for a while."

"Yes, but where will we live?"

"We'll find a place."

"You're a fool if you think we can find a place we can afford that's big enough for us all."

Bess pulled the blanket over her head and tried not to cry. What she had feared for months was real. They had to leave. She hoped Mr. Schuster wouldn't post an eviction notice on the shop door. The shame would be unbearable.

On Wednesday, the third day of Sukkoth, Bess went back to school and had her worst day ever. When she saw a C- on her makeup test, she ran out of Algebra class in tears. Mrs. Satterwhite scolded her when she lost her place in *The Mikado* for the third time. After rehearsal, Bess hurried home without waiting for Naomi. She couldn't bear to tell anyone the news of their eviction. Why were they having the Habermanns come eat in the sukkah, and why had she invited Phyllis? It would be hotter than Hades.

When she got home, Annabelle was leaving. She shook her head and said, "That baby is a pretty little thing, but can she ever howl."

Bess nodded in agreement.

"I done finished frying the latkes. Alls y'all need to do is heat them up in the oven. And your momma wants y'all to finish decorating the sukkah."

"Oh, all right." Bess had thought maybe her parents would cancel the dinner, but of course, they would never take back an invitation.

In the toolshed she found the box marked "Sukkoth" and the oilcloth with the cornucopia design and all the familiar decorations. She unfolded the cloth and put it on the long table and was about to get up on a chair to hang the paper chains and the banners when her neighbor Naomi walked in carrying a basket of fruit in one arm and a bunch of golden mums in the other.

"Hey, I waited to walk home with you and then Phyllis said she thought she saw you leave."

"I wanted to get home fast and finish up the preparations."

"Well, I thought you could use some help getting ready for the Habermann invasion!" Naomi laughed. "It's exciting to eat in the sukkah, just like the Israelites. Hey, you don't look so good. Is everything okay?"

"I'm fine. Just maybe tired."

"Well, there are plenty of chairs here, so sit for a minute." Naomi sat down and pulled Bess to sit next to her.

The minute Bess sat down, she told Naomi about algebra and about the awful rehearsal.

"Is that what's eatin' you? Bess, really?"

Bess broke into tears and blurted out that they had lost the apartment and the store, and she was pretty sure they were moving to be with Poppa's brother in Indianapolis.

"What? You can't move!"

Naomi put her arms around Bess and let her have her cry.

Everyone but Phyllis, who was always late, gathered in the sukkah at six. Bubby Adel, the five Toplanskys, and five Habermanns (one son was at the seminary and one was in the army). They lit the festival candles and did all the special rituals for the harvest feast. Pastor Habermann had to have a full explanation for the long shaft of palm and the willow and myrtle branches that Poppa gave him. Poppa showed him how to hold the branches in one hand and the special lemony fruit called the etrog in the other and wave them all in the cardinal directions.

Pastor had so many questions and Poppa answered them patiently while Calvin tried to get Johnny to protest with him. Bubby said, "Sha!" and Pastor gave them a dirty look and the explanations continued. Pastor said the symbolism of the precariousness of human dwellings was a fitting theme for the times. There were still so many across the nation living in those wretched Hoovervilles. His next sermon would be about the Jews dwelling in tents in the desert for forty years.

Finally, the meal was served, and the platters of potato pancakes with sour cream and applesauce were a hit as usual. Bess set aside a plate of latkes for Phyllis because she knew she'd show up eventually.

After the meal, they sang the long grace in Hebrew and then translated it. Pastor Habermann said he would like to say a few words. Momma looked a little worried but said, "Yes, of course, please, Pastor."

"May the Lord bless our good neighbors and keep them strong and healthy, and may they reap the bounty of all their hard work, even as we are reaping the harvest in this glorious season of the year. And as we look up to the sky, may we be grateful for the Lord's creation. . ."

"Amen!" Clara Habermann interjected. Pastor looked surprised at the interruption, but he and everyone else said, "Amen."

It was quiet for a minute and then Naomi asked them to sing their festival songs. Calvin said, "Let's sing American songs."

"How about America the Beautiful?" Bess offered. The Habermanns were used to singing close harmony—Naomi's older sister Ruth had a strong soprano voice—and Bess and her father followed their lead. Afterwards, Carl Habermann said that they should be going home as tomorrow was a workday.

"Vell, first I have some news." Poppa tried to stand up and Momma whispered, "Not now, Sol." Bess felt the latkes churning in her gut as Poppa rose. "I want to thank such good neighbors. We have lived side by side for nine years, and so we are sad to say that we are going to be moving away for a while. My brother needs our help, and so we are going to Indianapolis to help him with his business."

Bubby Adel slammed her fist on the table and stood up. "Ich vell nisht furren avek," she exclaimed. Then she turned and hobbled up the stairs.

Pastor and Mrs. Habermann were stunned.

Naomi whispered to Bess, "What did your grandmother say?"

"She said she's not leaving here."

"Oh," said Naomi not knowing what else to say. No one in the entire gathering, it seemed, had anything to say.

"Hey, sorry I'm late! Why's everyone so quiet?" Phyllis said, poking her head into the sukkah. "My goodness, look at the hair on the baby. She's a beauty. Can I hold her?"

Momma said, "I'll just take her up and change her and then you could hold her."

"Well, your timing is perfect, Phyllie. I saved you some latkes," Bess said.

"We should be getting home," Clara Habermann motioned to her girls to get up from the table. "Come, Naomi let's help clean up."

"No," said Poppa, "sit down and we'll enjoy the nice evening a little more. Phyllis come sit down by me," he motioned to the seat Momma had vacated.

"Have some lemonade or some mead what we make special." Sol pointed to a bottle of honey wine and motioned for Bess to pour it for everyone.

"We have so much to be grateful for. Our beautiful children, our good friends. I would like to thank you for being our guests tonight." Poppa rose slowly and raised a little glass of mead to the Habermanns and to Phyllis and said, "L'chaim."

Chapter 29
Into The Wilderness

"Sol, you talk to her. Maybe to you she would listen. My mother is stubborn like an ox." Mollie's dark eyes emitted anger and frustration. Toby started to wail, so Mollie snatched her out of the bassinet and took her into their bedroom.

Sol took a deep breath and walked over to Mother Adel's alcove. She had drawn the curtain, and although it was morning, he heard the squeak of her pulling down her Murphy bed.

The old woman was stubborn, but so was her daughter, and he saw he had no choice but to do as she asked. Sol went back to the kitchen and put a kettle of water on and planned his strategy. The cup rattled wildly as he set it on the table. His tremor was always worse when he was under stress. He looked in the back of the pantry for some jam. No jam. In the breadbox, thanks goodness, there was a soft roll, and if there would be butter in the icebox, it would be perfect. That would butter her up.

"Mother Adel," Sol said outside her curtain. "I would like to speak with you. May I come in?"

"Why not?"

Sol drew the curtain and found his mother-in-law lying in bed with her black shawl over her eyes.

"Mother Adel, what's wrong? Why are you going back to bed?"

"Tsss. It's not to sleep. I am praying to God to take me already. For me it's the end."

"But why? You are not so old."

Sol stood there and waited for Adel to answer, but she did not. "You didn't eat any breakfast, and you barely ate anything last night in the sukkah."

Silence.

"Maybe you would have a glezel tea with a nice roll and butter."

Silence.

"Mother Adel, please, let me help you get up."

Adel didn't speak, but she rolled over and sat on the edge of the bed.

"May I?" Sol extended his hand.

"The cripple helps the dying woman," Adel muttered.

Sol ignored her words and led her out to the kitchen.

"Please have a seat, and I'll pour your tea."

"No, you would spill it." She pushed him aside with a vigor that belied her claim to be on her deathbed and poured her tea. Then with a groan, she sank into a chair. "Oy vey," she groaned again.

If this were not so serious, Sol thought, it would be comical.

Seeing the roll Sol had put on the table, Adel shrugged. "Why not? One last meal? Sol, be so good as to pass me the butter."

Sol sat down next to Adel and leaned close to her. "Mother Adel, you love your Malke, no? Then why won't you go with us to my brother's family?"

"Live with a stranger? Take his charity? Never."

"But Mother, Abe is not a stranger. You know him. He comes with his family every year for the High Holidays and Pesach. And it's not charity. My brother, danken Got, has a successful business where Bess and Malke would work."

"I know all about his fancy restaurant."

"What do you mean?"

"Mrs. Waldman told me all about it. A shame for the goyim. He opens on the Sabbath."

Sol was beginning to understand.

"Yes, to earn a living, but he buys only Kosher meat. He serves no dairy."

"But now my daughter and granddaughter will work on the Sabbath."

"No, this they will not do. Abe promised they'll have Saturdays off."

"But would he have a rabbi to watch over it all? No. No rabbi would give his approval to a restaurant what opens on Shabbos."

"But their home is kosher. Completely kosher. And he closes for the High Holidays and Passover."

"Naturally, why would his wife want to clean and change dishes if she can come here?"

"Oh, Mother, you know Hettie is a ballabuste. I promise you the home is kosher."

Adel pulled a cube of sugar from her pocket and sipped on her glass of tea, the cube between her two front teeth. The soft roll was gone.

"Mother, I beg of you. We wouldn't travel without you."

"Gut, then don't travel."

"No, we have to. I know you think I'm a nogoodnik gambler, but. . ."

"No, Sol, I know you are a hard worker."

Mother Adel had never said that before.

"And it's good mine Malke married you and not that thief from Pinsk."

"Mother, thank you, but here's the truth. We need you in Indianapolis. We need you to make sure Toby is well taken care of while Mollie and Bessele work."

"That you could do."

"But not if I am working with Bar Mitzvah boys."

"So, you'll have a job?"

"Yes, thanks God. Now tell me, who rocks Toviah better than you? Who can help Bessele with her math? Who watches over that teivel Calman? Who makes the best holiday cakes?"

Adel got up to clear the dishes.

"All right, may God grant me the strength to live another year even in such a God forsaken wilderness."

Chapter 30
Exodus

SUNDAY, OCTOBER 3, 1937

Sol stood on the sidewalk trying to light a cigarette to no avail. Oh well, he probably shouldn't smoke anyway. The morning air was crisp and the sky was clear. There was very little traffic on Broadway. Everything upstairs was in a tumult, and he was just in the way, so he had come down to the shop one last time. He looked at the sign in the window, "Sol Toplansky, Tailor," and remembered how proud he had been to bring his bride and his kinder to this spot. A few churchgoers walked by. The men doffed their hats. A Mr. Eberhard stopped to shake his hand. "You see, I'm still wearing this." Eberhard touched the lapel of his gray tweed suit. "Well, safe travels, Sol. Best of luck." A good customer, he had been. Trim and easy to fit.

Sol put the cigarette in his pocket and walked into the store. The wooden cabinets and linoleum floor sparkled. They were all that was left of the business he and Mollie had built. Maishe Yoffe had bought all of his equipment and furniture. He knew their situation but didn't take advantage. He paid a good price, before even the goods were delivered. Such a friend his landsman was. Sol shook his head. How he would miss Maishe. He would miss Jackson standing over the steaming iron telling jokes and Mollie greeting the customers with a big smile. He missed that smile too. Since the eviction, she hadn't found anything to smile about. He closed the blinds and locked the front door.

As he approached the door to the apartment, he could hear Adel scolding everyone. "Hurry up and finish," she said over and over. That had been her motto all week as they sold off or gave away their things. "In a hurry and on one foot." She said that was how the Jews had eaten and prepared to leave Egypt. Sure enough, his family was standing at the kitchen counter and finishing their breakfast.

Sol reached for the baby, but Mollie shooed him off. "You haven't eaten a thing. Es epes."

"I'm not so hungry."

"Well, it's a long train trip, so you better eat anyway," Momma Adel said.

Annabelle walked in and looked around. "My my, this place looks strange. I guess there's nothing left for me to do."

"You could wash up and take these last things to Mrs. Habermann."

"Yes ma'am. And I'll stay here until my brother comes and gets Bessie Lee's piano."

"And make sure they don't scratch the walls."

"Yes, ma'am. Of course, y'all know I will. Y'all look like you going to a funeral. Bessie Lee you should play something."

Bess shook her head no.

Calvin said, "Annabelle's right. Play 'Get Happy.'"

"No, then we'll have that stupid song in our heads all the way to Indianapolis."

"What would be so bad about that?" Sol asked as he took Bess's arm and led her to the parlor.

"But all my music is boxed up."

"Enough! You know it by heart, so play already," Poppa said.

The little gilded piano that had enlivened so many gatherings stood alone in the parlor. Momma with the baby in her arms sat on the bench with Bess while Poppa and Calvin leaned into the piano and sang, "Forget your troubles, come on get happy. We're gonna chase all the blues away." The music echoed off the walls of the empty room.

By the time they got to "We're heading 'cross the river..." Minnie, Sam, and the kids arrived. Dotty stood behind Bess and belted out the chorus.

"No more singing. The train leaves soon," Momma Adel said.

"Momma, it doesn't leave for an hour." Mollie objected.

"But we need to pack the car."

"With what?" Calvin said. "We ain't got nothing left."

It was true. All they had were their valises and the lunch that Annabelle had fixed. They had so little, Sol thought with regret, but he could hold his head up high. They had paid all their bills and given money to the shul.

As they walked out to Sam's car, Bess stopped under the arbor and said, "Bubby, you missed a bunch." Adel opened her basket, so Bess could put the grapes inside. Calvin and Joe took charge of packing the trunk. Sol heard rapping on a window and looked up to see Miss Dodge waving to them. "Bess, your friend is saying goodbye. Wave to her. And look, here come the Habermanns."

"Well, neighbors, we came to say our goodbyes." Pastor Habermann, Clara, and Naomi were dressed in their Sunday finery. The pastor and Sol shook hands and Clara gave Calvin and Mollie a hug and a kiss. Naomi and Bess hugged tightly.

"Enough! We're going to be late," Adel ordered. "Let's go already." Annabelle was wiping her eyes with a handkerchief Mollie had made for her. She took the baby so Mollie could get in the car.

"Before you leave, might I say a blessing?" Pastor asked.

"Why not, if you please," Sol answered. He noticed the scowl on his mother-in-law's face. The blessing was cut short by Clara's amen, and Sol chuckled to himself that she was ending it before her husband could invoke the name of Jesus. Sam gave the word that they should get going. Dotty and Joe insisted on going to the station even though they would all be piled in together. They rolled down the windows and yelled goodbyes to their neighbors and Annabelle.

At the station Bess's friend Phyllis was waiting for them.

"Hey, you are early!" Bess said.

"I didn't want to miss you." She gave Bess a present. "It's just like my blue cashmere you like so much. It will be cold up North."

"Here's stationery and a whole sheet of stamps. You have to write me!" Bess said and then hugged her girlfriend.

"All aboard for New Albany and Indianapolis." There was a long whistle.

Sol and his family boarded. They found their seats. Sol sat with Mollie, the baby, and Calvin. Bubby and Bess sat facing them.

Adel had her goose feather pillow and basket on her lap. She refused to store them above in the rack. There was a scowl on her face.

"What wrong, Mother Adel?"

"Why did you let the priest say a blessing? That can't be a good thing."

"I don't think God would care who blesses our coming and going."

The train rolled out and Bess closed her eyes. She had always been afraid of the train bridge across the Ohio River. It was so high. What could you do? The girl was a worrier like her mother. Toviah, thanks God, was quiet, so Mollie sat back and took a deep breath.

"Where do you think you are going?" Sol grabbed Calvin's pants leg before he could run off. "Sit down and watch out the window."

As they gathered speed, Sol stared at the big Palmolive Clock on the Indiana side. Would he ever see the Ohio River again? Such a big river. And so calm today. A barge and a tugboat passed below. A few birds swooped for fish. So many family picnics and canoeing with friends. Such refreshing cold water when the heat of Louisville got unbearable. But also a plague. Less than a year ago, its muddy waters had submerged the city and destroyed so much. Sol thought of the water rushing up Broadway. Then he shook it off. They had survived the worst.

"Bess, you could open your eyes. We're over the river."

Part Five:

Indianapolis

Chapter 31
Green Street

OCTOBER 3, 1937, INDIANAPOLIS

As the train pulled in, Bess saw the family waiting on the platform. Cousin Pinkie trotted around Uncle Abe and Aunt Hettie waving with both arms. Poor Aunt and Uncle with such a wild fourteen-year-old. But where was Sarah? As they got off, Abe grabbed Poppa and hugged him as if he hadn't seen his brother in years. Aunt Hettie and Momma kissed and cried, and Pinkie crashed into Calvin's arms. "Calvin, Calvin," he yelled, "I gotta a new popgun."

"Oh, Bess, it's so good to have you here. Sarah had to help her girlfriend with homework, but she'll see you at home later," said Aunt Hettie as she gave her niece a hug and a kiss. Aunt Hettie made over the baby, cootchy cooing. "Here let me hold her. Such dark hair and eyes you have. Just like your mama. Oh, what a beauty."

Bubby disapproved of such fussing and spit on her forefinger to keep evil spirits away. Calvin and Uncle Abe stashed the bags in the Studebaker's trunk and off they went.

It was a short drive from the station to Green Street. Her aunt and uncle's dark brick house was, in Bess's opinion, the nicest one on the block. She remembered the swing on the front porch from their visit when she eight. One night she and Sarah had stayed up all night swinging and then sat on the lawn to watch the stars. The house sat across from a city park with miles of shady parkways. And directly in front of her aunt and uncle's house was a playground.

As Uncle Abe pulled into the garage, he said, "Welcome home."

They entered through the kitchen. Bess took Poppa's arm to help him up the three stairs that led to the kitchen. Everything was shiny and new. The sun poured in through starched white curtains. Calvin and Pinkie ran off to play, but the rest of the family followed Uncle Abe to the study that had been converted into a bedroom for Momma and Poppa.

"This room will be perfect for you two lovebirds. There are no stairs to climb. And you have a big bathroom right next door."

They walked Bubby up to the third floor and showed her a low-ceilinged room that had dormer windows on all sides of the house.

"We put in a washstand, so you could clean up without going downstairs."

Bubby didn't say a word. She just hung her hat on a hook, went to the front window, raised it, and said a prayer.

Down on the second floor there were three bedrooms and a big bathroom. Calvin would sleep with Pinkie in his room. Bess noted that there were bars on the window. Calvin wouldn't be slipping out on the roof anymore. Sarah's rooms had twin beds covered in pink satin bedspreads, a dressing table with a matching satin skirt, a dresser, and a desk. Aunt Hettie opened the closet and said, "See, Sarah made room for your clothes." Sarah's clothes hung according to color and season. Bess was embarrassed at how little room she'd need. "Well, I'll let you unpack," her aunt said and left.

Bess had always admired her cousin's bedroom. The satin bedspreads and matching drapes, the dressing table loaded with fine toiletries, the big closet and chest of drawers. She pushed aside the drapes and saw Sarah getting out of a car. Her cousin looked like a girl from a fashion magazine.

"Hello, Cuz," Sarah shouted as she walked in. She hugged Bess and said, "Hope you like your new room."

"You know I do, and thanks for making room for my stuff."

"Ab-so-lute-ly my pleasure," Sarah said with a wink. "We're going to have a nifty time."

Sarah helped Bess put her things away. "Oh, this is keen," Sarah said admiring the blue sweater from Phyllis.

"You can borrow it any time," Bess said.

"Oh, same with anything in my closet," Sarah answered. She showed Bess her collection of ceramic mice and a stack of records with all the latest hits. "The victrola is in the parlor, but I keep my platters here, so Pinkie doesn't ruin them." Arm in arm they went downstairs to see what was for dinner.

"It's just cold cuts," Aunt Hettie said apologetically. Calvin's eyes were fixed on a tray piled high with salami, pastrami, and corned beef and a double loaf of rye bread. Bubby whispered something to Momma, probably to check if the food was kosher. Momma shook her head yes emphatically. Bubby looked astonished that no one said a prayer before the meal, but she mumbled her blessing and pushed the food around on her plate.

After dinner, Bubby retired to the attic, and the rest of the family gathered in the parlor to listen to the radio. "See, there's space here for your piano," Uncle Abe said. "We look forward to hearing you play. No one plays 'Malagueña' like my niece." Bess blushed with pride.

 After the radio show ended, Aunt Hettie asked if Sarah had finished her homework. "And tomorrow, you'll show Bess around the school and introduce her to all your friends." The girls kissed all the adults goodnight and went up to bed.

As they put on their pajamas, Bess said, "Lucky you, to have a room all to yourself. Well, I guess now you don't." She giggled.

Sarah was quiet and then she said, "Well, I'd better get in my hundred strokes." Sarah sat down at her dressing table and began to brush her long wavy brown hair. "Do you want to borrow my curlers?"

"No, I have my own," Bess said as she stood behind Sarah and peered into the mirror to wind locks of her hair around rags. Then she pinned each curl hoping it would stay in all night.

"So, tomorrow I'll show you the ropes at Ben Frankin High. You'll love my friends," said Sarah climbing into bed.

As they lay in the dark, Sarah named and described the kids in her group, Bess didn't know how she'd remember them all. At Atherton she had Phyllie and Naomi and a few girls from music class. And Sarah seemed to know an awful lot of boys, and to hear her tell it, she had gone out with lots of them.

"Gee, I don't know if I can get used to going to school with boys," said Bess.

"The boys are swell. This boy Milton is dying to meet you. And Ted is a real pal. Jimmy K is a dreamboat. Tall, wavy blond hair. He gave Sophie Schreiber his football sweater, but she just up and left two weeks ago to go to school up north. Her parents have always thought they were too good for Indianapolis. Anyway, Jimmy has been awfully friendly at lunch. I think he's going to ask me on a date any day now. My parents don't like him, so don't let on that I do."

"Okay, I promise I won't. Well, I guess we should get some shut eye."

"Mmm. Nighty night, Cuz."

Sarah fell asleep immediately, but Bess lay there and worried about the new school.

Chapter 32
New Girl

The smells were different. Instead of Cashmere Bouquet and Coty's powder, there were men's hair pomade and a tangy smell like Calvin's before he showered. Bunches of boys clogged up the halls. The girls walked in twos and threes. Giggles, hoots of laughter, friends yelling out to friends. Students did not yell at Atherton. Miss Woerner would not put up with such behavior. What a maze! If Sarah hadn't taken her to the office, Bess would never have found it.

Bess waited on a wooden bench and watched the clock in the office tick away the seconds, then minutes. It was almost as if she had become invisible. She sure felt that way. At last, the secretary spoke. "Miss Toplansky, Dean Hearst will see you now." The secretary rose and opened the door marked Dean of Students.

Bess handed her records to the stern-looking woman seated at her desk.

"Have a seat Miss, um, Bess."

Dean Hearst dwarfed her office. Bess thought she might be taller than most men and just about as wide. Her gray scruffy eyebrows were knit into a tight frown. Bess held her breath as the dean opened her file and put on her glasses.

"Usually, we get some advanced notice so we can organize student schedules optimally."

"Oh, so sorry. We left quickly. I mean our family needed us here." Bess had told that story so many times that she almost believed it.

"Well, we shall try to place you so that you won't be overwhelmed. You are, after all, transferring from Kentucky."

That stung. Did they think everyone from Kentucky was a fool?

After a long silence, the dean opened her eyes wide and looked at Bess for the first time.

"I see now, you are ahead on state requirements, so this should not be difficult. You did well in Biology I, so I could put you in Anatomy, but they dissect animals, and so many of our girls faint at the sight of blood. What's more, there are only two other girls in the class. And as you have been in an all-girls school, I don't know if this would be appropriate."

"I don't faint. And I'm used to boys." Bess had seen enough blood to know she wouldn't faint, but she lied about being used to boys other than Calvin and her cousins. There was Walter of course, but he was such a gentleman— not a boy.

The dean continued shuffling through the file as though Bess had not spoken. "I see you have had lots of music courses, even piano theory. Miss Dunlap will be thrilled to meet you." As she scrawled out a note, the Dean read aloud. "Secretarial Education, Algebra II, Choral Music, American Literature, and Anatomy. That sounds right." She glanced at her watch. "You've already missed most of Secretarial Ed, so you'll go straight to Algebra." Dean Hearst pressed a buzzer and the secretary walked in.

"Betty, write up a copy of this schedule with the room numbers and show Miss, um, Bess, where to go. Best of luck to you, Bess."

"Oh my, you must be very smart," the secretary said as she led Bess to the second floor. "Algebra II. And we don't get many girls in Anatomy. Even the boys are kind of afraid of Miss Jacobson, but she's really a good egg. You'll learn a lot if you can tolerate cutting open the lab specimens. That wouldn't be for me. I don't even like to touch raw chicken. And Mr. Forest, your math teacher, can be a tough nut, but only if you step out of line. Here we go. Sit here, and when the bell rings you go in and hand him this sheet."

While Bess waited, a couple of stray boys met up and went into the lavatory. As they walked by returning to class, she could smell tobacco. Both boys took a long hard look at her, and then they mumbled something and laughed. Bess could feel herself turning crimson. When the bell rang, Bess stood. She was almost knocked over by the kids exiting the math teacher's room. The halls were suddenly flooded with bodies and laughter. When she entered the classroom, Mr. Forest was putting equations on the board. Her classmates entered by twos and threes, brushing past Bess as if she were not even there.

When the bell rang, the room got silent, and Mr. Forest began to take attendance. Then he noticed Bess, who still stood near the door, her schedule in hand.

"Oh, you are new. What is your name?"

The class laughed.

"I am Bess Toplansky." Bess handed him her schedule.

"Ladies and gentlemen, please welcome, Miss Bess Topolsky. Topolsky, find an empty seat. We are working on graphing equations. Berger, share your book with Topolsky."

Bess tried hard to keep up with the lesson. She understood some of the basics, but a lot of it was over her head. She felt that everyone was staring at her and prayed Mr. Forest would not call on her. She had never felt so self-conscious. When the bell rang at last, she asked Berger, the girl who had shared her book, where the music room was.

"I'm going right by there," she said. "Come on. My name is Melissa, by the way. I don't know why he uses our last names. He acts like we're in the Army."

At the music room, Bess thanked Melissa and said hopefully, "See you tomorrow?" She had a feeling it was going to be hard to make friends in this school, but Melissa Berger had been nice.

A familiar Broadway song drew Bess inside, where students were already up on the risers. Bess stood behind the teacher at the piano as she directed students. When the boys weren't singing their part, they combed their hair, joked around, and stared at Bess. When the girls weren't singing, they stared at the boys and whispered. When they all sang together it sounded awful. The teacher was a terrific pianist, but she had no control of her students.

After the song ended, a pimply-faced boy in the top row raised his hand and told their frazzled teacher about Bess.

"Oh dear me," Miss Dunlap said. "Welcome." She held out her hand, and

Bess gave the teacher her schedule. "Just find a spot to blend in there, in the front row, for now, and meet me after class."

The next number sounded more professional, and Bess thought she might enjoy this class after all. When they started on "Puttin' on the Ritz," Bess smiled. This one she knew inside out. Before long, the bell rang, and Bess met her teacher by the piano.

"Well now, Bess, isn't it? Have you ever sung in a chorus before?"

Bess explained that she had been in chorus since junior year, but her skill was as a pianist. "At my previous school, I accompanied the school operetta."

"That is the best news I've had all day. You're officially enlisted. Can you come to rehearsal this afternoon at three? We're getting our review ready for Homecoming."

"I'm so sorry. I can't come today." If Bess didn't walk home with Sarah, she would never remember how to get back. "I could play tomorrow, but after this week I'll be working after school."

"I'd be grateful for any help I can get. Oh, there's the bell. You're late for your next class."

"Actually, I have lunch."

"And I have to monitor the cafeteria, so I'll walk you there. "

The din of the cafeteria surprised Bess. It was so crowded, nothing like their dining room at Atherton. She craned her neck to search for Sarah. Finally, she saw her cousin at a big table near the windows surrounded by a knot of kids.

"Hey, look who finally showed up," Sarah said, scooting to make room on the end for Bess. "Everybody, this is my cousin Bess from Louisville. You know—Kentucky." Sarah chuckled and gave Bess a shrug as if to say, I'm only teasing.

Bess sat down and put her lunch bag on the table. Sarah introduced her to three girls, one was Jeannette, and two boys. Then there was a Goldberg, a Cohen, a Zarinsky, a Waldman. So many Jewish names. More than in all of Atherton's student body. Bess's head was ringing with the noise, the names, and new faces. A boy named Milton nodded to her, and another named Ted smiled and asked how she liked Old Ben. Jeannette asked if she had a horse but didn't wait to hear her answer.

Bess felt as though she was no longer there. Jeannette started teasing Sarah about swooning over Jimmy. Everyone joined in at once. Everyone but Milton, who sat across from Bess. He ate slowly but not elegantly, like Walter. His face wore a constant gloomy look. When a guy in a football jacket dropped by the table, everyone stopped talking. Sarah looked up at him and smiled. Then he tousled her hair. When he walked away, Jeannette and the other girls chanted, "Jimmy and Sarah sitting in a tree." Bess hadn't heard that silly rhyme since she was a child skipping rope in her backyard. So that was the famous Jimmy. Sarah was right. He was dreamy.

"Hey," Ted said, "I'll take that if you don't want it." Bess realized she hadn't touched the salami sandwich Aunt Hettie had packed her.

"You pig. You just finished mine," Sarah said. Bess smiled and handed him half, then took a big bite out of the other half. The bell rang before she could finish it. She wrapped it back in the waxed paper and put it in her bag so she could finish it after school.

Sarah whispered, "You can throw it away. We'll have snacks when we get home."

Bess tried not to show how embarrassed she felt. "Where should I meet you after school?" she asked. Sarah told her to wait at the front entrance. "And how do I get to the next class?" Bess didn't even remember what it was, so she showed her schedule to Sarah.

"You are not taking Anatomy? You will stink to high heaven. I mean carrying around your salami sandwich is bad enough, but dissecting dead animals? Honestly, Bess, are you trying to keep people away?"

Bess bit her lip and grabbed her schedule back. "Thanks a bunch." She hurried away into the hall and found her English classroom on her own. The teacher introduced Bess to the class and gave her a copy of the Emerson poem they were studying. Bess was still fuming about her cousin's mean remark when the teacher asked her if she knew what "the shot heard round the world" referred to. Bess actually did know, but she was caught unawares and couldn't get the answer out fast enough.

"Well, please don't be dreaming in my class, Miss Toplansky."

It was bad enough to be the new girl, being stared at all day, but to be called out like that was so humiliating, and after her teacher's cold remarks, Bess did not hear another word. When the bell rang, she ran out of class and headed for the third floor. By now, she knew where the stairwells were and how the rooms were numbered.

Her nose led her to her science classroom. It smelled like formaldehyde. The students, seated in groups at high tables, were so busy assembling their lab equipment no one noticed Bess in the doorway. Miss Jacobson brushed past her in a hurry and then turned and asked, "And who might you be?"

"I'm Bess Toplansky," Bess said. She handed Miss Jacobson her schedule. The teacher was just about Bess's height and very compact, like Momma. Her brownish-gray hair was pulled up into a lopsided bun.

"All right, Bess Toplansky. Let's put you with Anna and Katherine. They'll show you the ropes."

Anna and Katherine said polite hellos but didn't seem pleased to have a third partner. They showed Bess where to find gloves and explained what each tool was for. Then they proceeded to dissect a muscle. They showed her how it looked under the microscope. It was red and striped with white lines. It looked amazing.

"All right, move over now," Anna said. "We have a lab report to write."

Katherine added, "Girls are lucky to get into this class, so don't make us look bad."

After class, Miss Jacobson drew Bess aside and asked her if she thought she could handle the work. "This is an advanced class, you know," she said.

"Oh, yes, ma'am. It looks fascinating."

"Hmmm. All right. We shall see how it goes." Miss Jacobson gave Bess the textbook and an outline of the course. "We've already covered chapters one and two. There is a test in two weeks, but I can help you catch up after school if you need."

"Thanks, but I am sure I can catch up on my own."

Out in the hallway, Bess found her way to the bathroom. She hadn't gone all day. At the mirror, she stared at her face, flushed and sweaty. Her sandy hair had lost all the curls she had patiently put in with the rag curlers. Her head was spinning with all the new people and subjects and places. No one had been kind to her all day. Almost no one. And why hadn't she accepted Miss Jacobson's offer to help her? Bess felt like crying. At least the day was over.

Bess heard a toilet flush and then Melissa, the girl from algebra class, was next to her at the row of sinks. "Hi again, Bess. How is Old Ben treating you so far?"

Bess shrugged her shoulders.

"Yup, it's a lot. I transferred here last year. I'm from Kentucky."

Bess smiled. "I'm from Louisville."

"Well, hoopty do. A big city girl. I'm from Frankfort."

"I took a train there once. It's beautiful."

"Well, Bess, you won't be the new girl for long. I better skedaddle. My sister is waiting to walk home with me. See you in class tomorrow."

Bess felt better having talked to someone. She left the washroom and wandered a bit. At the end of the hall was the library. Sarah was at her home economics club meeting and Bess had to wait. She could use the hour to get started on her homework. Bess introduced herself to the librarian who asked if she could help her find something.

"Oh, no, thanks. I just need to study."

The familiar smell of books and the quiet were just what she needed. Bess opened her anatomy textbook to page one.

Chapter 33
School Days

OCTOBER 5-15, 1937

Bess's second day at Benjamin Franklin High was not much different from her first, but by the end of the week, she no longer felt lost, and she no longer thought everyone was staring at her. If anything, they ignored her. Her Anatomy partners slowly allowed Bess to take part in their labs, and in Algebra, Melissa was a godsend, helping Bess keep up. She'd been a good student at Atherton, and Bess tried hard to keep from "dreaming" in all her classes.

Sarah's lunchtime friends had accepted Bess as part of their group, and she enjoyed listening to their banter. The topic of the moment was the upcoming Harvest Moon Dance to be held at the Jewish Center. While Sarah waited for that football player, Jimmy K, to ask her, Bess realized she didn't want to be Cinderella at home with her old bubby and baby sister. But the only boys that were even possible dates were Ted or that sullen dope Milton, God forbid, who slugged behind them as they walked home each day.

On Friday, after Jeannette and Milton veered off to where they lived on a nearby street, Sarah said, "I think he likes you. Bess and Milton, sitting in a tree..."

Bess shoved her cousin gently in the ribs and walked ahead, moving her little feet faster towards home. She barged in the back door and into the kitchen. Right behind her was Sarah, still giggling. They put their books down on the table and said hello to Miss Violet, the Negro housekeeper, who was burping Toby.

"Now just git them books off my table," she said. The woman was brusk and bossy, but the baby had taken to her. With Toby on her hip, she fixed them a snack of milk and cookies.

"Why does Milton always tag along?" Bess asked. "He gives me the heebie jeebies."

"Well, beggars can't be choosers."

"That's not nice, Sarah."

"You're right. I'm sorry. I'm just so nervous about when Jimmy K will call and ask me to the dance."

Bess nodded. She had seen him in the cafeteria that day, eating with the other football players, but he hadn't stopped by their table. Sarah had felt the snub.

"Oh girls, good, you're home," Aunt Hettie said, bursting through the kitchen door.

She grabbed Bess's elbow. "Come, come, Bess. We have a surprise for you."

In the living room stood Bess's blonde spinet. She felt a rush of happiness as she sat down at her bench. She ran her fingers up and down the keys. It sounded terrible.

Aunt Hettie must have read her mind. "Not to worry, darling. The man is coming to fix it tomorrow. Your father told us it was out of tune."

Poppa walked in and hugged Bess. His hugs were important because sometimes she couldn't tell what he was feeling. Because of his illness, his facial expression almost never changed now. "So, now you can get back to your music." Poppa said.

"Yes," Aunt Hettie said, "and your uncle and I want to pay for your lessons."

"Thanks, Aunt Hettie," Bess said with a smile, but she wasn't so sure she wanted to saddle herself with another burden. She and Poppa had talked about her having an audition for the conservatory in the spring, but she knew how out of practice she had gotten in the last few weeks and the hours it would take to play if she wanted to be competitive. With schoolwork and her job at the restaurant, it would be hard to find time to practice. And yet, the blonde spinet was so dear to her, and having it here felt like a bit of their old life in Louisville had come along with them.

Sabbath at her aunt and uncle's house was quite different from their Friday nights at home. Naturally, Bubby had brought the charity box, so each cousin put in coins given to them by their parents. But they skipped the hand washing ritual, and the prayers were cut short. Her Aunt and Uncle allowed electrical things to be run. Even the record player.

After dinner, Bubby retired to her room. Sarah brought down her records and asked the boys to roll back the rug. She wanted Calvin to practice dancing with her, and he was happy to oblige. Cousin Dotty had taught him and Bess to Lindy Hop and Shag. Pinkie did everything Calvin did, so he grabbed Bess by the arm to dance. They laughed and jumped to the beat. Pinkie flung Bess with glee. Bess felt like she would go flying across the room and knock over one of Aunt Hettie's porcelain lamps.

Then Sarah put on "Dancing Cheek to Cheek." Pinkie grabbed Bess tightly and exclaimed, "Calvin, Bess has a chest like Momma." Bess smacked him on the face, and he smacked her back.

"Whoa," yelled Calvin as he yanked Pinkie away. "You are not allowed to talk that way to my sister, and you better not hit her."

"What's the ruckus?" Uncle Abe asked, rushing in. Momma, Aunt Hettie, and Poppa followed close behind.

"Bess hit me," Pinkie said.

"He was getting fresh with Bess," Sarah said. As much as Calvin could drive her mad, Bess realized how lucky she was to have him.

"That is enough craziness," Aunt Hettie said. She added, looking at Sarah and Bess, "I hope you don't do that dancing where everyone can see your undergarments." Sarah rolled her eyes, and Bess stifled a laugh.

Momma said Bess should play something classical, but Aunt Hettie had another idea. "You know how we love to hear 'Malagueña'. Why don't you play that for us?" Bess could play that piece blindfolded. With the opening chords, she remembered the quizzical look of the judges after she played it in Frankfort. Bess took a bow as the family applauded. Then she played a Chopin waltz. As always, Calvin wanted American songs, so Bess played a few hit songs from the movies. The men sang along. Uncle Abe's deep voice was beautiful, but Poppa's was now thin and wavery.

At 10:30 the adults shooed the kids off to bed. After they turned the lights out, Sarah was very quiet. Bess thought maybe it was because Jimmy K hadn't called to ask her to the dance, but she also suspected Sarah didn't like sharing the limelight. Or could she be jealous of the attention Bess was getting? Sarah had looked hurt when Aunt Hettie mentioned paying for piano lessons. Sarah was not easy to figure out.

On Saturday, Bess walked Bubby to shul. She met a lot of old women who made a fuss over her and said their grandsons would like to meet her. Bess was used to that, but the grandsons never materialized. It was possible she would never have a boyfriend.

After sundown Uncle Abe drove Momma and Bess to his restaurant.

"Well, all right, then, Bess, you would do Monday, Tuesday, Wednesday, and Thursday afternoons. Sunday you would do your schoolwork and have time to practice."

Uncle Abe asked two of the waitresses to show Bess around while he took Momma next door to see the bakery. The waitresses were friendly and patient about showing her the ropes. One of the women gave Bess a pot of coffee and told her to go around and ask the customers if they needed a refill. The customers were all friendly. This might be a decent job after all.

Then she spotted Jimmy K at a table in the corner with a few other football players. She wasn't keen for anyone at school to know she was working at Toppers as a waitress. Oh well, he probably didn't even remember her. But as she passed by his table he looked up and flicked a finger at his forehead and winked. Bess hurried away to the next table and avoided his corner the rest of the night.

When Bess got home, Sarah was in a foul mood. Jeannette had stopped by to wait with Sarah by the phone for Jimmy K's call. Bess decided not to say she'd seen Jimmy K with his buddies. She didn't know why. Maybe because of the wink. If Sarah asked her for details, she couldn't tell her about it. Bess didn't like keeping secrets, but Sarah sometimes took things the wrong way, and Bess didn't want to create even more tension between them.

By the following Friday afternoon Sarah was at her wits end. Rumor was that Jimmy had asked another girl to the dance. Sarah had bought a new lipstick, a new dress, and a matching purse. Ted had been her backup, but now he was taking Jeannette. At Atherton girls often went to the dances without dates. Bess offered that idea, but Sarah rejected it.

"Bess, that just isn't done here. I'm going with Jimmy or I'm not going."

Chapter 34
The Harvest Moon Dance

Saturday, October 16, 1937

Finally, Saturday morning, Jimmy K called and asked Sarah to go to the dance. After shooing Bess away, she tucked herself into the alcove under the stairs and pulled the door as tight as she could without crimping the phone cord. Ten minutes later, she emerged and plunked the phone on the receiver.

Bess had been waiting, dying to hear all about her conversation. What she didn't expect was for Sarah to announce that she would accompany Bess and her grandmother to services. It was the oddest thing. She said not a word about Jimmy.

On the way to shul, Sarah whispered to Bess that she had a plan, and boy was it an earful. "First of all, we are double dating, and you're going with Milton Cohen."

"What? No, I don't want to go with that nincompoop."

"He's really okay when you get to know him. His parents will drive us. They always go to the Jewish Center Saturday nights to play bridge."

"So are they picking Jimmy K up too?"

Sarah grabbed Bess's arm and pulled her close. "Jimmy and I are meeting at the Center. You know Mom and Dad don't approve of him, so don't you go tattling."

"Don't worry. But let's not say any more now. Bubby understands more than she lets on."

After shul, the girls primped. Bess decided to wear her cousin's blue satin dress. Sarah curled their hair with an iron and applied a bit of Calvin's Brill Cream to make their curls stay. Then they sprayed themselves with Emeraude so they wouldn't smell like boys.

The Cohens arrived to pick them up at 8 p.m. Unlike Milton, Mr. and Mrs. Cohen were very talkative. They knew a lot about Bess. They knew that she played piano and that she was a very good student. Sarah didn't utter a word, and Bess knew why. She had the jitters. The Cohens promised to drop them off in front of the Center so that no one would see them arriving with parents. Sarah had requested that.

"Well, kids," said Mrs. Cohen, "shake a leg and have a swinging time but remember, we'll pick you up in front at 10:30."

The auditorium was breathtaking. There were big round globes of light on each table and an enormous golden moon behind an orchestra decked out in tuxedos. They were playing swing. It was like a movie. Still, two and a half hours with Milton. Bess shuddered to herself. If she were in Louisville, she'd be able to count on her friends to get her out of this jam. Her brother would dance with her, or Cousin Joe.

They found their table and got a big hello from Ted and Jeannette. Jimmy K had evidently not arrived yet. A boy who looked familiar came up and asked Sarah to dance, but she turned him down. He shrugged and asked Bess. He was a good dancer. Great rhythm and a light touch on the swinging out and in. Bess hoped they would continue, but as the music ended, he thanked her and walked her back to her table. It was empty except for Milton.

The dance floor was crowded, but now she saw her cousin dancing with the swoonable Mr. Jimmy Koenigsberg. Phew. She didn't know if she could handle Sarah's mood if he hadn't shown up.

"So, where's the rest of the gang?" Bess asked her date.

"Refreshments. I didn't know what you would want."

"Oh, I'd love a soda."

Milton got up and Bess followed him. While they waited in line at the soda bar, Sarah and Jimmy K came up behind them.

Sarah giggled. "Jimmy, this is my cousin."

"Hey, I know you. You're the pretty waitress at Toppers."

"Oh, do you go there? I don't remember seeing you." Bess lied. She had to or her cousin would kill her for not mentioning seeing him.

"Well, the team likes it. Those goys don't know from corned beef and pastrami. You look great in blue, might I say?"

Sarah pulled at him and announced, "I don't want anything to drink. This is my favorite song. Let's dance."

Jimmy looked startled. "Okay doll. Whatever you say. Bess, see you around."

How did he know her name? He certainly was as handsome as any movie star. Bess thought about asking Milton to dance. It would be better than sitting with him at the table all by themselves. If only he would say something. She wouldn't mind if he said something stupid such as, "You have a kissable mouth," like the boy in the Fitzgerald story. When the orchestra took a break, she followed Jeannette to the powder room. She could not bear to sit at the table with stone-faced Milton another minute. Sarah came in beaming. Jimmy's snazzy outfit. His smile. His dancing. She was talking a mile a minute.

"He has a new car, a convertible, and he wants to take me for a spin and then to Shorty's for a bite to eat. Don't wait for me. Well, I mean, not here. If you get home first, just wait on the back porch."

"What? That will be weird. Calvin or somebody will notice." Bess was fed up with Sarah's ideas. "I'm not going to lie for you."

"Then just say Jeannette's parents drove us home. Tell that to the Cohens and to my folks." Sarah waltzed out before Bess could argue.

After the break, Bess walked around the auditorium, but she didn't see Sarah anywhere. In desperation, Bess asked Milton to dance. He agreed, but he was a horrible dancer. He shuffled about awkwardly and his hands were clammy. He was counting the beat to himself, but it was all wrong. It reminded Bess of a violin off-key. When Ted cut in, she was elated. He had a terrific smile, and he really knew his way around the dance floor. When they went back to the table, Milton sat like a statue.

Jeannette returned to their table after dancing with another guy. She introduced Bess but Bess didn't catch his name in all the noise. Then they were off, back to the crowded dance floor. She glanced at her watch. Only nine thirty. How was she going to endure the rest of the evening?

"Do your parents ever get finished with bridge early?" she asked hopefully.

"Not usually."

Bess excused herself and went to the refreshment table. In the line there were a few girls who had come without dates. So, it was done here. They seemed to be having a perfectly good time. Bess had also noticed guys who had come stag, and they'd not been shy about asking different girls to dance. She struck up a conversation with a guy in line behind her named Irv whom she'd met at school. Irv asked if Bess wanted to dance.

Irv was light on his feet. What a time she'd have had if she'd come with Irv instead. They danced a few dances and Bess almost forgot about Milton, until he walked up and said, "Time to go."

It seemed as if Milton couldn't wait to leave. Bess wondered just then if somehow he had been forced into asking her to the dance. He certainly had been miserable the entire time. He pulled Bess along with him outside where his parents were waiting in their car.

"Where is Sarah?" Mrs. Cohen asked.

"Jeannette's parents drove her home."

"Well, I bet you kids would love a bite to eat. How about we go to Toppers? We love your uncle's place."

"Oh, no thank you," Bess said. "I better just get home. My parents would be too worried if I stayed out past eleven." But the truth was, Bess would rather die than be seen anywhere else with Milton. Especially Toppers. When Bess got home, she tiptoed into Momma and Poppa's room to kiss them goodnight.

"Did you and Sarah enjoy yourselves?" Poppa asked.

"Oh yes."

"Well sleep well, Bessele."

Bess tiptoed up the stairs and headed to the bathroom. It was locked. Calvin popped out of his room and said, "She's in there crying. If you have to go bad, better go downstairs."

"Oh, okay," Bess said. As she headed to the downstairs bathroom, Bess wondered what would have her cousin in tears and how she'd gotten home so early.

When Bess opened the bedroom door, the light was off and Sarah was in bed, her blankets pulled up nearly over her head, her body facing the wall. Bess decided to try an upbeat approach.

"So, how was it with the dreamboat?"

Sarah didn't answer.

"Is everything all right?"

Sarah didn't answer.

"Sarah, are you okay? Calvin said he heard you crying."

"Just mind your own business and go to sleep."

Chapter 35
The Parties

MARCH, 1938

By early spring Bess was used to her new routine. Saturday afternoons she took a piano lesson with her aunt and uncle's neighbor. Most Saturday evenings, she sat home with her family and played cards. Calvin had figured out a contraption with clothes pins that held Poppa's cards steady. On Sundays Bess did homework and practiced. She had no household chores like back home in Louisville, so that was a relief. She didn't mind working at Uncle Abe's place because everyone was friendly to her.

Sometimes she went to events at the Jewish Center with her cousin, but when Sarah was invited to parties at her friends' houses, Bess stayed home. That was until she overheard Aunt Hettie giving Sarah an ultimatum: "Either Bess goes with you to the parties, or you stay home."

So, the next weekend Jeannette's parents drove Bess and Sarah to a party out in the country. On the way, Sarah and her friend talked about who would be there and about the feature in the newspaper about the Weissberg's new home. As they drove up a long gravel driveway, Bess saw a house unlike anything she had ever seen. So sleek and modern. Inside the furniture was leather and chrome. Mrs. Weissberg welcomed them warmly and showed them to a room where the coats were kept. Then she led them to a big room that had a dance floor, a baby grand, and an Audiophone that could play eight different records. "You kids have fun," she said and left.

Most of the boys were huddled around the Audiophone, but Irv, Sarah's friend from school, asked Bess to dance. And could he dance. He twirled her so her skirts twirled, and he lifted her for jumps. He was very strong for such a short boy.

"Another one?" he asked when the record ended.

"Sure," Bess said. Before long, they had an audience. Soon, Ted cut in and then other boys asked her to dance. When Bess finally sat down to catch her breath, her cousin came up and whispered, "They just want to dance with you because you are little. They can throw you in the air easily."

Bess knew Sarah was jealous and wanted to hurt her feelings, but for once, Bess enjoyed being little.

Sarah stood up and said, "Why are we playing that record contraption when my cousin can play all the big hits on the piano."

"Yes, Bess can play anything," Jeannette said. Then other kids urged Bess to play.

Bess wasn't eager to be sidelined from the dance floor, but the baby grand was a beauty and she had to admit she was dying to play it. Even the first few notes sounded rich. After her first tune, the crowd applauded wildly. "Encore," a boy she didn't know shouted. Bess had her hands poised to begin when she saw Sarah talking to Jimmy K. When had he arrived? He waved and pulled Sarah to the piano where they nudged their way into the group around the baby grand.

"Hey, cuz, we need some more good tunes," Sarah said.

"Maybe, Bess would like to dance," Jimmy winked at Bess.

"Actually, she prefers to play piano," Sarah said.

Bess wasn't surprised at her cousin's possessiveness. On impulse she played the popular tune "Jealousy," and grinned at her cleverness. When the song ended, Jimmy leaned in to ask "Why not play something with more swing?" He had green eyes and a wide smile. She played "Boogie Woogie Bugle Boy." She ended the song with a flourish.

Then, to her delight, Jimmy Koenigsberg sat down with her on the bench. With two fingers, he plunked out "Chopsticks," a childish song she had known how to play since she was seven. She giggled and acted coy, but why? As Jimmy's long arms reached across her to roll his fists on the bass clef, he brushed her breasts. Her face reddened. When he started banging his fists wildly, Bess motioned him to stop, but he just kept playing. She tried to follow his lead when "Chopsticks" morphed to ragtime. The kids loved it and yelled for more. Jimmy moved to Bess's left and whispered in her ear, "Too Marvelous for Words." She played and he boomed out the lyrics. Bess could smell alcohol on his breath. She saw Sarah standing with her arms folded across her chest.

When Jeannette said she wanted a turn to play piano, Jimmy said "let's dance." Bess was about to say, what about Sarah, when he yanked her out on to the dance floor. It was a swing number, and he knew what he was doing. His strong arms flung her out with flair, and then he reeled her back in and held her so tight she could barely breathe. Bess felt nervous. Everyone was watching them. Then she heard Sarah's voice, loudly requesting a song Bess knew Jeannette couldn't play. Jeannette looked dumbfounded.

"Bess knows it," Sarah said.

"Come on Bess," a boy said. "Don't just stand there. Give us a song!"

After playing the request and then an Andrews Sisters' hit, Bess looked around, but she didn't see Sarah or Jimmy anywhere. She wanted to dance again, but the crowd begged for more. After she played several Tommy Dorsey numbers, Sarah rushed up to the piano and announced that they were leaving. She pushed Bess to the door without saying goodbye to anyone.

Bess was confused. The party was in full swing. "Why are we leaving?" Bess asked as Sarah opened the door of a little sedan and motioned for Bess and Jeannette to get into the back. Irv was driving and Sarah sat up front.

"What's the hurry? I thought your parents would be picking us up," Bess asked Jeannette.

"Nope, I called them to say we had a ride," Jeannette said curtly and turned away from Bess to stare out the window.

They drove back to Uncle Abe's in silence. When Irv pulled up, Sarah jumped out and ran into the house. Bess followed quickly behind her.

That night in bed, Sarah didn't say a word to Bess other than to hiss, "Don't you ever, ever go out with Jimmy Koenigsberg."

"Who said I was interested?" Bess answered, but as she lay there, she was thinking about his green eyes and his dazzling smile and how it had felt when he twirled her around the dance floor.

Chapter 36
Off Limits

The following week, Jimmy K became a regular at Uncle Abe's restaurant. He sat at the counter drinking coffee until closing time. He joked with all the waitresses and left nice tips. He kept offering Bess a ride home. Normally she took the bus, but one night, she called Momma to see if it would be okay for Jimmy to drive her.

"Who is he?" Momma asked.

Bess could sense her mother's hesitancy. "He's a friend of Sarah's."

"Okay, but come straight home."

When her shift ended, Bess went outside to the parking lot and saw Jimmy leaning against a gleaming convertible.

"This is the prettiest car I've ever seen," Bess said.

He grinned, opened the door, bowed, and said, "At your service, ma'am."

As they drove, Bess was grateful that Jimmy kept up a steady banter. For some reason, as talkative as she was, she couldn't think of much to say. And it felt odd to be alone with him in the car. He zipped around corners, and she just laughed and held onto her seat.

When they pulled up to the house, Jimmy asked her to go to the movies with him on Sunday night. That stunned her. She felt her cheeks grow hot and was grateful it was growing dark.

"Yes, I'd love to," she said.

On Sunday night, Sarah burst into the bedroom as Bess was practicing her smile and checking her teeth for lipstick. "I'm telling you, don't you dare go out with him. He's off limits. He's bad."

"Is this the green-eyed monster talking? And might I have a little privacy, please?"

"Well it is my dressing table, and see that you don't touch my makeup," Sarah said, slamming the door.

When Bess went downstairs, her cousin was on the phone talking to Jeannette. As usual, Sarah was tucked into the alcove under the stairs. Bess went into Momma and Poppa's room to say goodbye. They were sitting in their chairs, reading.

"How pretty you look in that dress!" Poppa grinned and motioned for her to twirl around. "You work so hard at Abe's place. It's wonderful that you would go out tonight." Bess gave him a kiss as her mother stood to smooth her bodice and button her top button.

"Such pretty rhinestones," Momma said. "Ach, I remember you standing on stage in this dress with the blue ribbon around your neck. So thin, you've gotten. Too thin. It's not healthy."

"Momma, you always say I'm too heavy, and now I'm too thin."

"Is Sarah going with you?"

"No, but other kids will be there." It wasn't a lie since Bess was sure other kids would be at the picture show, just not with her and Jimmy. She hadn't told her parents she had a date, only that she was walking downtown to meet up for the movie because she still wasn't allowed to be alone with a boy.

"Well, don't be late," Momma said. "And take a sweater."

Bess smiled. "Don't wait up for me. We'll probably go out for shakes after the movie."

Momma's eyes grew wide with alarm. "Milkshakes, Momma," Bess laughed.

On her way to the theater, Bess practiced what she would say to Jimmy. She did not want to be the bump on a log she was when he had driven her home. She imagined him, tall and handsome, standing by the box office under the lights waiting for her, but when she arrived, Jimmy waited in his car out front, the top of his convertible down.

"Hey, there she is," he said. "Get in, and we'll go for a spin."

"What about the movie?"

"It's too nice a night to be indoors."

Bess shrugged, then smiled. She guessed a short drive would be okay. It was fun just being with Jimmy. As she pulled the door shut, Jimmy accelerated so fast that she felt pinned to the seat.

"Where are we going?"

Jimmy didn't answer, so Bess repeated her question.

"I'm gonna show you what this baby can do. It could win the Indy 500."

It was a nice night, clear, and the stars were shining brightly over the country road they were driving on. Bess laughed as they wound around the curves and over hills, and the more she laughed, the faster Jimmy went. Suddenly, he slammed on the brakes so that the car began to spin. She felt her stomach rise.

"Gosh Jimmy. Maybe you oughta slow down."

He laughed. "You think so?"

At a crossroads, Jimmy did a sharp u-turn and headed back toward the city. Before long Bess saw the lights for Shorty's Diner. Sarah's friends raved about the place. Tires screeching, Jimmy parked close to the side door.

"This is a great place for burgers," Jimmy said as he jumped out and opened the door for Bess. "Look, I've left my mark." He pointed with pride to skid marks on the asphalt. Jimmy combed back his hair. In profile, he looked slick and sleek, almost like a panther. Bess felt proud to walk into a teen hangout with him. He pointed to a corner booth, and they slid in, Jimmy sitting closer to her than her family would have.

After they were seated, the waitress rushed over, greeting Jimmy like a regular. Jimmy ordered first. "My usual burger and fries," he said. Bess had never eaten a non-kosher hamburger, so she ordered a shake. As they waited for their food, Jimmy told her about a drag race he'd won the night before. When the waitress brought his burger and fries, the smell was delicious. But Bess knew she had to stick to her milkshake.

"Wanna bite?"

Bess shook her head. "I'm fine with this," she said.

"Oh, come on. You haven't lived until you've had one of Shorty's famous burgers." Jimmy put the burger right in front of her face. The grilled onions smelled wonderful. She took a small bite and thought her grandmother would beat her silly if she knew. She pushed the plate back to Jimmy.

"What's wrong? Don't you like it?"

"It's good, but now I've not only eaten meat that's not kosher, I've mixed it with milk," she looked at her milk shake and knew she couldn't finish it.

"What your parents don't know won't hurt them. My parents have no idea what I am up to most of the time."

After Jimmy paid the bill, he said he wanted to show her the full moon. "I know the perfect place. Greenway Park. We'll be able to see it reflecting in the pond."

Of course Bess knew the park. It was by Uncle Abe's. And it did sound lovely, so Bess said it would be okay. She assumed they would take a romantic walk, maybe skip rocks on the pond, sit out in the moonlight and talk, but when they got there, Jimmy drove past the pond. He turned onto a quiet lane where a few cars were parked and then kept going to the turn-around at the top of the hill where they were alone.

He pulled to the curb and said, "Now we can get to know each other better."

Bess laughed nervously. There was not another soul in sight. She looked up, but it was hard to see the moon through the trees.

"Come closer," he said, "You must be cold."

"I'm fine," Bess answered and pulled her sweater close around her.

"Oh, yes you are fine. You are certainly fine." He leaned across her and took a silver flask from the glove compartment. After a big swig, he offered Bess a taste. She shook her head no. He shrugged, took another drink, and tossed the flask on the floor. Then quickly he reached over the gear box and pulled Bess closer. "There. Better, right?"

His breath smelled of onions and alcohol as he moved in to kiss her. Before she knew it his tongue was in her mouth, and he was pushing hard against her. It wasn't a movie kiss. She felt like she was choking. Then his hands tugged at the bodice of her dress. He ripped so hard that a button came off. Bess pulled away.

"Hey, don't be a prude." Once again Jimmy's hands were on her.

"Jimmy, please, don't."

Bess put her hand on the door handle and pushed. Jimmy's weight against her forced the door to swing open and sent her to the ground. She struggled, but as she stood and backed away, she heard Jimmy's door open.

"Where do you think you're off to?" Jimmy said, coming towards her. Then he was upon her, pulling her close and groping her breasts.

"Jimmy, you're hurting me." Her heart raced with fear as Jimmy pushed her hard against a tree. The rough bark cut at the back of her neck.

He grunted, then his hands were in her dress. She shuddered as he reached under her slip and her panties. While he unbuckled his belt and unzipped his pants, Bess wanted to run, but her legs weren't working right. He knelt to pull her panties down and tore them over her feet. He started to stand, and she pushed him away. He lost his balance and fell on his back. When he got to his knees, she butted her forehead against his face and found her legs at last.

"Jesus Christ," he yelled after her. "You bitch, you broke my nose." Jimmy's face was covered in blood.

By then Bess was running down the hill. She had to get away. She saw headlights. A few cars. Would they stop? Give her a ride to safety? She felt dirty. Too dirty to ask for a ride. She felt dizzy, nauseated, and out of breath. She told her feet to move. Faster. Headlights lit the ground. Her throat tightened when she heard Jimmy's voice.

"Hey, get in the car. I forgive you. It's no big deal," he was cruising slowly next to her as she reached Main Street. From there it wasn't too far to Uncle Abe's. "Look, Bess, if you know what's good for you, get in the damn car."

Bess started running, going through yards where Jimmy couldn't follow her. When she saw the playground, she knew she had reached Green Street, and Jimmy would have to leave her alone. But when she got to their corner, he pulled up next to her.

"I don't know why I took out a slutty waitress to begin with!" he yelled. Then Jimmy's tires squealed as he sped off.

The whole neighborhood must have heard him, Bess thought with horror. She stifled an urge to cry. She stared at the house from across the street and felt paralyzed. Her new fear was how she'd get inside without notice. The lights in the living room silhouetted Momma, Poppa, Aunt Hettie, and Uncle Abe. She couldn't face them. She trembled with cold. She buttoned up her sweater, went to the back yard, where she vomited in her aunt's hydrangea bushes. The nasty taste of the burger and milkshake burnt her throat. She huddled on the stone stoop shivering with cold until the lights went off, then went in the back door. The house was quiet as she tiptoed to Momma and Poppa's bedroom and poked her head in the door.

"I'm home," she whispered.

"Did you have a good time?"

"Yes. Sleep well."

She locked herself in the upstairs bathroom and vomited again. She washed her hands over and over to get off Jimmy's greasy pomade and the dirt and the gravel. She scrubbed her face. Her eyes were ringed with mascara, and there were big purple fingerprints on her neck. Her breasts hurt, but she couldn't look at them. She sobbed uncontrollably and no matter how she tried to stop, she cried more.

When she got into bed, Bess was still shaking. She knew Sarah pretended to be asleep and she was grateful, at least for that.

Bess lay facing the wall. She wanted to disappear. If only they had never come to Indianapolis. If only she could go be some other person in another place. She tossed and turned all night. When early morning light came under the curtains, she fell into a deep sleep.

She dreamed that she was on a roller coaster with Jimmy who was driving the car off the tracks. Then he was ripping her dress and she tried to yell but no sound came out. When the alarm went off, Bess was screaming and awoke to Sarah standing over her.

"My God, what did he do to you?" Sarah said in a panic. "I told you he was trouble. Oh my God, your neck! Bess, I am so sorry." Sarah went to her dressing table and grabbed a tube of pancake.

"You can put this makeup on, so no one will see the marks."

"I thought your things were off limits." Bess threw the tube on the floor.

She didn't want anything from her cousin and didn't want to talk to her, and if she could, she'd leave this house so Sarah could have her precious room back. Bess grabbed her school clothes and threw on a robe and hurried toward the bathroom to get dressed.

"Bess, is everything all right? Who was screaming?" Aunt Hettie was out of breath from running upstairs.

Bess pulled the robe around her neck and said, "I'm all right Auntie, I just had a nightmare."

"Oh, no, you poor dear. Well, breakfast is ready when you are."

"No, no breakfast today. I have to get to school early."

The morning was sunny but cool. Uncle Abe had been talking about the possibility of snow. Each step toward school felt shaky, and Bess constantly looked around, expecting Jimmy's stupid car to be creeping up on her.

When she got to school, she hurried up to the anatomy lab on the third floor. She tried her best to put on a happy face when she greeted her teacher.

"Oh my goodness," Miss Jacobson said with a worried look. "Are you all right?"

"I'm fine. I just need a place to be alone."

"Well, you've found it. I have to go to a meeting. And I'll leave the door unlocked during lunch if you need to come back. If you do want to talk, you can talk to me."

Bess nodded gratefully.

"Here," her teacher said, "put this kerchief around your neck."

Bess had forgotten about the marks on her neck, but now she burned with shame. "Thank you," she said, choking back a sob.

Throughout the day Bess felt as though everyone was staring at her, and she thought it might have been a better idea to have feigned sickness and stayed home, but Aunt Hettie would have hovered, and she would have seen the bruises and Bess would have been forced to reveal the truth. At least here, she could blend into the hordes of students in the hallways when changing classes.

At lunchtime, she saw Sarah was with her friends, huddled together whispering. Thankfully, Jimmy was nowhere to be seen. She backed out before her cousin's group saw her.

Bess went back to the lab. When Miss J popped in to give her a cheese sandwich, Bess nodded gratefully. Then she sat there staring at the waxed paper without making a move to unwrap it.

After school, she made it to Topper's somehow, but she was anything but on top of things. Bess dropped utensils and food orders on her tables. She was so quiet and sullen that a regular asked her, "Where's that sweet smile?" Bess asked Uncle Abe to let her off early, and she stumbled home.

"Hey, Sis, you're home early," Calvin called from the kitchen table. They were in the middle of dinner.

"Get up and get your sister a chair," Momma said. "Good you are home early, so you would have more time for the piano. Bess sat and ate. When everything on her plate was gone, Aunt Hettie put more roast and mashed potatoes on.

"Gosh, Sis, you're ahead of me tonight. Slow down. I'll want seconds."

Bess jumped up, shoved her chair under the table, threw away the uneaten food, and put her plate in the sink.

"What's eatin' Bess?" Pinkie asked.

Sarah said, "Just leave her alone. She's mad at someone at school."

"Is your school all right? Are you in trouble?" Aunt Hettie asked.

"No, I'm not in trouble."

"Do you want to tell me the trouble?" Poppa said, getting up slowly from the table. He motioned Bess to follow him.

"No, Poppa, I'm going to practice the piano and do my homework. Thanks for the meal, Aunt Hettie."

Bess played scales loudly and fast. A Schumann march sounded like troops were storming the streets. Then she stopped abruptly and said to herself, "I can't sit here another minute."

"I'm going to study at the library," she called out before she left.

The public library was three blocks away. It was big and imposing from the outside. Inside her footsteps echoed on the mosaic tiled floor. Bess avoided making eye contact with the librarian at checkout. The reading room was full, but Bess didn't know anyone. Good. She went to the second floor and roamed until she found an alcove where no one could see her and fell asleep at her books and didn't awaken until the announcement that the library was closing.

Chapter 37
Comeuppance

APRIL 1938

For a week, Jimmy K all but disappeared, but then he showed up at Toppers with his football buddies. He specifically asked to be seated in Bess's section. They had pie and coffee with refill after refill. Jimmy made rude statements about the competence of the waitstaff in general and Bess in particular, which made his buddies laugh. They left a penny tip.

In the anatomy lab the next day, Miss Jacobson asked Bess to stay after class instead of going to lunch.

"Bess, sit down. We need to talk. You haven't been yourself in days."

"I guess I'm just tired of everything."

"You got a D on your last quiz, and you do seem exhausted."

Bess didn't answer, but her eyes filled with tears.

"Whatever is bothering you, I am here to listen, and I have all the time in the world."

Bess began to sob uncontrollably. Miss Jacobson pulled her chair close and said softly, "It's all right. You'll be all right."

"Nothing is all right!" Bess blurted out angrily.

"Is everything all right at home?"

Bess shook her head no.

"Can't you tell me about it? Get it out. I promise, you'll feel better.

"Well, you know my whole family is living with my aunt and uncle and cousins."

Miss Jacobson shook her head no.

Bess was surprised. She thought everyone knew that they were living off her uncle's charity. She told Miss J that she didn't feel like she belonged anywhere and that her cousin had made it clear that she didn't want to share her bedroom or her friends."

"Well, I guess you'll have to make your own friends, and you'll have to face up to your cousin." Bess couldn't imagine fighting with Sarah, but maybe it wasn't such a bad idea.

"Bess, is that all that's bothering you?"

Before Bess knew it, she had told her teacher about her date with Jimmy Koenigsberg. How she had lied to her parents and how he had driven her to a remote place and attacked her.

"There there, Bess. You are a brave girl for telling me. I need to ask you a few questions. Was there blood in your panties?"

"No, well, I don't know. He tore them off me. I have bruises, not just on my neck.."

"So, he didn't rape you?"

Bess didn't know what that meant.

"Did he penetrate, I mean enter you sexually?"

Bess shook her head no.

"That's good. How did you get away?"

"I broke his nose."

"What? How?"

"I head butted his face."

"You certainly have guts."

"No, I don't. I can't stand to be anywhere in school, and I don't feel safe anywhere. Well, I do feel okay here."

"May I give you a hug?"

Bess nodded and leaned over to allow Miss Jacobson to envelope her in her arms. She began to cry again. "I feel dirty all the time."

"You are not the dirty one. He is. He has probably hurt other girls. Unfortunately, if you say anything, you won't get much satisfaction. He will deny everything, and you'll end up going through a terrible process for nothing. Your reputation will be dragged through the mud. Believe me, I know what I'm talking about."

Then Bess told her how he'd shown up and taunted her at Toppers. She thought she'd have to quit her job if he kept coming there. She couldn't stand how she felt when he was there.

"Well, that filthy thug needs his comeuppance."

Bess didn't know what to say.

"If you broke his nose before, you could probably do it again."

"I don't think so. That was lucky, and I would never do anything like that at work."

Miss Jacobson smiled and squeezed Bess's hand. She looked Bess in the eyes. "Of course not, but you'll figure something out. Bess I don't know what you need to do, but you can't let him control you and make you feel so bad. Somehow he needs to be punished."

Bess knew her teacher was right, but what could she do? She couldn't think of a thing, but the tight spot in her chest wasn't hurting her as much. She felt lighter after having told Miss J everything, but she still dreaded the idea of going to work the next day. After school, Bess avoided Sarah and the gang and walked home by herself, but she decided that she would give her cousin a piece of her mind that night.

Naturally at dinner, Sarah acted as if she and Bess were best of friends. She always did whenever they were with the parents. Aunt Hettie and Uncle Abe thought their Sarah could do no wrong. But Bess had seen a different side.

After dinner Bess got to the bedroom before her cousin, spread all her books on Sarah's desk, and began to revise an essay.

When Sarah came in, she stood over Bess, her arms crossed over her chest. "Hey cuz, I thought I told you never to touch my things."

"I guess it was okay for me to share everything in Louisville, but here you run the show. You have done nothing but belittle me ever since we got here. You whisper about me with Jeannette. You've turned your friends against me. You try to control every little thing I do. Are you satisfied?" Bess didn't pause for Sarah to answer. Now that the wound had been punctured, the pus would not stop running out. "You've made my life miserable. Well, I'll tell you this. I don't care if you run me off at school, or if you gossip about me with your idiot friends, but this is supposed to be my room too, and I'm not moving."

Bess stood up and said, "Maybe we should talk this over with our parents. Do you have a problem with that?"

Sarah was stunned. She turned and left the room.

Bess finished her assignments, got washed up, and went to bed. She was about to fall asleep when Sarah walked into the room.

"Are you awake, Bess?"

"Yes."

"May I sit on your bed?"

"No."

Sarah sighed and sat on her own bed.

"Bess, I am so sorry about everything. What can I do to make things right?"

"Well, you can call off Jeannette and the rest."

"I will. I'll do anything you ask."

"Well, there's something you can't fix." Bess stopped to take a breath and asked, "Why didn't you warn me about Jimmy K?"

"I told you not to go out with him."

"But you didn't tell me he was an animal."

"I couldn't talk about it. I'm sorry, Bess, but it was awful. I mean he tried stuff with me on the patio at the Harvest Moon Dance. When a few boys came out to smoke, I ran inside and asked the first friend I saw to take me home. It was Hank. It was so upsetting." Sarah paused and Bess kept quiet until her cousin resumed the story.

"Remember when Jimmy came to the party at the Weissbergs' house? He said he'd come especially to see me. After he danced with me, he said I was really the only girl for him. He said he knew he should apologize for getting fresh but said we should go outside where we could have some privacy."

"That was a mistake," Bess said.

"I know. He started with sweet talk and convinced me to sit with him in his car. Then he pounced on me. Luckily, Mrs. Weissberg heard me scream and came outside. I got out and he drove off."

It all sounded painfully familiar to Bess. If only someone had been there for her in the park.

Sarah asked, "Did Jimmy, um, did he hurt you? I mean force you?"

Bess shook her head no. "You saw the bruises, but that was all."

"I guess we were both lucky, sort of. Can you ever forgive me?"

Bess let her cousin hug her and said, "I think we should get some shut-eye. I have a quiz tomorrow."

Bess fell asleep quickly and slept soundly. She dreamt she was with her friends in Louisville. But when the alarm went off and she opened her eyes, she was still in Sarah's room in Indianapolis.

The next afternoon was Wednesday. There was no sight of Jimmy or his teammates at Toppers. What a relief. Maybe he was tired of bullying her. But on Thursday, there he was, with his thick-necked friends. Bess asked another waitress to take over, so she could take a break, but when she came back, they were still there. They were at it again with the same stupid insults, but this time instead of a penny tip, Jimmy put Bess's rhinestone button on the counter. Bess grabbed the button and put it in her pocket.

"Shall I tally your bill," Bess asked coldly.

"I guess I'd like a refill after all."

"Well, I'll have to make another pot."

"I don't have all day. Have you ever seen anyone so slow?" Jimmy said, eliciting more laughs from his buddies.

Anger bubbled within Bess, but she couldn't reveal her feelings. She answered with a smile, "Coming right up."

She stood with her back to the boys, gritted her teeth, and watched the coffee percolate. When it finished, she carried the pot over to Jimmy and poured hot coffee into his lap. He jumped up screaming and cursing. His buddies hooted with laughter as Jimmy ran out of the restaurant.

"Oops," Bess said.

If Bess was worried she'd be in trouble, she needn't have. One of the other waitresses helped her clean up the spill and said, "That jerk had it coming."

Chapter 38
Dear Bess

Owensboro, Kentucky

May 1, 1938

My dear Bess,

I am worried about you, dear friend. I wrote a few weeks ago and the letter came back, so I wrote to Naomi for news of you. She told me that your family moved to Indianapolis because your father is very ill. I am very sorry to hear it. She also said you were discouraged about your music studies. I hope that is not the case, because as you know, we made a promise to one another to play "The Spring Sonata" as a duet. I still hope someday we will. Meanwhile, I hear Indianapolis has a fine conservatory, and I'm certain they would take you.

Naomi told me all about the flood in Louisville. I survived in Paducah because of the kindness of a Negro family named Robertson. We sheltered at a church, but the conditions for the Robertsons were deplorable there. So, we left Paducah in their rowboat and went downriver to Metropolis. It wasn't so far as the crow flies, but the treacherous currents meant slow-going. In Metropolis, a Negro bargeman offered to take us to Owensboro where Mr. Robertson has a cousin.

It was difficult for us all at first, but we are doing well now. Mr. Robertson has a job working for a Negro doctor, and his daughter is going to a decent school. You would like her. She plays the violin beautifully, and I have helped her improve. I have earned money giving other people lessons, but I am tired of small-town life, and I feel I cannot impose on the Robertsons any longer.

It may please you to know that I have scheduled lessons with Mr. Parmer for the middle of May. If he likes what he hears, he and Mrs. Parmer might hire me to work with their students. Kindly, they have offered to let me sleep in their studio for as long as I need to. Naomi's family also offered me a room, but it will be better if I stay with the Parmers.

Please write soon. After May 15, you must write in care of the Parmers.

All best regards,
Walter

Chapter 39
In The Attic

Adel sat by the window and watched the street fill with morning light. She was bundled in the goose feather quilt her mother had given her as a bride. Gottenu, that was so long ago. And how long had she been in this place? Too long. In a month they would celebrate their second Peisach in this wilderness. Toby was no longer a baby. Adel couldn't keep up with her, and the girl couldn't keep still. She was a little dreidel. Spinning and spinning.

Oy gevalt, everything hurt her. She slept in the chair now because she couldn't stand that bed any longer with its metal headboard. Sol's sister-in-law had bragged that it was brand new, but to her, it felt like a bed in a prison. And yesterday she'd told her Malke how she felt. What a to-do. Momma, you ingrate. Ungrateful daughter. Spiteful. Hateful. So many curses and vile words they spat out. But to tell the truth, Adel was sorry for her Malke, not herself.

Poor Malke, working her fingers to the bone in her brother-in-law's bakery. Well, Adel thought, she herself had always worked. She could never count on her dear departed Calman's income as a scribe. Sometimes people needed scrolls, or documents, sometimes they didn't. And a big commission to write a Torah? That didn't come every year. So, she had always sold cheese, eggs, and vegetables from her garden.

Oy Calman, may your soul rest in the Garden of Eden, better you shouldn't look down here and better I should not have lived so long. I worry God will punish the kinder because they abandon Torah and disobey His word. They think I don't know because I'm up here all alone, but I hear music and radio played on Sabbath. I see lights go on and off. Calman, your namesake, rides bicycle on Sabbath. From my window I see Sarah go alone with boys in their cars. Never would I forget that shiny black car without a top. A miniature version of the car the Czar and Czarina used to parade around in. The same animal what followed Bessele. Oy vey. Truth be told, Adel was too tired even to worry. She wanted to spit, but her mouth was dry. She tried to get up and get a glass of water from the pitcher they left her every night, but she felt weak.

She looked down at her book of Bible stories. It hurt her eyes to read, but she knew the stories by heart. She turned to Deuteronomy and the book fell open to Moses' death. "And his eyesight was not dim." She put her hand to her heart. Her eyes were dim, but like Moses, she was dying.

There was a clattering of footsteps in the hallway. Into her room Bessele charged without so much as a knock or a zei azoi gut.

"Good morning, Bubby," Bess said with a smile.

"Gut morgen, mamale. Where is the cleaning lady?" Adel mumbled.

"She's getting Toby dressed, so I brought you your breakfast."

"Just put it on the table."

"Bubby, your water glass is full." Bess brought the glass over. Adel shook her head and Bess said, "Bubby, you must drink."

"Oy, Bessele, I don't want nothing. I don't need nothing. My time has come."

"That's nonsense. Let me help you up." Bess took Adel's arm and led her to the table. The cream of wheat was steaming hot. Adel usually threw it away, but today Bess spoon-fed her. Adel gritted her two front teeth and the cereal fell on her chin. Bess wiped her face gently as though she were a baby.

"Should I take you to the toilet?" Bess asked when she finished breakfast.

"You call that a toilet? A commode in my hallway? I was better off in the village going in the woods. Tell them to take that contraption away."

"Aunt Hettie bought that to help you out. If you would get up and walk more, you could use the bathroom downstairs like before."

Finally, Bubby let Bessele walk her to the wooden commode, help her with her garments, wipe her, and lead her back to her chair. Bess went to empty the portable toilet, but Adel chided her.

"Leave it. The black woman will be here soon to do that. You go to school and work hard and make your mother and father proud. Your momma told me about your good grades and about your nice teachers. You don't need me anymore. I'm only sorry I won't live to see what you become."

"Bubby, don't talk that way. I know it's hard being up here, but you know Calvin and I would help you come down for meals. I wish I could sleep up here. It's so pretty how they fixed it up for you. Fresh wallpaper. Nice curtains. Your own room! So, please, Bubby, make an effort."

"For what, Bessele? I feel in my bones that the Angel of Death is coming to this house. If you see him on the street, an old man dressed in rags, let him in Bessele, let him in and tell him where to find me."

Chapter 40
The Angel of Death

INDIANAPOLIS, MARCH 15-16, 1939

On Mollie's dresser sat a tinted photograph of Bess and Calvin in their sailor suits when they were little. Such angels they were. Well, compared to Toby. Oh my, they didn't have a portrait of the baby. What baby? She was almost two and ran around the house like a dervish.

Mollie buttoned the top button on her pink and white uniform and smoothed the collar. She powdered her nose, applied rouge and lipstick, penciled her highly arched eyebrows, and ran a comb through her hair. Oh no, a silver hair. "Only forty, I'm too young to go gray," she said as she plucked it out of her jet-black curls. She smiled at herself in the mirror. The same smile the customers loved. Work was easier than being home with Sol, Momma, and the kinder. At work everyone listened to her. She was the manager of Abe's bakery, after all. She slipped on her watch. Oy, it was late, and Sol was still asleep.

"Sol, wake up. I've got to get to work, and the kinder are soon leaving for school. Miss Violet is coming late, so you'll need to keep an eye on Toby."

She grabbed her raincoat. "Sol, it's raining, and Hettie is driving the kids to school. You must give an eye to the baby."

Sol didn't stir. Mollie bent over and shook his shoulder. "Sol, oy Gottenyu. Sol!" He did not budge or grumble. Mollie put her hand to his forehead. It was cold. She put her face to his and felt no warmth, no breath.

"It cannot be." His hand had no pulse. Mollie's chest seized with fear.

"No, no, no!" Mollie was shrieking.

Bess and Calvin ran in, "Momma, what's wrong?"

"Your father," she said her eyes wide with disbelief.

"What's wrong with Pop?" Calvin asked. Bess knelt to touch her father, but Calvin pushed her out of the way and put his hand under Sol's nose.

"Pop's not breathing!"

Mollie stood there not able to breathe herself, not knowing what to do.

Toby wandered in in her pajamas dragging her blanket. Mollie told Bess to take the baby out, but before she could, Adel came in hunched over her cane. "What's happened?"

Adel walked over and took Sol's cold hand. "Oy vey iz mir. It's my fault. I called the Angel of Death to come for me, and he took our Sol."

Mollie began to wail. Bess and Calvin sobbed, and Toby followed suit. Mollie knelt down by the bed and put her head on her Sol's chest.

"Calvin," Bubby ordered, "call your uncle and tell him to get home right away. Bess, take the baby out of here. Calvin, tell Aunt Hettie to keep her kids away." Then she ripped the collar of her housedress. "Mollie," she said, "stand up, so I can rip your collar." Mollie didn't respond.

That afternoon Mollie stumbled into the kitchen to find Abe making phone calls. When he got off the phone, he gave Mollie a hug and said, "Everyone is coming. Sam, Minnie, their kids, and the cousins from Chicago."

"Sit down, Mollie," Hettie said. "You have to have something to eat."

Mollie sat down and looked at the plate. She took a bite and began to sob softly.

"So, the funeral would be tomorrow afternoon," Abe said.

Mollie nodded.

Mother Adel walked in and said, "Who's with the body? Calvin, go stand watch." Then she sat down next to Mollie.

"Momma, what are we going to do?" Mollie whispered.

"We're going to what needs to be done."

Mollie began sobbing again. Adel leaned over and pulled Mollie close.

"Today you can cry, Malkele. Today you can cry." Then she asked Hettie if all the mirrors were covered and who would prepare food for the shiva.

"The mirrors are covered. Don't worry, and Violet will take care of the food for after the um, cemetery."

"It wouldn't be food from the restaurant?"

"No, Mother Adel," Hettie said, "It would all be dairy and made here in this kitchen. You can sit and watch Violet if you like. Our friends will provide the meals for the rest of the week."

"It would be kosher?"

"Yes, Mother Adel, yes. It will all be kosher."

The next morning, Hettie helped Mollie get dressed. She took Mollie's shears and cut a tear in the buttonhole of her black jacket. She gave her a kiss on the cheek and hugged her.

Abe knocked softly at the door and said, "The family has arrived. They'll be at Ruben's Funeral Home."

Except for Pinkie's sobbing, there was not a sound in Uncle Abe's car as they drove to the funeral home. When they arrived, Calvin helped Mollie out of the car. He and Bess led her in and flanked her in the first row of the chapel. She nodded as family and friends bent to hug and kiss her and say, "May his memory be for a blessing," "May he rest in peace," or tell her how sad and shocked they were. Tears fell on Mollie as Minnie kissed her. Bess moved so that Sol's sister could sit next to Mollie.

The quiet chatter in the room stopped when the rabbi walked in and chanted a prayer calling upon God to grant perfect rest to the deceased. After the Twenty-third Psalm, the rabbi spoke about Sol as a husband, father, brother, and friend. "I am told he was a skilled tailor. I know he was a fine teacher to our bar mitzvah boys." He asked Abe to lead the "Mourner's Prayer" and everyone rose.

At the cemetery, Abe, dressed in a black robe, led a procession chanting a psalm in his deep voice. Slowly they proceeded down the sidewalk toward the burial spot, stopping seven times. They led Mollie to a chair draped in velvet next to the open grave. When they repeated the "Mourner's Prayer," she could not stand. After the casket was lowered into the ground, Abe and Calvin helped Mollie perform the ritual of covering Sol's pine box with dirt.

When the burial service ended, the family drove home. Violet was waiting on the front porch. She helped Mollie perform the ceremonial washing of her hands after visiting a cemetery. Hettie and Minnie led Mollie to the dining room table for the mourners' meal of consolation. Afterwards, Mollie sat on a low stool that symbolized her suffering. At dusk the rabbi came and called the men to recite Kaddish again. Mollie asked Bess to help her to her room.

Mollie stood and stared at the bed she and Sol had shared for the last year and a half. She had no tears left, and she was exhausted. She collapsed on the bed face up and fingered her torn button-hole. The fine wool Sol had chosen. This was the last suit he had made for her before he became ill. She flopped over on her belly and pounded the pillow with her fists. Then she slept until the room was full of light.

Chapter 41
A Big Decision

March-April 1939

Friends and family paraded through the house the week of Sol's death. Condolence cards came from Abe and Hettie's friends and from old friends in Louisville. Mollie stacked them up unopened on her dresser. She knew what they would say.

After a week, the remembrance candle, lit on the day of the funeral, burned out, and the sheets came off the mirrors. Mollie looked at herself and saw dark circles under her eyes. The house was quiet. It would remain that way for a month. No radio. No music. Abe, Calvin, and Pinkie would go to shul every morning to say Mourner's Kaddish for Sol.

After the first thirty days of mourning had passed, Mollie still didn't feel like anything was real. It was so strange to live in her brother-in-law's house without her Sol. Yes, they were family, but something felt wrong. She felt restless, so she washed her face, combed her hair, and put on her uniform. When she got to the bakery, Abe wanted her to go home, but she refused. "We'll talk tonight," he said.

That night Abe asked Mollie to come into the kitchen. Before he could close the door, Mollie blurted out, "We'll pay you back for everything, no matter how long it takes."

Abe waved his hand, "Mollie, please, wait a minute."

"But we owe you so much, so it will take us time to repay you. Calvin will get a better job. Bess could leave school."

"Mollie, dear sister, please, just listen to me. Bess wouldn't leave school. Now sit down and be quiet. Ever since Bess was born, I decided to put a little away every month for your family. My brother, God rest his soul, was a sweet and talented man, but we both know he couldn't resist to play cards. When Calvin was born, I convinced Sol to get life insurance. I told him I knew a fine broker here. You know, just in case. But Sol made the payments every month until he got sick, so then I used the money I'd put away to pay for the policy. So, you see, Mollie, you wouldn't have to work, not for now. And you're not going anywhere. We're your family and this is your home."

Abe handed her the envelope with the insurance policy. Mollie took it and looked at her brother-in-law in disbelief.

"Go ahead, open it," Abe urged.

She sighed, then, with shaking hands, opened the envelope. She unfolded the paper and looked at the amount. So much money, she had never seen in her life. $2,000. If her Sol were alive, he'd want to play cards to double the fortune. She laughed and cried.

"So, you see, Malkele, everything is going to be okay." Abe put his hands on hers.

"Abe, I don't know what to say. Thank you. Thank you. Sol always said you were the best brother a man could have."

"Stop it. Hettie, come in and help me."

Hettie burst through the door. She hugged Mollie and said, "So, you will stay here, and Bess will prepare for auditions at the conservatory."

Mollie stood and said, "I am so grateful to you both, but I need to think this all out. I need some time."

Abe said, "Of course. You think about it. Take all the time you need, and whatever you want to do, that's what we'll do."

Mollie said, "And the kinder. I must talk to Calvin and Bess. And to Momma."

"Of course."

After Abe and Hettie retired for the night, Mollie paced in the bedroom. What should they do? Bess was about to graduate high school. Calvin was right behind her and, thanks God, he was passing all his classes. Since Sol's death, Momma had started coming down to have meals with the family again. She still didn't eat any meat, but she didn't make remarks. Momma hadn't done well at all in Indianapolis. She was almost an invalid. In Louisville, she had gotten everywhere on the trolley, but here she complained everything hurt her and stayed like a hermit in her room.

But Abe and Hettie had been so kind. They never said a word about how insulting Momma could be. They treated Bess and Calvin like their own two kids. And Toby and Hettie were inseparable. Hettie would be heartbroken if they left. How could she hurt them by leaving. Besides, even though Bess didn't like working at Toppers, Mollie loved managing the bakery. Abe said Mollie could sell her customers week old bread covered in mold. And the other workers liked Mollie's smile and her imperturbable manner. Even though she worried constantly about her family, at work she was unflappable.

That night Mollie noticed the pile of condolence cards on her dresser, and she sat down to read them. Card after card said the same thing. All expressing sadness and how much Sol would be missed. Oy, a card from her dear Fanny and Jake. Ah, a card from Maishe Yoffee. She opened it. So sweet. He wrote that Sol was like a brother and that he was sorry he couldn't come to the funeral. He was busy because he was about to open a new tailor shop in the Highlands in late June. In fact, he said that if Mollie wanted to be his manager, he needed someone at the downtown store. Mollie put the card down and wondered if he had maybe already given the job to someone else. The card was dated March 17, and it was already mid-April.

The next day Mollie told Bess and Calvin to be sure and be home for dinner. She had somthing important to speak with them about. After Sarah and Bess cleared the table, Mollie asked her kids to come to the bedroom. The kids had such serious looks on their faces as they sat on the bed.

"Your poppa, may his soul rest in the Garden of Eden, had life insurance."

"How much?" Calvin asked.

"Enough. Maishe Yoffee has offered me a job, but I won't answer him until I know how you both feel. Do you want to go back to Louisville?"

 "Yes!" they said at once.

"I know Momma is miserable here, so I'll go to the corner and call Maishe to see if the job's still open. Don't say anything to anyone yet."

As the coins fell into the box, Mollie's heart pounded. She knew the number by heart. How many times had she called their landsman to find out where Sol was?

That night at dinner, Mollie said that she had been offered a job in Louisville and that they would be going back there after Bess and Sarah's graduation.

"Calvin can't go," Pinkie whined. "If he goes, I'm going too!"

Hettie asked, "But who will take care of the baby if you work?"

"I not a baby," Toby said.

"God spared me for a reason," said Momma Adel. "I would take care of Toviah." Abe's family was silent.

"It's the right thing. Sol, alev hashalom, would want for us to go home," Mollie said.

Part Six

Back to Louisville

Chapter 42
House Hunting

INDIANAPOLIS TO LOUISVILLE, JUNE 6, 1939

Bess sat across from Calvin on the train to Louisville. He didn't look like the Angel she knew and loved. He looked serious. She felt mixed emotions. Happy to be going home but nervous about everything she and Calvin would have to take care of alone. Momma had stayed behind to train the new bakery manager. Besides, Bubby wasn't fit enough to house hunt if the place the Habermann's parishioner was offering didn't work out.

"Hey! Angel, we're free. No more being Pinkie's keeper." Bess grinned at him as the train pulled out of the Indianapolis station.

"What about you? No more lugging trays bigger than you at Toppers."

"Oh, it wasn't terrible. The waitresses were a great bunch, and Uncle Abe was so good to us." Bess was trying to put a positive spin on it. But she had hated it when Sarah's clique came and acted so friendly and then snubbed her at school. She decided to gloss it over. "I mean, I guess I never felt quite right at Old Ben."

"Well, you showed 'em all. Top prize for biology and music."

"Yeah, graduation was swell, wasn't it? Momma almost popped with pride."

"And I haven't seen Bubby smile so much in a long time." They both laughed thinking of Bubby's toothless smile.

"If only Poppa could have been there."

"Yup," Calvin answered looking as though he would cry. "Hey, Sis, how about I get us some refreshments."

"Nothing now, thanks. I'm going to read."

Bess didn't open her book. Instead, she looked at the list Momma had made of all they needed to do in Louisville.

1. confirm rent
2. check utility costs
3. check transportation
4. arrange for furniture

She and Calvin had to do all of that and Bess needed to find a job. She put the list in her purse and pulled out the corsage that they had given her for playing piano at graduation. It still smelled sweet. She dug deeper and looked at the savings bond Miss Jacobson had handed her at graduation. Twenty-five dollars. How would she have made it at Old Ben without Miss Jacobson? Indy hadn't been all bad. She turned her attention out the window. The buildings of downtown Indianapolis rolled by. Before she knew it, the train was flanked by green fields, and she felt her body relax.

Calvin sat back down and gave her a cold root beer and offered her half a sandwich. "Hey, Sis, you wanna give me a loan?"

She still held the savings bond in her hand. "It doesn't mature for ten years. You think maybe by then you'll mature?"

"Fat chance."

"I'm just joking. In the fall you'll be a senior at Male High. A big man."

Calvin shrugged and finished his sandwich. He yawned, unbuttoned the top button of his shirt, leaned his head back, and before long he was asleep.

He'd been out late with Rosie, his latest girlfriend. Poor Rosie had looked like she was going to die at the station. She wasn't supposed to come because she wasn't Jewish, and Calvin didn't want Momma to know about her. Oh well, Momma was too distraught about her children going to Louisville alone to take much notice. Sarah certainly gave Rosie the evil eye though. No doubt Calvin would soon forget Rosie. He'd be Angel again, running with his friends, girls and boys.

Bess smiled and thought of the boyfriend drama at Old Ben. She had gone to the senior prom with a nice boy, Sarah's friend Ike, but he still had a crush on her cousin, poor boy. He was doomed to suffer because Sarah thought he was too short. Even though Bess was sensitive about her own height, she too liked guys who were taller. Like Walter. He might be boyfriend material. She had worried that Naomi would get first dibs on him, but that hadn't gone anywhere. Naomi assured her that they were just good friends. Bess would see Walter as soon as she got everything set up for her family. His last letter had been very positive. He had his own little studio, now, but he didn't have a phone. Bess was to call the Parmer's to get him a message about when she could see him.

But there was so much to do before she'd have a moment to do that. Bess opened the window wider and picked up her novel. The rhythm of the train and the warm air made her sleepy.

"Hey, Sis," Calvin said, waking her. "They're announcing New Albany. We'll be in Louisville before you know it."

As they passed the giant Colgate Palmolive Clock, Bess thought how proud Poppa had been of Louisville. How he had loved the Ohio River.

"Hey, there's Fontaine Ferry," Calvin said, pointing upriver at the roller coaster. "Oh, come on, Bess, don't cry."

Bess couldn't help it. She was so sorry to be going home without Poppa. He had left a hole in her life that no one could fill. It would be great to see her friends, but everyone would be getting on with their lives, and she had no idea what her future would bring. She needed a job but what could she do? Teach piano for the Parmers and play concerts or be an accompanist? Walter had written that the pay wasn't great. Naomi was about to start nursing school, and she had begged Bess to join her. Cousin Dotty wanted her to work with her in Uncle Sam's pawn shop. It had doubled in size since they'd been gone. Phyllis was teaching tennis at the YMHA summer camp in Henryville. After that, Phyllis had no idea what she'd be doing either, but she didn't really need to work.

Bess took a deep breath as they crossed the river, then she stood to retrieve their parcels. As they stepped off the train, they were surprised to see Naomi waiting on the platform. She had a bouquet of flowers for Bess.

"Oh, Bess, I am just so happy you're back." The girls hugged tightly.

"Calvin, you are now the man of the family. We are all so heartbroken about your father. He was a wonderful man." Naomi stretched out her hand to Calvin.

"Thanks, Naomi, Poppa really liked your father. Momma said to thank him for all his help finding us a place."

Naomi led the way to the street.

"Hey, look who's driving! Naomi, will you teach me?" Bess said as they got into Pastor Habermann's beat up sedan.

They rolled down all the windows. It was a hot, hazy morning, but Louisville looked beautiful to Bess. Most of the reconstruction and repair after the flood was finished. Naomi turned off Broadway at Second Street. As they got further away from downtown, the homes were bigger, and the street was lined with trees.

"So, you'll not be far from your music teacher, if you take this place," Naomi said as she slowed down by a big house on the corner of Second and Magnolia. The trolley line runs right near here. The owner is picky about whom she would rent to, but Father told her that there are no better people than the Toplanskys. Anyway, he thinks she might bring the rent down for you if she likes you. Her name is Mrs. Neumann. She's a widow. I don't know her very well. She never stays to socialize after services. But Father admires her work in the community."

"Well, that says a lot," Bess said.

"Here. She gave us a key in case she's late. She said it's okay to go in and look around. I gotta scoot. Mother needs the car. Mother and Father want you to eat with us tonight."

"Oh, that's so sweet but we're expected at Aunt Minnie and Uncle Sam's. I promise we'll come by soon." Bess waved as Naomi drove off then she turned her focus to the big brick house with the wide front porch.

"The front yard looks pretty rough," Calvin said. "Not excited about having to mow this."

Unlike Uncle Abe's front yard that was flat and small and could be mowed in under ten minutes, this yard was deep, and it sloped sharply up toward the front entrance. And it hadn't been cared for. The grass was sparse, and weeds grew untended.

"I'm sure you're up to the challenge, man of the family," Bess said with a smile. The house itself was large. It might be too big, but it was in better shape than the yard, at least from the outside. As she walked up the steep front steps, Bess knew Bubby would struggle with those. But maybe the back entrance would be easier.

Bess rang the bell, but no one answered. She turned the key, and they stepped inside. Calvin plopped their bags down and dust flew up into the air. They looked around in dismay. There were cobwebs on the light fixtures. But she liked how spacious it was. It just needed a mop and some paint.

"Whoo hee," Calvin shouted, his voice echoing in the emptiness. "I don't know, Sis. It sure ain't no home sweet home," Calvin said.

"Well, let's not make a hasty decision. Let's see if we can afford the rent."

They looked around trying to imagine how the place could be livable. There was a big living room and dining room with high ceilings and a parlor with empty bookshelves on one wall and a bay window on another.

"It'll cost plenty to heat," Bess said remembering how coal had disappeared from their basement on Broadway so quickly.

The kitchen looked suitable. The stove was enormous and old but in good condition. Bess peered out the back window into the yard. It had a fence. "This will be a nice place for Toby to play and Bubby will be able to get into the house easily from here." There was only one step up to the back porch. Unlike the front yard, the back was well tended with flowers and trees and had a sunny area with a truck garden. Was that a coach house or a neighbor's house? It was a neat little place with window boxes spilling over with petunias.

On the second floor were three bedrooms and a big bathroom. One of the bedrooms had a sunny bay window looking south. Calvin liked the looks of that. Bess was making a mental note of who could sleep where. Three bedrooms and a parlor. Who would be the easiest to share a room with? Bubby snored, Momma was a restless sleeper, and Toby loved getting into Bess's things.

The third floor was sealed off, so they went back downstairs. "Calvin, take a look at the basement and see what's down there."

He yelled up. "You won't believe this. There's a new furnace."

Bess walked into a kitchen pantry and then a laundry room with a big sink and lots of space to dry things in winter. Back in the kitchen she noticed a door by the refrigerator. It led to a narrow room with its own sink and shower. She pulled up the blinds and opened a window to let a cool breeze blow in. It faced north and was shaded by a stand of pines.

She thought this room would work for Bubby. No stairs. But then Bubby would be taking care of Toby, so it might not work, after all.

"That was Maureen O'Grady's room. Best cook I ever had."

Startled, Bess turned to see a tall slender woman in a well-cut linen dress. She took off a big straw hat and fanned herself. Her silver hair was tied back in a bun.

"I'm Helen Neumann, and you must be Miss Toplansky. Pastor speaks highly of you and your family."

"A pleasure to meet you. I am grateful for Pastor Habermann's high regard."

Bess was sizing up the widow. She didn't look like she needed to rent the place. Bess wondered if she could be persuaded to lower the rent or make any concessions considering the condition of the house. Bess picked at a spot of peeling paint and the widow nodded.

"There's a bit to do in here, I'm afraid. I just let it go after my Harold died. Then the neighborhood changed, and I didn't like being in this big house at this stage of my life. The coach house in the garden is fine for me."

"Oh, so you live in the pretty house in back."

"Yes, and I apologize again for the state of this place. I couldn't justify the cost of keeping it clean."

Bess said, "It just needs some scrubbing, sweeping, and paint."

Calvin walked upstairs with a bag of golf clubs. "There's a lot of sports equipment in the basement. Even a canoe."

"Oh, I'm sorry," the woman said to Calvin. "I shall have that carted away if you like. Those clubs were my first husband's. I've outlived three husbands and two of my children. My baby is an officer in the Navy, and I rarely see him." She paused and said to Calvin, "I am Mrs. Neumann." Bess realized she should have introduced her brother, but the woman intimidated her.

Calvin introduced himself.

"Of course, if you'd like to make use of any of that equipment, feel free," Mrs. Neumann said.

"This is such a beautiful house," Bess said. "It might work for us if we could afford it. What are you asking for rent?"

"Does twenty-five dollars a month sound fair to you?"

"Yes, ma'am, it does," Bess said. "But could you go even lower if we were to take care of the grounds?"

"She means me," Calvin laughed.

"Yes, what would sound reasonable?"

"Twenty dollars a month?"

Mrs. Neumannn agreed and said that she would cover the cost of materials for any improvements they made as long as they consulted with her first.

Mrs. Neumann held out her hand and said, "Shall we shake on it?"

Bess shook Mrs. Neumann's strong hand and was sure this was a good decision.

"Well, Miss Toplansky, when will you moving in? As you can see, there's no one here to displace."

"As soon as we get it cleaned up and get some furniture, our mother, grandmother and baby sister will join us."

"That's just fine. I hope your family will be happy here. I look forward to meeting them."

When Mrs. Neumann walked out, Calvin and Bess looked at each other incredulously.

"She drove a hard bargain," Calvin said with a grin as he propped the golf clubs on the wall. Then he noticed the open door to the servant's room and headed toward it. Bess cut him off.

"Oh, no, you're not taking it. You are sleeping upstairs. I don't care if it is the cook's room and it's next to the kitchen. I am going to have my own room."

Chapter 43
Spring Sonata

Bess was relaxing in bed and reading for a bit in her room. Calvin had painted it a pale robin's egg blue. She was on a rollaway bed Naomi's family loaned them. Momma had already bought fabric for drapes and curtains and would make them at Maishe Yoffee's shop after hours. Bess told her she didn't need curtains. The trees gave her privacy. Her own room. She could loll about here forever, but she thought about her list of things to do for the day.

Oh goodness, she had to go to the bank for Momma and then she was going to Mrs. Parmer's school to meet Walter. They had talked by phone a week ago and decided they would play the "Spring Sonata" as a lark without fanfare or preparation at the Parmers' music school. They planned their debut for a time when Mrs. Parmer would probably be out. Bess had worked on the music in Indianapolis, but she'd never had time to get it up to tempo, and her piano hadn't arrived yet. Walter was such a perfectionist, but he hadn't had much time to work on it either since he'd taken a job teaching for the Parmers.

After opening the bank account, Bess stopped at a thrift shop and saw a kitchen table and a rocking chair for Bubby. The shopkeeper said that for a little extra, they could deliver. Bess asked them to hold the things until the afternoon so her mother could decide. Fourth Street was bustling as she headed south. The Oak Leaf Café was still there! She remembered how Calvin loved to have a soda there with Momma while they waited for Bess to finish her lesson with Mrs. Parmer. That seemed so long ago.

Bess stood at the door to the Parmers' home and music school. She could hear the sounds of student violinists from somewhere up above. They were playing "The Emperor" by Mozart. They sounded good. Just as she was about to knock, Walter opened the door.

He pulled her to him, and they embraced. "Oh, Bess, it's so good to see you."

"It's wonderful to see you, too, Walter."

He motioned for her to follow. "You look really good, Bess. I can't believe we're finally together after so long." They walked through the entryway and ascended the stairs to the piano studio, where everything was familiar.

"Yes, five years later, we'll finally play our duet. It's too hot today for a 'Spring Sonata,' but the weather isn't going to be our only problem. I haven't had much time to practice," Bess said.

Walter waved off her objection. "You'll play beautifully, I'm sure. But how are you? How is your family?" Walter asked as he led her to the piano.

"Everything is fine. Momma, Bubby, and the baby, I mean Toby, just got here a few days ago."

"How old is Toby now?"

"She's almost two, but she's quite lively, and she loves music."

"Do you have a picture?"

Bess felt embarrassed to say, "Seems like we haven't had a chance to take pictures of Toby, but she's pretty. She looks like Momma."

"If only I had my baby violin."

"Oh no, I don't think she could ever sit still enough to play an instrument. And who can stand a beginner? I only listen to concert violinists like you."

"Hah. You are in for a shock. I am teaching a lot, but aside from paying gigs, I am devoting myself to piano jazz." He ran his fingers along the keys of the baby grand and played a minor riff. Then he sat down and played the opening of "When They Begin the Beguine."

Walter played so effortlessly. When he stood to take a little bow, Bess applauded and said, "Oh, Walter, is there anything you can't do?" Her old friend had grown taller. She saw now that he was a man.

He grinned and his blue eyes focused on her. "You haven't changed a bit since I saw you last. Still my sweet Little Bess."

"Now you are in trouble," she said with a laugh. She lunged at him, and he ran around the piano.

"I surrender," Walter said waving his handkerchief. "Come on, let's warm up and get this over with. I am making dinner for you at my studio, so, we'll celebrate our reunion no matter how badly we play."

It was worse than bad. Walter lost the place. Bess missed sharps and flats. The tempo was ragged. But they soldiered on to the end.

When they finished, Mrs. Parmer popped her head into the room. "That was godawful," she exclaimed.

Walter looked at Bess, and all three burst out laughing.

"Oh, Mrs. Parmer," Bess cried. She jumped up to greet her beloved teacher. Mrs. Parmer was quite pregnant. "Oh, my," Bess said as she hugged her carefully.

"Bess, Bess, I do declare, I've missed you so much. Look at you. You are all grown up. Come downstairs and have iced tea. John is just finishing with his junior quartet."

They sipped their tea and Bess got caught up with the Parmers, who now insisted on being called John and Althea. Walter easily called them by their first names, but Bess found it difficult. An hour later, Walter and Bess said their goodbyes. Bess promised not to be a stranger.

Walter's studio apartment was a few blocks away in an old house in St. James Square. He had a back entrance up a metal staircase.

"Welcome to my palatial abode."

"Walter, it's lovely." Bess didn't know where to look first. "Your artwork is beautiful."

"All prints and secondhand frames," Walter said.

"This is an original, though, and an amazing likeness of you, despite the crazy brushwork."

"That's by my friend Jacob," he said. "Have a seat." He pointed to a sofa covered in red brocade.

"I think I'll need your help with our place. It's enormous, and we are struggling to furnish it on a tight budget."

"My pleasure," Walter said. He grinned and bowed. "Would you like an aperitif."

"Sure, if you tell me what that is."

"A bit of dry sherry."

"Yes," Bess said, thinking sherry sounded sophisticated.

Walter poured the amber liquid into a little glass. "Try it. If you don't like it, I have something sweeter." It smelled great, but she didn't like it.

Walter pulled out a tiny silver flask. "Would you like a taste of your local bourbon?"

"No thank you." The silver flask reminded her of that animal who had assaulted her in Indianapolis. She shook off the feeling. Walter could never be like that.

Walter took a long sip and said, "Feel free to look around while I fix dinner. You can freshen up over there."

Bess stepped into the bathroom. Walter had nicer colognes than she did. She picked up the tiny colored soaps. Lavender, rose, carnation, spices she didn't recognize. She washed her hands and face with the spicy smelling one. She reapplied her powder, rouge, and lipstick. Louisville's humidity could really destroy a girl's makeup. "Not bad," she said to herself. Here she was in the studio of a man who was better looking than most film stars. Why was she nervous? Walter was one of her oldest friends. But he wasn't a boy any longer, and she found him even more attractive. Back in the living room, rather than sit, she looked at Walter's record collection. Louis Armstrong, Count Basie, Billie Holliday. She asked Walter if she should put on a record.

"Oh, yes, whatever you like." She found "Maple Leaf Rag." Poppa had liked ragtime. She put it on.

"Bess, would you have wine with your dinner? I've made schnitzel. Not veal. Chicken, and I salted it overnight so it's almost kosher."

Bess laughed. She'd written Walter about eating unkoshered chicken out in Indianapolis. How thoughtful of him to consider that.

At dinner Bess had a glass of Riesling. It was sweet, almost like the Passover wine that Poppa used to make. Walter had put flowers and candles on the table. Everything looked sparkly. The food was delicious. Bess relaxed as they talked about music, about the Parmers, about the future.

"So, our dear Naomi has started nursing school. She is so serious," Walter said as he cleared the dishes. Bess jumped up to help.

"Yes, she doesn't have time for anything else, but she is the happiest I've ever seen her."

Bess washed, and Walter dried. Of course, Walter had placed a little step stool by the sink for her. Exasperating but sweet. She asked him how he liked working at the music school.

"Music classes don't pay well, and as you say, beginning violinists drive you up the wall. I do make some money as a piano accompanist. I don't play as well as you but well enough."

Bess said with a sigh, "I guess Mrs. P gave the verdict on my future in music. Trouble is, I hate waitressing, and I don't qualify for much else."

"You wrote me that your father left you a nest egg. So, you don't have to hurry do you? What about college?"

"Well, that nest egg has to last and there are five of us. The money is quickly being eaten up in furnishing the place and fixing it up. When winter comes, it's going to cost a fortune to heat it. I hope we haven't made a big mistake."

"You could do a quick course at secretarial school and get a decent job."

"Ugh," she said. "I learned how to type in Indianapolis, but I hated the noise and the tedium."

"Well, my friend Jacob manages his father's department store where lots of young people work. Do you want me to ask him if they need anyone."

"Oh, Walter, I could kiss you!"

Bess turned and kissed him on the lips. Walter stumbled backwards. He looked stunned.

"My, my, Little Bess. That was a very nice kiss. Very nice, indeed."

Bess was surprised too. She had thought Walter would kiss her back.

Walter said, "Let's leave the dishes. I can do them later. I think perhaps we need to talk."

Bess sat on the couch and Walter pulled up a chair to face her.

"I don't know where to start, Bess. This isn't easy for me to tell you. You may not want to be my friend anymore."

"Walter, whatever you say, we'll be friends. I promise." She was sure he was about to say he had a girlfriend or a fiancée and braced herself for disappointment.

Walter explained how difficult life had always been for him. He never had felt that he fit in anywhere and he never felt he was what his father wanted him to be.

Bess had felt ebullient while they were doing the dishes, but Walter's somber mood confused her. She listened to Walter, but she was embarrassed about the kiss.

He continued, "What I am saying is that all of my life I have been trying to deny something about myself."

Bess said, "I am not sure how true any of us are to ourselves. Poppa always wanted to be a singer, but he became a tailor. I am not sure what on earth I want to do."

"Please, Bess, this is difficult. Just let me talk. I have always been attracted to men. I mean I prefer men." Walter paused and Bess stared at him wide-eyed. Walter resumed. "Do you understand what I'm trying to say?"

"Not really," Bess said. "Do you mean you don't like women?"

"I loved my sister Charlotte, more than life."

"And your mother."

"Yes, I love my mother, and I pray she is still alive."

"But you are not interested in me."

"Of course, I am. I was so charmed by you in Frankfort. You were so spunky and talented. I so wanted you to beat that unbearable girl." Walter paused. "And I think I was infatuated with you."

"Really? With me? I was so. . . awkward." Bess remembered how plump and unattractive she had felt then.

"I guess it was the idea of you. You were friendly and not anything like the wealthy girls in Paducah whose fathers were so interested in me because I was a German Jew. I wanted to be in love with you. I wanted to be in love with a girl and not be attracted to boys. Father was delighted that I was writing to you. And I spent most of my life trying to win his approval. My whole life he tried to make me more manly. He taught me to swim, to box, to hunt. When it was obvious I would never excel at those manly sports, he became a tyrant about the violin. I loved the violin, but I lived in fear of not being the best. In Berlin I had the support of my mother and sister. But Paducah and Cincinnati were unbearable. I lived in fear of his discovering I would never be like him."

"So that is why your letter sounded so bleak and you stopped writing for so long."

"Bleak. Yes, I gave up on life."

"But surely it couldn't have been that awful."

Walter looked at the floor and then he stood and took a deep breath. "It was worse. Father discovered me kissing a boy, another violinist. The only friend I had in Cincinnati. Father physically threw him out of our apartment. This I never told you, but after that, I tried to take my life."

Bess gasped.

"So, Bess, I am so sorry to ruin our celebration. Please, say you don't hate me. Surely, you have met men like me before."

Bess shook her head no.

"I'm sure you have. You just didn't know it."

Bess sat quietly not knowing what to do or say. Then she faced him. "Walter Schreiber, you are my friend, and you always will be."

Chapter 44
Keeping the Peace

Bess sat at the Brown Hotel Coffee Shop waiting for Phyllis and Naomi. Since the Habermanns didn't do anything much for birthdays, Bess wanted to do something special for her friend. She hoped her girlfriends would get along. If she could steer the conversation away from the war in Europe, there might not be fireworks. Naomi was adamant that the United States should be fighting Germany, while Phyllis and her family wanted to stay out of war at all costs.

There was another reason Phyllis and Naomi might argue. Naomi felt that nursing school was the ideal way for a woman to help the world. Phyllis took a more lighthearted approach to life. She liked working at Wasserman's Department Store. Walter's friend Jacob had gotten them both jobs, and Phyllis had met a wonderful guy named Irv. Bess liked working in cosmetics. Just yesterday she had sold a woman a whole line of makeup and perfume. Her commission would help when Christmas bonuses came out. Bess also enjoyed the guys who worked there. None of them swept her off her feet, but it was fun to go to a dance or a movie. Just today, Irv had introduced her to a nice-looking guy named Eddie. Nice enough but so quiet.

The truth was, Bess was getting bored with the silly gossip about who was going out with whom and the routine at the department store. Naomi had convinced her that nursing school would not only be fascinating, but it would lead to a life of adventure. Bess had arranged everything with the dean just yesterday. She glanced out the window to see Phyllis strolling down Fourth toward the Brown.

Phyllis scooched in next to Bess in the red leather booth. "Lucky you to have a day off. The new manager wouldn't let me get out early. Jacob Wasserman would have let me go in a heartbeat. What a sweetheart he was. And handsome. All the girls at Wasserman's are dejected now that he's left for New York."

"Yes, I imagine," Bess said. She'd not been surprised when Walter had called to give her the news that he and Jacob were moving. They staggered their departure to avoid generating suspicion. True to her word, Bess hadn't mentioned a word to anyone about his relationship with Jacob.

Naomi walked in and said, "Sorry I'm late. Gosh, this place smells great. I could eat a side of beef." She sat down and smiled at Phyllis. "Hey Phyllis, nice to see you. Pretty sweater."

Good, Bess thought, Naomi was trying to be friendly. If they could keep the conversation on clothes.

Phyllis beamed and said, "A benefit of working at Wasserman's. Did you know Bess has bought a whole set of dishes for her family."

"Yes, I'll miss those benefits," Bess said.

Phyllis turned and shot her a quizzical look, "What do you mean by that?"

Oh dear. She had let the cat out of the bag first thing. "I mean that I have to quit after the first of the year to start nursing school."

"What? Are you crazy? I thought you needed the money. Can you afford the tuition?" Phyllis could be so blunt.

"Well, they are not only letting me into the program in the middle of the year because of my advanced science credits, but they are also offering me a stipend and room and board."

"And doesn't your family need your wages for that big house you live in?"

"No need to worry, Phillie. Everything is fine."

Phyllis scrunched up her face. "If you say so. I'm only concerned for your well being, you know."

An elderly Negro waiter walked up and greeted them. "Would you ladies like a cocktail before lunch?"

Bess knew Naomi didn't drink, so she ordered iced tea. Naomi ordered lemonade. Phyllis shrugged her shoulders and said, "Well, I guess I'll have a

Coca Cola since y'all are being such party poopers."

The lunch was delicious, and the conversation was light and friendly. As the waiter cleared the dishes, Naomi brought up the situation in Europe. Bess cringed. Now they were in for it.

"You've seen how Hitler broke the Non-Aggression Declaration. We can't let him take over Europe and then the world," Naomi said.

Phyllis glared at her and said, "Yes, but do we have to let a crazy man turn our country upside down? He is never coming here."

"I wouldn't be so sure. But in the meantime, my brothers are serving in the Army, and they are ready to join the fight against the Nazis. I plan to enlist myself."

"Look, Naomi, my father fought the Kaiser in World War I, and he lost an eye doing it. He does not want my brothers sent to die over Europe's problems." Phyllis had an answer for everything.

"And my father's best friend is sitting in a Gestapo prison and will probably be executed as a traitor just because he won't swear loyalty to Herr Hitler."

Bess sighed. There was no way to put this cat back in the bag. Then the waiter arrived and bailed them out a second time. He carried a chocolate cake lit with lots of candles.

After they sang "Happy Birthday," Phyllis shrugged her shoulders and smiled at Naomi as if to say a truce had been called. Bess gave her friend a pair of kid gloves and a tube of the newest hand cream. Phyllis gave her a card and wished her the best. "We may disagree about Europe, but we can still be friends. Happy birthday."

Then she turned to Bess, "You may leave Wasserman's but I'm not giving up on you and Eddie. He's terrific. You'll see."

Chapter 45
Another Move

While Calvin lugged Bess's bags out to Maishe Yoffee's truck, she took one last look at her robin's egg blue room and sighed. "Well, I had my own room for five months." She wondered what it would be like sleeping in a room full of nursing students.

On the way to the residence, Calvin told her that he'd tried to enlist in the Army, but they wouldn't take him because of his crooked thumb.

"That's crazy. You can do anything anyone else can do. But still, Momma really needs you now. Maybe it's for the best."

Calvin shrugged. Bess knew he was champing at the bit to be out on his own. Living with so many women. Even Toby was bossy. Bess felt eager to be free of them herself. Before long, Calvin was slowing down, looking at the street numbers.

"This is it." Bess braced herself as Calvin put on the brakes.

"It looks swell," Calvin remarked carrying her bags up the front stairs.

As they walked inside, a voice called out, "No men allowed beyond this point." A girl Bess's age added with a sigh, "Well, except the last Saturday of the month. Come back then," she said. "By the way, I'm Gladys."

"I'm Calvin, but my friends call me Angel. I'm her brother."

Gladys turned to Bess. "And you must be our new student, Bess Toplansky."

"Yes, nice to meet you, Gladys."

"Welcome, to your new home. I'll help you with your bags."

Bess thanked her brother and hugged him goodbye. Gladys said, "Don't forget, Angel. We have an open house party at the end of the month."

Calvin winked and said, "You betcha."

The house smelled of furniture polish, women's cologne, and coffee. The big oak stairway was carpeted and full of light. Bess liked the place already.

Gladys skipped up the stairs with Bess's bags in tow as though they were filled with feathers. "This is it, Bess. Welcome to Shangri La."

There were eight beds in the room. The walls were festooned with posters of Hollywood Stars and clothing hung on hooks in an alcove.

"Looks like a barracks, but you'll get used to it. Here look." She pointed across the hall at an identical room.

"We share a bathroom. That's pretty crazy. Mrs. Knightly doesn't like us to use her bathroom on the first floor, but you can when she's not here. And you can always run to the basement in a pinch. There's a commode and a shower down there. There's also ping pong and a pool table in the basement. Here, this bed has your name on it."

Gladys dropped Bess's bags by the bed.

"You can unpack later. Let's go downstairs, and I'll make us some coffee."

"It's really quiet here."

"Don't get used to it. It's a madhouse when we're all together. The rest have a shift at Norton's Hospital, and I have a day off. So does our house mother."

The kitchen appliances, floor, and sink shone. As the coffee percolated, Gladys showed Bess where everything was stored. A sign over the sink said, "Let's keep this place spotless." Gladys poured their coffee. "Come on, I'll show you around and we can relax in the parlor."

The dining room had two big tables. In the living room there was a fireplace, tables with lamps for study, shelves of books, two large sofas, and an upright piano. Bess ran her fingers over the keys. Not bad.

"Hey, do you play?"

"Not so much, lately," Bess said.

"We roll up the rug for our parties and dance in here and the front hall. Everywhere but upstairs. Mrs. Knightly keeps an eagle eye on us. You'll meet her tonight."

Bess was relieved to hear about parties. Naomi had said a career in nursing would lead to a life of adventure, but all her friend did was study and work.

Nursing school was demanding. After three weeks of classes, Bess was doing well, all except for Advanced Chemistry. But help was on the way. She watched out of the living room window for Naomi, who had promised to come by to check her lab notebook. If only Naomi lived in the student residence with her, things would be so much easier, but she had decided to stay at home. She had to make sure her father was taken care of now that her brothers and sisters were all out of the house. Naomi's mother worked full-time at St. Anthony's in the Emergency Room, and ever since Annabelle's mother had quit, they hadn't gotten any more help. Mrs. Rowan had moved to Chicago with her daughter and new son-in-law.

"Hey, come on in," Bess greeted her friend. "You are one good egg. I wouldn't be passing chemistry without you."

Bess motioned to the table by the fire where she had her books.

"Let's get to it," Naomi said.

"You're going to see that I don't get this stuff at all."

After a few minutes, Naomi looked up from circling mistakes and asked, "How ever did you win the science award in high school?"

Bess grinned at Naomi's teasing. "Miss Jacobson wanted me to have the money. I was good in biology and anatomy."

After Naomi explained the concepts patiently, Bess corrected her lab manual. "Phew, that was tough. By the way, are you coming to our party tomorrow night?"

"Nope. Father needs someone to type his sermon, and I haven't had a minute to spare."

Bess knew it would be useless to try to change her mind. Naomi tended to avoid big parties. As awkward as Bess sometimes felt about being short, she was sure her old neighbor hated being so tall.

Saturday night the two bedrooms were a rollicking mess as the nursing students shared perfume, hair creams, clothes, and shoes. They jostled to inspect themselves in the mirror in the hallway. There was laughter and loud conjecture as to which of the med students was the handsomest and which would show up for their party.

The housemother called upstairs, "Ladies, your guests will be here soon, so you'd best stop dillydallying and get down here and set up the refreshments. And I better not find a mess if I go upstairs to inspect."

Actually, Bess had learned that Mrs. Knightly never came upstairs if she could help it. She preferred to read magazines and drink coffee or sneak a cigarette out on the back porch.

All sixteen girls trooped downstairs at once and went to their preassigned stations. Bess had volunteered with Gladys to take care of the punch. No one knew she could play piano, and she liked it that way. At the punch bowl, she could meet guys without having to wait for them to ask her to dance. Then when she had a break, she'd maybe play ping pong in the basement. She was pretty good with a paddle.

Bess was delighted when Phyllis showed up with Irv and Eddie in tow. They were both in uniform.

"Can we crash this party?" Irv asked.

Bess's new friend Gladys said, "Soldiers are always welcome here."

"Bessie, what are you doing at the punch table? You should dance with Eddie," Phyllis said.

"It's my turn to serve the punch."

"Oh, malarky! Irv and I can run this stand for a few minutes."

Irv didn't cotton to the idea. "Don't be long," he said.

It was a slow lindy. Eddie's hands were clammy, and he had barely managed to say how nice it was to see her.

When they went back to the refreshment table, another girl had taken over. Bess invited Eddie to sit in the kitchen. Maybe he'd be more comfortable where it was a bit quieter.

"So, you have enlisted. Where are you stationed?"

"We're at Fort Knox."

"Do you think you'll actually get a chance at the Nazis?"

"Yes, I think so. Otherwise, I've marched and hiked in the mud for nothing."

Bess grinned. She liked his attitude and his sense of humor.

Gladys ran in. "Bess Toplansky, your secret is out. Report to the piano immediately."

"Oh dear, I've been recruited. Will you excuse me?" Eddie rose and followed her to the piano in the front room. She played "It Don't Mean a Thing if it Ain't Got That Swing" and Benny Goodman's "Sing, Sing, Sing." Eddie clapped to the music and sang along.

A med student Bess had met in surgery pushed Ed aside and sat down on the piano bench. "Hey nurse, you're not bad. Let's play two-piano. Do you know 'Lady Be Good?'"

Bess jumped up. "Maybe you should play it. I don't know it so well." She walked out the front door and sat down on the porch swing. Eddie followed her out. Phyllis and Irv were right behind him.

"That guy just wanted to horn in on your show," Phyllis said, and Irv agreed. Eddie stood there with a bewildered look on his face.

Irv said, "Why don't we blow this place and listen to some jazz. There's a hot new club on Jefferson Street."

"I need to stay here with my classmates, but thanks for coming to the party. Nice to see you again, Eddie." Bess hopped off the swing and held out her hand to shake his.

"I'm not in the mood for clubbing," he said. "I'll stay here for a while if it's okay."

"It's a free country."

Everyone laughed, but Phyllis leaned over and whispered, "Give the guy a chance."

Bess invited Eddie to sit on the steps with her despite the chill in the air.

"So, why did you enlist?"

"You know what they say, 'Join the Army and see the world.' How about you? You are a first-class musician. Why are you studying nursing?"

"I really liked science in high school, and I like helping people. Does that sound corny?"

"Nope," he said. "I understand completely."

Unlike most boys, Bess had met, Eddie asked questions and listened to the answers. The time passed quickly. Bess glanced at her watch. "Hey, it's getting late. The party will be over soon, and I'd better go in help with the clean up. The place has to be spotless for the housemother's inspection."

Eddie thanked Bess for a great time and said good night.

She walked up the porch steps and turned to wave goodbye. Eddie was still standing watching her. He came up the stairs.

"Bess, I just wondered whether..." He twisted his private's cap in his hands and shuffled from foot to foot.

"What, Eddie? What were you wondering?" Bess tried not to laugh at his discomfort.

"I wondered whether I ... I really would like to write to you."

Bess grinned. "Yes, of course. And I'll write back."

They said a quick goodbye and Bess watched him walk away into the darkness.

Another nursing student was brushing her teeth as Bess went into the big bathroom. "Who was that fellow you danced with?"

"Just someone I met when I worked at Wasserman's."

"He's nice looking and seemed like he was sweet on you."

Bess shrugged, "It's hard to tell. He's kind of quiet."

Chapter 46
Dear Walter

OCTOBER 1941

On her days off Bess answered letters from Eddie and Walter. She opened Walter's letter first and read it quickly. He had gotten his citizenship, and he and his friend Jacob were planning to enlist in the armed services.

Dear Walter,

Congratulations on becoming a Yank. But I am worried about you. If you end up enlisting, they could send you to Germany, and won't it be dangerous as a Jew? Please do think about this carefully.

To answer your first question, yes, Momma and Poppa are from Bialystok and yes, the Courier Journal had a front-page story about Nazis killing Jews in the main square in Bialystok. It was in April, I believe. If Poppa were not already dead, that news might have killed him. He loved Bialystok.

To answer your second question, I am very happy in my training. As second-year students, we have a lot of responsibility. We do the dirty work like cleaning bed pans and changing beds. We're short of staff, so everyone pitches in. I love working with patients. The first shift of my second year was in the department of psychiatry at Louisville City Hospital. It was disturbing to see such lost people. Naomi had told me about shock therapy, so I knew what it entailed, but I didn't realize the people would be so desperate. I learned that psychiatry was not something I would like to pursue. I loved pediatrics at St. Anthony's. It was great fun to be taller than my patients. But Jewish Hospital was the best experience, so far. I was on General Surgery. Would you believe the very same doctor who delivered me showed up on my first day in the suit Poppa had made to pay for his services? Dr. Rubel is a joy to work with. He is so patient and takes so much time to explain everything. He loves that I'm so quick with the instruments. Not all the doctors are as kind as he is.

The Parmers send their love. Your goddaughter Lucy is adorable. She turns two next week, and I'll go to her birthday party, if only for a few minutes. She already plays "Twinkle, Twinkle, Little Star" on the piano.

Please write soon.

Your friend,
Bess

Next, she opened Ed's latest letter. She laughed out loud. He'd just been put in charge of the mechanics at an air base in Mississippi.

Greenville Army Airfield
Greenville, Mississippi

Dear Bess,

I've never worked on anything other than a crossword puzzle and the guys know it. I don't let any planes go unless they look exactly like the pictures in the manual. Yesterday two pilots locked me in the storeroom and took off without my authorization. Everyone has had a good laugh about that except the base commander who doesn't know it happened.

Thanks to your recommendations, you have turned me into a Gershwin fan. You are the world's best music appreciation teacher.

Bess put Eddie's letter on the bed for a second. She knew what he would write next. How pretty she was. How smart. They had spent so little time together, and he was getting too serious. She picked up the letter again.

Looks like I've finagled a weekend leave, and I'm coming to see
you even if I have to spend most of the weekend on the train.

Bess picked up a pen and considered her words carefully. She didn't want to lead Eddie on. She felt he was rushing her, so she'd best keep things on an even keel. As always, she wrote to him about her training. She said how much she dreaded her new rotation, the maternity ward. Gladys had warned her that the head nurse at General Hospital was a martinet and wouldn't put up with even minor infractions of the rules. Bess closed by saying she was happy he had a weekend pass to come home.

She was happy, but she also wondered where this relationship was going.

Chapter 47
Maternity Ward

OCTOBER 1941

Gladys was right. The head nurse on maternity was a tyrant, famous for getting nurses dismissed. Despite Bess's worry about measuring up to Nurse Wagner's impossibly high standards, the work was rewarding. It was lovely to roll in the babies for the mothers to feed. When the crying subsided, the anxious mothers calmed down. The little blue and pink bundles pulled at their mothers' breasts or sucked energetically at their bottles.

Sadly, a few mothers had a rough time. The painkillers administered after delivery left them lethargic. Other mothers had no one to visit them. Bess felt sorry for the mothers whose husbands were not there to bring potted plants, candy, and flowers. Maybe they were in the service.

A few weeks after she'd started on the ward, Nurse Wagner called Bess aside and put her in charge of a woman, a girl really, who had just arrived.

"The baby died just after birth. Methemoglobinemia. The mother's from outside Louisville, from Okolona. You know where that is?"

"No, ma'am."

"It's a dirt-poor place just to the south. She probably drinks contaminated well water."

"Oh dear, poor thing." Bess had studied blue baby syndrome, but she thought death was unusual.

"Well, just keep a close watch on her. She's unmarried. She could be trouble."

Bess bristled at Nurse Wagner's words. It wasn't the patient's fault she was poor. She went to the patient's bedside. The black curls matted to her pale forehead reminded Bess of her mother when she'd lost a baby.

"Good morning, Mandy, I'm a student nurse, Bess Toplansky. I'm here to take your vitals and make sure you are comfortable. How are you doing?"

"Porely," Mandy answered.

"Does anything hurt you?"

"Everything."

Bess was extra gentle with Mandy's care, and when lunch came, she put a daisy on her tray.

When she came around to help the woman go to the bathroom, she saw Mandy's flower on the floor, so she put it on her bedside table. Her act of kindness backfired.

Mandy shoved everything off her tray and yelled, "I don't need no flowers. I jist want to git out of this durn place."

The crashing plates and Mandy's outburst frightened the mothers whose babies started wailing. Mandy shoved Bess away and tried to get out of bed alone.

Nurse Wagner had observed it all. She rushed in to restrain the patient. She ordered Bess to administer a sedative. As the head nurse closed the leather straps on Mandy's wrist, Bess thought of the patients in the psych ward. Mandy thrashed as the head nurse buckled her legs.

"This place is worse than a prison," Mandy yelled. She cursed the nurses, the doctors, the fool babies, and the mothers until the sedative took effect.

When the shift ended, Nurse Wagner called Bess aside and asked her what had gotten Mandy so upset.

"I don't know. I gave her a flower and it had fallen on the floor, so I put it on her tray, and she blew up."

"Why did you put a flower on her tray?"

"I felt bad for her. The only woman in the ward without a baby."

"You can't help patients heal if you feel sorry for them. You are their nurse, not their friend. You are in charge, and keeping order is the most helpful thing you can do."

The next day Bess returned to the hospital determined to be extra careful. The nurse going off duty filled her in on the ward. She said Mandy had had another outburst. Bess looked at the girl's chart. She'd been administered a heavy dose of painkillers and was still tied to the bed. It was unsettling to see a patient this way.

Bess took Mandy's temperature. Normal, but her eyes were hollow, and she looked like she had been crying.

"I hear you got upset last night." Bess whispered, "I know how sad you must feel. My mother had three miscarriages."

"Your mother lost babies. So what. I bet your momma had a husband and other babies to home. I ain't got nothin', so just keep your stories to yourself."

"Mandy, you are young, and you will have other babies. You need to rest and get strong."

"You don't know chicken scat about me. Jist leave me alone."

Mandy's words stung. Most of Bess's patients loved her. How on earth was she to respond. And the woman still needed to be examined. How was she going to do that now? If she asked the head nurse for advice, she would be in trouble for sure. She was on her own.

"Just remember who's in charge," Nurse Wagner had said. So, Bess lifted Mandy's gown. The girl was all skin and bones and had yellow bruises up and down her legs. She checked her stitches and was glad to see the wound was healing. She stuck a thermometer in her patient's mouth while she took her blood pressure. Her temperature was normal and blood pressure good. A relief. Still, she felt helpless to do anything for her.

That afternoon Bess checked Mandy's lab results and saw that she was still anemic. She hadn't been turned or bathed in two days. That wouldn't do.

After removing the restraints, Bess turned Mandy on her side and began to wash her very gently. The girl was so full of tranquilizers and pain killers that she didn't move. Bess was worried about Mandy's wrists. She was getting sores from the restraints. She needed ointment and gauze on her wrists. Where was the damned gauze? Her supply cart was just outside the room. As she stepped back into the room, Mandy's bed pan crashed to the floor. Mandy was screaming. The other patients were terrified. Mandy slid off her bed, limped over to her shelf, and pulled her suitcase down.

"Mandy, get back in bed. You're in no shape to be walking around."

"Git outa my way, girlie. I'm leaving this durned prison."

Bess grabbed the suitcase so hard that Mandy was left with the handle and fell to the floor.

"What in the name of all that is holy is going on here? Miss Toplansky, call the orderlies, and wait for me in my office."

Bess waited in the office for what seemed an eternity. Nurse Wagner's grimace, when she walked in, was etched in stone. "Well, Miss Toplansky, you handled that well."

"I am so sorry."

"Look, apologies mean nothing. If you cannot assert authority, maybe you need to find another profession."

"But the patient needed to be turned and her wrists were abraded."

"And so you left her alone? Was she better off falling? Did you think of that?"

"No, Nurse Wagner."

"That woman may have needed your attention, but you have the responsibility for the entire ward. The well-being of all the patients. That girl could have hurt someone or herself. I will have to write this up in your record. You should think good and hard about whether you have what it takes for this work. See me on Monday. For now, you are dismissed."

Bess went straight to the stairwell and had a good cry. Then she went to the bathroom, washed her face, and finished up the day. She needed to give her best to the babies and the mothers. She avoided looking at Mandy and somehow made it to three o'clock.

As she walked back to the residence, her mind buzzed with worries. She knew she should not have left Mandy unrestrained to get the gauze, and the more she thought about her poor judgment, the angrier she got at herself. It was a mistake a nurse should not make. She had let her emotions get in her way. But she could not believe how cruelly Mandy was being treated. And she didn't know how she could work under Nurse Wagner's eagle eyes for three more weeks. That woman had made her roommate Gladys's life miserable too. Bess worried about being thrown out of the program. It would be a shame for her and her family. She wasn't ready to go back to the residence, so she walked a few blocks and then a few blocks more. She felt chilly as the heat of the Indian Summer day dissipated, so she headed back to the residence.

She was startled to see a soldier sitting on the front steps.

"Hey Bess, I was just about to send a rescue party."

"Oh, Eddie, my goodness. I didn't think you'd be here until tomorrow."

"Well, I just got in, and I wanted to see you before I went home." Ed started to stand but Bess slumped down next to him.

"How was your day?" Ed asked.

"Next question."

"That bad?"

Bess started to sob, and Ed put his arm around her. A nurse skipped down the steps and said, "Hey, no smooching on the front porch, Bessie."

Ed said softly, "Let's go someplace quiet and talk."

They walked in silence to the park, the sun glaring in their faces. There were still a few kids playing tag and climbing on the swings.

"Allow me to buy you a drink," Ed said with a bow as they passed the water fountain. She laughed and took a sip. They sat on a bench and watched as the sunset turned the treetops red then purple then a soft gray surrounded them.

"Would it help to talk about it?" Ed asked.

Bess told him she thought she might not be cut out to be a nurse.

"I have a hard time believing that. You love nursing. Tell me what's wrong."

Bess told him about Mandy's condition. "I just don't know how I got that girl so upset. I only wanted to help her. Poor thing, no family there to support her and surrounded by mothers with their babies and their doting husbands."

"Tell me what you said to her again?"

"I told her about Momma's three miscarriages, and I said she was young and could still have babies. That was what set her off."

"How young is she?"

"Her chart said seventeen."

"And you said she had bruises on her body?"

Bess nodded. Eddie was quiet and after several moments said, "The girl was right. You don't know anything about her. You just can't know what other people have been through. Sounds like maybe she had been abused. Maybe her home situation isn't so great. Maybe she was relieved to lose the baby and felt guilty."

"Well, it gets worse. They restrained her with leather straps and the restraints were digging into her wrists."

"That sounds terrible."

"It was. Anyway, she needed to be bathed and turned and since she was calm—well, I thought she was calm—I took off the straps, moved her to her side, and gave her a quick sponge bath. I wanted to bandage her wrists, but I was out of gauze, so I walked away for a second to get supplies."

"And the patient was unrestrained?"

"Yes, but just for a second and I was only a few feet away. Suddenly, she was up throwing things and yelling. Then she and I wrestled with her suitcase, and she fell. Nurse Wagner came in to find utter chaos."

"Whoa, that is bad."

"Nurse Wagner wants to see me on Monday to discuss my future. I have three more weeks with that woman, and I'm on her bad side. She has kicked other students out of the school."

"You have one more year, right?"

Bess started crying again. Ed gave her his handkerchief.

"Don't cry. You may have done the right thing in taking off the restraints. But you didn't have the authority to do it. You aren't even a nurse yet."

"I'm not a nurse, but I know when a patient is being mistreated."

"Okay, okay. You may be right, but sometimes being right doesn't help your situation."

Bess was silent.

"You need to list all the ways you messed up to this head nurse. She's a bully and she'll stomp all over you if you don't. If I've learned anything in the army it is to just own up to your mistakes and move on."

Bess shook her head in agreement.

"Three weeks until you finish maternity and then you go to other rotations. You keep up the good work. You know Bess, the rules are always the rules."

"Look, Eddie, I'm tired and I just want to go back to the residence."

"Have I hurt your feelings?"

"No. I just think I'm not going to be much fun tonight."

They walked back to the residence in silence. Ed rubbed her shoulder and Bess pulled away. She was both angry and chagrined. Sobered by Eddie's words.

The porch lights were lit, and a few nurses were outside on the porch smoking or chatting with their boyfriends.

Bess took Ed's hand, "You rode the train all the way from Mississippi to see me, and I'm down at the mouth. Sorry."

"Well, I had something to tell you. Well to ask."

"What is it?"

"I'm being moved to a base in Massachusetts, and we leave Sunday morning."

"Oh, goodness, so soon?"

"I just wanted to know whether you would come to visit me there."

"Oh, Ed, I don't get many days off, and when I do, there's always so much to do for Momma."

"I understand," he said. "But you'll keep on writing me, right?"

"Of course. I love your letters. Your stories amaze me."

"May I kiss you goodnight?"

Bess nodded.

He lowered his face, and when their lips met, she felt her worries disappear.

Chapter 48
Declarations

DECEMBER 7-8, 1941

Bess was home for the third night of Chanukah chatting with Phyllis. The fire in the hearth was blazing and Bubby Adel was nodding off to sleep. The candles on the mantle had melted all over the menorah. Momma was sitting on the couch pulling the basting out of a hem. Toby wanted to play dreidel, but Phyllis didn't know how. Bess explained the Hebrew letters on the four sides of the old wooden top Adel had brought from Bialystok.

"I can't believe you've never played dreidel!" Bess said as her friend flubbed the first spin. Soon Toby was jumping with delight. She was winning and had a pile of matchsticks in front of her.

Angel walked in with Cousin Joe who asked, "Hey, why are you betting with matchsticks? Didn't we used to play with pennies even when we couldn't afford matches?" He threw a pile of coins on the table and said, "Let's have some real action here."

There was a loud knock at the back door, but before anyone could answer it, their landlady Mrs. Neumann ran into the dining room. "The Japanese have bombarded our naval base in Hawaii," she cried. "Quick, turn on your radio. Mrs. Roosevelt is going to speak."

Bess smiled remembering that Poppa always said Eleanor should be the president. She turned on the Zenith to hear the First Lady's words.

> *Good evening, ladies and gentlemen, I am speaking to you tonight*
> *at a very serious moment in our history.... We know what we have*
> *to face and we know that we are ready to face it. ... Whatever is*
> *asked of us I am sure we can accomplish it. We are the free and*

unconquerable people of the United States of America....

...

> *To the young people of the nation, I must speak a word tonight.*
> *You are going to have a great opportunity. There will be high*
> *moments in which your strength and your ability will be*
> *tested. I have faith in you. I feel as though I was standing upon*
> *a rock and that rock is my faith in my fellow citizens.*

When the speech was over, everyone sat there stunned. Mrs. Neumann was the first to speak. "You know what this means. War will be declared."

"I'm enlisting tomorrow," said Calvin.

Bess wished she could do the same. The Army had been recruiting nurses since the first days of her training. Mrs. Roosevelt had inspired her to think again about joining up. Bess was sure they would take her brother now, crooked thumb or not. And what about Eddie? Where would he be sent? If they could serve their country, so could she.

Cousin Joe hugged everyone and said his goodbyes. "I better get home to Mom and Pop with this news. I'm sure they'll be shipping me out soon."

There was a somber mood at the hospital on Monday. Everyone was talking about Pearl Harbor, a place they had never heard of before now. At 1:30, nurses, doctors, orderlies, and janitors gathered around the radio in the break room to listen to the President's address to Congress. The hospital had gone silent as had the members of Congress as the president began to speak. The legislators erupted in applause at several points. Then FDR concluded with these words:

> *With confidence in our armed forces, with the*
> *unbounding determination of our people, we will*
> *gain the inevitable triumph. So help us God."*

Everyone in the break room cheered along with the hoots and cheers in Congress. Energized by FDR's determination, the staff charged out to resume their duties.

That night Bess came home to have supper with her family. She told her mother that since the Armed Services would recruit nurses for their training while they were in school, she intended to apply.

"No, that you would not do. You'll be here with us. The Army is no place for a woman. And especially, no place for a Jewish woman. Anyway, Dr. Rubel's wife told me that as soon as you graduate, they want you at Jewish Hospital."

Adel walked into the kitchen and shook her finger at Mollie, "Listen my daughter, I don't want our maidele to be in danger, but think of our history. What if the Jews hadn't fought the tyrants? Would we have survived?"

"But the women didn't fight." Momma was as stubborn as Bubby.

For once, Bess got the last word, "Those were other times. You heard what Mrs. Roosevelt said last night about the women. 'We must 'rise above our fears.'"

Chapter 49
Nurse Cadets

Monday through Thursday for nine weeks Bess and the other army nurse cadets were bused down Dixie Highway to Fort Knox. Then they worked in Louisville hospitals all weekend. No days off. At Fort Knox they trained in battle wound dressings, general surgery, plastic surgery, and orthopedics. The girls usually got some shut eye on the hour drive. As soon as they arrived, they divided up and went to their assigned posts.

There was no special curriculum. The students just shadowed nurses in three rotations. The first week they watched, the second week they assisted, and the third week they had to sink or swim. In the afternoon, there were lectures and demonstrations. They learned how to set up a field hospital and how to evacuate it. On the bus home, full of caffeine and new knowledge, they sang all the way back.

Bess had plastic surgery last rotation, and she was amazed at how noses and jaws could be reconstructed. She surprised herself by being able to make tiny sutures. Having a tailor for a father and a seamstress for a mother paid off. Today they had reconstructed the ear of a man who'd been shot in basic training. First, they harvested cartilage from the soldier's ribs. Then they took a bit of skin from behind his ear. Bess closed the wounds on his chest. "That's it nurse," the surgeon said, delighted at how quickly and well she closed.

The soldier's surgery took three hours in total. Everyone was elated that the young man would look normal. He'd have some hearing loss, but that would improve over time. On morning rounds the next day, the surgeon and his students checked the soldier's ear and chest.

"This nurse has stitched you so well," the surgeon said, looking at Bess. "No one will ever know you were cut into."

Bess felt grateful for the colonel's kind words. But more than that, she'd never forget the soldier's smile.

Chapter 50
Pinning, Graduation, and Commission

The pinning ceremony was an intimate early morning ceremony with the faculty in the Board Room of Jewish Hospital. The fifteen students each had invited one guest to do the pinning. The young women rose together to take the Florence Nightingale Oath.

> *I solemnly pledge myself before God and in the presence of this assembly*
> *to pass my life in purity and to practice my profession faithfully. ...*
> *With loyalty will I aid the physician in his work, and as a missioner*
> *of health, I will dedicate myself to devoted service for human welfare.*

Bess Toplansky was last in line, so she watched with pride as the women she had worked and lived with lit their candles and received their nursing pins. Clara Habermann pinned Naomi. Tears streamed down Bess's face as Momma pinned the caduceus symbol on her.

Graduation was at ten a.m. A boisterous outdoor affair. Chairs had been set up on the lawn of the hospital.

Uncle Sam and Aunt Minnie had driven Bubby and Toby and arrived early to get seats up front. Uncle Abe and Aunt Hettie sent a telegram. They couldn't come because of gas rationing. Eddie's father called to say that Eddie had gotten leave but most likely would not get to Louisville in time for her graduation. Mrs. Neumann showed up with a bouquet of roses from the garden. Bubby had a new hat and dress for the occasion. She looked so small in the crowd even though she still stood straight. Bess looked for them as she filed onto the stage.

When Bess's name was called for honors, Uncle Sam cheered as if she'd hit a home run. The only sad note for Bess was that Poppa wasn't there to see her. And Calvin was in Texas and couldn't be there.

The reception was at the student residence. Family and friends filled the house and the front yard. Her classmates wanted her to meet their families, their beaus. Everyone wanted a picture with everyone else.

As the guests began leaving, Bess went upstairs to gather her belongings. There were so many teary goodbyes. Bess loved these girls like sisters. Some of the new nurses would be staying in Louisville. Others, like Bess, had been recruited into the service, although they all were heading in different directions. Naomi was heading for London that very evening, and Bess would leave for Washington, D.C. soon. She held up the Army uniform she'd wear that afternoon for the commission ceremony. Everything was happening so fast, but she was excited for the future.

Bess took her bags home and had lunch with her family and Mrs. Neumann in the garden. Bubby called Bess "meine doctorin" because in Bialystok, only Catholic women were nurses. Mrs. Neumann corrected her, and Bubby laughed. The two women had become fast friends over their well-tended victory garden. Dotty and her beau, a lieutenant in the Navy, arrived in time for dessert. Mrs. Neumann brought out her old victrola, and Toby entertained them by dancing and plucking daisies for everyone.

Then Bess changed into her uniform and took a cab downtown to the Armed Services Office. At the door stood Eddie. He looked different. Tan. Muscular. His hug felt great. She was proud that he had come for her induction.

After the brief ceremony, Eddie wanted to hear all about graduation. He wasn't surprised that she had graduated with honors.

"My family wants to meet you. Can you come for dinner?"

Bess nodded her head yes, but she dreaded dinner with Ed's family. The one time she had called his house, Mrs. Middleman hadn't been friendly at all. Ed had told her that his brother-in-law Wolf Berliner was a bit of a bully, although he doted on his sister. Ed's other sister would be there too, as well as his great uncle and Eddie's nephew and nieces, a toddler and two babies. Add in Mr. Middleman, and that was a lot of Middlemans and Berliners to deal with all at once.

Eddie's sister and brother-in-law were hosting dinner at their apartment. The Cherokee View Apartments stood atop a hill with well-tended shrubs and old shade trees. As Bess and Eddie ascended the long stone stairway up to the building, Bess felt as though she were going to Buckingham Palace to meet the queen.

"They must have a grand view."

"Yes, you can see all of the park."

Eddie's sister Gerta opened the door and gushed. "Oh, Bess, it's so good to finally meet you," she said as she drew Bess close to her impressive bosom. His sister Rosalie, an infant on each hip, said with a twinkle in her eyes, "You can't possibly be as great as Eddie says you are, but if you're even close. . ." Mrs. Middleman shook her hand, and Mr. Middleman gave her a hug. Uncle Shimmie greeted her in halting English. Gerta led them to the dining room table where Wolf sat at the head. He got up and greeted Bess with a big smile and a hearty handshake. She could see how he could be intimidating. With dark eyes behind thick glasses, bushy black eyebrows, and a booming voice, she sensed that Wolf was used to getting his way.

The table was set with fine china and silver. A Negro woman in a black uniform and a white apron and cap brought in platters of food.

"This is Miss Hattie, Bess. Miss Hattie, y'all make sure Bess gets plenty to eat," Gerta said.

"I will. I will. I heard all about y'all, Miss Bess."

Everyone talked at once. Adding to the confusion, Mrs. Middleman translated for her brother Shimmie, who spoke no English. The little boy sat in his aunt's lap and recited nursery rhymes, and the babies fussed. The sisters put them down to sleep. Things got quieter as Miss Hattie brought out a platter of meat. Bess put a small slice on her plate.

"What's that all about?" Wolf exclaimed. "We aren't rationing here. Hattie, give her more."

Toward the end of the meal, Bess heard Uncle Shimmie ask Mrs. Middleman in Yiddish why the girl wasn't eating anything. "Who knows? I don't think her family is used such fancy dining," she whispered in Yiddish.

"Ver iz ir tate?" Shimmie wanted to know who Bess's father was.

"Der schneider, Shlomo Toplansky."

"Yo, er iz geven oich a chazzen." He remembered that Poppa was a cantor at the Jacob Street Shul. Then he muttered that her father was a big gambler and lost everything.

Bess stiffened. She felt anger rise in her throat but she bit her tongue.

Ed said, "Y'all know I don't know Yiddish, but Bess does."

Mrs. Middleman turned red. She smiled at Bess with a smile that looked as though she smelled something rotten.

Ed stood up, "Sissie, Wolf, this has been great, but Bess and I have to stop by her family, and we haven't had any time alone."

Wolf roared, "Nonsense, sit down. We haven't had dessert yet."

Despite Wolf's order, Bess stood and pushed her chair under the table. She thanked Ed's sister and brother-in-law.

"Wait," said Gerta as she got up from the table. She threw Ed a set of car keys. "Here, show Bess around in style. There's a full tank of gas."

As they walked down to the underground garage, Ed asked what his uncle and mother were saying in Yiddish.

"Oh, they were just pinning down my family tree."

"Is that all? You looked fighting mad."

"Boy, can you read me," Bess said, and then she told Eddie that they said that Poppa had lost everything gambling which absolutely was not true.

"I know," said Eddie shaking his head. "Since Gerta married Wolf, Momma thinks we can put on airs. There's nothing fancy about us. We lived over our grocery store in Smoketown. Momma made corned beef and Pop sold bootlegged beer and schnapps to the workers from the baseball bat factory across the street. We're not blue bloods, that's for sure."

Bess grinned.

Chapter 51
A Ride

"This is a long ride, so get comfortable," Eddie said. "If it goes as planned, I'll show you something remarkable." They headed west on the parkway to a part of Louisville Bess had never seen. Bess asked about his transfer from Mississippi to Massachusetts.

"I couldn't be happier. I am sick of seeing how the Negroes are treated on base and off. I hope it's better up north."

"Will they put you in charge of the airplane mechanics again?" Bess said with a laugh knowing that Eddie was now editor of the base newspaper.

Eddie grinned.

"You are a terrific writer," Bess said. "Your letters make me feel like I'm there with you."

"Thanks, Bess, but I want to do more. I tried like heck to get into the new Officers Services School, but I just didn't make the grade."

"I, for one, am glad. I worry like crazy about Walter. I think he's probably somewhere in Germany undercover. What if I had to worry about you too?"

"I guess the army figures I'm not cut out to be a spy."

Bess didn't say anything, but she agreed with the army.

They pulled into a wooded area at the southern edge of the city limits.

"So this is Iroquois Park. My favorite spot in all of Louisville."

Ed drove up a steep, winding hill and parked the car.

"Are you ready to do some hiking? We have to move pretty fast. We're behind schedule." At first, they walked up a pine needle path in silence, then Ed started humming some marching songs and Bess joined in.

When they got to the top of Iroquois Hill, the sky was bright red. You could see for miles. In the distance, the lights of the city started to flicker on.

There was a big rocky outcropping where Ed invited Bess to sit. They sat and watched the sunset in silence.

"Ed this is the prettiest place in Louisville."

"Nothing less for you."

"You say the sweetest things."

"Only for the sweetest person I know.

"Come on, you know I am far from sweet."

Ed laughed and then turned to face Bess. His blue-gray eyes looked straight into hers.

"Well, you know how I feel about you, but the question is how do you feel about me?" When Bess didn't say anything, Ed braved on. "I know the going will be tough for the next year or so. Who knows what we'll face. We'll be apart. It is likely I'll be shipped to London or Paris to work for *Stars and Stripes*. You could be sent anywhere."

Bess nodded. She would be leaving any day for Walter Reed and from there who knew? She put her head on Ed's shoulder and he put his arm around her. Gently he pulled her chin to him and kissed her. Bess turned to put her arms around him. In that moment, Bess felt that Ed was the part of her that she never knew she was missing.

"So, Bess, I want to ask you to marry me. And I don't want to wait. We could go to a justice of the peace."

Bess stiffened a bit and said, "Oh! Eddie, I do love you." Bess was surprised to hear herself say that. "But…"

"What's the but?" Ed's eyes showed he was hurt.

"You said it yourself. We don't know where we'll be. That's no way to start a marriage."

"Then we should get engaged. We should think beyond this war." Ed clasped her hand and put a ring into it.

Bess saw the diamond sparkle in the waning light.

"How can you afford this?"

"My mother wants you to have it. It was her engagement ring."

"Are you sure your mother gave it up willingly? For me?"

"Well, Pop gave her one with a bigger diamond."

Ed took Bess's laughter as a signal to put the ring on her finger. They kissed again and walked back to the car hand in hand, stumbling a bit in the path.

On the drive back Bess held out her hand. The diamond sparkled in the streetlights.

Chapter 52
Union Station

JUNE 6, 1943

On the morning Bess was to leave for Walter Reed, news had just come out about a terrible accident in Baltimore Harbor. A ship loaded with explosives had been rammed by another American vessel. A hundred sailors had burned to death. Bess knew that in addition to their injuries, the survivors would be shell shocked. She felt an urgency to get to D.C.

She was going alone to the station because she knew it would be packed with military personnel and not a good place for her teary-eyed mother. Momma had been moping all morning. As she cleaned up from breakfast, she pulled up her apron and dabbed her eyes. Momma was certain she would never see Bess again. She started crying, and Toby joined in.

"Please don't cry. It only makes it harder," Bess said as she hugged them both tightly. She picked up her bag and went to the back door, where Bubby waited to say goodbye.

"Gute maydeleh. We very proud," she said. Bubby now spoke English but generously mixed with Yiddish. "You will be in danger, but you are shtarke, very strong."

At least Bubby didn't worry about her. "Please, Bubby, convince Momma I'll be fine."

Bubby spat three times. "You'll be fine. You have a good head on your shoulders, so God willing, you would save lives and help our soldiers kill those beasts, who should rot in Gehenna."

"Oh, Bubby, I'll miss you."

"Maybe you would never see me again, so I want you should have something from me." Bubby Adel handed Bess her book of Bible stories in Yiddish. "I can't see to read it no more, and anyway I know it by heart."

Bess brought the book to her face. The soft leather binding smelled of Bubby's hands. Bess kissed her grandmother. "It's a precious gift, Bubby. Thank you."

"Go, go," Adel said, pushing Bess away. "Don't miss your train, and don't thank me. Just be well."

Bess took a cab to the station. As she had thought, it was jammed. There were posters and banners and all kinds of uniforms. She was proud to stand among them in her own uniform. She was checking for her departure gate when she saw a slim woman in a cream-colored linen suit surrounded by luggage. It was Mary D. Bess turned away quickly hoping her old nemesis hadn't seen her. But of course, she had.

"Bess? Bess Toplansky? Is that y'all?" Mary D hurried over. A Negro porter followed, hefting her bags.

Bess smiled. "Well, Mary Dianne Porter, how are you?"

"I do declare, I almost didn't recognize you. Y'all look so fine and slender in that uniform. I mean I just wasn't sure it was you."

Bess answered, "You look lovely too, Mary D." It wasn't quite true. Up close, Bess realized her old rival looked gaunt and tired.

"So, where are you off to, Bess?"

"Washington, D.C., to work at Walter Reed Hospital. No doubt, I'll be shipped overseas within a few weeks."

At that moment a soldier bumped into Bess, and then seeing her bars, he saluted her. "Excuse me, ma'am," he said.

Bess saluted back.

"You're an officer?" Mary D asked.

Bess nodded. "They give all the nurses the rank of lieutenant, but it doesn't mean much. The men really don't have to salute us. Where are you headed, Mary D?"

Mary D laughed. "Nothing far away and glamorous like you've in store. Just some parties in Lexington before the big auction. Y'all know Daddy's horse Miss Dogwood?"

Bess shook her head no. She had to suppress a laugh. How would she have met a horse?

"Land's sake, she raced here and won the Kentucky Oaks. I mean it was in the papers all around the country. Anyway, they're selling her foals."

There was a call for the train to Lexington.

"Well, I'd best hurry. We have so much to do in Lexington, what with my husband—y'all remember George—looking to get us a young filly. We despise this war, but it has been good for family business. Whiskey, tobacco, and horses. They keep George busy. What would we Kentuckians do without them?" Mary D shrugged her shoulders and sighed. Bess and Mary D hugged, and her old classmate hurried off.

"Whiskey, tobacco, and horses, indeed," Bess muttered indignantly. And if George was George Watterson Clay III, Mary D's high school beau, why was he buying horses and not in the service like every other able-bodied man his age in the country.

Bess heard someone yelling her name. She turned to see Calvin running toward her. She still swelled with pride seeing her Angel in uniform.

"How on earth did you get off base?" Bess asked.

"The sergeant owed me one. Here. You'll need pin money." Calvin stuffed a wad of cash into Bess's pocket.

"Uh oh, you've been gambling again."

"I always win."

"Thanks, Calvin, but shouldn't you give this money to Momma?"

"Don't worry, I'll take care of Momma. You take good care of yourself."

At the first call for her train, Bess and Calvin clutched one another.

"I'm so proud of you, Sis. You be careful."

"You take care of yourself. And stay out of trouble, Angel."

Bess boarded her train and found a seat in a sea of uniforms. There wasn't another woman in the car. As the train pulled out of the station, Bess took off her gloves and put them into her army-issue satchel. She put the money from Calvin into a zipper compartment. She stared at the sparkly filigree ring on her finger. She took it off and put it into a little velvet bag. For now, these were the skilled hands of a surgical nurse.

ACKNOWLEDGEMENTS

"War Stories" was published online in *Flashquake* and nominated for a Pushcart Prize in 2011.

"Mrs. Parmer's Dress" appeared online as "Mrs. Parmenter's Dress" in *The Jewish Literary Journal*, 2014 as did "The Substitution" in 2019.

There are innumerable people to thank for their help in getting this book finished. From the time I was little, I heard my mother Ethel Cooper Baer's stories about The Great Flood, about the golden garden, the grape arbor behind their home on East Broadway, and the Lutheran pastor's family next door. Mom didn't mind that I called her Bess, since she'd never liked the name Ethel. She generously allowed me to veer from the truth: she turned down an invitation to play a recital at the Pendennis Club. She was delighted when "Mrs. Parmenter's Dress" was published. It was the last story she read. She would have been so proud that I maneuvered my way into the Pendennis Club by telling the manager I was writing about the club during the '37 Flood. The Pendennis was converted into police headquarters because it was on the highest spot downtown. The manager gave me a tour of everything from the top floor ballroom to the basement sports club, except of course the men's dressing room. (They didn't have a ladies' locker room because women still weren't allowed to have full membership.)

My other informants were Mom and Dad's dear friend Gladys Pope, whose detailed memories of the flood and of things Mom told her were invaluable. Her daughter, historian Gwynne Tuell Potts, pointed me to Carol Ely's work on the Jewish community of Louisville. My Aunt Toby Kahn revealed the story of how a soldier saved my bubby, Edith Kagan Cooper, on the train from Bialystok to Hamburg. Laura McCrea, the granddaughter of Pastor Carl A. Eberhard of Concordia Lutheran Church (the model for Pastor Habermann) found my story "Mrs. Parmenter's Dress," contacted me, and has rooted for this story ever since. Laura kindly allowed me to see her grandmother Naomi's scrapbooks. The many letters Naomi Eberhard got from around the world gave me the idea for the "Pen Pals" chapter.

The librarians at the University of Louisville archives helped me maneuver the vast collection of photos, maps, newspapers, and personal accounts of the 1937 Flood. There I also discovered Mom's music teacher, Althea Stephens Parmenter's M.A. Thesis for the English Department at U of L. Before she married John Parmenter, a violinist and teacher, Mrs. Parmenter began teaching Mom. A saint, she also gave me and my brother piano lessons. I changed her last name to Parmer to feel free to invent her thoughts and actions.

The archivist at Concordia Lutheran Church, still on East Broadway, showed me everything they had about the flood including a photograph of my grandfather Solomon Cooper's shop with his name atop the building. My mother's story that the flood came to within half a block of their shop was verified by a photograph of flood rescue boats docked a few feet from their door. The librarians at Lake Forest College, especially the director Kim Hazlett, helped me get materials on interlibrary loan and provided workspace and encouragement.

I am ever in debt to readers who tackled huge chunks of the novel: colleagues Carla Arnell and her family, David George, Gizella Meneses, and the late Richard Mallette. Friends Ellen Birkett-Morris, Michele Heiman, Beth and Nestor Sánchez, Paulie Beutel, Becky Ruth, Dr. Maceo Ellison, and Dr. Nutan Vaidya read early versions and cheered me on.

Dennis Lohmann was a meticulous reader and fact checker and Chloe Phillips, a fine copy editor. Michael O'Connor contributed his sensitivity and knowledge of the Great Depression and World Wars I and II. Of course any mistakes are entirely my own.

The Writer's Workspace in Chicago (now defunct due to COVID-19) was where I wrote much of this novel and enjoyed the support of so many members. I especially must thank its director Amy Davis for her friendship and wisdom. It was there I met Amin Ahmad, who invited me to join a critique group with Vimi Bajaj, Rachel Gottlieb, Nada Sneige Fuleihan, and Natalia Nebel. How grateful I am to these accomplished younger writers for their honest and sensitive critiques.

Ghassan Zeineddine's critique of the opening chapters at his fiction workshop at Kenyon College Writers' Workshop was most beneficial.

Heartfelt thanks to my writing group for almost twenty years–Kathleen Dohrmann, Karin Gordon, and Cynthia Hahn. We laugh and cry when we write together.

I appreciate the support of the Deerfield Poetry Workshop led by Herb Berman, M.J. Gabrielsen, Judith Kaufmann, and Jacky Harris.

Mary France Schneider and I have written together on Zoom during the pandemic, and you won't find a pushier or more sincere partner.

My sister-in-law Judy Wertheim, my daughter Emily, my son-in-law Erin Ruth, and granddaughter Norah are discerning readers. But most of all, my husband Lew encouraged me and was an invaluable editor through this long process. Thanks for everything.

Dawn Hogue made me dig deeper into my story and convinced me that Bess is not my mother but a character in a novel to whom anything can happen.

Further Information and Sources

Notes on Yiddish

Yiddish usage in this novel will inevitably jar the sensibilities of many because I have attempted to recreate the language of my own family. The Yiddish that Edith Kagan Cooper—my own grandmother and the model for Mollie—spoke certainly carried the dialectical idiosyncrasies of Bialystok; however, since my bubby came to the United States in 1920 at the age of twenty, she no doubt picked up other influences. She would have spoken Yiddish with close friends who came from other parts of the Pale of Settlement. They all would have adopted many southern sayings and even incorporated aspects of Louisville's unique registers. Just as there is no one correct way to say Louisville, there is no one way to pronounce Yiddish.

The Yiddish Research Organization, YIVO, has created a standard Yiddish which is used for teaching academic courses in the language which incorporates aspects of northern and southern Yiddish. Although I have consulted YIVO's transliteration system, my goal was to make the Yiddish accurate to the different speakers in the novel. For example, the grandmother Adel, spoke almost no English until very late in her life, so she would use the correct grammatical forms whereas her children and grandchildren might Americanize pronunciation and disregard rules for case, gender, or pluralization. Many words in Yiddish come from the sacred language Hebrew; however, pronunciation of those words varies widely. For example, those who know Yiddish and those who don't often invoke protection from the the Evil Eye using the same phrase. My family said "Kenehora," but I've heard a myriad of pronunciations, most of which retain the second N in "Keyn eyn hara," the Hebrew phrase that the Yiddish word stems from. Another example from the book is the grandmother's insult for Yankee thieves, "Yankee gonevim!" She uses the plural form from Hebrew. But other speakers, especially contemporary speakers pluralize the word goniff as goniffs. I have attempted to spell Yiddish words consistently throughout; however, occasionally there will be discrepancies due to differences in speakers.

Family History

- *Louisville Courier Journal* online archives provided photographs and articles about my grandfather Solomon Cooper and my mother Ethel Cooper Baer. I hadn't known about many of their public performances including my grandfather's on radio at WHAS.
- Concordia Lutheran Church Archives
- University of Louisville Archives

Jewish Communities of Louisville and Indianapolis

- Carol Ely, *Jewish Louisville: Portrait of a Jewish Community*, 2003
- Herman Landau, A*dath Louisville: The Story of Jewish Community*, 1981

The digital collection at the Indiana University Library in Indianapolis provided:

- *The Jewish Post* 1933-03 - 1946-07-26
- *Kentucky Jewish Chronicle* 1937-05-14 - 1938-12-30

The Great Flood of 1937

- Rick Bell, *The Great Flood of 1936: Rising Waters–Soaring Spirits*, 2007
- Carmel Lile, *A Winter's Flood*, 2016 is one of the only novels about the Louisville flood.
- John Ed Pearce and Richard Nugent, *The Ohio River*, 1989
- David Welky, *The Thousand-Year Flood: The Ohio Mississippi Disaster of 1937*, 2011

The Great Synagogue of Bialystok

My family never talked about the massacre of Bialystok's remaining Jews when Hitler's army reached the city in 1941. The synagogue was burnt down by Germans on June 27, 1941, with an estimated number of 2,000 Jews locked inside. *The Louisville Courier Journal* reported that 5,000 Jews were shot in the square, but the news about the immolation and destruction of the grand synagogue was not generally known to the public until after the war.

I am also grateful to Rebecca Kobrin and her book *Jewish Bialystok and Its Diaspora*, 2010

Nurses' Training

- Jewish Hospital (Louisville, Ky.) Records, 1905-2008 are available online at The Filson Historical Society
- "The Nightingale Pledge" is from Wikipedia

The Great Depression and World War II

President Franklin Delano Roosevelt's Fireside Chats are available at the digital archives of the Franklin Delano Roosevelt Presidential Library hosted by Marist University.

Eleanor Roosevelt's Speech on the day of the Pearl Harbor Attack comes from the digital library of the Eleanor Roosevelt Papers Project hosted by The George Washington University.

Racehorses

Tom Hall, "Miss Dogwood Bloomed in 1943 With Keeneland on Hiatus," appeared on April 1, 2020 online at *BloodHorse*.

About the Author

photo by Ed Levin

With degrees from Georgetown University and Middlebury College's Spanish School and a Ph.D. from University of Kentucky, Lois Baer Barr lives in Riverwoods, Illinois with husband Lew and Goldendoodle Aggie. Barr is a literacy tutor for recent refugee children in Chicago. Her chapbook *Biopoesis* won Poetica Magazine' s first prize in 2013, and *Tracks: Poems on the 'L,'* was a finalist in the New Voices Contest and was published at Finishing Line Press. An emerita Spanish professor at Lake Forest College, Barr's books include a study of Latin American Jewish Literature and a work of short fiction from Red Bird Chapbooks, *Lope de Vega's Daughter*. Her poems and stories have been published in English and Spanish here and abroad. *The Tailor's Daughter* is her first novel.